Freak Trilogy: Book 2
Freak Unleashed — The Trumpets

FREAK UNLEASHED

Journals of the End Times

A novel by Dave Cheadle

Headwaters Christian Resources

Headwaters Christian Resources
PO Box 175
Englewood, CO 80110

www.FreakTrilogy.com
Cover art and Book design by Joe Anderson

ISBN: 978-1-945413-98-8

10 9 8 7 6 5 4 3 2 1

To my family, friends, and readers,
who are sharing the journey of the ages towards
the End of Days... and the Return of the King.

"Then they will deliver you up to tribulation,
and put you to death;
and you will be hated by all nations for my name's sake.

And then many will fall away,
and betray one another, and hate one another.
And many false prophets will arise and lead many astray.

And because wickedness is multiplied,
most men's love will grow cold.

But he who endures to the end will be saved.

And this gospel of the kingdom will be preached throughout the whole world, as a testimony to all nations; and then the end will come."

Matthew 24:9-14 (RSV)

PART I

SUMMIT COUNTY

The explosion left me dazed.

Impact was above us, on the west side of the lodge, gutting through a wall of windows facing some of the most spectacular ski runs in Colorado.

I may have blacked out for a few seconds and buckled to the floor. Then blindly staggered to my feet.

Hours later, both my knees were swollen and darkly bruised. One leg had apparently bled for quite some time. A cracked scab and a black trickle clung to my shin. A tar-like ooze disappeared into a blood-caked sock that stank of death when I finally was in a place where I could peel it loose.

I'd left our suite, walked the long hall, and had just stepped from the elevator into the lobby on the ground floor of the Elkhead Lodge. The initial blast was upstairs at our suite, rattling the entire building. Thick glass lobby windows shook. Several cracked. A few of the enormous panes shattered and collapsed into heaps of jagged rubble and deadly shards.

Cold air and a dozen screams immediately filled the foyer.

The second blast was much closer.

Twenty steps outside the entrance. A dead hit, lifting and slamming the armored military command vehicle in a raucous fireball. It detonated in shrapnel and carnage and a powerful, deafening wave of shock that flung and leveled anything or anyone anywhere near the front doors.

By some miracle, I somehow kept my wits through the second explosion.

I knew I needed to act quickly, before the next strike. I shook my head. Cleared my eyes. Looked for Freak.

He was sprawled at my feet, easy to spot, even in the dust and thick smoke. His orange parka glowed through the blizzard of snow suddenly swirling everywhere, sucked in from the storm outside.

I grabbed the stunned prophet, emptied my lungs in a couple shouts for Saundra and Steve, then instinctively began to charge... deeper into the burning resort. Into the bowels of the massive, shuddering structure that within minutes would collapse and bury any who had not already fallen.

I dragged Freak by his sleeve, hauling him through debris and the panic of the bewildered journalists who had been able to regain their feet. They were blindly groping, punch-drunk. All reeling or fleeing the wrong way.

Without looking, I called her name again, hoping Saundra would hear and follow.

By the next explosion, we had reached the loading dock area at the far end of the long service corridor. We crashed out of the building, letting the door slam behind, then hearing it explode from its hinges in the third blast that scrubbed to ashes the lobby we'd just escaped.

Last night, I had somehow known something horrible loomed.

Yet in the morning's light, I had reverted to my usual ways.

I'd become distracted.

I had let the frightening premonition slide.

Perhaps lives could have been saved.

Lord... have mercy.

1

INTO GOOD FRIDAY: EARLY TO RISE

I awoke on the massive sectional couch, perpendicular to the snoring Steve.

"You're awake?" called Agent Wilcox, rattling a spoon into the stainless steel sink across the room. "Good. We need to talk."

I pushed the heavy Elkhead Lodge blanket aside and slowly lowered my feet from the leather upholstery onto the rich carpet. Steve could sleep through anything. But the smell of brewing coffee and the brilliant sunrise bouncing from the towering Breckenridge slopes west beyond our balcony had put an end to my few hours of restless tossing.

"In a few minutes," said Wilcox, "room service will be here with breakfast. Before everyone else gets up, you and I should touch base on a few things."

I flexed my toes, then rolled my head and cracked my neck.

"Right."

I needed clean socks. And underwear. And a shower.

"Heather," said Wilcox, "is still asleep." He pointed his coffee mug at the entrance to what had recently been my exclusive domain. "Let's leave her alone in there for now. After she gets up, you two can do whatever you want. Meanwhile, you and I should compare notes and discuss a few things in private while we still can."

The door to Heather's bed and the private bath of the master suite was tightly closed, and I could hear nothing from within. I would have to wait for my steam shower and fresh clothes until she was up and out of there anyway. Might as well catch up with the man in the suit.

"Hang on," I sighed, rising, steadying myself, then moving towards the common bathroom adjacent to the sprawling TV room and the living area where I'd spent the night. "What about the sheriff... will Andy be joining us?"

"No. Not for another half hour. Sheriff Dekker is briefing with his team down in the main conference area."

I glanced toward the enormous stone fireplace at the far end of our vaulted room. Freak was no longer there. He must have finished praying and gone to bed sometime after midnight, after I'd fallen asleep. My gaze drifted up along the open wooden stairs and pine handrail to the loft. The door to Saundra's suite—as well as the entrance opposite of hers that led into Freak's double room—showed no signs of anyone coming or going.

"Hey, Wilcox," I quietly called over my shoulder, fumbling into the bathroom. "Would you mind digging through the first aid kit? I need something for a headache. My aspirins are in Heather's purse, beside the bed. I'd be happy to go in there and get the bottle, but if Heather happens to wake up, it might be a while before...."

"Right," he snapped. "Just do your business in the bathroom, and I'll get some aspirins from the kit on the pool table in the game room. Stop dawdling. We don't have time for that today."

2

OUT OF THE BOX

When I emerged, Wilcox was planted at the massive kitchen bar. A pill bottle, a sugar bowl with a spoon, a small dish of creamers and a mug of steaming coffee were all neatly arranged, all waiting for me across from him on the tiled countertop. I moved toward the most central of the four empty stools opposite of him.

He let me sidle in and pop open a thimble cup of creamer before breaking the silence.

"Last night," he said, "Reverend Jacobs unleashed a monster."

Hmm.

I poured a second creamer, added sugar, stirred.

"Wilcox," I said, tapping my spoon, "Freak doesn't see it that way." I took a long, sweet sip. "According to Freak, none of this was his doing. It's all *'God's work.'* It was the Lord who snatched him from the jaws of death on the Day of the Falling Skies."

Wilcox raised his mug. He matched my sip with one of his own, then met my eyes.

"Freak is crazy," he said. "Reverend Jacobs scrambled his brain when he crashed through those branches before he hit the ground. You know that, right?"

I studied the government man long and hard. He had identified himself as a special agent with Homeland Security, but clearly there was more to him than that. I never actually saw what was printed on his badge. He never offered to show it up close, nor to explain the details of his assignment other than that he and his team had been jetted into Colorado to cover the Summit County terrorist incident. And to handle the fallout of Freak's survival from the mid-air explosion.

"Bill Jacobs," I said at last, "is out of control... maybe." I lowered my mug to the counter. "But he's not crazy. Freak makes sense. He throws around a lot of disturbing claims, but he is logical, consistent, and convincing. If the pastor was crazy, then we wouldn't have anything to worry about today. We could end this conversation right now."

"I didn't say," said Wilcox, "that he isn't convincing. That's what makes him so dangerous. He's got half of the nation convinced this morning that angels have begun blowing trumpets to release the wrath of the apocalypse."

"Half the nation?" I gave Wilcox a quizzical look. "What have you heard? Have you been watching the news already this morning?"

"Not me. Didn't have to. I've had crews monitoring the networks and tracking social media for me all night. Our Washington team sent me an up-to-date summary and a set of color-coded charts and graphs less than an hour ago." He waved his coffee at a beige file folder near the middle of the countertop.

"What's the word?" I asked.

"Chaos. We couldn't contain it. Freak's prophecies went viral last night from coast to coast. The tension is rising by the hour. Video clips of his outrageous claims are showing up everywhere. Even in Japan and Europe."

"It has begun," I said. "Pandora's box."

Wilcox started to say something, then cut himself short.

"So," I asked, "why are we even having this conversation? This is between you and your Washington boss. And Freak. I'm just the guy who saw Freak hit the tree. Saw the plane explode. Dug him out of a snowdrift and took him to the hospital." I grinned. "I'm a nobody. A week ago, I'd hardly even heard of W.B. Jacobs."

"Knock it off, Mark. You know everyone who watches television considers you his right-hand man. People think you're the guy who leaked the videos. You're the champion of the free press, the courageous high school English teacher who smuggled out the prophet's most catastrophic predictions while the networks cowered behind protectionist policies and institutional fear."

"But I didn't...."

"The truth is beside the point. What matters is what people think. What Freak thinks." Wilcox shook his head. "We've got a powder keg here. I need to know where you stand on all of this."

"An apt mix of metaphors," I grinned. "You've placed me standing on a powder keg."

I took another sip.

"You are. And it's going to blow."

"Probably."

"So, are you going to step off, or are you just going to watch the fuse burn in your direction while you stand there?"

"It's funny," I said, "you keep putting it that way. Freak asked the same thing last night. He challenged me to decide where I stood... if I was with him, or not."

"Fine. And what was your answer?"

"I'm still trying to decide."

"Well, you'd better decide soon. Millions of people are scared to death San Francisco will be in ruins by the end of the day. They're starting to believe Freak's predictions, and they're worried that global judgment has begun. Whatever position you take publicly towards Freak's prophecies could make a lot of difference in some communities. How you handle Freak could make the difference between calm streets... and panicked stampedes." He let the image linger, then finished. "So do you think you can lock your buddy down, or not?"

"Listen," I said, chilling the word, "it would be a lot more comfortable between you and me if you would stop always trying to force things to go a certain way. I don't do well with badgering."

He waited.

"To answer your question," I said, glancing again toward Freak's door at the top of the stairs, "maybe I'll wait to see how today goes."

Wilcox checked his watch.

"Top-of-the-hour news," he said, "starts in fifteen minutes. That's also about when breakfast arrives. The others will be joining us any minute."

"Great," I said. "So finish what you've got to say."

"We both know," said Wilcox, "that Freak is going to try to get back on the air again. If he does, that puts you back in the spotlight with him."

"And?"

"I'd like to give you some pointers on how to proceed."

Wilcox wrapped his hands around his coffee. He leaned across the counter, intentionally stretching himself into my space.

I straightened. Reached for the pill bottle. Shook out a few and washed them down with a rich swig.

Stared into the depths of my cup.

I finally raised my head, then looked around from empty stool to empty stool.

"Looks like we've got a whole room full of control freaks," I sighed. My gaze finally returned to meet his eyes. "Maybe even one too many."

Wilcox glanced around the empty room. "There's nobody here," he said, "except for...." He scowled, then irately tapped his mug.

"Relax," I said. "I'm thinking."

Behind the closed door of the master suite, the shower jets kicked into a distant, high-pitched spray. Heather was finally awake. I allowed myself to picture her letting the water heat, letting the room fill with steam. It felt good to get my thoughts as far away from Freak and Wilcox as I could.

I caught myself staring at her door.

Wilcox cleared his throat.

"Girlfriend troubles, eh?"

"No," I said. "Heather and I are just taking a little break. We're good."

We both listened to the muted hiss of the shower.

Again, Wilcox cleared his throat.

"You've been with her," he asked, "for what... a few months?"

"More or less," I replied.

"And you like her, right?"

"Of course I like her. I'm not going to walk her down the aisle, but she's okay. Most of the time." I leaned forward. "Stop jerking me around, Wilcox. What are you trying to say?"

"Mark," he said, "I know you're not as stupid as you act. I'm going to share something to make myself absolutely clear. You need to settle down and get with the program." He tugged on his freshly shaved chin. "If you ever quote me on this, I'll deny every word of it. I'll say you made a lucky guess."

"About what?"

"Yesterday," he said, "we tracked your entire walk with Heather. GPS. And audio. We followed every step of your hike around the ski village. You never left our sights. We had glass on you from several strategic surveillance blinds, plus cameras... you name it. And we recorded every word you two said. I know all about how you two argued over going back to her apartment in Denver."

I started to sputter a protest.

"She begged you," continued Wilcox, "she pleaded that you both should leave the lodge immediately." He shot a glance towards Steve to make sure the pudgy Channel 5 News cameraman was still asleep. "But you insisted you needed one more day at the lodge to see if Freak was right about San Francisco."

For a moment, I wanted to imagine Wilcox was kidding, that he was trying to intimidate me or to bluff me into supporting his efforts to quietly shut Freak down. Then I remembered the little high-tech two way radio devices that one of his men had clipped onto our collars before letting Heather and me slip out through the loading dock bay and past the dumpsters around back. They had instructed us how to turn the gadgets on to call for help if we encountered any more violent protestors. They told us to use the devices as a sort of panic button, in the event something came up and we needed immediate security assistance.

Now, it was obvious. The on and off switch was a decoy. Heather and I were broadcasting the whole time.

I swore.

"It gets better," he said. "This whole place is bugged. Spy cams in every room."

I shook my head.

"The other night," he smiled, "I even got to sit in my team's control truck and watch a replay of your morning's pillow fight with the lovely Saundra Paige from Channel 5 News." He tossed his nose upward. "When you two were up there... on the loft couch."

I thought about throwing a punch. Thought better of it, then swore again.

I glanced up to the ceiling. Ran my eyes along the tops of the window frames. Studied the central chandelier.

"Stop it," he laughed. "Don't make a bigger fool of yourself than you already have. Even an expert couldn't spot any of our bugs from here. You'd need a ladder. And an electronic detector, with a whole lot of time."

I shook my head.

"I'm telling you this," said Wilcox, "off the record... but in no uncertain terms. You heard it last night, but let me remind you again today. Even the President is concerned about what you and Freak are up to. Many lives are at stake. Not to mention the health of our economy and the stability of the world."

My mind kept looping.

"Every room?" I asked. "You've bugged every room in this townhouse... up and down?"

"Mark, we're precariously balanced atop a mountain peak. Not just the terrorist attacks last weekend, but the entire global system. Fanatical and fringe religious movements are already escalating the violence. Law enforcement agencies could quickly become overwhelmed. The military could over react. Worse yet, some overly cautious general could fail to respond until it's too late."

He seemed to enjoy imagining the scenarios.

"All of the major markets," he continued, "almost every financial institution is only one or two very bad headlines away from total collapse. One little mistake or nudge in the wrong direction, and it all goes down. America. Europe. Asia. All of it."

"How could you plant cameras in our rooms and still pretend as if...."

"Grow up, Mark. Haven't you been listening?" Wilcox stood from his stool and recharged his coffee from the kitchen's countertop brewer. "This is bigger than the Constitutional rights of a few individuals. Freak is correct about at least one thing: millions of lives are at stake right now. The last thing we need is a self-proclaimed loose-canon prophet making matters worse. Freak is rapidly becoming a real problem in the midst of an already extremely volatile situation."

I closed my eyes and took a deep breath.

"Increasingly volatile," I muttered, "is *right*."

Deep down, I must have guessed that the place might be rigged with surveillance equipment. Why else would the government have been so quick to get us specifically into the Elkhead Lodge... and so willing to pick up the exorbitant tab? This place was expansive enough to hide whatever they needed, and with its full range of services, we'd had little excuse to ever leave.

"You told us," I said, fighting my anger, "that you and Andy were assigned to us for our own protection. That you were staying here day and night with us for our own safety."

"Yes. That, too. The threats I outlined on our first day together are totally real. But I've also been tasked to make certain that things don't get out of hand...."

"What do you mean? Are you supposed to put a bullet in Freak's skull if he says something the folks back in Washington don't want to hear?"

Wilcox stared.

"Not," he said at last, "a bullet... *per se*. But I do have the authority to do whatever I deem necessary to pull the plug and shut this whole thing down immediately. With a single word, I could have you both whisked off and held in isolation all the way until the next election. If there ever is another election."

I lowered my coffee to the bar and shook my head. "I don't believe you."

Wilcox resettled onto his stool across the counter. He made a point of eyeballing the placement of my mug.

"Sure you do." He sniffed, then puffed a wisp of rising coffee steam in my direction. "You know they've given me total discretion. They had to. Too much is at stake to leave anything up to chance. You and Freak have been on a much shorter leash than you even realized. And you need to fully cooperate from here on out... or the party is over."

"Seriously?" I asked, unable to let it go. "You've been spying into every room?"

"Yesterday morning," he smiled, "when Heather threw you out of the shower, you claimed that you mistook her unlocked bathroom door as an open invitation." He took a sip. "She didn't buy it."

It had been several years since I'd swore so many times outside of a locker room.

"Come on," he smirked. "You're the clever boy with all the great one-liners. Surely you can do better than that."

I felt my fists tighten. I looked down at my white knuckles. Tried to relax.

"Even the shower?" I asked at last. "You've been recording even in the bathroom?"

"Of course." There was a nasty edge to his voice I'd not noticed before. "If we're going to bother to bug anything, we're certainly not going to skip the Jacuzzi and the shower. The bathroom is often where some of the biggest stuff comes out. So to speak."

"Jerk," I spat.

"Let's talk about a few days ago. Your little attempt to disguise Freak and smuggle him out of the hospital. Do you remember that fiasco in the parking lot... when Freak was first spotted?"

"What about it?" I asked.

"After we rescued the three of you from the media frenzy, I told you that you'd beaten my team to the hospital by less than an hour. I apologized for how we weren't able help you any sooner because we were not yet in place. That we were not yet fully operational as a team."

I glared. "You lied? You were watching us get mobbed and humiliated the whole time?"

"Of course," he laughed. "We watched the whole thing. We wanted you to experience what would happen if you didn't accept our help and guidance. We've been in complete control here every moment, playing you—and our cards—as needed."

He carefully placed his mug on the bar, intentionally bumping it lightly into mine.

"I'm telling you this for your own good... so you'll start working with me. Either that, or so you'll dump Freak and leave him to the pros. That would be best, you know. For you to run back to Heather's apartment in Denver the way she asked. And for you to let me handle everything from here on out. In my own way."

He locked onto my eyes.

"And, just so you know," he sneered, "it was one of my men who shouted to the media and pointed to Freak in the parking lot. It was my guy who let everyone know it was Bill Jacobs who was moving across the parking lot in that stupid orange parka disguise...."

My fist shot towards his jaw.

With the counter between us, Wilcox leaned back and easily avoided contact.

He grinned. Then casually retrieved his mug for another sip.

I shook with rage.

Closed my eyes.

Realized what he was doing. He was playing me. Just like he said.

I slowed my breathing.

I'd won scholarships. In sports and academics both. I was better than this.

Another breath.

I forced myself to picture falling snow. I opened my eyes and imagined large fluffy flakes falling and melting into my coffee.

I lifted my eyes to the man smugly grinning across from me.

"Okay," I faintly smiled. "I see what you did there."

I took another deep breath. "You've made your point."

Wilcox studied me. "Sorry about that. But you've been testing me ever since the first day we met. You told Heather you wanted to punch me out, and you just had your chance. I figured it was about time I brought some wolf pack alpha male clarity into this relationship."

"A relationship," I said, "of unequals. That's how you see it, isn't it? That's what you think you've just proved."

My lunge against the overhang of the bar had cost me a couple of tender ribs, but I wasn't about to give Wilcox the satisfaction of rubbing my side.

"Look," he scoffed, "you're a civilian. An amateur. I'm a professional when it comes to situations like these. You could probably beat me in your favorite game of ball, but this is not a ball game. You need to let me take the lead right now... and you need to follow and do as you're told."

"Perhaps," I said, reaching again for my own coffee, "but I'm not leaving. I promised Freak one more day. None of your little tricks are going to get me out of here any sooner."

"Fair enough. Listen, Mark, I hope you understand that none of this is personal. I'm not judging you or any of your choices. With Freak. Or with the ladies. But I have an assignment. I have my orders. And I'm responsible for a lot more than what happens here in Colorado, let alone what happens just inside these few rooms."

He leaned into the bar, eyes intense.

"Freak," he said, "is a bit like the insane man who waves his arms and shouts 'Fire!' in a crowded theater. Except in this case," he leaned back, "Freak's theater is the entire planet."

"Hang on," I said, holding up my hand. "What if Freak is correct... what if there actually *is* a fire?"

"Look," said Wilcox, "another earthquake in the Bay Area is a very real possibility. After yesterday's disaster in Petaluma, many experts are saying that severe aftershocks—and even related earthquakes—are likely. We can anticipate what's next. Something else will go wrong in California, and then people will start thinking Freak somehow knows the future."

"And...?"

"A few kooks will start believing Freak has a supernatural hotline to God." Wilcox's voice turned hostile. "And then, suddenly, people might start doing everything this preacher tells them to do. This has the potential to mushroom into an End Times cult practically overnight. Or worse, a fanatical broad-based movement that tips the sanity of the world over the edge."

"You still haven't answered my question."

"What question?"

I didn't blink. "What," I asked, "if this *is* the end of the world?"

"Mark," he said, "has Freak suckered you in now, too? You're playing with fire....."

"Freak," I interrupted, "says we all are playing with fire." I shook my head. "And, just a minute ago, you said there wasn't any fire."

"Word play," said Wilcox, looking grim. "But this is not a game."

"Let's talk again," I said, "at the end of the day. We'll know more then."

Room service interrupted with a breakfast knock.

Wilcox drew my eyes. "Remember," he frowned, heading to the door, "I'll deny every word of it. This conversation never happened."

"What conversation?" I grinned. "For the life of me, I can't remember anything you've ever said."

I stood, turned my back, then headed towards the television remote on the low table beside the couch.

Steve stirred. He struggled to untangle from his blanket and rise, probably already sensing the hot food cart beyond the bolted door.

"Good morning, Sunshine," I smiled. I reached past him and picked up the remote.

Wilcox turned the locks in the other room and opened the door.

I clicked to Channel 5 and tossed a pillow in Steve's direction.

"Breakfast is on, my friend, and so is the news."

3
DRAWN DRAPES

Freak looked awful.

"Whoa," gasped Saundra, leaping from her end of the couch.

She rushed to Freak and gently took his elbow.

Perhaps because the man was running on so little sleep, Reverend Jacobs had overdone his shower... with the handle cranked too far into either the hot or cold.

However it was, the plasticized ridges and the deep troughs of his scarred left cheek flamed in unnatural reds, purples and pinks. Even the healthy, unscarred right side of his face looked battered and raw.

His dark hair was combed, but his clothing was rumpled and his feet dragged as he crossed from the bottom landing of the loft stairs to join the rest of us in the TV area.

Eating together in front of the news had become a ritual. At various times, each of us had appeared on the screen over the past few days. Not only during Saundra's lively Channel 5 interviews, but also via wobbly handheld parking lot shots, cable station spotlights, and in numerous file portrait insets posted to the side of the screen during global network commentaries.

But the stories always boiled down to Freak.

I started to rise, then resettled as Saundra eased Freak into her spot at the far end of the sectional couch.

"Dude," I grinned, putting down my fork, "you look worse this morning than you did last weekend when you fell from the plane."

He nodded.

Wilcox rose from his stool behind the couch. "Good morning," he said, touching Freak's shoulder as he strode past the pastor and headed towards the closed drapes. For a moment, I thought he might pull the ropes and finally restore our balcony view. Instead, Wilcox merely drew aside one fold and peered through the slit.

Freak shifted his attention from Wilcox, then moved it around our circle, taking stock of how we were responding to the morning's news. How we were responding to him.

Heather flinched slightly when his gaze lighted on her. She quickly and awkwardly turned back to the latest updates from yesterday's earthquake.

"Here," said Saundra, bustling to the service cart. She lifted a large ivory thermos carafe with one hand, and an empty white cup with the other. "Maybe a little black coffee will help?"

"Thanks," he sighed. "I had a few rough moments last night. Another vision... a really bad one." He held the cup in both hands as she poured, then squinted towards the enormous flat screen television on the wall.

"Do you care to talk about it?" asked Saundra, stepping back.

"Not yet," Freak shrugged. "I'm still trying to discern where it all fits in with today's earthquakes."

A cable station was currently airing a 30-second highlight from one of the cell phone videos of Freak that had gone viral during the night.

The images were often shaky and pointed askew, but through the magic of some high-tech wizardry, the sound had been clarified and enhanced until it rang unmistakably clear.

"The entire world," said Freak in the clip, "will soon face judgments on the order of San Francisco. Running may buy an individual some time, but it will not reverse the direction history is now heading. For many thousands of Bay Area residents, tomorrow is the appointed day of their death...."

Steve chomped on a pastry and clicked the remote to another network.

A carefully disheveled Black female reporter stood atop a heap of rubble in a glowing safety vest and white helmet. Her bulky, handheld mic bobbed in the excitement of her live disaster update from California. Smiles and frowns punctuated her report, which was further authenticated by the brown and ruby vapors of a dying Petaluma fire far beyond her left shoulder.

Saundra appeared curious to see how the reporter would conclude her segment on the earthquake.

Heather was having a hard time touching her breakfast.

I glanced over to Agent Wilcox. He remained planted, standing on duty beside the pleated wall of thick jade drapes, splitting his focus in pivoting glances between the flat screen and the ski slopes beyond our sliding glass doors and snow-covered balcony rail.

"Hey," I called. "Anything new with the snipers?"

Wilcox shook his head in disgust.

"You know," I called again, "this is a huge lodge. With so many hundreds of windows and so many balconies, if anyone was out there, they'd have a hard time figuring out which rooms were ours." I laughed. "Unless, of course, it occurred to them to hunt for the only guests trying to hide behind drawn drapes."

Steve chuckled.

Wilcox dropped his hold on the thick green tapestry and returned to his stool. He leaned in my direction.

"Idiot," he whispered, barely loud enough for everyone in the room to hear. "If anyone is out there, they already know our unit. The drapes are pulled only to foil a clean shot. Maybe you should go out there and sit on the balcony for a while. Signal with a little grunt if you happen to take a bullet. I'd love to know whether or not my theory is correct."

Hmm. I rolled my head and cracked my neck.

Above our first floor curtains, the brilliant morning's light that had flooded the loft and bathed the vaulted ceiling through the upper windows was now shifting in hue down into a deep gray. Large flakes were beginning to swirl, thickening and clinging to the high glass panes.

"Wilcox," I said, nodding toward the darkening sky, "it looks like the big storm they all predicted has started moving in."

He eyed me suspiciously. "Yes. And the radar says it's going to get worse."

"Well," I said, "maybe you should brew up a big pot of hot chocolate and buy a bag of marshmallows. Get a stack of Styrofoam cups and find a snow bank. I heard them Arabs can't stand the cold. For fifty cents a pop, I'll bet you could catch yourself a couple of bucks worth of terrorists in no time."

Wilcox refused to turn his head.

Heather leaned close.

"What are you talking about?" she softly asked. "Are you saying we might have some terrorists out there?"

"No," I replied, "nothing like that. Wilcox has a job to do, and I'm just giving him a hard time."

"But you said...."

"I was joking." I patted her arm.

"What about that news story," she pressed, "where they showed all of the bloody stuff at the tree where Freak fell from the plane... where people cut off the bark and sacrificed those dead animals. Were those rituals and that curse they put on Freak all the work of a cult, like the reporters said, or were those animals killed by terrorists?"

I took Heather's hand. Squeezed it lightly.

"Shh," I said. "You're getting all worked up over nothing. That silliness at the tree was probably only a prank. Probably some high school kids from Denver out on a joyride after watching too many horror movies."

She dug her nails back into my squeeze.

"Yesterday, Mark, when we went for our walk... you told me it was protesters who were angry about the preacher, and that's why we needed Sheriff Andy and Agent Wilcox for security. But you didn't say anything about terrorists. And you certainly didn't mention any snipers...."

"A joke," I insisted, pulling back my arm and reaching for an English muffin. "Let's all relax and watch some more news."

Perhaps drawn by mention of his name, Andy drifted forward from the kitchen area with a cup of coffee in his left hand. He stood, hesitating, silently shaking his head. His right thumb absently rolled back and forth, caressing the worn black flap of his sidearm holster.

We'd been thrown together for less than a week, but we'd become a bit of an unlikely team.

His attention shifted from me towards Heather. He started to speak, stopped, glanced at Wilcox, then back at me.

"I don't like it," he said, lifting his hand and pointing at the television. "This is not good. For them, for us... for the world."

He turned, muttering as he disappeared from the room.

"I need to call my wife."

SAN FRANCISCO STIRRINGS

The networks began running rewinds of their top stories at the bottom of the hour. We shifted our attention to some of the coverage from other stations that we'd missed the first time around.

According to CNN, Israel faced investigative problems similar to ours in Colorado as they tried to recover evidence from the airline attack off their coast. Retrieving bodies and plane wreckage from the Mediterranean Sea was as difficult as fishing carnage from remote, treacherous snow-filled ravines.

Beyond Colorado—and Israel aside—the other seven crash sites were moving towards mop-up work.

In Europe, an unnamed Paris bureaucrat leaked that several more neighborhood sweeps, gun battles, and safe house raids had produced another 37 terrorist casualties and over 120 new arrests. Three terrorist cells had been successfully neutralized, and through interrogations, officials were able to finally positively confirm that the attacks were sponsored and coordinated by "a specific terrorist network supported by the Islamic State and based in the Middle East."

"Brilliant," coughed Steve. "Especially since those same Middle East guys were already on television bragging about the success of their deadly work within five minutes of the explosions."

"Not so fast," said Wilcox. "*Who* was bragging? Did they really speak for their nations, or even for their own little organizations? In situations like these, a half dozen or more groups might try to take the stage and grab credit for the attacks. Psychologically, religious extremists and terrorist cells all have a lot of skin in the game with this sort of thing. They need to ensure that infidels are afraid of them, and that they have the power to intimidate the rest of the world." He pointed at the television. "In truth, for all we know, these attacks were sponsored and executed by teams from China... or North Korea."

"Well," said Steve, "for China's sake, I hope it was those Middle Eastern guys. A few minutes ago, an American general announced that a dozen substantial military targets were now identified, and one of our aircraft carriers would commence with proportional retaliatory airstrikes within the hour."

Steve abruptly stood and tossed the remote my way. He stepped towards the pastries, and I clicked us back to Channel 5.

Again, it was Freak's face and a bootlegged clip from his last interview with Saundra that filled the screen.

"The world," said the fallen prophet, "is broken. It groans beneath the weight of humanity's mistakes... and it shudders in the shadows of the looming, ugly, painful consequences of our sins."

I glanced at Freak, shook my head, then tried another cable station.

"...if you live in the San Francisco Bay area," said Freak from the screen, "then you should pray... listen to what the Lord has to say. If He tells you to leave, do so immediately, before the bridges and roads fill with the panicked masses....

"Tomorrow, when an escalating series of ruptures, shakings, and judgments begins... help others. If the Lord has called you to stay and serve, pull your neighbors from the rubble. Show mercy...."

The video shifted to another cut.

"As certain as I am sitting here, God has shown me that a warning hammer of wrath will come down in America this year... on Good Friday."

I hit the mute.

"Oh, dear," whispered Heather.

If possible, she sank yet deeper beside me on the couch.

She was the one who had shot that video. It was Heather who had found Krissy's cell phone on the counter. Heather had idly fussed with the unfamiliar apps and camera settings, and she had unwittingly made numerous random recordings throughout the duration of Saundra's interview with Freak across the room.

When Krissy had returned to retrieve her lost phone, those recordings filled the gallery, waiting for Krissy to discover them. Once found by Krissy, the clips had been uploaded to Krissy's website and launched into the social media universe.

"Heather," said Freak, drawing her gaze to him, almost against her will. "It's okay. You did good. The Lord has used you to warn the city."

"But...." she wavered.

"It's okay. By the time Good Friday is over, thousands of people will owe you their lives."

She half nodded, then turned back to the silent screen.

"Heather," he softly called again. "May I pray for you?"

She glanced at him briefly, then nervously, almost violently, shook her head no.

"Okay," he whispered, nodding for her to turn back to the news.

She gladly obliged, overplaying her fascination with muted reports flowing across the screen, thankful to turn away from his scars.

Freak's lips quivered. His eyes closed as he silently prayed for her anyway.

"Hey, Heather," said Steve. "Mark says you're a teacher." He reached for the last croissant, giving her time to compose herself. "In Denver, right?"

"Preschool," she quietly replied. "The kiddos are very sweet."

They both let it go at that.

I looked back at the television. Even with the sound off, Krissy's enthusiasms radiated in the rebroadcasting of reporter Tom Jackson's interview with her from the night before. Once again, she was shown tugging on her T-shirt and explaining the meaning of the yellow happy face with its red patch scar representing Freak's wounded left cheek and the consequences of sin.

She mouthed her paraphrases of Freak's message, of how God had transformed the pastor's face into an embodiment of both Grace and Truth.

As found on her new line of shirts.

As available for purchase on her website, www. FreakFall.com.

In all sizes.

I finished the kill job, and the digital review of the past week's hype and horrors faded to black.

Heather excused herself to make a call.

Freak waited for the sound of Heather's lock, then turned to Wilcox.

"How many people have fled from the city?" he asked. "How accurately are they tracking the numbers for the Bay Area evacuations?"

Wilcox cleared his throat. He turned to Sheriff Andy, who sat beside him, then looked back at Freak. He leaned forward from his bar-stool behind the couch.

"Thousands," he said. "I received a text report from our San Francisco team a few minutes ago. It's hard to tell how many can be directly attributed to your predictions, but traffic camera data and bridge toll collections suggest a significant spike over comparable hours during last year's Easter weekend."

"Good," said Freak. "What kind of numbers are we talking about?"

"We're up on the order of 11,000 unexpected vehicles departures across the Oakland Bridge alone." Wilcox shifted towards me. "So far, no shutdowns or stampedes. A few extra rush hour jams, but the city is still up and running."

"Rush hour?" asked Freak.

"Well," said Wilcox, "Good Friday is not exactly a national holiday. As far as employers are concerned, today is still another work day. By best estimates, the spike in job absenteeism is significantly up, but that can be attributed mostly to yesterday's disasters in the North Bay region. Our team actuary has estimated that we are experiencing a rise of approximately six percent in job no-reports that could be attributed to your prophecies of a Good Friday disaster."

Freak lifted his cup near to his lips, then lowered it untasted.

"I need to get back on the air," he sighed. "And not just about what today will bring for the West Coast. There's more coming... horrors that will include the whole world."

He turned to Saundra. "But right now, more families should be getting out while they still can. Especially the children. The Lord has not shown me at what time today the next earthquake will occur, but it's urgent that we immediately start motivating those who are willing to listen. Do you think Channel 5 will let you do another live interview yet this morning?"

She hesitated. She glanced across the expansive sectional to Steve, who had instinctively dropped his hand to the camera bag at his feet.

"Yes," she said. "Channel 5 would never say no to another interview. The problem is what the station will do with the footage. As before, they won't stream it live. And I cannot guarantee what my producer will edit out. Nor can I promise the network will rebroadcast any portions of it later in the day."

Saundra shrugged.

She looked over to Agent Wilcox and Deputy Sheriff Dekker, who suddenly found it necessary to adjust a cuff button on his uniform.

Ms. Paige often had that effect on men. More than once in the past week, I, too, had been forced to examine a sleeve wrinkle or tug on a shoelace when under the laser scrutiny of her brown eyes. There's something unfair about a woman who accessorizes a perfect face and long blonde hair with flowing black lowlights and sparkling dark eyes. And a searing intellect.

Saundra focused on Wilcox.

"If we've learned anything," she said, squaring her shoulders, "we've learned that I don't always get to call the shots." She nodded. "Not here in Summit County. Not in Denver. And certainly not for the networks."

Andy looked as if he'd been scolded, but Wilcox sat unfazed.

"Saundra," said Wilcox, "you've done an amazing job this week on this Falling Skies story. I'm sorry so much of your work has had to be censored. For a professional journalist, I know this must be brutal."

She said nothing.

"On the other hand," he added, "there's no need to write off that Emmy so soon. I trust you have followed the pastor's advice and have kept all of your unused footage. Assuming that Reverend Jacobs is wrong about the end of the world, then you're already sitting on the raw material for one heck of a documentary... or one hell of an exposé."

Saundra glanced at Steve, who nodded.

"Freak," she said, catching the pastor as he finally took his first sip, "as much as I'd like another exclusive, I think it's in your best interest for you to hold an open press conference. My boss would fire me for saying this, but you'll get faster and better exposure that way than with another Channel 5 exclusive."

Wilcox started to object.

"I can arrange," she interrupted, "for a press meeting to be held later this morning in the lobby downstairs. Wilcox can handle security. We never have to leave the premises. All of the major networks already have mobile teams here on standby, and it's time for us to get them involved."

"Sorry," said Wilcox, "but I'm not going to be able to...."

"Agent Wilcox," she snapped. "In case you were sleeping on the job, the whole world figured out last night that someone high up has been grossly censoring their news. The disparity between my last edited interview and what the world saw an hour later on those Internet clips made a mockery of this whole Washington effort to control information. Right now, confidence in television news and faith in the government have *got* to be at an all-time low. And justifiably so."

She stood decisively, then motioned for Steve to grab his equipment and to follow her upstairs for phone calls and a planning session in her room.

Saundra hardly turned as she brushed past the two government employees on their stools.

"Wilcox," she said, "if you're going to want America to believe anything from the network outlets ever again—including any more of the government's future propaganda—then this press conference has got to happen. In one hour."

Saundra started up the stairs, then called over her shoulder. "Think about it. If you play this wrong, then you will awaken to a world where uncensored viral clips will become the dominant and most trusted source to which our nation turns for news... from here to whatever end the future might bring."

"Ms. Paige," called Wilcox, "I know you've pulled this sort of thing before. But if you think...."

She stopped at the top of the stairs and leaned over the pine rail.

"The Internet or this. One hour."

5
PRESS CONFERENCE PLANNING

Saundra said one hour, but she was forced to make it ninety minutes.

The other reporters and media crews needed the additional half hour to get things in place, as did the security teams. Wilcox threw himself into a flurry of security adjustments and instructed the Special Ops team from Fort Carson to position their two armored Humvees under the valet canopy immediately outside the main entrance.

The extra thirty minutes also conveniently pushed the press conference back to coincide with the 12:00 news for the millions of viewers who would be tuning in at the top of the hour from Chicago, St. Louis, Houston and the rest of the Central Time Zone.

I watched in fascination as the networks scrambled to prepare, and as they immediately began hyping the upcoming media event. Despite the countless times Freak had appeared on television in the past week, almost all of the professional grade clips were recycled from one of Sandra's exclusive interviews or were lifted from outdated file footage from the pastor's career as a television preacher.

Of more interest—but less quality—were the short paparazzi videos taken during Freak's parking lot adventures. Plus the dozen or so cell camera clips recorded by Heather with Krissy's phone, and the footage from inside the Blue River Bible Church sanctuary that had been shot without Pastor Jacob's knowledge or consent.

Not that he minded.

But nobody in the world, outside of Saundra's team, had yet had direct access to Freak with steady tripods and their own live Q and A.

Freak had wanted a press conference like this all week. Right from the first hours after his fall from the plane, from the time when he awoke in the hospital with his freshly shredded face still wrapped in gauze. When he had declared during Saundra's first interview that God would heal him overnight, and that he would share the miracle with the world on live television the following day.

As it turned out, such a press conference never occurred.

But it would now.

The Fallen Prophet would finally speak directly to the world.

Live.

As usual, Freak spent more time in his room praying than he did picking out his wardrobe. His options were limited to begin with, confined to the donated branded sportswear he'd been given at the hospital, plus the one reasonable outfit that the Wilcox team had managed to scrounge together from the outlet mall in Silverthorne.

His familiar regular wardrobe for media appearances had been in a suitcase on his plane. It was now strewn and buried in the snow with tons of wreckage. Everything he had brought was now scattered with the debris of almost three hundred deceased passengers, spread across a couple hundred square miles of Summit County forests, jagged peaks and inaccessible gorges.

Freak finally emerged from his room twenty minutes before show time.

Heather, who was trying to straighten up the living room, simply shook her head.

He stopped at the kitchen counter, a strange mixture of awkward self-awareness and excited anticipation. He wore a bright green pair of overlarge sweat pants. Not exactly the GQ look required for a man striving to garner respectability among legions of critics.

The real problem, though, was above his pants.

He appeared focused and reenergized by his time in prayer, but it was hard to take him seriously because he was wearing one of the gaudy silkscreened T-shirts Krissy had dreamt up earlier in the week. One of the ones she and her artist boyfriend had rushed into production shortly after Freak's impact a few miles from the liquor store where she worked.

In a flash of marketing genius, Krissy had donated the shirt to the Freak Power movement only a couple of days ago. The night when Krissy, Saundra and Heather had all met for the first time, sizing each other up amidst angry misunderstandings, jealous assumptions, and way too much alcohol.

At least that was the way I remembered it. What I could recall of it.

Not everything was clear from that night, other than that by the end of the party, I had been demoted from my king bed to the couch.

"Preacher," I said, pointing at Freak's chest, "what an ungodly combination. Even the orange parka would have been a better choice than that."

"Thanks for the confirmation," Freak nodded. "I'm glad it creates such a strong impression." He moved to between me and the television. "By the way, where is that orange parka of yours? I need it for continuity. It'll provide a powerful connecting element for branding my message and generating maximum visual impact."

"Your face," I grinned, "it already reflects a maximum impact. And you don't need a fluorescent jacket to be instantly recognized. By now, over a billion people have seen your scars. CNN says your left cheek currently has more global recognition power than the golden arches."

"All the same, the day-glow coat adds a little extra punch. I intend to wear the coat when I walk into my press conference. It'll be unzipped, flapping wide open over the top of this shirt. People *will* remember. It is critical for the world to hear and to remember… and to respond appropriately to the warnings of the Lord."

The T-shirt was printed with large lettering. Above the chest was "Silverthorne, Colorado." The image printed at the center of the shirt was of Freak, depicted as a yogi. He was shown dressed in an orange hooded coat, plummeting to earth, his legs crossed and hands folded, elbows on his knees. Beneath his rump were two flying cherubs, each extending pine branches to form an X.

Printed under the X were the words: "Ground Zero."

Krissy had designed and begun selling the controversial shirt in local shops and on her web site shortly after Freak's airliner had been detonated by terrorists in the skies above Summit County. Thanks to Freak's notoriety as the miraculous lone survivor who claimed to have been saved by two angels, and his instant global audience as the presumptive End of Days prophet for the Lord, sales had been brisk.

I'd seen the shirt's effect on the public. The incongruence between the absurd graphics and the tragic New York towers Ground Zero mythos never failed to bring a puzzled frown… or an angered wince.

"Krissy," I said, "is going to love you. She's going to sell out of the rest of those shirts in less than an hour. In all sizes."

At the mention of Krissy, Heather paused. She shot a quick dart at me, then at Freak and the shirt. Finally, she resumed her cleaning, gathering several stray cups and loudly piling them onto the room service cart. She stacked them with enough violence to nearly chip and crack a few of the breakfast plates, if not quite shatter them all.

"Heather," I said, "relax. Forget how it looked with Krissy and the towel. I already told you... nothing happened. And for gosh sakes, don't break *all* the cups. I'm going to need more coffee in another hour. I hardly slept at all last night."

She looked up, glaring.

"The couch," I grinned, "is very lumpy."

Heather scowled and returned to clattering a few more saucers.

Freak watched for a moment, then finally let go and turned back to me. "Krissy's yellow 'Freak Power' shirt would have been a better choice for this press conference. But I don't have one of those yet."

"Freak," I said, "you're acting like you bought shares in Krissy Corp last night. If I didn't know better, I'd fear that you'd been sucked into the cesspool of capitalistic opportunism. Or shameless cross marketing. Maybe even worse."

"What could be worse?"

"Televangelistic fundraising."

I threw up my hands in a wild hallelujah, then dropped them into an exaggerated thigh slap.

"As you know," I smirked, straightening, "the theatrics on those television circus shows are as low as it gets."

"We do owe her," nodded Freak. "But my point is not to promote her business. My goal is to visually reinforce the fact that I'm not just another preacher in a suit. What I've been assigned to announce is huge. The Lord has convicted me—yet again a few minutes ago while I was praying—that I'm supposed to leverage the miracle of my survival from the fall as a sign of His supernatural grace. The world needs to be reminded of God's power to save. And they need to accept the Lord's divine approval of the message I now speak on His behalf."

"Wow," I whistled. "That's a lot of freight to be carried by one little shirt."

"But the shirt does it. Krissy got this one right." Freak touched the bright yogi on his belly. "There's a lot God is saying... right here." He rubbed the image, then laughed. "This signature little guy might not look like much, but he'll capture the imaginations of millions of folks who will be unable to shake from their heads the fact that God saved a spiritual man with a message from heaven. Consciously or not, this shirt will convey a truth from God. Don't underestimate the power of an icon. As you know, even the rocks can declare the glory of the Lord...."

"Well," I nodded, "Krissy isn't exactly a *rock*. But I had no idea she was so theologically astute."

"She is *not* theologically astute," snapped Heather. "She just got lucky."

Heather clinked a couple juice glasses and shuffled a few forks on the far side of the cart, as distant from Freak as possible. "Krissy is way too young to even know what she's doing.... I'm sure she's never even been to college."

Hmm.

"You're probably right," I said. "I'll bet she's gotta be a least two years younger than you. But you do have to admit, she *is* pretty clever."

Heather stopped her fussing. "Did you say, 'pretty clever'?" She frowned. "Or did you really mean, clever... and *pretty*?"

Freak raised his hand. "Please, you two, I know this week has been hard on your relationship...."

"*Seriously?*" Heather yelped, wheeling in Freak's direction. "Do you have *any* idea how much trouble you're causing? Not just for me and Mark, but for the whole world?"

"I'm sorry," he said. "I didn't mean to start something...."

"Well, you did. If it wasn't for you, Mark wouldn't have even met those other two women. And we wouldn't have to be thinking about snipers. And if it wasn't for you, people in California wouldn't all be scared and rushing away from their homes worried to death that it's the end of the world." She turned toward me, utterly resolved. "We've got to go. I need to get out of here. Now!"

"Honey," I pleaded, suddenly unbalanced in a wave of genuine concern. "I know how horrible this has been for you. But we agreed to wait until tonight. We agreed to give this one more day, to see what happens in San Francisco...."

"I drove my own car," she said. "I'm leaving as soon as I can pack and get out. I'm tired of trying to convince you. If you know what's good for you, then you'll follow right behind me." She pointed at Freak. "That man is dangerous."

She lowered her hand, trembling.

"He's going to get people killed," she said, her eyes filling. "I just know it. Maybe even you. But not me."

Heather turned and scurried toward her room.

Within five steps she had lost the battle against her sobs.

6
CALENDAR QUIRKS

"The orange parka," I told Freak, "is in the closet by the front door. I suppose it's about time we headed down to face the world."

He raised his head from his hands at the other end of the couch, signing off from one last prayer.

"Right," he said, taking to his feet. "Let's do this."

I flipped off the news.

We would leave the screen dark until after the press conference, when once again the enormous digital portal would open back into our room, at times bigger than life, flowing with Freak's quotable quips and his dire warnings for a world he painted with strokes of doom.

Freak hesitated, then met my eyes. "Before we go down," he said, "I need to quickly run something past you." He lowered himself back onto the couch.

"Yes?"

"Last night, while I was praying over there by the fireplace... what do you remember? Were you aware of anything unusual as you were drifting off to sleep on the couch?"

I thought.

My keys. For some reason, as I fell asleep, I kept seeing myself grabbing keys. The keys to my red Ford Expedition. My beastie.

Hmm.

"Unusual?" I finally smiled. "Sure. But of course, every hour with you is nothing but one Facebook status update after another."

"What about last night?"

"Last night, it was the sight of you kneeling in front of a gas log fireplace... looking like you were trying to light the darn thing with a match."

He smiled, faintly.

"Seriously, Mark. Did you see, or hear... or feel anything out of the ordinary?"

I cracked my neck. Studied him. "Why do you ask?"

"Do you remember our first night, around the big table, when I prayed for our meal... how when we opened our eyes, Saundra saw the angels?"

I sniffed. Grinned. "If you will recall," I said, "Saundra recanted. The next morning, she confessed that she probably only imagined those two big fellas because you had planted the idea in her head while she was drinking. And because *you* were so confident they were there."

"Or perhaps," he smiled, "she denied seeing the angels because *you* were so confident they were *not* there."

"Okay," I sighed. "What about those angels?"

"Last night," he said, watching for my response, "they returned."

I glanced around the suite. Saundra and Steve were gone, downstairs finishing their setup for the press conference in the lobby. Wilcox and Andy were double-checking security throughout the lodge. Heather was locked in her room. Maybe packing.

"Right," I sighed. "You know I don't believe in any of that stuff. Why do you keep bringing it up?"

"I thought you might be curious," he said, "to know what they were up to."

"Fine," I said. "I'll take the bait. What were your two angel pals up to last night when they returned to the lodge?"

"For one," said Freak, "I'm not sure they ever left. Sometimes I see them, sometimes I don't. I'm pretty sure they get to decide when I can and when I can't. It's their call. If I had to guess, I'd say they've been with me this whole time. Ever since my drop from the exploding plane, when they flew with me all the way down and guided me into the branches of that big tree...."

He paused.

For a moment, we both drifted back to the massive ponderosa pine, thick with bending boughs, heavy with snow. A saving net through which Freak crashed and tumbled, the snapping branches slowing his fall until he plunged feet first into the deep snow powder at the evergreen's base. Until he slid down the steep pitch of the mountain to the place where I found him... and dug him free. The miracle tree that was later defiled in some bizarre, occult blood ritual. Where bark had been stripped and deep cuts and ancient curses carved.

I sniffed again, maybe fighting a cold. I met Freak's gaze.

"Okay. So why are old Mike and Gabe buzzing around this time? Are you planning on making another leap of faith?"

He smiled, ironically. "These two warriors are certainly not the archangels Michael and Gabriel. But I'm glad you've come around to giving my two celestial companions names. One of them—and they have not told me who they are—sat with me last night while I prayed. He again bathed me in waves of encouragement. But he also challenged me to listen carefully and to be prepared to adjust. He revealed to me a few more shocking images of things this weekend that are yet to be."

"*Things yet to be...*" I smirked. "I love it how you always start sounding all King James-ish whenever you slip into your preacher mode."

Freak served up one of those odd stares that he only dishes out to me, and only on special occasions... only a couple of times each day.

"The other angel," he finally continued, "drifted throughout the townhouse. He entered every room, then finally came back here... to you." He motioned towards where I'd slept. "The angel stayed with you for quite some time."

Hmm.

"What," I asked, curious, despite myself, "what do you suppose the angel was up to?"

"For one... I think he was clearing the place of Dark Riders."

"Demons?"

"Yes. Could you feel it... the freedom? When he came to you, I saw two or three flee in terror. They've returned, I would imagine. But for at least a while, you were free."

"Okaaay..." I sighed. "Are we going back to that again? Because if we are, then I need to remind you that the press conference starts in about ten minutes, and it's probably time we go down."

Freak stood. "Then have it your way, Mark. It's just that from the manner in which he was stroking your forehead, I would have guessed he was giving you some kind of message. Perhaps showing you an image or something."

"Naw," I said, rising to my feet. "I woke up this morning with a headache. There weren't any angels poking my brain last night. If anything, I'm guessing my brain might have gotten jabbed by one of those Dark Riders you seem to think I'm so attached to."

"You're not attached to them. I never said that." Freak moved towards the closet to retrieve the orange parka. "What I said... is that *they* are attached to you. And they will continue to ride you until you do something to throw them off and be done with them."

Hmm.

I took a few steps, then changed course.

"Hold the elevator," I called. "I'll be right there."

I couldn't help myself.

I had to grab my keys.

Freak remained on the threshold rug, waiting for me, his hand on the doorknob, twisting tensely back and forth.

"Okay," I said, returning with my keys.

He was unnerving, standing inside a warm room in that heavy outdoors parka.

"Fine," I said, opening the closet. "I guess I'll grab a sports vest. I don't want you to be the only one downstairs looking foolishly overdressed."

I selected one of the new ski-branded donations we'd been given at the hospital. I snapped the dangling tag off and slipped it on.

"One more thing," said Freak. "Something horrible is going to happen this weekend, but I'm still trying to work out the timeline. I believe it begins after the West Coast earthquakes."

Inside the closet door hung a full length mirror. I took a quick glance, then tugged the dark fleece garment snug to my chest and closed the closet.

"You," he said, "were the last person to watch the news this morning. Before we go down, I need to know what's going on in the Bay Area. Are there any breaking stories I should be aware of?"

"All quiet on the Western Front," I said. "A few nasty aftershocks, but the bridges are holding, and Nob Hill still stands cocky—proud and tall as ever."

"Interesting," he replied. "A lot has got to happen in the next twelve hours. The Lord has made it abundantly clear to me—over and over—that San Francisco will be devastated today... this year on Good Friday. And then it would begin."

"Having some doubts?" I asked.

"Not exactly. But the word the Lord gave me was very clear. The destruction and devastation would be unleashed by mid-morning and would last far into the night. So I would have thought the horrors would have begun by now."

He opened the door. We stepped into the hall, let it close, and then started towards the elevator.

"It's probably a time zone thing," I kidded. "Was that mid-morning in New York, or was it 10 AM in California? Or did the earthquakes start at noon in Israel?"

Freak stopped cold.

The part of his face that wasn't locked in flaming scars drained quickly into a deathly hue.

"Crap," he whispered.

I wanted to rib the preacher about his use of vile profanity, but I sensed something was suddenly earthshakingly wrong.

"I'm an idiot," he whispered again.

He lifted a hand to his forehead, then spread and squeezed his fingers into his temple. He massaged rigorously enough to work out a few wrinkles, then hard enough to buckle up a few more.

"What an arrogant fool," he said, his voice suddenly empty, dry.

I sized him up. "You, or me?"

He met my gaze, then looked away. "Me. I am the arrogant fool."

"Sure," I said, trying to coax out of him whatever it was that had grabbed him by the throat. "We all know how you are. That's what makes you so special. But what's wrong? If it wasn't for your scars, I'd wonder: *who is this man... and what has he done with our ever-endearing prophet of doom?*"

He lowered his hand, eyes blazing.

"No jokes," he spat. "We're screwed. I did it again."

I waited.

Freak stretched an arm to steady himself against the wall. His other hand returned to his temples."

"Did what?" I asked.

He muttered something. Maybe curses. Maybe prayers.

"Look," I said at last. "Whatever it is, it can't be that bad. Pull yourself together. By now, everyone downstairs is probably wondering where you are. Saundra is probably fit to be tied. We've got to go."

He ignored me, trembling off and on for what seemed like forever.

Then, slowly, the fallen prophet straightened. When he turned, the fire in his eyes was gone, doused. His cheeks and scars glistened in a couple of moist streaks.

"Mark," he said, "it's not today." He closed his eyes. "Every time I predict a date, this happens. You'd think I'd learn."

Hmm.

"The Lord told me that judgment would escalate on Good Friday. I received a vision of the bowls of wrath pouring out on San Francisco… on Good Friday."

"Freak," I said softly, stepping close. "You're not making sense. Sunday is Easter. Today is Good Friday…."

"It's not!" He jerked back. "Everything is messed up." He shook a hand at nothing. "It's this damn pagan calendar of ours."

"Huh?"

"Through Moses, the Lord established festivals for his people. The whole rhythm of God's work is set to the timing of his special days, calendars set to the moon, not to some arbitrary piece of paper in Rome. At the center of it all is the celebration of Pesach… the Passover."

"Right," I agreed, trying to get him moving. "That's the whole Moses thing in Egypt, with the angel of death passing over the homes with the lamb's blood smeared around their doors."

He didn't respond, so I continued.

"And that's where the Last Supper comes from, when Christians remember Jesus was killed at the time of Passover like a sacrificed lamb. But Jesus was supposedly raised a few days later on Easter... with the cup of wine representing the saving blood of Jesus and all of that. For Christians, Passover is the same as Good Friday, and they're both celebrated on the same day because... ."

Freak shook his head.

"Wrong." He gently kicked the wall. "How could I have missed this...."

"How," I said, "could today not be Good Friday?"

"It's complicated," he interrupted, "but the Hebrew calendar is different from the Western calendar. Kings and courts have been moving dates around for the past thousand years."

"So," I said, scratching my head, "you're saying the real Good Friday has not yet arrived...."

"This year," said Freak, "The Jewish Passover won't arrive for a few more weeks. Using that calendar, Good Friday is still a ways out."

He let it sink in.

Finally, it did.

After considerable reflection, I found a little spot of light.

"The silver lining," I said at last, "is that San Francisco has now got a few more weeks to prepare. That's a good thing, right?"

"The bad thing," he growled, "is that in my prideful haste to grandstand for the world—and to play the prophetic role—I have utterly compromised the integrity of God's assignment. Thanks to me, this could be a horrible blow to the faith of millions of people who might otherwise have been willing to listen and obey."

I considered his words.

I couldn't quite figure out why I cared so much.

Then it hit me.

"More good news." I forced Freak to meet my eyes. "Believe it or not, you are perfectly positioned for this. We can catch it right now. You've got a lobby full of cameras downstairs waiting for your big entrance. In a few minutes, you'll be on the global stage. Explain it. Tell the truth." I lifted my voice to sound as hopeful as I could manage. "Freak, you're the one who was making such a big deal about truth and grace. Krissy even put it on a shirt."

"And?"

"Explain to the world about this whole crazy calendar thing. Tell them God let you and everyone else think that the big shaking would start today just so folks in California would have a little more time to escape. Or to repent... or to do whatever it is you think they should be doing to get ready for the end of the world."

Freak considered.

"Go ahead," I finished. "Spin this. Salvage what you can."

I put a hand on his shoulder.

"Who knows," I added, "maybe this was God's plan all along. Maybe he's still in charge after all."

Freak gave me another one of his trademark odd stares.

"Okay," he finally nodded.

He took a deep breath, then turned towards the elevator.

"You're right," he said. "Let's go. Let's see what God is up to this time."

7

GOING DOWN

Exactly as it opened, I stood at the wall panel pumping the elevator button for the third time.

"Going down?" grinned Steve.

The small back-up camera from his equipment bag was leveled and steady at his eye, blocking a corner of his round happy face. Steve's usual camera was probably patiently waiting for us on a tripod downstairs. Rigged with a live feed to the truck for the "official" media event that would soon begin.

This special behind-the-scenes footage upstairs was another Channel 5 bonus exclusive.

Flanking Steve were Deputy Sheriff Andy Dekker and Channel 5's increasingly-famous hot-shot reporter, Saundra Paige. Somehow, she'd managed to slip in a few moments for yet another wardrobe change, this time donning a billowing red blouse that was tightly tucked into pleated khaki slacks.

Saundra held up her hand. "Hold," she directed. "Okay, step forward… now!"

Before she could drop her arm, Andy had already brushed past and into the hallway.

"Where," he demanded, "is Heather?"

"In the room," I replied. "Maybe packing. What's wrong?"

"Packing," he said, "is the best idea I've heard all morning. She needs to get out of here. We all do. The armored trucks are outside of the lobby doors, fired up and ready to roll."

"Not so fast," said Saundra. "We need to shoot a few more seconds of B-roll here. And then we've got the press conference downstairs in two minutes. Wilcox agreed that nobody has to leave until after the Q and A."

"Bad idea," complained Andy. "I'll go see if Heather is okay. I'll fill her in and make sure she gets packed and ready. The rest of you will have to leave your stuff in the rooms for now. After the press conference, we need to jump straight into the Humvees and get the heck out of here. We'll send a couple of our men back to clear the rooms later."

"What's going on?" I asked again, glancing from Andy to Saundra.

"Go!" said Andy.

Freak and I stepped into the elevator as Andy disappeared down the hall.

Saundra frowned at the closing doors. "Wilcox is really getting out of hand. He claims that one of his men spotted something suspicious up the hill. Now his security people are trying to tell everybody else what to do. And I do mean, *everybody*."

I took her to mean, *Saundra*.

That Wilcox was trying to tell Saundra what to do.

Good luck with that.

As the elevator began to descend, she continued, ignoring the quiet text ping from the phone beneath the oversized flap of her back pocket. "The way this storm is building out there, I don't see how anyone could have seen anything. I looked outside a few minutes ago, and I could hardly see across the parking lot. Loveland Pass has already closed, and the chain laws are going into effect all over Colorado. It's a good thing the networks already had their teams up here before this storm hit."

"Probably a tree," said Steve, still recording. "I'll bet what the security guys saw was a few branches bobbing in the wind. Something like that."

Instinctively, I dropped a hand to my front pocket to check for my keys.

"Lord..." whispered Freak.

He squeezed his eyes. "Lord, have mercy."

The elevator doors parted, revealing over a dozen bobbing cameras and almost as many outwardly thrust microphones, all awash among a sea of intense faces.

Wilcox himself buffered their advance, barking a few orders and drawing us out into the lobby. One of his men stepped alongside, and together they escorted us towards a podium that had been pulled from a side room. The stage was positioned in front of a mountain mural painted in bold pastels on the southwest wall.

Half way to the podium, we were joined by Agent Wright, the head of the lobby's security team that I'd met the previous day on my walk with Heather.

As Wright fell in, Wilcox peeled off, presumably to reestablish control of the event from his agency's command room in the adjacent conference suite. Wilcox grinned and nodded my attention back towards our destination ahead, then disappeared.

That's when the first explosion hit at the other end of the lodge.

In one breath, it obliterated the executive suite where I'd spent the past week.

We later learned the entire assault was conducted by only a handful of strategically placed men. Three teams of two, each armed with shoulder-fired, rocket-propelled missiles.

And each projectile had been loaded with a thermobaric warhead.

The RPGs were probably Soviet made, but the grenade launchers could have passed through any number of military arms brokers or terrorist camps before finding their way into the hands of our assailants.

Before finding our lodge.

Before finding a hundred civilians within their deadly sights.

When I regained my wits, the lobby was in chaos.

Then a second blast rocked everything, striking the armored command vehicle twenty steps beyond what had once been the resort's beautiful glass entrance.

The Humvee exploded into a massive fireball.

An enormous shock swept through the foyer, followed by a sucking heat fist that smashed and scattered everything anywhere near the door.

Freak staggered and collapsed before me, an arm's length away.

Despite the gritty smoke and the snow that immediately swirled into the lobby from the blizzard outside, his orange parka made for an easy target.

My voice joined the screams of a dozen or more others as I grabbed Freak by the sleeve and bellowed the names of Saundra and Steve.

Black air filled my nose and throat, but my mind kicked into that hyper-speed clarity sometimes experienced by athletes or warriors in the anarchy of a free-for-all moment.

I saw what needed to happen.

And got it done.

By the third missile, the explosion that gutted the lobby and vaporized over thirty journalists in a single flash, I was crashing out through a back door, out through the service entrance at the rear of the building. I'd been there before, with Heather, striding up from the sunken ramp of the loading dock bay and heading towards the corner of the lodge.

But this time there was no sunshine. No pretty lady on my arm.

This time I was weaving between cold steel dumpsters under the cover of a storm, dragging Freak by the coat and scampering fast and low on a long-shot scramble to save our lives.

I glanced back only long enough to confirm that Saundra, and somehow Steve, were both following closely behind.

"Quick," I hissed to Freak, pulling him down between the second pair of dumpsters. "Get that parka off." I got him started, then unzipped and yanked off my vest.

Saundra and Steve ducked in beside us.

"Here," I said, tossing Saundra my vest.

Saundra was dressed for cameras, not for a mountain war zone.

She started to protest, heard another explosion, then wordlessly slipped my dark vest over her thin, brightly colored blouse.

"Catch your breaths," I whispered, keeping my voice low below the wind. "In thirty seconds... we run. Heads down. I'm parked over there."

I pointed to a remote edge of the parking lot. My red SUV was covered with enough snow that it was all but indistinguishable from all of the many other 4-wheel drive vehicles on the lot.

I jammed a fist into my pants pocket and withdrew my keys.

Freak handed me the orange parka.

"Your phone," I softly barked. "You need to give me your phone."

Puzzled, he quickly complied.

I rolled the phone into the parka, then stuffed the wad beneath the dumpster.

"Listen closely," I whispered, addressing them all. "Follow tight. Stay low. I won't be looking back, and I won't be able to wait. If we drag this out, we die. All of us."

Saundra shook her head, composed. Steve trembled.

"My headlights will automatically flash when I trip the remote, so I'll have to wait until the last possible second to unlock the doors. I'm going to need a few moments to clear the front windshield, and then we roll. Don't draw attention by slamming your door. I hope you're all inside and on the floor by the time I hit the gas."

Freak looked at the keys in my hand. "How did you...?"

"No time." I glanced to confirm that Saundra and Steve were about as ready as they could get.

They were.

"No shortcuts," I urged. "We'll need to zigzag a bit. Let's go!"

Our timing was good.

The second military Humvee from Fort Carson had just begun returning fire.

Almost instantly, an anti-tank missile connected, blowing the armored vehicle into flaming scrap only seconds after we'd leapt from the dumpster's shadows. No doubt all enemy eyes were squinting through the wind-driven snow towards that end of the fire-engulfed lodge. Towards that end of the parking lot. And in the vicinity of the only recognizable escape route from the resort back to the main road.

We darted, then slid down onto the asphalt lot that was slicked and padded by a couple inches of fresh wet snow. The four of us crouched and sprawled in the lee of an oversized truck.

Moments later, another explosion rocked the crumbling mid-section of the resort. We took our cue, dashing low past a media van and several more vehicles.

Within seconds, we had ducked behind an Escalade. I could see my beastie, patiently waiting, one final spurt away.

I raised and quietly rattled my keys for encouragement, then gave the others thirty seconds to finish clearing their lungs from the dust and smoke and to catch their breaths.

Despite the cold, they were all flushed. Hair wet. Sweating and melting the snow as fast as the flakes hit their cheeks.

Raising a hand, I finger counted down from five.

Then ran.

I led the charge, flying straight for the driver's side of the windshield.

With a few swipes of my fully extended arm, I cleared the snow from most of the glass, then dragged off with my hand what I could from the high end of the hood. Even though it would expose some red, I needed to minimize the blowback of snow and limit the whiteout once we started to move.

At the last possible instant, just as Freak reached for the nearest handle, I clicked the remote.

Headlights on.

Thankfully, the thick snow and the diffused midday light minimized the headlights' glow. Within seconds, I was inside and had snuffed the beams.

Freak, then Saundra and Steve, all piled in. By the time I found the ignition, they'd all pressed themselves as low as possible.

Beastie jumped to life.

Some absurd CD began an autostart, but I killed the sound before the second note.

I jammed the SUV into 4-Low, then gunned her straight ahead towards the steep mountain grade behind the lodge, ignoring the exit path that led towards the main road that serviced the front of the resort... the exit route that passed across the expectant crosshairs of enemies unknown.

"What are you doing?" cried Saundra, not seeing so much as feeling the lurch as we dropped from the asphalt drive and began climbing the steep hill.

"Trust me," I softly called.

A few days prior, at the Frisco Trauma Center parking lot, I'd learned my lesson. At that time, our exit from the hospital had been intentionally blocked. My SUV had been ambushed by the media, and then we'd had to hunker down behind rolled windows, trapped like fish in a bowl as the journalists circled like sharks.

I'd sworn to not be caught like that again. After the hospital, when I'd parked at the lodge, I'd anticipated the need for a possible emergency evacuation.

I had plotted this backdoor escape route, just in case.

But at that time, when I had spied this unplowed service road winding up from by the dumpsters, I had imagined myself eluding zealous reporters with handheld cameras shooting paparazzi film.

Not RPGs firing subsonic missiles with incinerating warheads.

4-WHEELING

Lights off, my beastie hauled herself up the narrow drive.

Almost quietly, without complaint, she dug in with her 20 inch custom chrome wheels, surging into the thick forest and through the churning white flurry of the almost-blinding storm.

Ahead, our gravel service road crossed one of the many ski trails that snaked along the base of the slopes. A complicated network of such trails connected the outlying lodges and parking areas with the ski lifts and the village tourist center to the south. During the off-season, these trails doubled as bike paths, and they were intentionally maintained to the width of a golf cart.

Or to the size of a 4-wheel drive vehicle that could slide off and still pull herself back onto the path in the case of an emergency.

Based upon the direction of the incoming shots, I figured whoever they were, they'd probably snuck up from the village under the cover of the storm, driving in from the left on the trail that crossed in front of us. Hopefully, they had driven past the service road intersection and had parked their vehicle further to the right around the long bend, higher up the slope, somewhere to the north of the crude junction just ahead.

With any luck, they were far enough to the right that with the increasingly poor visibility and all of the pandemonium below at the lodge, they'd not yet taken notice of my approaching rig.

I was counting on catching them off guard. It had only been a few quick minutes since they'd launched their attack. With any luck, for a few more moments they would still be concentrating on finishing their assault—not yet pulling back. Not expecting anyone to be coming up from the back of the Elkhead to challenge their position.

"Hang on," I called.

There was no way to make the 90 degree turn from the narrow unplowed service lane onto the even more narrow trail without dropping at least one wheel.

Thankfully, I had four, and my beastie was able to give me a little more speed.

We chunked down hard into the turn, then violently popped up onto the ski trail. With a bit of inertia and clawing power to spare, I corrected our swing, pulled another wheel up from of the shallow ditch, then straightened for a downhill run away from the lodge and towards the gondola hub at the center of town.

Over my shoulder, I caught movement in the second seat. I glanced in my mirror only long enough to catch

Steve's camera, swaying, periscope style, at the top of his up-stretched arm.

Then movement ahead.

A parked vehicle.

A large SUV, red taillights off, liftgate open. A dark figure wobbling, awkwardly wrangling some heavy gear.

Loading to pull out.

Blocking our escape.

"Brace yourselves," I yelled, not turning my head.

I jammed into 4-High, then gunned for the right corner of their bumper.

The powerful winch below my push bar would be useless today. If we lost our grip on the trail and became stuck, we were as good as dead. There would be no time for hooking to a tree and pulling ourselves free.

He saw us at the last moment. The driver dove from the trail as I rammed hard. The Suburban's liftgate slammed and bounced back up, unable to latch, torqued askew from the mangling crush of my impact.

Thankfully, the trail was slick and pitched downward towards the village.

And the momentum was all mine.

We kept smashing through, my push bar shattering the molded cosmetic pieces around the Suburban's bumper and creasing its rear end.

I cranked my wheel hard left, then yanked right.

Then planted my foot on the brakes.

I controlled my skid as best I could, holding to the trail.

Their vehicle spun 45 degrees, dropped two wheels, then slipped three quarters of the way off from the trail.

I released the brake and hit the gas again, to the floor.

We rammed through, popping the high end of the big Chevy that was still on the path, knocking it aside. Setting it back at least a few minutes if it had any inclination to follow.

"Holy...." muttered Freak.

I checked my mirror.

The End Times Prophet was in the back seat, bent over and shaking with Steve, who despite the lurching, appeared to be trying to re-hoist his little camera periscope up to the window, still keeping his head low.

Saundra was in the passenger seat, up front with me, arms and knees braced between the dash, the console and the door.

I hadn't really noticed her until then.

"Saundra," I ordered. "You'd better buckle up... or drop to the floor. It's still not safe."

She reached behind the seat and snatched the camera from Steve.

"Keep driving," she growled. "You do your job. I'll do mine."

She latched onto the handhold above her door, then with her free hand, she recorded more, filming as best she could as we jostled down the trail.

She pointed the lens at me, then the others. Then through the back window to the crunched Suburban that had somehow kept its wheels and not rolled to its side on the grade.

The trail head swerved in a dogleg.

I took the bend as fast as I dared, then picked up steam, creating as much distance and as many trees as possible between our team and theirs.

By the time they got another rocket off in our direction, we'd put enough trail and obstacles between us and them to waste the warhead.

The concussion and the fireball of trees and vaporizing snow hit close enough to shake our rig, but we never lost speed.

Our trail dumped into a side street that fed into the center of town. Within moments, we found ourselves on smooth wide roads with snow-covered curbs and blinking lights.

Sirens wailed throughout the village.

Confused clusters of tourists with shouldered skis pointed in random directions, guessing from where, to where, and what now.

Visitors stepped from shops and lunch tables, craning their necks to the north through the blowing snow, the direction of our burning lodge and the half dozen or so thundering explosions that had rocked the valley in the past few minutes.

I slowed my beastie and merged into the bewildered village, blending with a few other moving vehicles still debating whether to flee or to find a place to park.

"Sorry," I said, turning to Saundra. "I know this is going to hurt like hell. But I need your phone."

She hesitated.

"Now!"

Saundra reluctantly released the handhold above her door and shifted her weight enough to slip fingers beneath her back pocket flap and retrieve her phone.

"Here," she said, her face pained.

I took it. Studied it. Stopped at the next intersection.

A short-bed Nissan with a roll cage and chrome light bar was turning, coming my way.

I pressed the automatic *down* button for my window.

Then tossed her phone into the snow-filled bed of the truck as it ambled away.

"What the heck!" Saundra all but dove through my window to get it back.

She flung her head around as the truck disappeared at the next corner.

"Stop, damn it!"

"Shh!" I said, raising a finger to my lips and shaking my head.

She blinked, then leaned back.

"Any more phones?" I asked.

Steve shrugged. "Mine is still at the lodge... stuffed inside my camera bag. If there's anything left back there."

"There's not," I said.

We drove another three blocks in silence.

Then, slowly, I began meandering the side streets towards Swan Mountain Road, the least conspicuous route to the other side of Dillon Reservoir, to Highway 6, and then to Silverthorne. That would keep me off the radar to my end of the valley, where I knew every cutoff and every curve in the road all the way north forty miles on Highway 9 to Kremmling.

And then from Kremmling fifteen miles up Highway 40 along the Colorado River.

All the way to Hot Sulphur Springs.

9

SWAN MOUNTAIN ROAD

Shortly, we'd turned east from Breckenridge onto Swan Mountain Road.

Steve pressed forward from the back seat.

"What about Heather?" he ventured, tentatively. "Maybe we should have done something. Maybe we still can. For all we know...."

I reached to the climate control panel on the dash. I dialed the blasting defrost down two notches, then cranked the intermittent wiper back a click.

The cab fell all but silent.

I was eager to leave the valley, but the asphalt was unplowed and visibility was poor as we began the winding climb. We eased along, not risking a drop into the ditch. Or hitting some cocky little Subaru.

One rear-end collision was enough for the day.

"Listen," I eventually said, addressing them all. "With this storm and all of the snow we've had in the past couple of weeks, only a few roads are going to be open out of Summit County. Based upon what Wilcox said the other day, I'm guessing we just dodged a roadblock in Frisco, but we'll still run into some kind of checkpoint within the next fifteen minutes or so."

Steve settled back. "I'm just saying," he sighed, "that we really don't know what happened at the lodge. Maybe...."

"One of the roadblocks," I continued, "will be on I-70, probably up at the Eisenhower Tunnel. Loveland Pass is already closed, so that would seal the entire valley to the northeast. To the southwest, they've probably locked things down on I-70 at Copper Mountain. And then Highway 9 to the southeast... maybe a closure around Hoosier Pass."

"Mark," said Saundra, softly, leaning toward me from my right. She had lowered the camera and buried it in her lap. "Are you okay?" Her voiced cracked. "I can't believe...."

"Sure," I said, tilting forward, tightening on the wheel. "I'm fine. But I'm kinda busy right now."

"Well," she said, "I guess...." She swiveled in her seat to face me head on, her eyes searching. "Back there... some of those people were my friends. Not just Andy and Heather, but reporters that I've known ever since I moved to Colorado. Friends that I met at events, people I went out with for drinks...."

Her voice trailed off with a hungry little tremble that I could not afford to feed.

"Sorry," I said. "You're right. What happened... it sucks."

I nodded towards the road ahead. "To the east, there aren't any winter roads out of the valley. So that only leaves Highway 9 to the northwest, which, if anyone cares to know, is exactly where we're headed. I'm guessing they'll put the Highway 9 checkpoint right there at Gilford's church, right at the edge of town. I know the terrain, and I know all of the roads... and that would be the most logical place."

I slowed for another tight curve.

A hand from the back seat gently squeezed my shoulder.

It had to be Freak's hand... Steve would know better.

"Mark," he said, "you did good back there. Back at the lodge. Thank you."

Despite the blowing snow, I caught the flash of a red traffic light a half mile ahead at the Highway 6 junction.

"You saved our lives," Freak continued. "If you had done anything differently, we'd all be dead. The mission would be over."

"Sure," I sighed.

I gave my neck a quick twist and crack, and then I took a glancing inventory of my companions.

No surprises. Somber faces. Fixed, wet eyes. Shock.

"Here's what I need," I said, suddenly louder than I intended. "You all need to give me another hour. If you want to help, then do whatever I say... and leave me alone."

I glanced at Saundra. "And then—once we get safely out of Summit County—then we can park this rig and we can all have ourselves a good cry. Maybe even a group hug."

Saundra blinked hard a couple times, then abruptly swung away. A moment later, she lifted a wrist and smudged a shaky swirl into her side window. Then stared off into the storm.

"Right now," I continued, "I need to think. Unless there are any more objections, I'm going to focus on getting what's left of us out of this valley alive."

I brushed Freak's hand from my shoulder.

"And as for you, Reverend Jacobs...." My voice was more bitter than I could help. "Freak, why don't you please fold your hands and lay low. If you have to talk, then talk to your God... for all of the good that ever does. But keep the rest of those conversations to yourself. Do it silently from now on. If you even want to bother."

Freak withdrew back into his seat.

"I still believe in listening to God," he said, quietly. "I still believe prayer makes a difference. And I've been praying from the moment we stepped onto that elevator."

"My point exactly."

Ahead at the traffic light on Highway 6, a few cars were creeping east and west through the storm. On my light's green, I finally turned left to join those who were headed down from Keystone Resort back into Dillon.

Freak cleared his throat. "Getting out alive," he said, "that was another miracle in God's plan. Mark, you know this, right? Nobody can deny that what happened a few minutes ago was another miracle. The four of us should have all died back there with the rest of them...."

"Should have died? Listen to yourself."

"You know that's not what I meant."

"Look, Freak. I know you're a bright guy. But think before you preach. Do the math. Answer me this: why were *any* of us even up there getting blown to pieces in the first place?"

I inhaled. Slowly. Deeply.

"It's bad enough," I said, "that all of those reporters and security people had to die. Especially the good guys, like Andy." I glanced at the mirror. "And innocent bystanders... like Heather."

I took another deep breath.

"But what about the families... folks who had booked vacations at the lodge months ago? Families who came up this weekend to hang out together and to have a good time? Kids on spring break, for crying out loud...."

"The Lord," he whispered, "will have mercy. But things go like this during times of judgment...."

"Stop it!" I pounded the steering wheel. "You've got an attitude, Freak. I can almost hear you mouthing it: *If you want to make an omelet, you've gotta break some eggs.* I'm on to you, Freak. I think you can hardly wait to see more people die. The more people who die, the more you'll interpret it all as some sort of twisted validation. A confirmation of you and your jacked-up version of God's plan for the End of Days."

"Mark, you know that's not true. I don't want people to die...."

"Do I?" I flashed him a glare through the mirror. "It's one thing when you start getting all excited about earthquakes and the death of strangers a thousand miles away in California. But this is Colorado. My home. The rest of us here know some of those people who just got crushed or burned alive...."

"Mark, San Francisco is *my* home. I don't want people I know back there to die...."

"Hey, words are cheap. Like I said, innocent children died this morning at the lodge. I wonder if you'd be sitting there with that same *'God is good'* attitude if one of those families had been yours. If it had been your wife and kids burning and screaming from that rubble back at the lodge."

I resisted the urge to stab him another glare.

"Then again," I mumbled, "maybe you could live with that just fine."

Freak started a protest, then quietly slumped even lower into his seat.

"Thanks to you, Freak, people are dying. And the rest of us are running for our lives."

"I'm not running for my life," he said, his voice quiet, but firm. "I'm running for my mission. To complete an assignment from God that I didn't sign up for any more than you did for yours."

He reached towards my shoulder again. Stopped. Lowered his hand.

"Here's something," he said, barely loud enough for me to hear, "that you might want to consider. You can curse me for who I am and what I've done... but I've just been trying to be faithful with this mission God has thrown me into. And you've been doing the same thing, every day for the entire past week. And you still are. God chose *you* to be my witness, and you've testified to the miracle of my survival on global news. And *you* are the one God chose to save my life back there... so that I may continue to be the Lord's prophet to the very end."

He patted my shoulder in spite of himself.

"Like it or not, Mark, you were called to be my wingman. And you've been doing a damn good job with your assignment."

Given the road conditions, I squeezed my eyes closed far longer than was safe.

Maybe I was hoping that with a little luck, I might fly off a mountain curve.

There were only four of us, but our clothing had collected snow in the parking lot. The last of that snow was melting, and we'd all been breathing hard. An icy humidity filled the cab.

A blur of frost was growing on the inside of my windshield, working its way inward from the corners of the glass. Gradually constricting my view.

"Mark," pleaded Freak, "I know you don't want to hear this, but there is something else the Lord has shown me. Something you really need to know...."

I flipped the defroster back up to an obnoxious full blast.

Checked my mirror.

"Mark...."

"I see you're still here, Freak." I adjusted the mirror. "Even worse, I still hear you."

I flipped on my sound system and dialed to KOA NewsRadio.

"Go ahead," said Freak, raising his voice above a familiar commercial. "Tune me out. But after we arrive at the ranch, you'll learn the power of prayer."

I couldn't remember mentioning the ranch.

"I started to pray," he said, "as soon as we stepped into the elevator. And do you want to know why?"

I shook my head no.

"I started to pray," he said, "because I was *told* to pray. Not asked to pray. Told!"

I glanced toward Saundra as she turned my way.

Her face was wet. She'd been listening, crying out the window harder than I would have guessed. I had not heard so much as a sniffle. She pivoted further, lifting her head to see more clearly over the seat. To meet Freak's eyes.

"It wasn't me," she said. "I was only trying to do my job. I didn't have any idea something bad was going to happen. I didn't ask you to pray."

Steve shifted uneasily as her gaze moved to him.

"Don't look at me," shrugged Steve. He folded his arms atop his stomach and hunched his shoulders tight. "If you'll remember, I was filming B-roll at the time."

"Great," I sighed. "Who told you to pray, Freak? Another angel, right? Or did we scare them all away?"

Freak waited.

Finally, I lowered the volume on news.

"Mark," he said, "you keep trying to make this all about me. But right now I'm trying to sort out visions that concern every person on this planet. Don't fight me. You became part of this with me the moment you dug me out of the snow."

"Hey," I said, "my mistake. Please stop rubbing it in my face. No good deed goes unpunished, right?"

"Good deed?" Freak shook his head. "Are you really that dense? This is much bigger than a few good deeds. This is the Apocalypse… the end of the world…."

"Fine," I interrupted. "Then why don't you just put your head down and see if you can get us some more help from the Lord. Seriously. Take all the time you need. I'll fill you in later if you miss anything."

Saundra put herself straight again within her seat.

Steve looked away.

Freak sighed. "Fine. I'll just shut up now and pray. And I'll quietly continue to pray until the Lord gets us all safely to Hot Sulphur Springs."

I redirected my attention back to the road.

And tried to remember if I'd actually mentioned hiding out at Hot Sulphur Springs.

10
THROUGH THE LIGHTS

"Listen," I said, breaking the silence as we rolled towards the T-bone junction ahead. "It hasn't even been half an hour yet. Chances are good that with this storm, most people down here are still in the dark about the explosions up at the lodge."

I slowed, then halted at the Highway 6 red light.

"If we get stopped on the other side of Silverthorne—and we most certainly will—play dumb." I looked at Saundra. "Even you, Saundra. Play blonde for a change… not like you're the smartest person in the room."

Her face remained unmoved.

The light changed. I eased through my left turn and headed northwest towards Dillon.

"When we come to the roadblock," I said, "it might be the police. But at this point, it could even be the National Guard or something. Whoever it is, we can't afford any breakdowns. For the sake of getting out of here, I need everyone to save the rest of your PTSD episodes for another time."

As soon as I said it, I wished I could take it back. Through the mirror, I saw Steve shake his head. I reset my focus on the road ahead.

A truck turned into a gas station in front of us. I glanced down to confirm we still had three quarters of a tank.

"Until we're out of this," I said, "we all need to be on the same page. Our story from now on is that the four of us are all up here from Pueblo. We've been skiing. We're staying with cousins who have a cabin up at Green Mountain. We were skiing this morning at Keystone, but the weather froze us off the slopes. Steve, you're my brother. Freak, you're name is Bill, but you're tired. When it comes time, you'll need to press your scars into your shoulder and pretend like you're asleep."

"It's hardly noon," he said.

"It's plenty late," I said. "You're exhausted from the altitude... and from too much effort impressing ladies on the slopes... and from drinking too many Bloody Mary's at the bar while eating brunch."

Freak shook his head. "A bit of projection there, eh?"

"Saundra," I said, "for the next hour, you're my wife." I forced a smile in her direction. "Your name is Betsy. If anyone hears the name Saundra, it'll set off a whole string of alarms."

"Betsy?" She studied me.

"And, by the way," I added, "if anyone wants to see your ID, the story is that you and Freak left your drivers licenses back at the cabin."

"Betsy?" she asked again.

"Yes. My grandmother's name was Betsy. Elizabeth, really. But my dad always liked to call her Betsy. She's my mom's mom."

Saundra touched my arm.

"Maybe we should just go to the police," she said. "Or if anyone stops us, then maybe we need to simply tell them who we really are."

"Fine," I grinned. "If you don't like the name Betsy, then pick your own name. But not Saundra. The name Saundra is already taken. With any luck, the name Saundra is already dead and hidden under a ton of bricks back at the lodge."

She withdrew her hand. "Betsy will work."

"Don't forget," I added, "to be affectionate towards me. Stroke my knee or something. That will really throw them off."

She shook her head. "What's going on, Mark? If we're going to lie to the police or to the military, then we have the right to know what it is that you're not saying."

I slowed for the light at the west edge of Dillon. It was green, and it stayed green long enough for me to get through without having to halt.

"Right now," I said, "we might catch them off guard. Another fifteen minutes, and perhaps not."

"Them?" Steve's voice quivered.

"I don't know who," I said. "But what happened at the lodge indicates a substantial network of dangerous military types with deep pockets. I also know Wilcox never put all of his cards on the table. Wilcox had spy cams and bugs all over our rooms. And that snake was into our phones. Probably tracking GPS for movement, as well as monitoring our calls."

"Surely," said Freak, "you don't think Wilcox assisted in what happened at the lodge?"

"What about Sheriff Andy?" Saundra interrupted. "He couldn't have had any part in the attack. I don't think there is any way that Andy—or anyone else—could have escaped from the second floor alive...."

Saundra managed to not mention Heather's name.

But the unmentioned name hung like the red light dead ahead.

This time I had to stop.

We slowed to a rest only a couple of blocks from the big elevated I-70 interchange. We waited in the blowing snow, watching as a few vehicles pulled out from the shopping center to our left.

"If it helps," I said, "even the guys at the checkpoint are going to be a bit in the dark right now. At least for a while. When they check us out, they'll be looking for terrorists on the run. Not goofball tourists. Or a brand new bride and groom."

The light changed, and I eased ahead.

We passed under I-70 and into Silverthorne, then swung northwest on the Highway 9 parkway.

Suddenly, a police cruiser appeared from nowhere.

Sirens screamed, lights flashed, and it tore south, straight towards us.

The police car whipped by, slowing only enough to make the turn onto the ramp that led up onto I-70. Behind him roared another set of sirens and flashing lights attached to an emergency response vehicle.

Behind that, a blaring fire truck.

Then another screaming, flashing SUV.

Breckenridge must have called down for additional support, a fourth or fifth line of assistance for the mayhem up at the Elkhorn Lodge.

I glanced at the clock in my dash.

It seemed like hours since the first explosion, but it was barely over thirty minutes.

The last of the flashers cleared, and I pulled forward.

I decided we could spare a few more minutes. A few minutes that could make a big difference if we ran into trouble at the roadblock.

I turned into a surplus store, then drove around to an isolated corner at the back of the lot.

"Guys," I said, "wait here. Freak... time to go to sleep. Scars down. I'll be right back." I opened my door. "It's time for a little misdirection."

Saundra started to complain, but I was gone before she could finish.

Inside, I grabbed four cheap jackets from a closeout rack by the register. A few steps later, I dug several assorted wool caps from a discount box against the wall.

In a final glance around the store, I spotted a heavy wire bin filled with Styrofoam mannequin heads; their vapid forms mingled and tumbled about, each seasonally adorned in a shimmering black polyester trappers hat. With snapping ear flaps.

Readymade for Freak.

I paid with cash and slipped into my new jacket and wool cap before leaving the counter. Then I stepped back out into the biting chill of the drifting parking lot. Freak's hat swayed in one hand, a huge bag of coats and caps rocked in the other, swinging in the sideways snow.

"Here," I said, opening a back door and dumping the contents of the bag into Steve's lap. "New coats and caps for everyone. Let's cover up. Merry Christmas."

I reached past Steve to Freak. "I bought this one special," I said, handing him his Soviet-style fake fur hat. "Flaps down. Turn it a half twist to the left to cover your scars. You know the routine." I grinned. "It's Russian Sherpa time."

He reluctantly took the hat and immediately began working on the flaps.

I stepped back and shut the door. Then I circled to the front of my rig to re-clear the windshield and inspect for damage. My push bar had effectively navigated our recent collision. Through the caked snow and ice, there were no noticeably fresh dents, and the headlights remained unscathed.

Snow partially covered my license plates, so I packed them each with a few more handfuls until what remained of the numbers was completely obscured.

Then I restarted my beastie and pulled away.

11
ONE LAST STOP

We came to flashing red and blue lights and no surprises at the edge of town.

Thankfully, only two Summit County Sheriff vehicles blocked the road, both SUV's. No military. Probably reserves who'd just been called in from off duty.

As I'd guessed, they'd established their checkpoint in front of the Blue River Bible Church, just beyond the Last Stop Liquors store, right where the parkway bottlenecked down into a two-lane road. With the bad weather and the time of day, the frozen gravel lot was empty, but drifts were beginning to creep from the plowed snow banks upwind.

I wheeled up tight, directly in front of the little shop's entrance.

"Steve," I said, turning to the back seat and passing him my keys. "You're the driver now. Remember our story. Look fat. Sound stupid. We're from Pueblo. We rented our skis this morning in Keystone, and we're picking up beer to bring up to a cousin's cabin on the Green Mountain Reservoir."

He nodded.

"Here's the plan," I said. "More misdirection. Freak sleeps right where he is. Saundra and I will go inside for the beer. Steve, you amble over and make small talk with the cops. Ask what's up. Look surprised and scared when they tell you. Act dumb... and make them feel smart. Make them believe we're nobodies from out of town just picking up some booze for the weekend. With any luck, they'll wave us through after Saundra and I return with our bags."

"Are you sure," asked Saundra, "that we should be going inside? What if Krissy...."

"We're going to need her help again," I said, settling the matter. "And her web site."

Saundra hesitated, then frowned, resigned, starting to get what I was thinking.

I gave them all quick glances. "We good?"

They nodded, and I slid out into the storm.

Saundra met me at the store's entrance as Steve made his way towards the cops.

The tiny silver bell tinkled overhead when we crossed the threshold as husband and wife.

"Look who's here!" Krissy jumped from her stool and started to bound around from the back of the counter.

"Hello," I called, thrusting up my arm, cutting her short.

I brushed my nose and gave my head a hard little jerk toward the security monitor above. "Betsy and I decided to come back for another bottle of that vodka you sold us the other day. You remember my new wife, Betsy, right?"

My recruited bride threw herself onto Krissy before the baffled clerk could blink. Saundra hugged the young lady with abandon, slapping her back, whispering something soft and sharp into Krissy's collar and flowing hair.

Then let go.

Then stepped back to my side with a grin.

Hmm.

I tugged on my new wool cap and glanced around the store.

"Betsy, what flavor of vodka was that... whipped cream, right?" I turned to Krissy. "It's hard to believe, but this pretty little thing really goes wild for that whipped cream stuff you sold us."

Krissy hesitated.

She glanced from me to Saundra. "Sure," she said, struggling to muffle her confusion. "Whipped cream vodka. It's over here."

She led us to a double-sided island shelf unit lined with vodkas, gins, whiskies and rums. She selected one, then presented it to my outstretched hand."

"Yes," I said. "That's the stuff. I'm embarrassed to admit this, but we finished the whole bottle last night at my cousin's cabin up at Green Mountain." I slid by arm around Sandra. "This has been one heck of a honeymoon."

Both women produced odd expressions, for each other, and for me.

It felt good to be back in my element.

"Hey," I said, turning back to Krissy. "How are those crazy new Ground Zero T-shirts of yours selling?" I nodded at the display depicting Freak as a yogi. "Has anybody seen that guy lately? Did you hear all of those sirens a few minutes ago? The radio says there were some explosions or something up in Breckenridge, right where that maniac preacher man has been staying."

Krissy stepped back, surprised. Unsure how to play against that line.

"Probably a rumor," interjected Saundra. "Who knows if there really was some kind of attack or not."

"That's right, honey," I agreed, giving her a squeeze. "You can't trust anything you get from the news these days."

"You know how journalists are," Saundra said, adding a small cough of disgust. "Some of those reporters will do anything to get a good a story."

Despite myself, I smiled.

Saundra turned toward me, smirked, then reached down and pulled my hand from her hip.

"Well, Kristen," continued Saundra, "I have to admire the way you've been promoting your web site. I'll bet you've been getting a lot of orders for your Freak stuff. A lot of email, too, huh?"

"Yes," said Krissy, still waiting for more clues as to what she should say. "The web site has been very busy."

"Who knows," concluded Saundra, now looking bored. "Maybe I'll drop you an email or something myself when I can. Just to see how things are going."

Krissy nodded, unsure.

"Beer!" I said. "Steve will kill us if we don't pick up some more of his favorite brew."

I passed the vodka to Saundra and headed towards the familiar Dillon Beach cooler.

"This one," I said, pulling out a six-pack, ignoring the pinup art that graced the labels. "This is Steve's new favorite. Wicked Wheat. He swears that this is the only beer that makes any sense to him anymore." I joined the two ladies as they approached the counter, Saundra in front, Krissy trailing.

"Steve says the world is wicked and dangerous everywhere these days... even in Colorado. And he says if that's the case, then there might as well be some Wicked Beer in his belly, too!"

I slid the beer across the counter and reached for my billfold.

"Maybe that would make a good new T-shirt design for you, Krissy. *It's dangerous and Wicked everywhere....*" I pointed at my chest. *"Even here in Colorado."*

Krissy started to reply, then silently finished ringing the sale.

"Okay, then," I said, scooping up our purchases. "Betsy will probably reach out in the next day or two. From the both of us. Just to see how things are going."

"Right," said Krissy, shaking her head. "See you in the funny pages."

"The funny pages," I agreed, shaking my head, turning to the door. "Or maybe even the front page. You never can tell."

Steve met us at my beastie.

"I think we're good," he whispered, climbing in behind the wheel.

I opened the front passenger door for Saundra, closed her in, then climbed into the second seat, beside the slumping Freak.

"Saundra," I said, shutting my door, "you make for a great bride. You did good in there. But we're not done yet. When we pull ahead, try to keep your hair tucked in. Sink your chest, and pull your collar up like you're cold." I put the Vodka and beer on the floor. "Look normal, my dear... try looking a little less like Saundra Paige."

She darted a look over her shoulder, then smiled stupidly and turned to Steve.

"That husband of mine," she said, "he is always *such* a tease. Why, if I didn't think he might beat me with a snowshoe, I'd say I might have married the wrong brother."

She gave Steve's knee an affectionate, lingering squeeze.

Steve glanced in the mirror, fumbled with my keys, then finally got us rolling.

"Like I said," he muttered, "I think the cops bought my story."

We rolled the short distance forward to the checkpoint.

Steve lowered his window.

"Hey again," he smiled, ironically. "How can I help you, officer?"

An older man in a dark uniform stuck his head into our window, perhaps as much for a break from the wind as to see who was inside.

"I count four of you," he said. "Are you all going to the same place?"

"Sure," I shrugged from the back seat. "Unless you want to buy us a night at one of them fancy places in Keystone. What's going on, officer?"

"Can't say," he sighed. "Where are you headed?"

Saundra leaned towards him, across Steve, looking her lovely, innocent eye-batting best.

"We have relatives," she smiled. "They own a cabin up by the Green Mountain Reservoir. With this storm and everything, we decided to call it a day. We just bought all of the makings for a long party, and we're heading home to hunker down for the night."

"My new bride," I said, leaning forward and stretching a hand to touch her cheek, "Betsy and me... we're on our honeymoon. And believe me... me and Betsy do like to hunker down."

"Okay, then," he said, nervously pulling back into the wind. "The roads are still open as far as Green Mountain. Beyond that, I'm not sure." He patted the door. "It's getting nasty out there. But Steve says he has done a lot of Colorado driving in this sort of weather. So I guess you'll be okay."

"We'll be fine," I agreed.

"Sure," he added, giving my Ford a parting swat, "it's a good thing your brother Steve is driving the right sort of car."

"Rig," I whispered as we pulled away. "She's not a car. She's my beastie."

12
UP THE BLUE

I gave Steve the first few miles of the treacherous road, then pointed to where we could safely pull over in the blowing storm and quickly switch seats.

"She handles well," said Steve, slipping down from behind the wheel, "but you can have her back. I hate negotiating with the mountains in weather like this."

I nodded.

Resumed control.

Cracked my neck and focused on the drive ahead.

I was tempted to take a left at the Rock Creek turnoff, to swing by my cabin for some clothing and gear, but I knew we couldn't risk it. Someone was probably monitoring the property, and we needed to keep moving even if they weren't. It was imperative that we get out of Summit County while confusion still reigned.

With a little more luck, we would be over the next pass before anyone confirmed our bodies to be missing from the smoldering carnage in Breckenridge.

The road was quiet. Eerie in the swirls of frozen white. Desolate.

A couple of chain-clambering county road trucks heading south to Silverthorne approached like tanks, indifferent, washing us in a bath of splashing ice, browning our windshield in a salty, dry film of sand and chemistry doled out sparingly only on the most deadly of grades and curves.

Otherwise, we hardly saw another human being.

We made surprisingly good time as far as Green Mountain. There we were forced to gear down and grope and slide a bit back and forth on windblown curves through a few miles of brief whiteouts and patches of black ice. North of the reservoir, visibility improved and I was able to resume a decent speed.

According to the radio news, aside from a few aftershocks, California was holding firm; the cleanup from Thursday's earthquake was progressing as well as could be expected given the soaking rains that were now expected to continue along the entire coast through the remainder of the holiday weekend.

Reports about the nine airline attacks were limited to crisp summaries, occasionally spiced with a brief human interest sidebar story. The identity of the terrorists groups behind the plane attacks was still being confirmed, but governments were boasting that investigations would soon provide clarity. Promises were made that the forthcoming military responses would be swift and decisive.

Closer to home, confused reports were flooding down from Summit County.

The media was trying to sort out details on another Colorado terrorist assault. It was supposed that the target had been the Reverend W.B. Jacobs, but it was not known whether he was among the many dead being removed in the storm from the waning flames and wreckage of what had been the elegant Elkhorn Lodge.

Five miles from Kremmling, I slowed, silenced the radio, then snapped off the defroster.

"Guys," I said, eyes fixed ahead, knuckles growing white, "I'm worried that we've got a problem. The more I think about it, the more certain I become. Unless we're dealing with complete idiots—and we know that's not the case—then someone is probably tracking my beastie. I'm guessing we've got a hidden GPS device inside a door panel or something. Maybe even an audio bug in the ceiling, monitoring everything we say."

Saundra glanced up and swallowed hard.

"The good news," I said, "is that my rig has been pretty quiet since we left Silverthorne. That'll suggest we must have ditched Freak somewhere along the road. Maybe they'll start searching the snowbanks and ravines and leave us alone."

Freak put his hand on my shoulder.

"Are you sure we're being tracked?" he asked.

"Rats." I pulled away from his hand. "So much for *that* ruse. No, of course I'm not sure we're being tracked. But here's the thing. From now on, let's watch what we say. Assume the worst."

We drove a minute in silence.

"Guys," I said at last. "We'll get through this. But for the rest of today, we need to forget about the lodge."

Steve leaned forward. "You can do that? You can just forget...."

"Of course I can. And you can, too. Sometimes things get ugly. That's when a person needs to block it all out and force himself to keep moving...."

"I'm not sure...."

"Steve... come on, bro. Suck it up. Freak. Saundra. You two like to pray. Go ahead and ask your angel pals for a little bit of help. Whatever it takes. But right now, we need to concentrate on doing whatever we must to finish this day in one piece. Even if they know exactly where we are, they're still some place behind us. Nobody can use an airport in weather like this, and we've got a good lead on anyone who might have scrambled to follow."

"Do you think," asked Steve, "that they'll catch up with us?"

"I know these roads better than any of them, and I've got exactly the right rig. I've been driving about as fast as these slick roads will allow. As long as we keep moving, we're probably far enough ahead of them to stay safe."

Steve rustled awkwardly in his puffy jacket.

"I hate to bring this up," he said, "but if anyone bothered to plant a GPS tracker or an audio bug, then they might have planted something else, too. Especially if these are the same folks who brought down the airplanes."

I met Steve's eyes in the mirror.

"For all we know," he finished, "your beastie might be packing a bomb."

Saundra looked at me, then turned back to the window.

I drove another long mile.

"So," I said, "that bridge up ahead is the Colorado River. Kremmling is on the other side. It's been an insane, exhausting morning. And maybe I've been a little harsh at times. But getting the four of us alive across that bridge has been my only goal for the past forty miles, and it looks like we're going to make it." I tapped the steering wheel and gave the horn a light beep. "Come on, everybody, cheer up a bit, okay?"

Freak cleared his throat, but that was all I got from any of them.

"We missed lunch," I continued, "and I almost wet my pants an hour ago on those Swan Mountain curves. Maybe we should stop."

More silence.

"How about you, Steve?" I said, speaking through the mirror. "Can you make it another thirty minutes?" I shook my head sideways. "Or do we need a quick pit stop in Kremmling?" I bobbed my head up and down in exaggerated encouragement.

"A sandwich," he said, his voice soft, "would be nice. A steak, better. A urinal, divine." He adjusted his hat. "But how can we dare to stop?"

"If you ask me," I said, "a ruptured bladder is probably more painful than a bullet. Let's gas up and hit the toilets. I know a classic old quick-stop service station on the edge of town. Steve, you pump the fuel while Saundra and I dash inside. We'll grab some Twinkies to go, and then you can use the bathroom. We'll be rolling again in under ten minutes."

I took my eyes from the road long enough to smile Freak's way.

"What about you, ol' buddy?" I asked. "Can you sleep through another adventure... or are you going to need your turn at the potty, too?"

"I'll make it," said Freak, twisting his ear flap. "The more distance between us and them, and the sooner we're off this road... the better."

We crossed the bridge.

I flicked my blinker and took a right on Tyler to avoid downtown and any stoplight cameras that might be rolling along the normal route to the US 40 junction. I decided to err on the cautious side. No sense making it any easier than we had to by showing up on a city street cam that someone with the right clearance might have access to.

"Saundra," I said, completing my plan as we pulled into the station, "this time you can play my sister. That way you'll be free to flirt and distract whoever is at the cash register. Depending upon whose shift it is, our attendant is probably going to be either a cowboy... or a cutie. I've gassed up here a lot over the years, and as clever as you are, you'll be able to handle either one of them just fine."

"What in the world," she asked, "are you talking about?"

I pointed at the ceiling.

"Tuck in your hair and pull down your new hat. I'll tell you on the way to the door."

13
SERVICE STATION QUICK STOP

I pulled tight to the furthest pump.

"High octane," I instructed Steve, again feeling the fleeting satisfaction of at least a flickering pretense of control. "We'll pre-pay with cash inside at the counter."

He turned up his collar, rolled out the door, then headed for the gas cap.

"Listen," I whispered to Saundra, reaching into my wallet as we approached the store's entrance. "Here's a fifty dollar bill. You need to get the clerk to turn on the pump for Steve right away. Then you'll need to distract the attendant for as long as possible. I'm going to try to make a phone call that might save our lives."

"But our phones...."

"They've got an old landline here. I'll use the gas station's phone. Play along, okay?"

I pushed open the door and let her lead us to the attendant.

"Hi," beamed Saundra, instantly up to speed. "Pump number four."

Saundra extended my fifty dollars over the counter as if it was a gift.

To the large woman behind the register. No cowboy hat. Not at all cute. The stranger was dressed like she'd just moved to the mountains from someplace near a South Carolina beach.

"Cash for the gas," smiled Saundra. "But we'll also be buying some Twinkies."

The smiling clerk nudged her smudged granny glasses with a hairy dark knuckle.

"Sure, honey," she said. "What a storm, huh?" She reached down and pressed Steve's pump to life with a quick firm poke. "Where are you folks headed to in a storm like this? Ain't hardly nobody out in this kinda weather."

Saundra head-checked my direction. "My husband and I," she smiled, "Bobbie and me are headed over to Utah. We left Keystone an hour or so ago with my two brothers. But with the storm raging like this, I'm not sure how far we're going to get tonight."

"Right," I said, pointing towards the oversized *Bucks* and *Does* plaques on a pair of nearby matching doors. "Thankfully, at least we made it as far as your set of restrooms over there."

I rolled a few steps towards the hers and his toilets, then wheeled around. "Say, ma'am... do there happen to be any good motels here in the Kremmling area? Maybe Betsy and me should count our blessings and sit the storm out right here where we're at."

"Good idea," said the clerk, "we've got a couple nice places right close by." She took the fifty dollar bill from Saundra. "Betsy and Bobbie. How cute. I'll bet you love introducing yourselves at potlucks."

The woman swabbed the fifty dollar bill with a marker from her drawer, then placed General Grant face down on the counter and gave him a light spank.

"How long have you two been married?" She tossed a crooked-toothed smile at each of us. "Are you gonna need one big room for the whole truck of ya, or are you gonna need two rooms so you can have your married-folk privacy? You really make a sweet-looking couple, ya know...."

"One room," blurted Saundra. "We don't need our own room. We're way past that. Our honeymoon ended a long time ago. Actually, I think it was over before it ever got started."

"Darling," I said. "Them's family secrets. Show some respect to this kind lady, and leave a tiny something to the imagination."

The clerk gave us each another grin.

"To be honest," I said, "I'd kinda like to consider all of our sleeping options. Betsy can be kinda moody... but if I find the right place, maybe I can talk Betsy into letting us get two rooms tonight after all. Betsy's two brothers snore something awful, and my nights just ain't the same when they're in the room. Do you happen to have a list of all the area motels and such? I'd love to take a gander."

"Sure, honey." She pointed to a brochure rack by the door. "We've got a few good ones here in the valley. You go and take a looksie. See if you can't find one Betsy might warm up over a bit."

"Not likely," said Saundra, half laugh, half threat.

"Not likely," I agreed turning to walk toward the rack.

"Seems like with the storm," cooed the clerk, "it'd be a waste not to have a good snuggle on a night like this. I know I'd take a good snuggle tonight... if an offer ever came my way."

I could almost hear the clerk winking.

"Come on, missy," she hoarsely whispered. "He's a looker. If yer a smart girl, you'll give him another chance. And he's gotta have a good job." I glanced back and caught the clerk nodding towards my beastie out at pump number four. "He's gotta be making real money to be driving you around in a big new rig like that."

I smiled in satisfaction as I buried my eyes in the brochures.

She'd referred to my Ford as a *rig.*

A couple dozen or so illustrated advertising tri-folds lined the rack's five rows, with several repeats. Near the bottom, I spotted a salmon-colored copy machine flyer from the Colorado River Valley Consolidated Regional Chamber of Commerce.

I snatched it up and quickly scanned through the alphabetized listings.

Showing no favorites, the flyer listed every lodging option for every small town for fifty miles in either direction, each listed democratically in the same bland type.

There it was: Diamond K Ranch, Hot Sulphur Springs.

I made my way back to the counter.

"Of course," said Saundra, her voice barely audible, "when my Bobbie has been drinking, it gets even worse."

She turned my way. "Why, Bobbie," she said, raising the volume as if she hadn't once again been leaking family secrets, "how did you ever find us a motel room so quickly?" She batted her lashes. "My, you *are* an eager one."

Hmm. It took me a moment to gulp past those teasing brown eyes and the perfectly straight line of Saundra's flashing white teeth.

"Ma'am?" I asked, shaking my head, turning my focus back to the clerk. "Is there any chance I could use your telephone? I found a couple of places here on this sheet that might work for the night. But I forgot my car charger at home, and my cell phone is plumb down for the count."

"I'm not sure if I should help you or not," the clerk frowned. "Bobbie... your missus here tells me you can turn mighty selfish. Even rough."

I grimaced.

"Here." She reached below the counter and hoisted up an old black telephone leashed to the floor on a long gray cord. "Bobbie, I'm going to let you use our phone... but I want you to promise not to hit this pretty girl any more. At least not tonight. Not while you're in our town. If you so much as lift a finger against Betsy, she's gonna call me, and I'll have our sheriff on you in no time."

I endured her censoring glare, tried to sputter a promise, then pulled the phone as far down the counter as the cord would stretch.

"Thank you," smiled Saundra, reaching to squeeze the woman's hand. "I'm sure that'll help. At least for tonight."

"My pleasure, honey. Is there anything else I can do for you?"

Saundra was feigning embarrassment as I looked down to begin dialing in my numbers.

"Ma'am," said Saundra, "thanks for asking. Maybe there is something else. Maybe it's what helps explain my mood." Saundra leaned forward and whispered something into the big clerk's ear.

The cashier leaned back, glowing.

"Now I see," she chuckled. "I was wondering if part of your mood might be something like that." She stepped from behind the counter. "We don't have much, but I'll show you what we've got."

The two of them headed, practically hand-in-hand, towards the hygiene and paper goods aisle.

After three rings, he answered.

"Hello?"

"Hey, Mister K. I gotta be really quick. It's Mark. Brian's friend."

"What...?"

"I need help. We need help. Right now. No time to talk."

"I'm listening...."

"Mister K.... have you been watching the news?"

There was a pause.

"Is *he* with you?"

"Yes."

"And you want to come here?"

"Yes. But I'm hoping you can meet me over at the old hotel. Downtown."

"How soon?"

"We're at the big junction right now. Leaving soon. I'm not sure about the roads."

"A half hour will get it done." He coughed. "Are you sure about this?"

"For the love of the King," I whispered. "Do it for the King."

"Got it," he sighed. "For the King. Anything else?"

"The Handyman," I said. "And also bring the Hired Help."

I clicked the line dead.

Saundra returned chattering to the counter with her escort. She clutched a small box to her chest, her eyes laughing, her free hand fluttering like a sparrow.

Steve came in to take his place in the restroom rotations, and I grabbed four bottled waters from the cooler. We paid, and were back on the road shortly.

Resettling into the front seat across from me, Saundra looked like she wasn't sure whether to laugh or gloat over her improvisation with the cashier.

She'd done well, and knew it.

It occurred to me that Saundra was good at improv... quick and clever, even bold and courageous, spontaneously adjusting to every changing situation, responding amazingly well to even the worst of it.

For the past week, we'd all been improvising. Making up our lines and responses on the fly. Doing the best we could as we fumbled forward, taking our prompts from wherever they came.

Managing both comedy and horrors alike.

Hanging in there. Together, sort of.

I turned my head. Met her eyes. Smiled.

"I did good," she winked, "right?"

I nodded. Then pointed my freshly uncapped plastic bottle towards the roof and summoned a good-natured scowl.

"Shh."

Saundra grabbed the camera.

"For posterity," she giggled. "Even if we don't make it, maybe this camera will. The world has a right to know we survived this morning's attack. And that Team Freak has got some spunk."

She filmed a quick pan of my beastie's interior, then focused on our backseat prophet. She gestured for him to give a thumbs up, and he obliged with a twitch and a smirk.

As she panned the cab again, she lingered briefly on each of us. We took turns mugging for the lens in our goofy discount store hats and closeout coats. Steve hadn't opened his water yet, so when it was his turn, he put the bottle to his ear and tipped his head sideways, pretending to douse his brain.

Finally, Saundra lowered the camera back to her lap.

"Thanks for indulging me," she said. For a fleeting moment, her voice was light. "Thanks for everything, Mark. For such a big *jerk*, you've done a pretty good job today. Who knows, with a little luck, we might still make it out of these mountains alive...."

"Shh," I said, pointing again at the ceiling.

Saundra lifted a finger to her lips. "Shh," she replied. Then she dropped her finger and pointed at my nose. "Shh," she said again. "Baby needs her sleep."

With that, she made an exaggerated show holding her water with both hands and drawing a few big gulps baby-bottle style. Then she folded her hands into a pillow, batted her eyes closed, and tucked herself into the door as if for a nap.

I eased my beastie around another treacherous corner. I remained tight lipped, but for the next few miles, felt somehow pleased.

14
HOT SULPHUR SPRINGS

We made it to Hot Sulphur Springs with minimal conversation.

The increasing fury of the storm began to wear on us all, and I caught each of us casting fleeting peeks up at the ceiling and down the road behind us, fretting about high-tech bugs and impending detonations.

Much relieved, I eventually slowed and left-turned off Highway 40 onto the sleepy four-block side road that doubled as the little burg's downtown drag.

"You're going to love the food here," I said, directing my voice towards the roof. "The Hot Springs Hotel has reigned in obscurity for over a century. It's a clapboard classic.

This is the real Wild West... right out of a John Wayne movie. Minus *The Duke*."

I pulled to a halt in front of a weathered, snow-topped curbside hitching post.

"And the menu," I added, "includes takeout. We can get anything we want to go. Everything from buffalo burgers and mule steaks to rainbow trout and Rocky Mountain Oysters."

"Oysters?" Freak pulled his collar and flap into place and opened his door. "Is there some kind of Colorado fresh water species? I've never heard of raising oysters at such a high altitude."

"Sure," I said. "Ranchers harvest them from along the grassy streams every autumn. You're going to find them amazing. Flatlanders always do."

Steve flipped me a wry wink.

We all piled out, slammed our doors, then stepped onto the snow-crunching boardwalk porch.

"Hang on," I said softly, lifting my hand, halting our party in the wind near the hotel's front door. "I'll explain later. I just wanted to make them think we stopped for food. But for now, we'll have to wait outside."

"Wait for what?" asked Steve.

"We're going to meet some friends of mine. The ones I called from the gas station in Kremmling. They always have food, open bunks, and extra sleeping bags at their ranch. We'll hole up with them for a day or two while we try to figure out what's going on and where we should go from here."

I turned to Saundra.

"I hope you're not allergic to beasts," I said. "They might have us bunking down together in the hay in the loft of their barn."

She studied me, trying to parse out how much of what I'd said was meant to be a joke.

"No," she said at last. "No allergies. Although I am starting to suffer some detox tremors. I can't remember how many years it's been since I've gone two hours without a hit from my phone."

"Are you sure," pleaded Steve, "that we can't wait for them inside here at a table? Sitting with a steak and a beer sounds pretty safe to me."

"Nice try," I said. "The answer is no. My friends will be here any minute."

I'd barely finished before an imposing black 4x4 Ford F-350 ranch truck with a raised front plow blade wheeled up and parked at the bottom step of the porch. A blue Ford Explorer with a Diamond K logo on the door immediately pulled in close to the pickup's side. The smaller rig was wrapped in scratches, dents and dings, but the oversized custom wheels and fancy off-road accessories hinted at the driver's pride in his ride.

Both vehicles stayed put, idling, waiting for me to make the first move.

The Handyman.

And the Hired Help.

"Guys," I said, pointing to the big rig's back cab doors, "you three sit behind. I'll be sitting in front. It's time for you all to meet Colorado's Mr. K."

We climbed into the spacious warm compartment. Positioned behind the controls was an enormous white-bearded man in a buckskin vest and a dark cowboy hat with a rattlesnake band.

Hanging from his mirror was a finely braided leather chain dangling down to a whittled, fist-sized wooden cross.

"Hey," he grunted, leveling the thick stub of an unlit cigar towards my face. "Long time."

He pivoted in his seat to eye Freak and Steve as they closed their doors. Saundra tried to nestle between them, clutching her camera with one hand, dragging her wool cap off with the other. Her hair fell loose into her collar and down the front of her shoulders, all except for a single long lock that tangled up into something close behind her right ear.

Saundra lifted a hand and swiveled to disengage the snag.

Then winced.

Her uptown feathered highlights were hopelessly snarled in the rifle scope of one the three high-caliber weapons racked in the window several inches from her head. She fumbled to set herself free from the Remington .30-06, then broke a few precious strands to finish the task before her performance could digress into a deeper farce.

"Mark," grinned the driver, still turned in his seat, "it's a good looking posse you've got here,"

"It all depends," I said, "on what you're into." I shifted. "Steve might look like a doughboy, but you'll want to cut him some slack. He made it out, and he keeps up. He's the cameraman."

The driver tapped the rim of his hat towards Steve.

"And," I said, "you probably recognize Saundra from the news. She's the one sitting in the middle... holding all the hair."

"If he's the cameraman," said the rancher, waving his cigar, "then what's she doing with his camera?"

Saundra started to speak, but he tonked his cigar to the brim of his hat and cut her short.

"Preacher," he said, bobbing towards Freak's conspicuously twisted left earflap, "let's see what's under that lid of yours."

Freak hesitated, then removed the trapper hat without a word.

The rancher studied Freak's scars, squinted, took a drag from his unlit cigar, then swung back around to face me.

"Interesting," he snorted. "Like I said, a good looking team."

I shrugged.

"So what's up?" he asked. "Why two rigs?"

"Everybody," I said, not bothering to turn, "I'd like you to meet Mr. K."

"It's Jack," he said, planting the tobacco stub between his teeth.

"Next to us," I said, pointing to the Explorer, "is Jack's son, Cal." I tossed a casual salute through my window. Cal tipped his head and tapped the bill of his Rockies cap in silent reply.

"We're going to have to make this quick," I resumed. "With any luck, we'll all get to talk more later." I looked at Saundra. "And I haven't forgotten about our boo-hoo party and the big group hug I promised us all for later tonight.

But right now, we're going to invite Mr. K. to get us the heck out of here."

Saundra again started to protest, but was cut short, this time by Jack's deep laugh.

"Young lady," chuckled Jack, "hang tight. You'll get to say your piece soon enough." He pointed his cigar back at me, suddenly firm. "Spill it. I'm guessing you're being tailed?"

"Not sure," I said. "Probably a GPS tracker planted on my rig. Maybe an audio bug. I might even be packing a bomb."

Jack shook his head.

"If we've got a tail," I continued, "it's hard saying how far back, or even who they are. Could be terrorists. Could be our own government. It might be the folks who attacked the lodge up in Breckenridge. Or it could be someone else I haven't even thought of yet."

"Give me something we can use," he frowned.

"I know I gotta ditch my beastie. That's why I asked for Cal. I'm thinking you should get these three out of here pronto. The Hired Hand can follow me up to Winter Park. I'll stash my rig in the middle of one of the big outer lots near the ski lifts, and then I'll throw some more snow on the plates. Cal can give me a ride back to the ranch. If someone's tracking us, they'll waste a lot of time trying to hunt through every motel and lodge in Winter Park. It might take another day or two before they guess we're not there."

"Do you think," asked Jack, "that it's safe to climb back into your rig? Maybe we should leave her right where she sits."

"Too close to the ranch," I replied. "If we leave her here, they'll sniff us out for sure. There just aren't many options in this neck of the woods."

Freak cleared his throat, but said nothing.

"I don't know," said Jack. "I'm worried about you driving that far. If you've got a bomb, it's a long drive all the way up to Winter Park."

Freak coughed, then leaned forward.

"What is it, Freak?" I asked. "Are you getting messages from the angels again?"

"From God," said Freak. "He showed me a few things during our drive."

Jack lifted a bushy white brow.

"Such as?" I asked.

Freak hesitated. Squeezed the cheap trapper hat in his hands.

"She's going to blow, Mark. I saw your car explode."

"Rig," I sighed.

Freak looked sincere.

"Okay," I said. "Freak, since you're the only source for intel we've got right now, I'm going to play along with you one more time." I met his eyes. "During this vision of yours, was I in it? Was I killed when my rig went boom?"

"No. It was empty. But it was rolling, flipping over and over. Tumbling down the side of a mountain."

"Great."

Jack pulled his cigar, turned, then squinted into the back seat.

"Are you sure about this, preacher?"

"Yes. I've seen it."

Hmm.

"From God?"

"Yes," said Freak. "From the throne. From the King."

Jack considered. "The King?" He gently bumped a knuckle against the cross dangling from his mirror.

"Yes. The vision was a gift... a gracious gift flowing... with the love of the King."

I wondered how Freak had known to use that language. When I'd mentioned the word "King" on the phone at the gas station, he'd been sitting outside in my beastie.

"New plan," said Jack, swinging back to me. "Cal will drive your crew back to the Diamond K Ranch. Pronto, like you said. But scratch Winter Park from the plan."

"And?"

"And... you and me gotta take Highway 40 east to 125, just outside of Granby. We'll go north a ways along Willow Creek, then we dump your beastie there. I know the perfect spot."

"Come on," I said. "You've hardly met this guy...."

"No time, Mark. My gut says we gotta move." He turned to the second seat. "Everybody out. Now!" he barked.

He turned to me.

"You, too... city boy."

OVER THE EDGE

I hoisted myself down from Jack's big rig and scuttled to my beastie.

Melting snow had already frozen and glazed on the outside of all the glass, especially the windshield. I opened my door and reached under the front seat to retrieve the long-handled ice scraper Mom had given me for Christmas. I made short work of the worst of the ice scabs, then quickly circled my rig, opening and slamming each of the doors, ending at last with me sitting inside and behind the wheel.

"Quiet!" I ordered, addressing the ghosts of passengers past. I cranked the ignition and turned the radio as loud as I could stand. "Eat your burgers, and not another a word. We've got to make up some lost time... and there's no sense giving eavesdroppers any more clues about where we're headed."

I put it in gear and rolled out behind Jack's big Ford.

Cal was already moving the other way, loaded with Saundra, Steve and Freak.

It was down to me, my beastie, and my one-way run to the end of road.

The highway had become almost impassable, even for the most rugged of 4x4's. Occasionally, Jack was forced to drop his snow blade down half way to knock the peaks off the larger drifts to make sure I wouldn't high center as we groped northward towards the Rabbit Ears and the Continental Divide.

Finally, he stopped the Handy Man in the middle of my lane. And stepped out.

As I slowly rolled forward, Jack gestured for me to keep moving, then waved both arms towards the narrow shoulder to the right. He stood there like an airport referee on the runway, silently directing my jet to the gate where I should dock.

He'd picked a good spot. Right in front of a guardrail that continued up on a long climbing curve. The drop-off was so abrupt and close to the side of the road that only a foot or so of plowed snow bank clung to the edge before spilling over the mountain's lip.

I geared down to crawling speed, 4 Low.

Reached for my long-handled ice scraper.

Wedged it between the gas peddle and my seat.

I opened my door, turned the wheel, and then rolled out into the snow just as my beastie dropped her front claws over the granite slide.

We stood there together, Jack and me, watching her dive, flip, tumble, summersault and crash into trees somewhere near the frozen creek hundreds of feet below.

When my beastie finally lit up with a modest flash and boom, the explosion was such that I'd hate to even put money on the cause. She might have been packing a collar of C-4 near a fuel line, rigged to a fancy electronic detonator.

But she might have just ruptured her gas tank and sucked in a spark.

We listened. We sniffed the burning rubber and oil plume and watched. Neither of us bothered with words.

Heather....

I shuddered, suddenly chilled.

At least Heather had died instantly... not like this... not like....

She must have burned. Perhaps she'd been horribly disfigured by the blast. There would be no open casket. Probably no coffin at all.

I wondered how she would have felt about not being buried in a yellow dress. Maybe she preferred cremations anyway. Maybe she was in heaven now. Maybe not....

I shuddered again, this time at the realization that I knew Heather's lips better than her heart.

I stooped, then gathered a handful of snow.

I packed it firm and round. I gave the snowball a blind heave out over the bottomless ravine.

It was a good throw. On a level green field, it was the sort of toss I could have enjoyed tracking all the way from the outfield into the catcher's mitt at home plate.

But we were standing a month away the spring thaw, and a couple thousand feet above the nearest green grass.

My farewell gesture was quickly swallowed by the storm, lost to sight long before it finished its plunge into the swirling white abyss.

I sighed, then turned away.

"Sorry about your rig."

"Thanks. She was a good one. I'll miss her."

Jack pulled his eyes from the storm long enough to send a brief sympathy sigh. He nodded across the empty seat between us, then focused again on getting us back to the ranch.

"Any suggestions," I asked, "about how I should explain all of this to my insurance company? I'm pretty sure my policy doesn't mention *kamikaze* dives under its listed coverages."

"I'm sure you'll come up with something good," replied Jack. "You've always been able to spin your way out of anything."

Hmm.

"She was paid off, right?"

"Sure. But I'll need to buy another set of wheels as soon as I get back to Denver. And it's not like I'm sitting on a lot of bank right now."

"Maybe Cal will sell you his rig for a decent price. He's been itching for another upgrade." Jack smiled. "Do you remember your first beastie... the one you took home one summer from the Diamond K? She was an ugly 1968 Ford Bronco. Not much to look at, but before you totaled her, Cal and I had given her a lot of good miles. She was Diamond K's first Hired Hand."

"Of course I remember. Cal was running out of duct tape. He sold that old piece of junk for whatever spare change I could dig out from the bottom of my duffle bag."

"Her motor was still good."

"Her transmission... not so much. Thankfully, it was mostly downhill from the ranch to Denver. If there'd been any steep climbs, I probably would have rolled backwards all the way back to your porch. Like the Swallows returning to Capistrano."

Jack smiled. "You made it over Berthoud Pass just fine. Switchbacks straight up the side. But your point is well taken. All the same, I know for a fact that you loved the old girl."

"Love is blind. Especially a guy's first crush... his first set of wheels."

Jack turned the wipers up a notch.

"Maybe," said Jack, "you won't need a new 4x4 beastie. If your prophet buddy is right, your next chariot might have a set of wings."

We drove the next five minutes in silence.

"On the bright side," I said at last, "with my beastie dead and buried, maybe I can upgrade to one of those Shelby Raptors I've been fantasizing about for the past few months. They're saying that even with only the V6, the twin-turbo F-150's are still hitting over 450 horsepower."

"Sure," said Jack, rolling the cigar stub between his lips, "sounds like a lot of truck." He glanced my way. "Listen, I've got ten sandbags under all that snow behind us in the box. We've got good traction—all the way around. We'll get back in good order."

"Ten minutes?"

"Sounds about right. But the weather reports have been getting worse all morning. Now they're predicting snow straight through into next week. It's our annual last big snow dump of the season. If it keeps falling like they're predicting, it'll probably be Monday or Tuesday before this road reopens again for regular traffic."

"That's fine with me. Maybe I'm due for a quiet weekend."

"Mark, let's talk."

"Sure. But I'm afraid I already know how your talks can go. You're going to make me forget everything and question stuff I don't even know. So before I forget or change my mind, thanks for coming to fetch us."

"For the love of the King." Jack knuckle-bumped his small swaying cross.

"Right."

Jack waited a moment for me to touch his cross, then risked another glance my way.

"Come on, Mark. How can you still be holding out on God after watching that preacher walk away from an exploding airplane?"

"All he did is fall," I said. "Any ape could have done the same thing. The preacher got lucky and landed in some soft branches and deep snow. And, just for the record, Freak didn't exactly walk away. I carried him out. By myself. The whole way."

"By yourself? The way I heard it, Reverend Jacobs has got angels."

"How much do you know?"

"Well, we've all been watching the news. And reading the articles about his predictions. And then that whole thing with him supposedly healing some guy's cancer the other day. We know what we've been told."

"You don't know the half of it," I scowled.

"When I called Brian, he shared a little more. Not that you've exactly kept my son in the loop on all of your latest adventures."

"I've been busy."

"So I've heard."

"How is Brian?"

"He says he owes you some winnings from a few college basketball bets you two placed."

"I haven't been able to keep up," I said. "How much of the tournament has even been played?"

"Well, since the planes went down, air travel everywhere in the world has been in complete chaos. And, as you can imagine, officials wanted to take a few days off to honor the dead... and whatnot. But the NCAA did manage to reschedule and play a few eliminations since Wednesday. Some of the games they could manage with bus rides."

"What a mess. I've totally lost touch."

"You've been busy."

"So I've heard."

The Handy Man lurched slightly through a drift, then stabilized and resumed churning steadily up the last three-mile grade to the ranch.

"The preacher," asked Jack, "can we trust him?"

"You're asking the wrong guy." I massaged my right knee. "Sometimes Freak prays in tongues. And he says he sees angels and demons. And he says he hears from God."

"Demons?"

"Sure. He calls them 'Dark Riders.' He says they're all out to get him. And that they're out to get me, too."

"Psychological hellhounds, eh? Memories and wounds from past sins. Bad habits and stupid mistakes, right?"

"No. *Real* demons. Evil spirits. Freak says I've got two or three of them attached to me... all my own. He's been preaching that I need to get rid of my Dark Riders before they do me in."

"Makes sense." Jack pulled his unlit stub and thrust it in my direction. "Based upon what my son has been saying, I'm inclined to agree. When Brian was home for Christmas, he said you've been having girls over day and night. Party, party, party. And no church."

"What? You think just because I stopped going to church I must have a demon or something?"

Jack gave his cigar another twist.

"Brian says you've got a new girl who has been leaving her toothbrush and panties on the sink. He said her name was Hester, or some such name as that."

"Heather," I mumbled.

"Right. Heather. So is it serious with this Heather girl, or is she just another one of your many flings?"

My mind flashed to how earlier in the day, as we drove away from Heather and the explosions, Saundra had lifted a wrist to the window to swirl a small portal into the frosted glass. How she had numbly stared at the passing trees.

"Mark," repeated Jack. "Is it serious with your friend Heather, or what?"

A man's wrist must be strung a little differently than a woman's. I could not quite replicate Saundra's motions on Jack's window to my right. I dropped my wrist from the glass, then switched to my elbow. I cleared the whole window with a couple wide hard strokes.

"Naw," I said at last. "Nothing serious. No future with Heather. We're not together anymore."

"Oh." Jack shifted the Handy Man down into 4 Low. We turned off County Road 55 onto a private drive and began following the fresh ruts left by Cal up the Diamond K's winding ranch lane. "A good relationship takes a lot of hard work. Was it her decision to bail, or yours?"

"The decision was Freak's."

Jack shot me a puzzled glance.

"Heather was staying at the lodge. Not that I invited her to drive up and join us or anything. She just showed up at the door. Totally unexpected." I took another look out the window. "If it makes you feel any better, I was sleeping on the couch. It ticks me off, though. I never even told her good-by."

"The lodge? You mean, she was staying in Breckenridge with you and the preacher?"

"Right. With all of us. But Heather's one of the folks who didn't make it out. She was probably killed in the first explosion. The rocket that hit our suite right after me and Freak had left the room."

"Oh." Jack flowed a hand over his beard. "May the King show mercy." He bumped his cross. "Sorry."

"Sure. Thanks."

"Was she a believer?"

I stroked my knee. It throbbed, unexpectedly tender.

"Maybe. Not like you, though. But probably more than me."

"Well, as I said... I'm sorry." His voice was sad. He may have slipped into a whispered prayer.

"Don't worry about Heather," I sighed, pulling back my hand. "She was a good girl. A little flaky sometimes. But good."

"Good?"

"Of course. As good as any of us. I'll miss her." I struggled for something to add. "May she rest in peace."

Jack cleared his throat. "Lord have mercy."

I stumbled over an *Amen.*

My gaze drifted forward to the familiar structures now emerging from the storm in the last light of the day. The big welcome sign with its cross on the hill. The massive log house, the scattered barns and the outlying bunkhouses of the Diamond K Dude Ranch.

A lot of good memories could be kicked up around here.

From the morning... not so much.

16
HOME ON THE RANCH

It felt strange to be trudging up the old wooden steps, shuffling into the rustic reception room of the main house without a duffle bag over my shoulder... without even a set of keys jingling in my pocket.

My only gear was a cheap winter jacket from a second-rate discount rack.

What a day.

Jack held the door as I stepped onto the braided rag-rug entrance mat and stomped an icing of wet snow from my soaked shoes.

"Welcome back to the Diamond K," he smiled. He softened his customary backslap. For once, I got a shoulder pat that didn't jar my knees. This slap was more like the flank rubbings I'd seen him apply to new-born foals.

"It's good," I said, "to be back."

"Your home away from home."

I mustered what I could of a grateful smile. Jack stepped to the high shelf by the door and dropped his cold cigar stub into a juice glass beside several aging others.

Before I could decide my next move, Rex Jr., the ranch's black Lab, came charging from the other room to greet me at the door.

"Whoa, boy," I said, lowering my palm. Rex skidded to a stop on the worn wooden planks inches from my feet .

Almost everything on the ranch was made of mountain logs and sturdy pine timbers. Inside and out. Walls, stairs, tables and chairs. Everything. Just like they claimed in their ads and on their web site. The floors were warmly stained spruce: dented, scratched, and functionally a bit of a hockey rink for the rambunctious Rex.

Just as they'd been for Rex's dad, Rex Sr.

Rex waited impatiently. His tail wagged wildly and his mouth slobbered around his newest tennis ball. He squirmed on his haunches, cocking his head from side to side, gingerly gumming his prize. By instinct or imagination, Rex presented the round toy as if it was a nicked duck struggling to flap free.

"Drop!" I commanded.

He immediately did. Then stepped back. Waited.

I slowly picked up the ratty green ball. Studied it carefully.

"Down," I said, pointing to my left ankle.

Rex found his place and forced himself to lie, tail twitching, shoulder pressed lightly against my leg.

I gave the ball a high, long underhanded toss towards the other room. I forced Rex to watch, to wait until it had completed its first bounce.

"Fetch!"

Rex exploded, picking up speed as he bounded past the ancient roll-top registration desk and into everyone's favorite room of the house. There, the grandest hearth of the ranch flickered and blazed beneath the exposed rough-hewn beams of the sprawling great room and guest lounge.

Frozen beneath those timbers in various postures of thaw were Saundra, Steve, Freak, and Mrs. K. They'd all stopped mid-sentence—mid-sip or mid-bite—to greet me with awkward stares from the log furniture around the fireplace. They remained still as I completed my ritual with the ranch mascot.

Rex snatched the ball mid-air on its third bounce, well before it reached their ring. He swung wide and looped back my way without breaking stride.

My finger shot in an outward thrust toward the distant sun room. "Kennel!"

Rex caught himself mid-stride, then reluctantly changed course. He obediently loped off with his ball to his slatted pine box beneath the windows at the south end of the sprawling log home.

Feeling as reticent as Rex, I redirected my gaze towards my companions from the past week.

Saundra, eyes red and hair mussed, clutched herself around an unsteady glass of wine. She glanced self-consciously between me and the others.

Steve reclined in a horse blanket. He held a beer in one hand, half an apple in the other. He looked serious... except for the one plump pink toe that poked through the end of his dirty right sock.

Freak nodded, hat off, his flaming scars glowing and shimmering in all of their hideous glory. Mrs. K smiled, awkwardly, half rising from her chair, hesitant as to whether to rush me or to concede more time for me to finish my coming home rites.

Saundra was the first to look away. To rediscover the fireplace.

I was the second.

It was a good fire, but it looked like it could use another log. It was all I could do to keep from going outside and digging through the snow until I found just the right one.

Instead, I began tugging off my coat and shoes, doing my best to pretend that none of them were there.

"Hey," said Jack, slapping me again. "Let's get you something to eat and drink." He glanced affectionately towards his wife in the other room. "Mary! This boy could use a little love. How 'bout you hook him up with some grub while I go tend to my horse? It's been a long ride."

Mary quickly finished finding her feet. "Heavens," she cried, scurrying my way. Her untucked flannel shirt flapped over well-worn jeans. "Mr. Hanson, how long has it been?"

"Too long."

I opened my arms and scooped her up as she landed.

"Mark," she purred, burying her long gray curls into my chest. She squeezed, locking her hands behind my back. "I'm so glad you're here…. I'm so sorry about this morning."

She wouldn't let go.

The hug was familiar, but the trembling was something new.

Finally, I gave her back to her Western boots and pried myself loose.

I leaned and kissed her seasoned cheek.

My lips withdrew salty and moist.

"They told me about your girlfriend. And your car."

I caught myself stifling a wince.

"It's going to be okay," she sniffed.

"Of course," I whispered. "Life goes on."

"Yes, but…."

"Hey," I called, throwing my voice around the room. "It's time for everybody to lighten up. We made it, right?"

Saundra and Steve interpreted my celebratory tone as permission to snatch a couple nervous nips from their drinks.

I gave the hostess another hug. "How ya been, Mrs. K?"

Mary raised her chin another two inches and met my eyes.

"Oh, Mark, you little rascal," she murmured. "It's been too long since anyone has called me Mrs. K."

She stepped away, rearranged her shirt, then turned to the others.

"When Mark was little," she explained, "he thought the Diamond K Ranch was named after me and Jack… he thought that our names were Mr. and Mrs. K."

"How sweet," smiled Saundra. She reached for her phone.

I recognized the motion, Saundra's instinctive journalistic habit of jotting key words into her notepad app for use in future stories.

As her hand hit her hip, her face dropped.

She caught my grin, then forced herself to return my acknowledgment of her loss with an fittingly faked pout. She resettled her loose hand into her lap, apparently resigned to gimp along for a while as best she could without her usual electronic props.

"Sweet," said Saundra again, turning her attention back to Mary. "Mark is like that, isn't he? Saying such charming, innocent things."

Steve coughed a chortle into his left hand.

Mary laughed. "Charming, yes. Innocent? Not since the first day he tossed a string of firecrackers into the horse corral. By the end of Mark's first summer, me and Jack had both turned gray... and we still haven't finished all of the repairs."

Saundra smiled. "But if the K is not for your last name, why do you call your ranch the Diamond K?"

"Is the K for *King*?" ventured Freak. "Or perhaps the K stands for our Lord's *Kingdom*?"

Mary's eyes sparkled. "Yes! Both."

Jack remained planted, thumbs hooked in his belt, studying Freak.

"Two thousand years ago," said Jack, "the Romans had a vast and powerful kingdom. And they had a king—a Caesar—who demanded to be served and worshiped as if he was a god."

"But," added Freak, "Jesus declared that all of our earthly kingdoms come and go. Persians, Greeks, Romans...."

Jack stepped into the circle.

"Back then," said Jack, "the most basic profession of the Christian faith was very direct... and to the point. Costly, but simple."

Freak nodded. *"Jesus is Lord.* Jesus is the one and only true King."

"Christians," finished Jack, "declared under penalty of torture and death that they ultimately served only one Master. King Jesus."

Jack tapped a fist to his heart. Then he turned and left for the bathroom.

Freak smiled, then called behind him: "Jesus is Lord!"

"Yes," said Jack, continuing to walk. "And that's why we give our King Jesus the loftiest room on the ranch." He raised a finger and pointed straight up to the open balcony above the bathroom he was about to enter. "Our modest little prayer chapel. The upper room. It's our King's throne on the Diamond K."

Jack passed through the door, then shut himself into the loo.

The indicated loft reigned down over the guest area. But it also commanded a high view through the soaring great room windows. On a clear day, a person could see southward over the rest of the ranch and far into the valley below. A short balcony handrail ran along the open face of the loft, and above that rail dangled an imposing letter strung from heavy chains. The letter had been cut from lodge pole pines, stripped of bark, then encased within a diamond-shaped frame of crudely hewn logs. The entire logo was lashed together with strips of mountain steer rawhide in a fashion that directed one's gaze to the center.

To a gigantic letter K.

Saundra smiled at Mary. "It's a powerful gesture... naming this place the Diamond K. Dedicated to the King."

Mary glowed. "We try to keep things around here comfortable, but special. A place where our King can feel at home whenever he checks in on us. Or whenever he sends us another one of his special guests." Mary touched her heart the same way her husband had, then turned back to me.

"Mark, honey," she asked, "what can I get you from the kitchen? Your friends say you didn't even stop to eat."

"Why would I spoil my appetite," I smiled, "with the Diamond K chuck wagon grill at the end of the trail? Whatcha got on the menu tonight, Mrs. K? Scratch biscuits, apple pie, pork and beans, and a bubbling cauldron of bull elk stew?"

"Not tonight," she laughed. "Until an hour ago, I was only cooking for three. The family that had come up for their cross-country skiing vacation left early because they didn't want to get snowed in for a week. We had a pair of honeymooners and a big family reunion on the calendar, but they all canceled on account of the highway closures. Lots of empty bunks. You and your friends picked a good time to show up without reservations."

"You know me," I grinned. "Ever the opportunist."

Mary smiled in agreement. "Well, the fridge and freezer are full. But your friends thought a pot of chicken sounded good, so that's what's heating on the stove right now."

I took a hard sniff.

"Yup," I laughed. "Carrots, celery, onions, *three secrets*... plus two pounds of cornmeal. Smells perfect. I'll have a hog trough full of your belly-busting chicken stew. With two quarts of milk... and pie with a six inch slab of cheese... if you please."

Mary proudly shook her head. Suddenly, she spotted a blackish-red stain on one of my socks. "*Heavens,*" she pointed. "Were you shot?"

I followed her finger and was as surprised as she had been. I lifted my pant leg and traced the congealed blood trickle to a fresh dark scab on my knee. At the sight of it, I became aware of a distant throb of pain.

"It must have happened this morning at the lodge," I said, tugging my pant leg down into place. "It doesn't hurt. No big deal."

Mary stepped forward. Her brow was knotted with concern. "Let me take a look. You don't want any infection. Lord knows...."

"Mrs. K, if you don't mind, I'll just wash it off and help myself to some clean socks from Cal's room. Really, it's no big deal."

"Fine," said Mary, reluctant to let it go. "But at least let me put together a plate for you while you change."

"Wonderful," I said. "I'm getting hungrier by the minute."

Mary shuffled off toward the galley. She worriedly glanced back as she vanished through the swinging double doors.

I resisted the urge to follow her into the kitchen. To let her treat my knee. To return to the comforting sights and clanging sounds and delicious smells I'd savored for so many years.

"What a delightful woman," said Saundra, her voice nudging me back. "Mark, you really do need to tell us more about this place."

"Wouldn't it be nice," said Steve, "to take a vacation here. Minus the blizzard."

"Minus the threat of terrorists," said Saundra.

My gaze reluctantly returned to the other room.

"It's a spot of heaven," I said, not moving. "I hope we haven't ruined it for them by dragging our hell up from Breckenridge."

Freak met my gaze. "They love you," he observed, "like a son."

"Sure," I said. "I grew up alongside their boys. I was out here on their ranch every chance I could get. And then, sometimes, Mr. K would let their boys spend time with me and my family in the city. Or, other times, at my family's ski cabin over in Summit County. Brian, their youngest, now lives with me in Denver."

"Huck Finn," said Saundra, "except that you kicked around in the mountains instead of on a river."

"Sort of." I shook my head. "Back then, it was nothing but good times."

"I'm guessing," said Steve, considering his apple for one last bite, "that back then you were a whole lot more relaxed than you are right now. I'll bet it's a whole different experience when you're not trying to dodge rocket launchers and outrun terrorists."

"Back then," I said, my knees suddenly growing weary, "most of us had never even heard of terrorists."

"Or..." said Freak, meeting my gaze "the Apocalypse."

Hmm. I closed my eyes. I rolled my head and cracked my neck behind squeezed lids.

"We'd all heard," I said, "of the Apocalypse." I opened my eyes. "Just like we'd all heard of zombies, Mad Max, and the Munchkins of Oz."

"*Toto*," grinned Steve. He knocked a knuckle against the log armrest of his chair. "I've got a feeling we're not in Kansas any more."

Saundra scooted on the couch, clearing more space. "Mark," she said, "come have a seat. You look like you're about ready to fall over."

I knew the feel of that couch, how it could cuddle around a guy and put a little slack back into the taut wires in a fellow's neck and spine. But what I really wanted was to sink deeply into about twenty feet of goose down mattress... and to not have to worry about anything, or to even say another word for another week.

I opened my eyes again to find Freak leaning ahead, balanced in his rocker, waiting.

Saundra blinked, then lowered her gaze into the nearly empty wine glass in her hands.

I'm not sure what she saw in my face, but I know what I felt, and it was more than a little grim.

And still, I couldn't move.

The standoff ended with a soft slam from the bathroom door.

"Hey!" said Jack, striding into the morgue-like mix, assessing the situation as he moved. He didn't stop until he reached my side. Until his huge arm was draped around my shoulder and neck, tenderly roughing me up like I'd just been thrown from a spinning tire swing.

"What's the matter with you people?" he demanded. "After everything you four have been through this week, I would have thought you'd all be friends by now."

"We are," insisted Saundra. She sounded way too hurried and apologetic.

"Where's Cal?" I asked, still resisting any tugs towards the circle. "I'd like to thank him for bailing us out. It was good of him to be out there for us in a storm like this."

"Chores," volunteered Freak. "Cal went straight to the barns as soon as we got back. That Cal is a good fellow. We had a very enlightening talk on our way back to the ranch. I get the feeling that for Cal, growing up beneath the shadow of that hanging K," Freak nodded towards the loft, "has made him a righteous man."

"You and Cal," said Jack, turning to me, "you two can catch up soon enough." He ran his appraisal down to my feet, then back to my eyes. "Mark, you go freshen up in the bathroom. Empty your trash. Splash some freezing mountain well water on your face. Then come join us again out here when you're ready. Meanwhile, I'm looking forward to having these three friends of yours all to myself for a spell."

He glanced at Freak.

"Sorry," said Jack, winking. "I guess maybe *spell* was a poor choice of words. I heard about those blood sacrifices and that whole pagan curse and spell business up at the tree by Mark's cabin."

"You're fine," said Freak, leaning back with a half grin. "God has assured me that it's all been handled. The spell is off. We're clean."

"Clean, huh?" Jack found the seat closest to Freak. "I'd like to hear more about what you saw at that tree. They say you thought you saw...."

Saundra shuddered. "Just a black crow," she interrupted. "It was only a big black bird."

"Hell of a bird," added Steve.

"Or…" said Freak, "a bird from hell."

I took my leave. "Have at it, Jack," I said. "They're all yours."

REFLECTIONS

I dawdled, in no hurry for whatever was next. I peeled off my blood-caked sock, sponged off my knee and shin, and put on the clean pair that I'd borrowed from the dresser in Cal's room.

The doctor's advice about splashing cold water helped, but I knew my weariness could not be washed away or assuaged short of a couple of cold beers and a dark ocean of sleep.

I scrubbed my cheeks with a coarse green towel from the doweled rack. I pressed aggressively, trying to coax some life into whatever remained of my wits.

I blinked a few times, then sighed, then let my mind roam about the ranch.

Beyond the sink mirror, a half-sized, younger Mark returned my gaze. He blinked back at me from beneath his first cowboy hat; his eyes brimmed with naive wonder and soaring expectation. This ranch. The mountains. The barns. The snorting horses and the long, dusty wagon rides.

Tin cups of beans and plates sagging with the weight of barbecued smoked pork.

The mesmerizing cadence of Mr. K's passionate prayers over the food and the harvest... and his closed-eyed pleas for millions of hungry children in lands far away.

The embellished campfire tales of heroic Bible kings and lowly servant saints.

Parents nodding in approval. Driving off, leaving me in a week of heaven.

Leaning back into sweet wrist-stinging bales of fresh-cut hay.

Soft guitars, wild banjos, and crisp country fiddling.

Lyrics laced with laughter. Stomping boots, and songs of simple faith.

Jesus the rancher. The King.

The Spirit... the wind.

God... the old man with a pen, writing his story of heaven and earth.

Of mountains and moms and dads and spoiled kids.

Of me.

I selected an upright clean water glass from the assortment on the weathered plank nailed beside the sink.

Filled it with Mrs. K's world-renowned unfiltered Rocky Mountain pump juice.

Closed my eyes and drank deeply, really deeply, for the first time in a few years.

Filled my cheeks with a second draught. Rolled my tongue in the remembered cold. Let it warm within my mouth. Let it leak in tiny wet trickles to stir a neglected dry throat.

I lingered in the dark, resisting what I feared to see when I opened my eyes.

Finally, the water gone, I blinked and returned to my day.

Reality.

I replaced the cup, then killed the light.

And stepped out to join the uncertain circle around the ebbing fire beyond the little room's door.

18
HEARTHSIDE HUDDLE

"I'm just saying," complained Steve, "that Jack makes a good point. Right now, we're off the grid. Below radar. Nobody has a clue where we are. If we lay low, it could be a week or two before we need to worry about making our next move."

"This is *not*," objected Freak, "about our own personal comfort and safety. It's about God's mission. As I have repeatedly made clear, millions of lives are at stake. God's plan is much bigger than the pleasantries of a handful of us hiding out in the secluded mountains of Colorado. While we drink hot chocolate in the warmth of this cozy fireplace, entire cities are on the verge of collapse.

Thousand of souls are balanced between the glories of heaven... and the fires of hell."

I cleared my throat. "That's being a little melodramatic, wouldn't you say?"

Freak jerked at my sudden appearance.

"Mark," demanded Saundra, "where have you been so long?"

"We about gave up on you," said Steve. "Did the toilet monster grab you by the outhouse, or what?"

"That," I replied, "is a rather personal question. But if you really want to hear about it...."

"No," grinned Steve, waving his hand. "I'm sorry I even asked."

"Seriously," I joked, "I know it sounds painful—and it is. But a guy has never really lived until he's been grabbed by the outhouse...."

"Enough," frowned Jack. "So I guess you're feeling better now? Are you ready to rejoin the living?"

"Or the dying," mumbled Steve.

"Not exactly," I sighed. "But I don't think it particularly matters *what* I'm feeling these days. The show must go on... with or without us clowns."

"Great. We need your input on something. Saundra and the preacher here are determined...."

"Freak," interrupted Freak. "Please, I really would prefer it if you'd call me by that name."

"Fine," said Jack, giving me a wink. "Freak over there," he tossed a thumb across the hearth, "he says it's imperative for him to do an interview... to release a statement. He says he's gotta get the word out, and he wants to film it right now, with Saundra and Steve."

Freak turned to Saundra, trying to coax out some additional support.

"I know," said Saundra, "it sounds dangerous. But we've got an idea about how to do this, and it seems really important."

"Besides," Freak added, "if we follow the Lord's plan, he will protect us. Exactly as he did this morning…."

"Another round," I grinned, "of exactly what we got this morning? This is your idea of encouragement?"

Freak frowned. "You know what I meant."

"We've already determined," said Saundra, "the Diamond K Ranch has the Internet capacity for uploading digital files to Kristen's computer back in Silverthorne. I figure if we can send a few files to her in the next hour or so, then she should be able to have them uploaded onto her website by tonight."

"I just need," Freak said, "to make a few brief statements. Nothing too extensive or specific at this point. Mark, it all comes back to what we were discussing in the hallway this morning. If we don't explain this whole calendar confusion and why the big earthquakes that I predicted are not happening in California today, then folks are going to question everything else I've said. And, even worse, it's going to be twice as hard for them to believe anything new that the Lord gives me to say about what is coming next. Let alone the hard things they should do in preparation for his return."

Hmm.

"On the other hand," said Jack, "I'm concerned about the attack this morning at the lodge. I'm worried about people being able to trace things back to this ranch through the liquor store girl. They'll figure it out in a hurry and be here in no time. We're talking about professional killers. A fully equipped militia...."

"*Rodney*," I said, dropping myself at the near end of Saundra's couch. "As much as I can't stand him, Rodney is the answer. We need to get another preacher into the mix."

"Pastor Gilford?" Saundra shook her head. "Why in the world would we want to get him involved?"

"Look," I said, "Jack is right. We need to slow them down and buy some time to let this go viral. By now, Kristen's web site has been hacked and is being monitored every minute. I doubt they'll have cut her off yet, but whoever they are, they'll be watching and tracing everything coming in or out of her IP address."

"Yes, but...."

"Saundra, what you need to do is to pull up Rodney Gilford's church website. Get his contact information, and then send your files to him. Tell him to copy everything onto a Memory Stick. Then have him personally walk the flash drive over to Krissy at the liquor store."

Steve smiled. "That way, there would be no easy cyber trail to trace from Krissy's computer back to our location here at the ranch."

"Precisely. Freak's location will remain off the grid for as long as Krissy can hold out and refuse to give Gilford up as her source. And if she immediately and simultaneously sends copies to all her friends and multiple web sites, the files will get out there before they discover what's going on."

"But," objected Saundra, "why would Pastor Gilford help us? And do you think the liquor store would even be open during this storm...."

"Of course," said Freak, rising to his feet. "Brilliant."

He took two steps, then spun towards Saundra. "Rodney is full of the Lord right now. He was just miraculously healed of cancer. The Spirit will confirm for him that this is his role in God's plan." Freak smiled. "He'll do it."

"And," said Steve, "the liquor store will be open. With the weather this bad, sales will be going through the roof. Everyone is going to want to settle in with their favorite...."

"What I meant," said Saundra, "is that I'm worried the roads might be closed...."

"The plows," I said, "will keep the roads open to the edge of town. They might not scrape out into the boondocks, but for emergencies and things like that, they will keep the main roads in town open no matter what. The county road trucks will use the liquor store and Gilford's parking lot as their terminus. During blizzards, that's where they always turn around and head back into the village. The liquor store will be open, and Krissy will be there."

"I like it," said Freak. "We could probably only use Kristen once, but if she moves quickly, that might be all we need."

He leaned forward. "So, Jack... what do you think?"

Jack tugged his beard.

"It's a good plan," said Jack. He looked towards me. "But for some reason, I'm not feeling any confirmation in my gut. I can't put my finger on the problem."

"Well," asked Steve, resigned, "should I start setting up for an interview, or not?"

Saundra nodded yes.

Freak's scars began to flush. "Jack," said Freak, "if you're worried about somebody recognizing the ranch, maybe we could hang up a big white sheet backdrop or something. Nobody would ever be able to guess where we're filming."

"It's not that," said Jack. "Tell me again... what exactly is it you feel you need to tell the world?"

Freak returned to his seat. He bobbed his head for Steve and Saundra to begin setting up a makeshift studio.

"As you know," said Freak, "in my interviews, I've been warning the world that San Francisco and the West Coast would be experiencing a series of catastrophic earthquakes this year on Good Friday." He glanced at me. "Today."

"The *problem*," I continued, filling in for Freak, "is that today is Good Friday. And so far, we have *not* had any apocalyptic shakings. We have not heard the screams of the dying masses. Except for here in Colorado, nobody has suffered. All is quiet on the Western Front. And, ironically, that is a problem."

"No," corrected Freak, bumping a knuckle against his brow. "The *problem* is that when the Lord told me to prophesy about these disasters, I surged ahead without waiting for confirmations. My worst assumption was about the date. I assumed that Good Friday was Good Friday, as the holiday is found on our Western calendar...."

"As opposed," interrupted Jack, "to the time of Passover... the Passover that is defined by the moons of the Jewish calendar."

"Exactly."

Freak again rose to his feet. He raised a hand. "That is why it is imperative we get on the air, and as soon as possible. Yet today. We need to apologize and to explain to the world that many thousands of people are about to die, but just not...."

The front door burst open.

Cal pounded into the entrance. He swayed, framed in a blast of cold air and a swirl of huge spinning flakes.

"*Yo!*" He yelled, slamming the door.

"Turn on the TV!" He kicked off his right boot. "Now!"

"Cal!" cried Mary, scurrying in from the kitchen, hands fluttering within her apron. "What on Earth is the matter?"

He kicked off his other boot, tossed his ball cap onto the coat rack, then hurried our way. He dropped an arm from a parka sleeve as he reached the couch.

"You're not going to believe," he panted, "what I just heard in the barn," he dropped into a chair, "on the radio!"

"What?" exclaimed his father.

"Just turn on the darn TV!"

19

SEVEN BOWLS OF WRATH

No cable on the ranch, but the Diamond K sported a satellite dish loaded with all of the major networks, as well as all of the most popular Denver stations.

Not that every channel wasn't providing continuous coverage of the same scenes.

Live disaster stories from California… and from around the globe.

Freak had been wrong about being wrong about Good Friday.

The devastating succession of "washboard shakings" he had predicted for California in the wake of yesterday's

Rodger's Creek Fault release had suddenly begun. A tag team of extraordinarily violent Hayward Fault ruptures in the north and south Bay Area were quickly followed by a Great Calaveras earthquake surpassing 8.0. The powerful series of erratic aftershocks was proved to be deadly and cataclysmic for structures already compromised by previous disturbances.

The fall of San Francisco had begun... with mudslides, fires, and the pandemonium of failing evacuation routes in the midst of heavy rains and the chaos of an overwhelmed emergency response system.

It was all playing out now on live television exactly as foretold.

Including residential looting, panic, and lawlessness in the streets.

But there was more.

Competing for airtime with the mayhem and lawlessness in San Francisco were horrific bombings and battle stories from Europe, North Africa, Indonesia, and the Middle East.

Scenes of deadly explosions and burning cities were flowing non-stop across the screen. We could hardly keep track of whether we were witnessing the carnage of a drone strike in London, watching a live stream of a collapsing storefront in San Francisco, or reviewing footage from the unraveling of a Frankfort siege.

It was numbing.

The nightmare images.

The sounds and reports.

The fatalities.

For the first thirty minutes or so, we huddled close to the television, speechless, trying to take it all in. Slowly, we began leaning back. Slumping away from the images. Checking the time. Asking simple questions and whispering short observations.

Rex ventured out from his kennel. He sniffed around our circle, glanced several times at the television, then curled against Freak's feet.

After an hour, Jack rose from his chair and walked to the screen.

He clicked the monitor dead. He killed the barrage of horrors the old fashioned way: with a stiff finger-punch to a small black button at the TV's base.

The big rancher turned where he stood.

"Freak," he asked, "what's going on? People aren't supposed to act this way. *Martial law*... the governor is already talking about imposing martial law to empower the military to handle the anarchy... in San Francisco, of all places! It makes no sense...."

Freak hesitated.

Saundra quietly ventured into the conversation, her head shaking.

"I agree with Jack. After 9/11 in New York—even during Hurricane Katrina in New Orleans—it never got like this. When cities were bombed during World War II... people pulled together...."

"This," sighed Freak, "is not a couple of skyscrapers in a safe city filled with millions of well-wishers. This is not even World War II." He ran his fingers through his hair. "This is the Apocalypse."

Steve cleared his throat. "I'm not even sure what that means. I've seen plenty of apocalyptic movies and television shows, and I've read a few books, but in the real world...."

"In the real world," said Freak, "we have entered a season without precedent. There is nothing comparable since the days of Noah. In sheer numbers, the scale and the nature of these shakings on the West Coast are already unlike anything in the history of our species."

"When it comes," I said, "to apocalyptic hysteria... I'm no expert. But I know a little bit about the whole martial law business. If I remember right, martial law has already been imposed at least once in the city of San Francisco... after the 1906 earthquake. And before that, martial law was enforced in response to the Great Chicago Fire in the late 1800's. Even here in Colorado, a hundred years ago our governor pulled the Colorado National Guard off the Coalfield War and turned the whole thing over to federal troops. He was forced to declare martial law in the mining districts because of the Ludlow Massacre. All of the usual rules of order were collapsing under the pressure of bloodshed and fear."

"Maybe," said Jack, "but that was a long time ago."

"Jack," I asked, "how about in your own lifetime? Not that long ago, the governor of Alabama declared martial law in response to the mobs and lawlessness surrounding the Freedom Riders."

Freak met Jack's eyes. "Do you realize," he said, "that even under martial law, soldiers will be unable to enforce a curfew tonight? Too few apartment buildings and homes are still standing. The entire city has collapsed, along with other cities up and down the coast. Tens of millions of people are without power and running water, injured, cold, wet... waiting for help."

"Yes," said Saundra, "but they've got to know that within a few days...."

"Within a few days," said Freak, "many of their worst fears will be confirmed. The criminal element—and many of the survivors—sense what is yet to come. Deep down, they fear. And they know."

"Know what?" asked Steve.

"They know," said Freak, "that their days are numbered. They know the judgments and the destruction they are currently facing will be escalating to a global level. They know their city is *beyond* saving. It will not be rebuilt. They will not be rescued anytime soon. They will need to scavenge for food. They will never have another home, and they will never work again. In short, they know their world is coming to an end."

The room fell still.

"And that," said Jack, with a clap of his hands, "is enough of *that*. At least for now."

To his credit, Mr. K paused long enough to field any objections.

There were none.

"Okay, then," he continued, "let's eat." He turned to his wife, who had long ago turned the chicken pot down to a simmer. "Mary, dear, do you need some help setting out a few bowls or anything?"

"No," she stammered, rising from her chair, "I'll only need a minute." She turned from her husband to face Freak, who eyed her expectantly, waiting for her question.

"Reverend Jacobs," she asked at last, "it really has begun... hasn't it?"

For once, Freak resisted the opportunity to correct an innocent bystander for failing to address him by his End Times prophetic handle.

"Yes," he softly replied. "It has begun."

Instead of eating in front of the nightly news, as had become our custom at the lodge, and rather than sitting around the massive ranch dining hall table, we quietly gathered in the kitchen to eat.

But not before we had prayed.

As we filed away from the television for our supper, Mary fussed and mumbled quiet apologies for not having put together a few side dishes and a dessert to round out our slabs of honey-yellow cornbread and steaming bowls of stew.

"Sorry," she said again from her station behind the counter, "I just got so caught up in the news...."

"Please," protested Steve, "no apologies. This looks and smells absolutely delicious. Thank you for all you've done." He smiled at the huge chunk of white meat Mary had just dolloped into his bowl. "After what I lived through this morning, and with everything that is going on out there in the world tonight, I feel like the luckiest man on the planet. And this feast just perfectly rounds out my luck."

He said it like he meant it.

"Hush," said Mary, kindly. "There is no luck. Only the grace of our Lord... the mercies of our King."

"Well, thank you all the same," he said, saluting her with his bowl.

"It is good," said Jack, waiting for us to settle ourselves into seats around the kitchen's plank table, "that we thank Mary for preparing this wonderful meal."

I knew the routine. What Jack would say next. He had been leading versions of this same liturgy for longer than I could remember.

"We say *thank you* to the cook," Jack continued, "for having prepared this meal." He slowly moved his gaze from chair to chair. "But it is our King who has given us this day, this ranch... and this food. Mary did not make this food, but she *did* skillfully rearrange what the Lord first made... that which our King entrusted to her care."

Jack gave his wife a tender wink and nod. "It was Mary who prepared this feast... and it was she who put a little fresh heat on it. Thank you, Mary."

"Thank you, Mary," I echoed, reciting before I could even question my role in the familiar rite.

"Yes," said Jack, "even as we thank our gracious cook, it is also right and good that we should thank our gracious Lord... our heavenly Father who made this food of which we shall now partake." He closed his eyes and raised his hands.

"Let us pray."

It was a stirring prayer.

Heartfelt, as always, but somehow it transitioned from the food into something utterly contemporary to the hour. Relevant to our planet's most traumatic Good Friday in the past 2,000 years.

I listened. Felt. Squeezed my eyes in spite of myself when he thanked God for the four of us who had survived the morning's explosions at the lodge.

Somewhere in there he starting praying some pretty specific sentiments, using names and pleading for mercy towards the unnamed others from the lodge—and from around the world—who had been hurt or killed. For those in pain. For the lost. For Sheriff Andy. Heather.

Saundra started to sob softly, and then one or two of the others joined in muffled tremors of their own.

I lost track of the time, then caught myself forgetting to breathe... forced myself back to the darkly grained wooden slab of the Diamond K olive-stained butcher-block table.

He finished.

I believe we all instinctively confirmed with a somber *amen.*

20
CHICKEN STEW

As we spooned deeper into our bowls, subdued comments eventually gathered misplaced heat, then flared into an increasingly steamed give-and-take debate.

"If we hadn't over-reacted to 9-11," insisted Saundra, "then the Islamic extremists would have lost their ability to recruit new members. It was only after we invaded Iraq and began to occupy their lands that...."

"*Come off it*," Cal growled. "If the United States had failed to invade, then Muslims everywhere in the world would have perceived us as too weak to follow through in our own defense. Americans would have had targets on their backs everywhere, even here at home. The Islamaicists have a stated goal of a one-world religion. And, unlike Christianity, their accepted methods for conversion include threats, torture, and war."

"Now honey," corrected his mother, "you know it's not fair to lump people together with negative generalizations like that."

"The American people," said Saundra, "were ready to withdraw from Iraq. The election and all of the polls were conclusive on that. The majority of us were ready to get on with our lives and to bring our soldiers home."

"If you ask me," Cal retorted, "pulling out of Iraq was a chicken move. It was our cowardly retreat that encouraged the fanatics to take it to the next level in the first place. If we'd voted in a President who wasn't a Muslim sympathizer, then maybe...."

"Maybe," I said, "if the Republicans had come up with a better set of candidates, then at least we could have...."

"*Enough!*"

Jack didn't need to slam his fist on the table to cut us short. He had always wielded his *Enough's* that way. With the force and skill of a swordsman.

"I've tried to remain silent," Jack continued, "but this little blame game is getting out of hand. Not just you folks, but everyone. The media. Politicians from both sides of the aisle. Religious organizations. I'm getting sick of these senseless, finger-pointing, endless debates."

I dropped my attention to the bottom of my all-but-empty bowl.

"I agree," said Freak. "Jack is right."

They met eyes.

"At this point in history," said Freak, "blaming people will accomplish nothing." He moved his gaze around the table. "Nor will trying to fix it. We're past the point of being able to fix any of this."

"What do you mean?" asked Steve. "If we suffer another attack on American soil, like those we saw tonight in Europe...."

Freak sighed deeply, loudly. It was his own understated version of Jack's *Enough.*

"Steve," said Freak, sighing again. "All of you. What we are now witnessing is from the Lord. There are supernatural forces behind these events. Not just the uprisings and the attacks, but the earthquakes in California... and all that is soon to come. We are experiencing the signs and wonders of God. As well as the work of angels and demons...."

"Freak," I said. "For once, I'd like to have a rational conversation that doesn't...."

"Wait," he said, holding up his hand. "I'm not finished. You all need to know there is an irresistible cosmic momentum behind what you're seeing on the news. What you've been caught up into. An inevitability of sorts...."

The phone rang on the landline at the registration desk.

Rang again.

Rex barked once, then was silenced as he caught Jack's frown.

"I'll get that," said Mary, rising from the table. "It's probably just some Texan wanting to book a family cabin for next July." Mary's face did not match her tone as she ambled towards the still-ringing phone. "I'm sure it's nothing important."

It was Brian. He wanted to know if his folks had seen the news. He wanted them to pray for the world. Asked them to pray for his missing roommate.

Me.

Thankfully, Mrs. K handed the phone to her approaching husband before she could tangle herself up and rat me out.

Jack's voice was calm. He avoided any direct lies about my whereabouts. He prayed into the phone, then concluded with a sky-sent word of thanksgiving and hope. He hung up while reminding his son that he was loved. And that his destiny was secure in the Lord.

Jack returned to the hush of our table.

"Brian," he said, facing me, "is pretty convinced you must be dead. Denver news has been evasive about what happened this morning at the lodge. A lot of Colorado field reporters were killed in the explosions and fire, so the information that is coming out of Breckenridge is a mess. Mostly unprofessional and second-hand. The only surviving news people were a handful of technicians who were outside in the trucks."

Saundra lowered her head.

"Thanks," I said, "for not telling Brian that we're here." I looked at Mrs. K. "It had to be hard for both of you to hold that information back."

"Of course," sighed Jack. "But we need to be very careful until we know what we're up against. No sense risking wire taps and putting Brian or the ranch at risk."

Mary shook. "It's unbelievable," she said. "A week ago, who would have thought...."

"Hush," said Jack, gently touching his wife's hand. "We've always known such a day could come...." He bumped a fist to his heart. "The King warned us. He said it would get like this before his return."

"Yes," she agreed. "But here... now... so soon?"

"The downward spiral," said Freak, "was inevitable. Because mankind has turned away from the Lord, the die has been cast. The script...."

Jack shook his head. "You're forgetting," he interrupted, "about free will. God always allows us to make choices. To respond. That's the whole point. I wouldn't go so far as to call it all some sort of pre-determined script...."

"I'm sorry," said Freak, "but I believe some things *are* ordained. In the book of Revelation, we are warned that during the End Times, certain scripts *will* play out. Trumpets will be blown in heaven, and bowls of wrath will be released upon the earth. The focus will shift from what the fallen world is doing... to what the Lord is doing."

"So," asked Saundra, raising her gaze, leaning towards Freak, "do you believe the earthquakes today are the ones from the book of Revelation? The ones that go with the 7th Trumpet?"

"No," said Freak, directing Saundra's attention over his shoulder to the television in the other room. "What we were witnessing tonight in there was not the Seventh Trumpet. Nor even the pouring out of a Bowl of Wrath. Today was a final warning shot over the bow. The Seventh Trumpet does not come until the end. That blast will unleash destruction far beyond anything we've yet seen. Or anything that has ever been seen in all of recorded history."

"Then what," she asked, "*are* we seeing? Where are we today in the Bible's timeline? How far are we from Armageddon...."

Saundra drew in her quivering lip, held it a moment, then slowly released it, moist and uncertain.

"How close are we," she asked at last, "to the end of the world?"

Freak put down his spoon.

He shifted his gaze from Saundra to the rest of us around the table.

"As I said, today's chaos comes as a warning shot. A wake-up call to the world." He returned his focus to Saundra. "Today's shakings and violence will continue throughout tonight and well into tomorrow. Saturday will be another frightening day." He took a deep breath. "But, believe it or not, the Lord spoke to me very clearly during Jack's prayer. The Lord has assured me that Easter will be calm. The Lord will give seven billion souls just enough time and space on Sunday to think. And to pray. To turn to him before the time of trumpets begins."

"Are you talking about the judgment of America?" asked Cal. "Or the shaking of the whole world?"

"Everyone," said Freak. "The entire planet. From here on out, we're all in this together. For those who are willing... this Easter will be the day of their salvation. A chance to attend a service. To worship. To repent. To accept forgiveness... and to obey."

"And then?"

"And then, after Easter... the First Trumpet blast of the Apocalypse."

Jack confirmed with an understanding nod. "Hail," said Jack, "mixed with fire...."

"Mixed with blood," finished Freak. "According to Revelation 8:7, our planet is headed for some hard times. It'll suffer an unprecedented series of disasters...."

I cleared my throat. "If God is love, then why would he...."

"Yes," said Freak. "God is love. But he is also real. That means he is not just some two-dimensional cartoon from a child's comic book. He's complex, and his wisdom and ways are often far beyond us."

"Nice answer," I shrugged. "When all else fails, forget logic. Just play the 'mystery' card, and then tell the rest of us to put our brains on hold."

Freak studied me. "Try this," he said at last. "People once feared death. They saw it up close around them every day. When Jesus rose on Easter from the dead, the message was good news to those who feared death. Their new hope was that by following the path of Jesus, they too would one day pass through death to glory. Some people embraced the hope of this promise, and they began following the truths and the ways of Jesus... no matter the cost."

Freak gazed around the room, then back to me.

"Today, however, many of us no longer fear death. Thanks to the lies of Satan, along with generations of watered-down Christianity, billions of people assume that life after death is an automatic upgrade. And, without a fear of accountability and judgment, people don't really pay attention to the true teachings of Jesus anymore. Let alone to the demanding path of service and sacrifice he has called people to follow."

"So," asked Mary, "you're saying God is sending disasters to make us fear death again? So that we'll start thinking about if we're really ready to die?"

"In part," nodded Freak. "God does love us. He'll do whatever it takes to humble us and to get us focused again on the truth."

Mary touched her bow. "Perhaps. But it all seems so sudden and drastic."

Freak met her eyes. "God will do whatever it takes."

"Are you sure?" protested Saundra. "I agree with Mary. How can these things be happening so soon? If God wants a revival this Easter, surely the Lord will not destroy millions of people the very next day...."

"Why not?" said Freak, his face fixed. "But actually, the Bible doesn't say how many humans will die as these shakings first begin. The Bible only addresses—and poetically at that—the initial magnitude of destruction for the planet as an ecosystem... as our garden home. The Lord has given us this Good Friday to get our attention. Easter will be a time to separate the flock into the sheep and the goats. People will self-sort. As Jack reminded us: free will. People will use this Easter to honor Jesus and to secure their relationship with the Lord... or not."

Freak sighed.

"And," he added, "it is *not*, as you say, 'so soon.' The Lord has been putting this day off for 2,000 years."

Jack cleared his throat. "Enough," he softly declared. "A few of you should help Mary in the kitchen. The television stays off for the rest of tonight. We can check it again for updates in the morning."

"What about Freak's interview?" asked Steve. "Are we going to film some kind of statement yet tonight, or not?"

"No," said Jack, his voice even. "Not tonight. His Good Friday predictions have already been proven correct. We all need to sleep on this. For those of you who know how to pray, I suggest you spend some quiet time with the Lord this evening. For those of you who don't know how to pray… I suggest you learn." Jack turned back to Freak. "What do you think, pastor," he asked, "shall we sleep on this?"

Freak studied Jack, then closed his eyes.

"Yes," he said, opening his eyes. "There is wisdom in what you say. I'm going to make *sure* I get my prophecies right this time. The stakes are too high on this next round. I'm going to need some confirmation."

Freak stretched out his hand. "Jack, I could use your help with this. I haven't had a Barnabas or a Timothy to pray with since all of this began last week. I've been shooting too much from the hip. After we clean up dinner, I'd like to spend a few minutes in prayer with you. And with Mary and Cal. With Saundra, too… if she is willing?"

Freak turned to where she sat. "Saundra?" he asked.

Saundra eased a glance as far as my napkin, then awkwardly nodded consent toward Freak as she dropped her chin and reached for her glass.

"Good," said Freak. "The five of us can gather again to pray in the loft in thirty minutes. I am also feeling some urgency to pray for my family. Who knows where Ellen and the kids are right now and how they're doing in this storm. Hopefully, they're safely holed up someplace between Nevada and Denver in a motel." Freak rose from his seat. "I sense with five of us praying together in that upper room, God will not let us down."

I started to protest.

For some reason, I wanted to sit in on their holy powwow. But I found myself unable to generate a single legitimate argument for anything other than my own humiliating exclusion from their club.

Thankfully, Steve said it for me.

"Hey," he objected, "what's the deal? Have Mark and I been voted off the island, or what?"

Freak straightened.

"Steve," asked Freak, "are you saying you *want* to pray, or that you just don't like the feeling of being left behind?"

"Well... I guess it depends upon what you mean by the word *pray*."

"Exactly," sighed Freak. "When we pray, we're not doing amateur therapy or something. We're inviting the Lord of the universe to sit with us... to listen to us... and to speak." Freak turned to Jack. "Did I miss anything?"

Jack smiled. "The only thing I might add is that if a person bothers to pray, and then he refuses to listen to the King's side of the conversation, then he is probably worse off than if he had never prayed in the first place."

Freak turned to Mrs. K. "Mary?"

"For me," she said, "it's very important to pray with other Christians who believe. The Bible says wherever two or three are gathered in His name...."

"...there the King shall be," finished Jack. "Jesus shows up. His Kingdom comes."

"Right," said Mary. "It becomes a special time and a sacred place. That's the way we always try to keep our prayer gatherings in the loft. It's a place we've set apart for holy encounters."

"Oh," puckered Steve. "You're right. I guess I'd better sit this one out."

Mrs. K looked sad. Looked at me.

"Mark?" she asked, her voice tentative. "Would you like to join us later when we pray?"

As hard as it was, I tore my gaze from Mrs. K and glanced at Steve instead.

"Naw," I said, reaching down to scratch Rex's ear. "It's been a very long, very rough day. What I really need is a good night of sleep. You can all let me know in the morning how your private prayer vigil went."

Freak stood. He leaned awkwardly over the table, lowering a hand to either side of his empty bowl.

"Tomorrow is going to be a rough day," said Freak. "Rough for the world. Difficult for those of us in this room." He turned to me. "And especially hard for you, Mark."

Despite myself, I gulped. I felt a little flare of red in my cheeks rising from embarrassment, anger... or fear. "Thanks," I said. "As if this week wasn't hard enough already. Did the Lord give you another vision? I already gave up my girlfriend and my rig today. What's it going to be tomorrow?"

Freak didn't blink. He did slowly wet his lips before answering. "Yes, Mark," he said, "you've paid a price. Thank you for everything you've done to help the cause. But tomorrow, it's going to be an internal explosion. You'll be contending for yourself, not for me. Nor for your friends. This battle will be yours. I'll be praying for you."

"Wonderful," I shrugged. "Do I need to sleep with a fire extinguisher and hose tonight, or what?"

"You won't need a fire hose," said Freak, straightening. "But a spiritual sword and shield might come in pretty handy. It's your call."

Jack looked alarmed. "Are we going to be attacked?" he asked.

"No," replied Freak. "We're safe. At least for another day. All of us except for Mark. He's the one I'm worried about. Not his flesh, but his soul."

"Whatever," I shrugged.

"Okay," said Jack, pushing away from the table. "Mark... you and Steve can sleep in the Esther. The heat is on, and the cabin is already guest-set for those honeymooners who never showed. You'll find fresh linens, towels, and everything you need. Saundra, you can sleep here in the big house, in the guest suite over there." He pointed.

He turned to Freak. "And for you, my prophet friend, we'll throw some clean sheets on Brian's old bed in the room at the end of the hall."

Jack rose from the table.

"Prayer upstairs in 30 minutes. Breakfast is at 8:00."

"Yo, Cal," I asked, "any beer in the fridge?"

"Sure," he frowned. "I've got an untouched six pack in the crisper. Help yourselves."

With that, we all shucked our seats and left the table in different directions.

Five sheep up... and a pair of goats to go.

21
INTO THE DARK COLD NIGHT

Saundra said it was powerful.

Later, she said their time together in the Prayer Chapel loft was unlike anything else she'd ever experienced.

Freak didn't say anything specifically about angels this time, but she said his eyes got big at one point, and she felt the spiritual presence of the angels more than saw them: Freak's two invisible pals had rejoined the sheep.

Kingdom warriors had arrived to contend for the flock in the midst of their prayers.

Of course, Steve and I didn't know about any of that at the time. We'd made our way back out into the dark storm wearing wrong-sized boots we'd borrowed from the lost and found closet. We'd clutched our beer, leaned into the wind, and filled our socks with snow from the piling drifts. We'd trudged the path past the barn lights and past the five lampposts that illuminated each of the five cabin porches in the night.

Steve grew more ornery with every step.

"That's it over there," I called, pointing my flashlight through the darkness and blowing snow. "The Esther."

"Shoulda told me it was in Utah," grumbled Steve. "I would have shoved Rex outside and commandeered his dog box for the night."

The Esther was the smallest cabin on the ranch. The Honeymoon Special... and the only cabin I'd never slept in before. A pot-belly stove for ambience, a tiled shower, a kitchenette, and an enormous antique bed for the endless stream of newlyweds who found their getaway bliss at the Diamond K.

Plus one reasonably comfortable pull-out couch.

I staked my claim on the bed, but I let Steve get one beer up on me while I arranged some kindling and fanned up a struggling fire. Steve watched in sullen silence as I dug out some blankets and settled him in with a few throw pillows on the sofa conversion.

"So, what do you think?" I asked, finally finished with the housekeeping. I reached to pop my first beer. "Is this the end of the world, or what?"

Steve lifted his silver can. "This tea water is nothing like those Dark Mamas you served at the lodge. But having to settle for a couple of diet beers is hardly what I'd call the end of the world."

I drudged up an empty chortle. "At least we've got six of them. At least that's enough to get us started."

"You said this was the honeymoon cabin, right?"

I followed Steve's gaze to the half-pint refrigerator in the kitchenette.

"Are you thinking," I asked, "what I'm thinking?"

Sure enough. A chilled bottle of cheap champagne was tucked inside the mini-fridge's door.

"Should we," asked Steve, "save this for tomorrow?"

"Why?" I replied. "Who says there's even going to be a tomorrow?"

We finished the fat green bottle, then switched back to the cans.

"Tell me," laughed Steve, "what's your *real* secret with women?"

Hmm.

"Well," I said, taking another drink, "it's been my experience that it boils down to two things with women. First, don't be stupid. Second, try to be as kind and gentle with them as you can. They really eat that up."

Steve lifted his hand. "Whoa," he objected. "I've got a buddy, and he's the most gentle, kindest guy you ever met, but he's miserable because his old lady is a real shrew. When he got married...."

"Rule number one," I grinned, "don't be stupid."

Half-way through the beer, we finally got half-way serious.

"When you and Heather took your walk yesterday," said Steve, "you were gone a long time."

"Not that long. To the village. A few shops."

"Did you two have a lover's quarrel?"

"Why do you ask?"

"It seemed kinda tense between you two." Steve took another swig. "It's just kinda weird, isn't it... a pretty girl like Heather, all innocent and everything, being dead all of a sudden today from out of nowhere?"

I didn't answer.

"Anyway," he continued, "this whole week has been weird. Way beyond weird."

Hmm. I studied him. "What's wrong?"

Steve took his time. Took another drink.

"*Freak*," he said at last. "Your buddy came out of his room while you were away with Heather. He said he wanted to talk to me while you were—and I quote—'not around to sabotage the conversation with all of your sarcasm.'"

"Hey," I grinned, "I love it when my best friend in the world talks like that behind my back. That's how I know he really loves me."

Steve didn't smile.

"We didn't talk about you," he said at last. "We talked about me."

"And...?"

"Freak said he is pretty worried about me. He said God has tolerated wickedness for a long time, but that we are now moving into a season of judgment. For everyone. Everywhere. He says that for the first time in history, television is going to make it possible for the whole world to watch at the same time as the judgments unfold. And for everyone to see Jesus return as it happens."

"Oh," I said with an exaggerated sigh. "Freak told me the same thing. Thanks to Judge Judy—and the

Apocalypse—Freak is predicting a whole new generation of in-your-face courtroom reality shows."

Steve smiled, faintly.

"What else did he say?" I asked, suddenly feeling more annoyed than curious. "Reverend Jacobs is one heck of a funny guy."

Steve carefully rolled his beer until the logo was centered between his hands. He frowned at it for a moment, then gave it another half turn.

"Freak told me that because the world is ending and everything, he is worried about my soul." He looked up at me. "He asked if I was saved... he wanted to know if I thought I was in a good relationship with... The Judge."

"Of course he did," I said. "That's his thing. What did you tell him?"

"I told him that I was... not sure." Steve took another drink.

"Bad answer," I said. "All a guy like Freak needs is to see an opening. He's like a great white shark. If he gets a sniff of blood in the water...."

"Mark, you're not listening. I'm really serious about this."

"Sorry," I said, closing my eyes. "This day has really kicked me in the teeth. Okay, I'm serious. What else?"

"He said he was concerned about all of my sins. About the way I make crude jokes about women... and how I eat and drink so much."

Hmm.

"There's more," said Steve. "The weird stuff."

"I'm all ears."

Steve glanced to the door, then back at me.

"Mark," he asked, "have you ever heard of the term, 'Dark Rider'?"

I might have twitched.

"You have?" he asked. "Everyone knows about demons and fallen angels. If not from the Bible, then from movies and books. But I'd never heard anyone talk about Dark Riders before."

"Let me guess," I said. "He told you that you had one, right?"

I tried to snicker, but somehow couldn't.

"How did you know?" Steve wetted his lips. "Yes, he said he saw one... that it was kinda attached to me or something. He said its name was 'Gluttony.'"

I shook my head. "Steve, you're really bringing me down, bro."

"What do you mean?"

"Look," I said, putting a hand on his shoulder. "Freak is a professional showman. This is what he does for a living. He's got the whole Darker Rider shtick down pat. He did the same thing with me."

"He did?" Steve looked confused.

"Sure. Freak said I have two or three Riders on me all the time... almost 24-7. He called one Lust. The other one was Pride. He said Pride was a big one, and the Pride Rider was really messing me up. Maybe there was a third Rider. I don't remember anymore." I took a drink.

"Ouch," Steve sighed. "Pride, huh? That's gotta hurt. How humiliating."

I had fallen from the mood to smile.

"So," he asked, "do you think Freak's whole conversation about Dark Riders was a con?"

"Maybe. If it is, it's a good one. A little later, when I was putting a lusty move on Heather, I could have sworn I started hearing a swarm of vaporous electric gnats buzzing in my ears."

"Bugs from the black tent, right? Freak used that metaphor on me, too." Steve looked down, shaking his head. "Man, he sure sounded like he knew what he was talking about."

"Freak is no dummy," I admitted.

"A con, huh?"

"Well," I said, "who knows? Maybe he's legit. He was right about those quakes in California today, wasn't he?"

"I guess."

"But," I said, "the whole Dark Rider thing creeps me out. It feels like it's probably all a power trip... a head game he uses to keep folks off balance while he shakes them down for donations." I reached for another beer. "Then again, what do I know? Maybe it's just my Pride Rider whispering doubts within my ears."

Steve took a long look at his beer.

He suddenly appeared to be in no hurry for another hit.

PART II

BLACK SATURDAY

The trek from the Esther cabin back to the big house seemed shorter in the light of day. Our tracks from the previous night had filled in, and another few inches of fresh snow had fallen, but we made decent time as we traipsed through the knee-high drifts and the dying wind.

"Bacon," I said. "I can smell it already."

We stomped our boots on the freshly shoveled porch. Cal had only bothered to clear the top step, plus a narrow path that ran down the porch along the cabin's outside wall to the south. His efforts terminated at the end of the porch in front of winter's dwindling stack of chopped wood.

I motioned to Steve. We each filled our arms with a few choice end-of-the-season split logs.

"Yo!" I called, dropping a hip to open the door. "It's Mutt and Jeff. And we've come bearing gifts!"

Cal let us in, somber faced. He mumbled a good morning and stretched his arms, cradle style. We loaded him down, then silently removed our boots and gear.

Beyond Cal's retreating back, the big television was screaming of natural disasters and playing terrorist terrors in the other room.

Mary shuttled back and forth between the kitchen grill and our dumbstruck galley of ringside horrors.

"Can I help you, Mrs. K?" I asked. "Would you like some company in the kitchen?"

"No," she said. "It's better this way. I can step out when I need to. In the kitchen, I can distract myself while I fuss over healthy fresh food."

Somehow, I felt oddly brushed off.

Dismissed.

I softly called to Rex. He rose from beside Jack's chair, started my way, then dropped himself at Freak's feet by the couch.

It turned into a late breakfast. A brunch, really. A lovely feast of far more poundage and flavor than any of us had the stomach or palate to absorb. In the other room, the TV had been clicked to mute, and in the kitchen, so had the table. For the most part, even Freak was dialed down to almost zero.

Cal pulled out his phone. It was making an odd chirping sound that, for all of his fumbling, he seemed unable to silence.

"Here," said Saundra, "let me help you with that."

He passed the phone, and it was hushed in an instant.

"This," said Saundra, her eyes eager, "is the new model. Same as mine... was." She shot me a disapproving glance, then refocused on the phone.

"I've got no idea how it works," confessed Cal. "Even the sales guy in Granby was pretty clueless."

"For starters," said Saundra, "you don't have to stream all of your Internet connectivity through your cell phone data plan. When you transmit directly from your phone to the cell tower, they can really gouge you for every gigabyte."

"Saundra," I said, "Slow down with that thing. You might accidently call one of your contacts. Every person you know is probably being monitored right now. The last thing we need is...."

She ignored me. "Cal," she asked, "you've got a password for the ranch's Wi-Fi, right?" She slid over tight against Cal's thigh. "Here, let me help you set up a few apps and alternatives for better functionality. Let's set you up so you can have the option of streaming both ways, via the cell tower and your computer line."

A nauseous pool began churning in the pit of my stomach. Probably bacon grease and undercooked egg.

They huddled, humped together over their stupid device, poking buttons, configuring, whispering, almost laughing... even as the world melted down in Freak's predicted flames.

"Don't get too excited," I observed, "with all of the shaking that Freak's predicting, who knows if the cell towers will survive even another week."

Saundra looked my way, then quickly dropped back to showing Cal the ins and outs of his new toy.

Finally, Jack reconvened.

"That's about enough gadget time for one meal." He turned to the prophet. "Freak," he asked, "have you observed anything surprising on the news this morning? Is this what you have been seeing in your visions?"

The pastor's scars seemed to have softened in the flush of the past hour.

Freak raised a hand and touched two fingers to his left temple. Then, slowly, the prophet traced the topography of his scars all the way down to his jaw. For a moment, he held his fingers there, pinching his chin with a thumb from below. One side of Freak's face was clean. Freshly shaved. He had done a good job, right up to the line where smooth skin butted hard against those signature pink dikes and ditches of frozen raw tissue.

Freak nodded.

"Yes," he sighed at last, dropping his hand. "No surprises."

"Good," said Jack. "Then I guess we're still aligned with the King's plan. Based upon what we heard from the Lord last night, I think it's time you got back on the air."

"On the air," I deadpanned, "is a bad idea. It looks like the jets are all wearing targets on their wings today."

Nobody laughed. Nobody even looked towards my place at the table.

Mr. K turned to Saundra and Steve.

"I'm okay if you still want to shoot your film in front of the fireplace. It's your call. No need for sheets."

"But," I objected, "your ranch website has pictures of that room. Of the fireplace. If anyone is looking closely...."

"Mark," said Jack, rising from his chair, "everything is in the Lord's hands right now. If we end up martyred for doing the work of the King, I gotta say... there's worse ways to go."

I found Jack's flip dismissiveness quite perturbing.

TRIAL BY FIRE

We worked together to clear the table. To fill, and then to empty the sink. To prepare things for Freak's podcast by the hearth.

While moving furniture, Saundra was all excited to tell me and Steve every little detail from their prayer vigil in the loft.

"We prayed for both of you," she said. "And for Freak's wife and kids. For California... for the whole world."

"For all the good that did," I said. "Didn't you see the news this morning? No, *wait*. How could you be expected to focus on a television screen. You must have had your eyes on Cal's fancy cell phone from the first minute you climbed into his truck."

"It was extraordinary," she blathered, ignoring me. "At one point in the prayers, I just couldn't stop crying. Even though I wasn't afraid, I just shook and wept. I felt both humanly weak and supernaturally strong at the same time. It was incredible."

"Incredible," I said, "is the operative word."

"Mark, I know you find it hard to believe," she continued, "but the presence of the Lord was so real...."

Blah, blah, blah.

"Right," I said. "I get it. Freak has tricked you into seeing angels again." I dropped my end of the couch. "Girl, you're absolutely hopeless."

Saundra stepped back.

"Mark, I didn't say I *saw* them."

"And to think," I continued, "that you call yourself a journalist."

She studied me.

Then, quietly, Saundra turned and slipped off to hunt down a better lamp from some other room.

By 10:30 the fireside studio was in place.

I slumped alone, at some distance, stewing in a lumpy chair.

Feeling hollow. Acid burning at the back of my throat.

Saundra and Freak sat hunched by the warmth of the hearth, reminiscent of their good times back at the lodge. They bobbed up and down over a notepad of prompts and talking points they'd hastily pulled together. Steve stood swaying between me and the celebrity rock stars, engaged in some final tweaking with the video camera he had jerry-rigged onto one of Jack's fully extended rifle tripods.

Cal was again in the barns, shoveling the only spot on the ranch deeper than where Freak sat. Jack was who-knows-where. If he happened to be up in the loft praying, at least he was keeping it down to a whisper for a change.

"I've got it!" Mary shrieked.

Mrs. K had busied herself on her computer at the registration desk.

"The church website," she said, addressing Saundra and Steve, "they had an information button with an email link to Pastor Gilford. I've started drafting him a cover letter to explain what we talked about for relaying video onto Kristen's website. You can edit my notes and attach your files once you're done filming. But the good news," she said, triumph in her voice, "is that I just checked the link. Within seconds, Pastor Gilford replied that the Lord put it on his heart to pray for Reverend Jacobs this morning. Pastor Gilford is standing by online even as we speak."

"Wonderful!" exclaimed Saundra. "This is going to work. Tell Gilford to dig out a big flash drive. We'll have something edited and packaged into a file for him by noon."

"Thanks, Mary," added Steve. "You've really saved us a lot of time. It's nice to have your help with this."

Hmm. *What about my help? Freak would be nothing but a buried stiff right now if it wasn't for me. Twice!*

Jack thumped his way down the stairs from the loft. He was carrying what had to be the heaviest Bible on the ranch.

"Here," he said, handing it to Freak. "It's more than a prop. If the King puts a verse on your heart, then feel free to flip to the passage and get it right. The text is all printed in oversized lettering. That way you'll be able to find your way around and read it without hardly having to glance away from the lens."

Freak smiled. "Thanks," he said, testing the heft of it. This reminds me of my pulpit Bible back home." He paused. Then, carefully, he put it down. "Or," he said, "what used to be my home. There's probably nothing left of our church and that Bible by now... nothing but ashes and dust."

Under the circumstances, I found his eloquence and sentimentality appalling.

"Why so glum?" I called from my chair. "I hope you're not going to start second-guessing the Lord. After all, this is all God's work, isn't it? He's in charge of all the tectonic demolitions and every black-bearded wrecking crew on the planet, right?"

Everyone turned my way.

"You know, Freak," I called again, "today has a special name. This Saturday during Holy Week is not just any ol' day." I rose from my chair and took a couple steps in his direction. "Today is sometimes referred to as Easter Eve. But the day after Good Friday is also known—in some traditions at least—as... *Black Saturday.*"

I took a couple more steps towards the crackling fireplace. "Black Saturday. Pretty convenient, eh?" I rolled my head and cracked my neck. "Maybe you can use that in your little speech. You can promise this whole Wal-Mart world of sinners that we can look forward to some unprecedented close-out specials this year." I faked an amused chuckle. "Don't miss this one-time shopping extravaganza... the greatest Black Saturday sales event in history."

"Mark," asked Saundra, her face searching, "what has gotten into you?"

"Pennies on the dollar," I said. "With a little elbow grease—and a nickel down—it can all be yours. Cash and carry for anything in the store... anything that is not yet crushed, soaked, looted or burned. Sales clerks included."

Jack took a step in my direction. "Whoa, boy," cautioned the big rancher. "Slow down."

I looked at Freak.

"What a lucky break, eh, preacher man? You've always wanted a bigger audience. Now, thanks to the wrath of God, the whole world is hanging on your every word."

A wince of humility flickered within Freak's gaze. A crack of self-doubt.

I found myself eager to set a wedge and drive it.

"You know, Freak, this really has been the opportunity of a lifetime. The politically correct media can't let go of you. Your face. Nobody in their right mind wants to see those scars, but in the name of political correctness, they keep showing you day and night so that nobody can accuse them of discriminating against people with repulsive features. Even a face that makes me want to gag."

I turned to Saundra.

"Saundra, you know how this works for the ratings, right? These Freak celebrity clips are like crack cocaine for the gullible masses. One hit, and they're hooked. This so-called prophet is like a slot machine lever those addicts keep having to pull: *Oh, wow! Here's that monstrous face rolling up on my screen again! Listen to that insane voice.... Maybe the next time he speaks he'll name my city. My sin. I'd better stay tuned.*"

Jack shook his head. "Okay, that's *enough*. I'm not sure what's going on here, but...."

"Hey," I said, "I can't help myself. Just ask the great Reverend W.B. Jacobs. The Devil is all over me. Satan's riders practically own me."

Jack glanced at Freak, then back to me. "Explain yourself," he demanded.

"Last night," I said, "Steve and I got into comparing notes. Apparently, it's now standard procedure for our prophet friend here to go around telling us sinners we've all got demons."

Jack gave Freak a questioning look.

"Dark Riders," said Freak. "And yes, I've spoken with both Mark and Steve about their issues."

"Issues?" I gasped. I slapped my forehead. "Oh.... No, wait. I distinctly remember you saying that I've got... *demons*. And then you pontificated that it's my own damn choice they won't go away and leave me alone."

I couldn't tell from where such anger was coming.

Nor why I couldn't stop.

"Listen, Saundra," I said, feigning empathy. "Freak told your poor friend Steve here that he's got a demonic attachment, a nastily chubby Dark Rider by the name of *Gluttony*." I pointed at the blushing cameraman. "And then, Freak told me," I swung my hand around to thump my own chest, "he says I'm possessed by even worse demons. Two of them. Maybe three. Pride and Lust, or so he says."

"Mark," said Freak, "you know I didn't put it that way. What I said, was...."

"Right. I guess it's just that darn Pride Rider making a boastful big deal out of nothing. Or making me all confused so he can stay in control?"

"Perhaps."

"What about my lust demon, Freak? The fun one. How about if you tell the rest of our friends here all about the joys of dancing with a lust devil. If memory serves, lust is where your expertise really kicks in."

Freak shuddered. He promptly closed his eyes and began to pray. In tongues, maybe.

Steve held up his hand. "Mark," he said. "You're losing it. Take a chill pill, pal."

"A pill? No, I'm way beyond taking a pill. What I need," I swatted my back pocket, "is to get laid. Thanks to our buddy, Freak," I waved my hand at him, "it's been way too long since I've gotten any...."

"Hey!" snapped Jack. "None of that talk under my roof. Especially not in front of the ladies. Where are your manners, boy?"

"The thing is," I said, now shaking, unable to stop, "I can't quite figure this all out. I mean, I can't whether the world ending is a good thing or a bad thing. On the upside, once I shuck this god-forsaken icebox, I'm going to have one hell of a good time back in Denver. Imagine that... with the world ending, there's no need to screw around with birth control. No worries about diseases and condoms. What's to slow me down...."

Jack was suddenly on me. He grabbed me by the shoulders. Shook. Hard.

"Stop it!" he shouted.

I swore. Then I yelled something, and then I added some curses. I don't recall any of the words, but I do remember how good it felt at the time to be letting it loose, unleashing the anger, getting it all out.

Rex started barking, then dropped back on his haunches.

Jack shook me again. "In the name of Jesus Christ," he commanded, "be still!"

It might have been Jack's hand.

It might have been something else.

I felt a whack against my skull that left me limp.

I tried to shake my head, to focus through the fog.

Freak was staring at me. From by the fire, his hand was instinctively pressing the cover of Jack's huge black Bible.

Saundra was sobbing.

Everything blurred. Jack's voice grew distant.

I guess I blacked out.

"Let go of me," I finally whimpered.

"Mark," Jack implored, adjusting me in my chair. "Have you lost your mind?"

"Maybe," I apologized, feeling vomit at the back of my throat. It was hard to lock in. "This past week has been insane. I guess I snapped."

"Do you," he demanded, "have any idea what you were saying?"

"Mr. K, you know I was only being ironic... only kidding."

"Only kidding?" Jack scowled. "You had us all praying our hearts out... over some kind of joke?"

"Sure," I said, trying to shrug. "The whole world is falling apart. You shouldn't get so bent out of shape because I tried to lighten things up and maybe got carried away and said something stupid by mistake."

Jack thrust a finger into my face. "Do I need to bunk you in the barn tonight?" he glowered. "Do I need to stick your head in a snow bank, or what?"

I felt my cheeks reddening.

"No, sir," I finally sputtered. "I mean, it's just that...."

"Forget the excuses, boy. Man up." Jack dropped a hand onto my wrist. "Freak is right. The Devil has gotten some hooks into you. Son, you need some Jesus help. And soon. You're in worse shape than you know."

Saundra shivered, then shifted her attention to her notes. Steve figured it was time to double-check his camera. Mrs. K adjusted her keyboard. Only Freak and Jack would not let me go.

"Sorry, Jack," I mumbled. "I forgot where I was."

"Not just *where* you are," he fumed, "but you also forgot *whose* you are. You've been baptized, son. You're better than what we just saw. You're a prince... a son of the King. You're not some pimp from the city dump. Show some self control."

"It's been a rough week. I'll try to be more careful." I took a deep breath and managed to raise my head. "Like I said, I'm sorry."

"Don't apologize to me," he insisted. "I clean stables for a living. I can handle mule kicks and potty talk. But you need to apologize to your friends. And to Mary."

It was another familiar routine. We'd trotted through softer versions of this script years before. Sitting there, I considered bucking what was about to come next.

Jack squeezed my wrist. "Come on," he said. "Fix this. Clean your mess."

Finally, I surrendered, half grateful that I knew my lines. That I knew how this conversation would soon end.

I forced myself to see them all, one at a time, the way Jack demanded a dozen times when I was young. I ended my gaze with Mary, the ranch queen, who fidgeted behind her computer screen. She was clearly once again lost in even more embarrassment than me.

"I'm sorry, everyone." I dropped my eyes. "Jack's right."

I hesitated, ransacking my memory for the exact all-but-forgotten words. The liturgy of confession. And the plea for grace.

"This is God's country," I recited. "This is the King's ranch. This is a sanctuary of peace. There is no place for potty talk and wicked nonsense at the Diamond K."

I focused on Mrs. K. "I'm sorry," I said. "Please forgive me."

She nodded.

I turned to the others. "I'm sorry... all of you. No excuses. Please forgive my poor behavior."

Saundra could hardly meet my eyes. Steve couldn't. Freak drilled.

"Okay, then," said Jack.

He released his grip and shifted his attention. "Some of you don't know how things work around here at the Diamond K, but we make a point of having short memories for honest mistakes... and no memory at all for forgiven sins. If you've been hurt by Mark, then you're going to need to let it go." He pointed to the big log Diamond K logo hanging over the loft. "For the love of the King."

Mary echoed in a whisper, even as my lips instinctively mouthed the refrain: "For the love of the King."

Jack turned back to me. "Thanks for coming clean, Mark."

"Sure. Sorry, Jack."

"You okay?"

I shrugged a yes.

23
BEHIND THE CURTAIN

Freak stepped to Jack and raised a hand to the big man's massive shoulder.

"He tried to pull us off," said Freak, addressing Mr. K, staring at me where I sat, confused, breathing hard. "He wanted to sabotage our recording session and to sidetrack my message from the Lord."

"I've known this boy a long time," said Jack. "He's had a few fits over the years, but it's never been this bad...."

"No," said Freak. "It's not Mark. It's the Devil. Satan tried to use Mark to derail this interview. To shut us down."

"That," Steve tentatively objected, "might be a little over the top, don't you think?" He stepped forward from beside his camera. "Are you saying that Satan was...."

"No," said Freak. "I don't mean the Devil himself was channeling through Mark. But demons have a way of exploiting our dark spots and messing with people... of using even the best of us from time to time. Lord knows the Devil has used me before."

Steve blinked hard. "I suppose if there is a Devil, but...."

"Satan is scared stiff about our podcast. He's worried even about you, Steve."

"Me?"

"He's afraid of you doing your job well today. Of your camera. And do you know why?"

Freak turned from Steve and met my eyes. He lowered himself to a knee beside my chair. I again began to tremble.

"This Easter," said Freak, "the Earth will experience the greatest revival in history. And Mark... the world, the flesh, and the Devil are not going to be able to stop this incredible move of the Holy Spirit." He smiled. "Like it or not, Mark, you're in the middle of it. And you're going to live through it... and you're never going to be the same. That's why the Devil is raging with all he's got."

Freak patted my arm.

"Right now, King Jesus is setting the stage," said Freak, "to pull you back... and to rob a million graves."

Mr. K and Freak guided me up, weak and unsteady, from my chair. They led me to the green couch. They stretched my legs, covered me with a blanket, then forced me to close my eyes and relax. They knelt beside me, put their hands on my throbbing temples, and they together prayed.

Mary came down from the loft with a vial of healing oil. She dabbed my forehead a couple times. Then she restoked their session by adding a few words of her own to their sometimes indecipherable prayers.

I let it wash over me. I felt too inexplicably exhausted to resist.

I let them finish. Let them finally drift off to pour coffee or to wander back to what they'd been doing to prepare for the podcast before I snapped. I watched them off and on, tentative. Grateful. Humiliated.

Uncertain.

Steve shifted uneasily, rechecking his camera yet again, working up the courage to speak.

"Jack," he finally asked, "tell me more about what happened there a few minutes ago. Why'd you come down so hard on Mark? Maybe he couldn't help himself. You kinda roughed him up a bit. I'm surprised he took it... that he didn't start swinging."

"Listen, Steve," said Jack. "You seem like an agreeable fellow. But there's some things you don't know. Mark over there is an exceptional young man." He nodded in my direction. "And Mark can help himself... any time he really wants to. Especially with all of the support he's got here at the Diamond K."

"Yes," ventured Steve, "but Freak said Demons...."

"I'm not disagreeing with the preacher," said Jack. "But, deep down, Mark still knows who the Lord is, and he knows Jesus is King. Even if he gets stubborn about it sometimes."

Mary smiled. "He'll work it out. Mark will come around."

"Mark," said Jack, addressing Steve, "he is one of the brightest young men I've ever met. Quick to learn. Often generous and considerate. A great athlete... a great shot with a rifle. He once dropped an elk with a plug straight through the heart... from over 200 yards across a ravine."

Jack swirled his coffee, ignoring it, not lifting his arm.

"Mark has always been everybody's favorite. But underneath all that bluster, he's a pretty sensitive kid. Self-absorbed, but sensitive."

My face burned. The sensitive kid was sensing where Mr. K was headed.

"The thing is," he continued, "Mark has lost his way. I don't blame just his mom and dad, but they had a hand in it. Once puberty hit, it was mostly the party crowd and the popular girls who got to messing around with the wiring inside of Mark's head. It was all too easy. Too fun. And then something snapped. I don't know what happened, but it's like Mark got broken all of a sudden."

I tried to ignore Saundra's discrete darting glance from across the room.

"And it didn't help having that fancy big-church youth pastor—Lord have mercy. And those arrogant half-educated teachers at school. Cocky college professors. HBO. The Internet. It's what Freak said: the world, the flesh, and the Devil. You name it. The crap and the clutter of everything ended up crowding out a whole lot of character and decency."

"Mr. K.," I protested, "I don't think Steve really...."

"Hold on, son," he said, holding up his hand. "I ain't finished. And this is important."

He glanced at Freak and Saundra, then turned back to Steve.

"Despite the good, like I said, our boy has lost his way. I can remember when he wasn't ashamed to call himself a Christian. Now he's grown cold and he says it's all a bunch of hooey. Freak is probably right. Satan has undoubtedly had a hand in this."

"Jack," asked Steve, "Do you see angels and demons... like Freak says he can?"

"Of course not. There's some kind of veil or something between us and them. I can't see a darn thing in the spirit world. But I've got a nose for evil, and a little while ago, I was sniffing it all over this boy."

"Hey," I softly complained, trying to lower my legs, to swing into a less vulnerable position. "I'm right here on the couch. Please don't talk like I'm not in the room."

"We all see ya, Mark," said Jack. "But we love ya, and we're too scared to pretend like everything is okay. Your parents did that, and it didn't work out too good for you at all."

"I'll be okay," I said. "All I need is some sleep."

Jack took a deep sip from his mug. "Mark," he said, "this is one of those times in history when ain't nobody can afford to sleep." He glanced at Freak, then lifted his mug toward Mrs. K. "If you can't tell, for some reason, Mary and me have always loved this boy."

Mary gently bobbed her head in agreement.

"So we need to speak some truth here. To do what we can to get Mark back on track."

Jack swung his coffee mug towards Freak.

"You, preacher. I admire how you and God nailed it with your face. 'Grace and Truth.' You know what I'm talking about here, right?"

Freak nodded. "Spare the rod and spoil the child," he softly concurred.

"For the past few years," said Jack, "I've seen this boy dodging his truth-checks, and also pushing off a lot of helping hands. But if the world is going to hell, then Mark is going to need all of the honest input and godly help he can get." He took another sip. "We all will."

Freak caught Jack's eye. "Jack," he said, "we're about ready."

"Good," replied Jack. "Think about it," he called to me on the couch. "You've got free will. You've studied 20th-century philosophy... consider this your "Existential Wake-up Call.' You've got to choose."

"Choose what?"

"No... choose *who*." He pointed towards the loft. "Who gets to be King in your life? Are you going to choose King Mark Hanson, the maker of illicit love, mischief, and wisecracks. Or the Lord Jesus Christ, the boss of the universe?"

"In philosophy," I weakly objected, "we call that a false dichotomy. It's a logical fallacy to even set it up like that."

"I didn't set it up. God did. Every person has got to choose if they're going to let God be the King of their life, or not. Mark, if you're not able to think your way to the right choice, then try praying."

"You know I don't pray anymore...."

"If you can't pray, and if you can't logic it out, then at least use your gut to mull on it for a while. This is too important to leave on the back burner. You need to put some real heat on this question."

Jack turned from the couch and headed toward the other end of the room, still addressing me as he walked away.

"If *you* don't put some heat on it," he said again, "then the Lord will. Maybe he already has. Jesus has got the power... as well as the last word. It'll go better for you if you let him be your Lord."

He didn't stop until he reached Freak's fireside chair. There, Jack settled in for a moment to pray one last time with Freak, who was preparing to speak.

The attention quickly shifted from me... to the Doomsday Prophet of God.

24

PODCAST PROPHECIES

Freak was on a roll.

He flipped through the Bible and delivered his message to the camera with such force and clarity I had to blink from time to time to remind myself I wasn't watching an edited production on a big screen TV.

Freak was only a few steps away from me. Large and in charge.

Live.

Waving a Bible. Foaming at the mouth, and spitting for the Lord.

"...and at the sound of that *mighty* trumpet blast, the Lord shook the city to its very foundations. The Lord collapsed those fortress walls of Jericho, and he leveled that wicked kingdom in a single hour. And then, by his own hand, the Lord built a new kingdom, a place within which justice and mercy was to reign. He established a kingdom among a people who were to be dedicated to the humble pursuit of *his* Grace and *his* Truth, not to the impulses and whims of self-serving rulers, nor to the short-sighted fumbling half-hearted efforts of the ever-fickle masses. The Lord called into being a set-apart people... a people who were *blessed* by him in order that they might *be a blessing...* to the entire world. Hebrew or not."

Without looking down, Freak fanned several hundred pages deeper into the book.

"But the Lord's people—in many ways—failed miserably. They failed to listen to their God and to obey. They failed to love and to serve their Creator. And they failed to love their neighbors with the passion their Lord had said was needed for a community to thrive in peace."

Freak glanced down and flipped back a few pages. He immediately found the selection beneath his fingertip, then lifted his eyes.

"We read in chapter seven, that the prophet Ezekiel," thundered Freak, "looked out over his nation, and he warned that a Day of *Disaster* was coming from the Lord. He warned the complacent multitudes to brace themselves... to brace themselves for a day when selling and buying would have no meaning. Merchants wouldn't live long enough to complete their sales... let alone to wallow in their windfalls. Consumers would not live long enough to make it home with their fancy drinks and their delicate pastries... let alone to grow any fatter."

Freak patted the open Bible.

"Ezekiel declared that where men and women had come to ignore God's truths and to carelessly defile God's mercy, the Lord would now inflict judgments that could no longer be ignored. Their card house of pride and self promotion would be shaken to the point of implosion... and the righteous winds of heaven's wrath would roar across the strewn wreckage of their homes... with a hurricane of vengeance."

Without looking down, Freak slid his finger a few inches lower into the column's text.

"Ezekiel goes on to speak of a trumpet blast... followed by the unleashing of God's corrective judgments. He paints pictures of flashing battles and plagues and famines. But he also holds out hope for those who might escape that first terrible round of justice... that they might have an opportunity to mourn their shortsighted sins and to contemplate the absolute power and the unsearchable wisdom of the eternal Lord."

Freak closed the Bible.

"If the Lord," he intoned, "would so harshly discipline the very people he had chosen and set apart back *then,* why would we expect any less of the Lord today?"

Freak paused, staring hard into the camera.

"Jesus himself," he finally continued, "declares in Revelation 3:19, 'I rebuke and discipline those whom I love.' Jesus insists that he chastises even his church. Perhaps especially his church. And why? I shake them up, says the Lord, so that while there is yet time, they might passionately turn from their cold-hearted indifference and repent of their *presumptuous, lukewarm, self-centered* lifestyles."

The End Times Prophet dramatically repeated his indictments, counting with his fingers, punctuating each accusation with such force so as to make each phrase a frightening sermon of its own.

Presumptuous.
Lukewarm.
Self-centered.

"From here to the end," Freak sighed, lowering his hand, "God will expose these sins... and demand reform."

I glanced at Steve.

The cameraman leaned dangerously hard into Jack's gangly rifle tripod. Steve's mouth was curled in, his lips pressed white between clenched teeth. His eyes were fixed, his breathing deep and slow.

The digital camcorder flashed an LED pulse of life. Faithfully and indiscriminately, the recording device captured the pastor's every gesture and word.

The human experience reduced to binary code. Yes's and no's.

Black and white.

"Jesus himself," Freak continued, "spoke of a Day of Disaster... of a great trumpet blast that would strike fear and weeping into the hearts of even the most bold. A cataclysmic season of correction that would drop even the most proud of rulers and the most vain of queens to their broken knees."

He opened the Bible to its final pages.

"And then," said Freak, "we again read of trumpet blasts in the book of Revelation. In the eighth chapter of

The Apocalypse of John, a scene is vividly described where, in the midst of catastrophic horrors... a silence falls. A short window of held-breath suspense."

Freak's finger flowed and probed the page until he had the phrase, though he clearly could have recited the passage without a prop.

"We read here of a day when the prayers of God's people will be mixed with the spiritual incense of heaven, and that together—this mixture of incense and prayer—will ascend before the Lord. Will *ascend before the Lord.*"

Freak rubbed the page.

"We have here," he said, "an image—the picture of a day defined by worship and prayer. In the very midst of calamities and disasters, we find God granting a pause. A break in the terrors. A time set apart for humble worship. A moment for reflection and repentance."

Freak closed his eyes and sighed so deeply that one corner of the open page lifted slightly in the passing of his breath.

For some reason, Rex chose that moment for a renewed interest in our guest preacher. The big black Lab drifted into the frame, nuzzled Freak's Bible hand, then surrendered himself to the floor beside Freak's leg.

I started to move to silently call off the dog, but I then caught Saundra's shrug. Hers was not so much a helpless shrug as it was an eyebrow drop and shoulder dip of curious resignation.

Freak lowered a hand to Rex's ear. The prophet's fingers scratched their way to a thick leather collar. Freak tugged the collar gently once, then met Rex's eyes and nodded towards me. The dog rose and padded his way to my outstretched hand off screen.

"And then," resumed Freak, his voice slow and sad, "we read that this pause of peace will be followed by peals of thunder. By flashes of lightning. And by a mighty shaking of the earth. After that heaven-sent interlude of worship and rest—of kneeling in prayer—things immediately spiral down into destruction and chaos."

His voice gathered strength.

"We read of a trumpet blast that is followed by hail and fire, a sky-falling cocktail of wrath mixed with blood... pouring upon earth so as to scorch and burn into ash a vast wasteland of what had once thrived with life."

He closed his Bible again, then somberly shook his head.

"From that trumpet blast to the end, the prophet John shares a vision, a succession of increasingly fierce judgments that are destined to unfurl. These judgments roll out, they pour down upon the Earth... upon all vegetation, upon all creatures of the sea, upon animals and humans alike. These horrors rise up from the natural realm, but the destruction equally emerges from the wickedness of Satan's army... and from the darkest hearts of humankind."

Off camera, Jack and Mary silently prayed. Their hands were tenderly entangled where they sat upon the heavy couch that had been dragged to the furthest wall.

Saundra stood, hardly breathing, a step behind Steve's shoulder. She occasionally leaned toward the viewfinder, but never for long. Early in her interview, Saundra had stopped asking questions. She had decided to slip from the frame, to simply turn the prophet loose.

"As you must know," said Freak, "the world is in the midst of an unprecedented meltdown. In recent years, the violence of the weather and of the earth itself has taken greater and greater tolls... tolls that God has reluctantly allowed. Tolls that have been tolerated by God in order to humble our arrogant species. The Lord has sought to awaken us through droughts, floods, tsunamis, volcanoes, tornados, earthquakes, and typhoons... unexpected disasters that might remind us that death is never more than a butterfly's wing-flap away."

"The escalating stresses of random shootings, bombings, revolutions, wars, and terrorist uprisings have pushed our minds and our self-definitions to the brink."

Freak slowly raised two fingers to his left temple. Then, with more melodrama than I'd ever yet seen him exhibit, he painstakingly dragged those fingertips down his scars, only stopping at last at his chin.

"It has gotten ugly," he sighed.

"I wish," he said, massaging his chin, "that I could tell you the worst is behind us."

He dropped his hand.

"But it is not. The worst... is yet to come."

He leaned towards the camera, stretching a hand the way a parent might draw forward towards a child on the verge of a fatal mistake.

"Whatever you have known of this world, and of your life," he whispered, "it is all coming to an end."

He straightened.

"A week ago, on The Day of the Falling Skies, the Lord plucked me from the air. He sent two angels to protect me in my plunge. To humble me. To open scripture to greater understanding. And to guide me as a prophet he himself had appointed... to bear witness to his Grace and his Truth in these, our planet's final days."

Freak held the Bible to the camera. Lowered it.

"The Lord told me of the earthquakes in San Francisco."

He paused.

"And of two more things that I shall now reveal."

"*Grace*," said Freak, pointing an index finger to his healthy right cheek.

"Tomorrow, God will give our planet a day of rest. For one day—Easter Sunday—God will let us catch our breaths. For those who are wise... this is a day to worship and pray. To humbly repent and obey. Our Lord Jesus Christ will soon arrive with his vast angel armies of heaven. I beg of you: turn to Jesus. Find an open church tomorrow. Read a Bible. Talk with a Christian friend. Accept salvation through Jesus Christ, who is the Lord of heaven, and who is the ultimate King of the Earth. He is the one to whom you must turn before you are swallowed in the days of judgment yet to come."

Freak paused.

Slowly, he returned two fingers to his scars.

"*Truth*," he whispered.

"After this Easter," he said, his voice suddenly resigned, "on Monday morning... the judgments will resume. Horrors shall be unleashed far beyond anything we've yet seen on our planet since the days of Noah."

He shook his head.

"Prepare yourselves... for in two days... our planet will shudder in the blast of the First Trumpet ... in our King's countdown for the End of Days."

25
OUT INTO THE ENDING WORLD

It worked.

With staggering effectiveness in minimal time, Steve edited Freak's podcast into three roughly equal segments. He also created a fast-paced four-minute highlights video titled: *End of the World? Ask Freak!*

Steve packaged the highlight footage to play like a movie trailer so that it could easily go viral around the planet. Which it did.

Within the first hour.

Pastor Gilford had received and promptly relayed the digital files to Krissy at the liquor store exactly as planned.

Later, Gilford relished retelling how surprised Krissy had looked when he'd walked in from the storm to hand his former nemesis a tiny silver thumb drive loaded with a few of the world's most important files.

"Mark and Saundra wanted you to have this," Gilford had said, passing her the drive. "These files contain critical prophecies for the end of the world. They want you to lock the store and to hurry home. Once home, you're to immediately upload these videos onto YouTube. Then, you're to quickly post everything else from this drive onto your web site. You're also to send copies to all your friends, as well as to *anywhere* else you can think to send the files."

"No way!" she'd exclaimed, examining the drive. "The end of the world? They're giving Freak's statements to me?"

"Yes. Do whatever it takes to get this information immediately scattered as far and as wide as possible. Send emails to all of the major television stations. Encourage them to check your website for the latest epic End of Days predictions from Freak. We need to get all of this information bouncing around in a hundred places before anyone can shut it down at a single source."

"Why would anyone want to shut it down?"

"I'm not sure. But Freak says you and your boyfriend should find a new place to lay low for a while. Things are going to get crazy, and you need to be safe. He also asked me to say that you two need to spend a little time getting yourselves squared away. You're supposed to study God's word. Especially *The Apocalypse of John...* the last book of the Bible."

"If the world is really going to end, maybe I should throw my boyfriend a big party. Why should we bother doing what Freak asks?"

"*Because* the world is going to end, you'd *better* bother to do exactly what the prophet suggests."

"Huh?"

"This assignment comes directly from God. If you've never met the Lord before, you soon enough *will*."

"And?"

"You've got a chance to stand before the commander of the angel armies and hear Jesus say, 'Thank you, Kristen. Well done. You really came through in a critical hour!' Or, if you fail to obey, you'll be weeping to explain all of the important other things you were doing that made his request seem like too much of a bother."

Krissy got it.

She abruptly reached for her keys and began to lock the store.

Propelled by hashtags like *#Apocalypse* and *#Freak*, the substance of Freak's disturbing sermon and his frightening predictions for Monday were lighting up social media venues unlike anything since the advent of the Internet.

By late-afternoon, choice phrases and short clips from Freak's podcast began surfacing in television newscasts. Several cable networks ran Steve's *End of the World? Ask Freak!* highlights video in its entirety.

"It's hard to know," commented one studio reporter, "whether to be thankful or irate about this footage coming from the disfigured Reverend W.B. 'Freak' Jacobs. This pastor claims to speak on behalf of God. Yet many of the pastor's most respected professional peers question both his reliability and his motives. His previous track record as a predictor of events is, at best, mixed."

"True," conceded the anchor, "but his predictions were amazingly accurate about many of the shocking events of the past 24 hours. And God only knows how he survived both an exploding airplane on The Day of the Falling Skies, and then that deadly terrorist attack yesterday at the ski lodge in Colorado."

And on it went.

Station after station.

Millions of people—those who were not fighting or fleeing for safety—watched live reports of disasters and violence from around the globe. The continuous coverage was peppered with Freak's dire predictions for more to come on Monday. And then salted with the prophet's passionate pleas for humanity to use Easter to choose whether to turn to Jesus... or to meet him unprepared.

CONFESSIONS

It all made me think.

Not the way I'd been taught to think in college, but again the way I'd learned to think long ago around campfires at the Diamond K Ranch.

I kept looking at Freak... his face. I tried to imagine any of my professors having the courage to talk about God's grace to a class of smug philosophy majors through the rawness of such scars.

I finally stood and awkwardly moved to the open spot beside Saundra on the couch.

"Can we talk?" I asked, keeping my voice between the two of us. "I know I've been a real jerk, but I'm hoping we can get past my mistakes so we can discuss some serious matters. Not just for the sake of my ego, but, more importantly, we need to work out a few of our issues... if only for the sake of the mission."

She studied me. "Sure," she said, "we can talk."

Saundra's gaze shifted from me to Freak, and then to the others. For the past hour, we'd all sat around the television gazing into the flickering monitor, sighing at the ongoing carnage of Black Saturday, viewing the barrage of scenes that blurred like a smoldering landfill, black with the smoke of human refuse and burning tires. At the moment, if any of the others in the room were eavesdropping, they were being discreet, and there was nothing I could do about their curiosity.

I took a deep breath.

"I've been thinking," I faltered, "about some of the things I said earlier today."

"Too little." Her tone was matter-of-fact. "And too late. You should have started your thinking before you began insulting and mocking me. And before you made a complete fool of yourself by ripping into Freak like that in front of every person in this room."

Nobody turned our way.

"Fair enough," I sighed. "You're right. I've been an ass, pretty much most of the time you've known me."

Saundra glanced at my hands, which were clenched on my knees, white knuckled.

I forced myself to continue. "You need to know," I said, "that Freak was right about me. I've been doing some fighting today. And I've been hearing his words about trying to pray and straighten up with God. I'm not sure where I'm at with the whole God thing, but I wanted to start by trying to get right with you."

Saundra's head tilted ever-so-slightly.

I squared to face her directly. "I'm sorry," I said, "for a lot of things. Not just for making fun of you this morning about angels and prayer... but everything. For all of my crude jokes. For not taking seriously your grief about losing friends yesterday in the explosion at the lodge. I've probably got some PTSD going on myself right now, but that's no excuse for making cracks about group hugs and boo-hoo parties... no excuse for blowing off your pain."

"Thanks for the reminder." Saundra squinted. "Are you being serious? Or are you just being ironic again?"

"No jokes this time," I said. "I actually meant what I said when Jack forced me to remember the words. I had to say it a few times when I was a kid here, too. 'There is no place for potty talk and wicked nonsense at the Diamond K. Please forgive me.'"

Saundra stared. Shook her head.

I bought time with another long breath. "There's more. I know it's obvious, but I'm a sucker for attractive ladies. Trust me when I promise that I'm not trying to hit on you right now when I say this, but you're one of the most beautiful women I've ever met. Jack was right when he said the wiring inside of my head is messed up when it comes to women."

Saundra remained composed, as if I was not the first ape to apologize for acting like an chimp in her presence.

"Here's the thing," I said. "I've been trying to impress you ever since we met. I keep wanting you to think I'm hot stuff. I need to get past that if we're going to get along as two real human beings who are stuck working together side-by-side in the midst of a burning world." I managed a weak smile. "I know it... I've been acting like another one of those obnoxious meatheads at the bar. Please forgive me. Let's get past that and move on. I'm really going to try to treat you better."

"Mark," she said, "sometimes you utterly baffle me."

"How so?"

"Forget it. What else were you going to say? You mentioned something about wanting to protect the mission. What do you mean when you say, *the mission?*"

"Look, I'm just doing the math. There have been too many improbable events and impossible coincidences. When they are all stacked in a line...." I slowed down. "Last weekend, I witnessed Freak's plane exploding in a clear sky. I saw him drop into my backyard. And then, as drunk as I was, I dug him out of a tomb of snow, and I somehow safely rushed him bleeding to death to the hospital... where he promptly healed over night. Sort of healed, I mean."

I forced a grin, then took another deep breath.

"Yesterday at the lodge, I felt the walls and glass blowing out all around us. And yet, somehow, I managed to get him out. Along with you, and with Steve."

Saundra crossed her arms and frowned.

"And then, in my mind, I clearly foresaw the roadblocks ahead of us while we were still miles away. And I somehow knew how to get us past the officials. To get us here... to the Diamond K."

I pointed to the television. They were rolling another clip from Freak's podcast. "Without me," I said, "the world wouldn't be listening to this guy right now."

Saundra rolled her eyes. "There you go again...."

"No," I said. "You're not letting me finish. I get it. This is *not* about me. It's not about what I choose, and it's bigger than what I could possibly do on my own. I'm in it, but I'm not the one who counts. You've played a big role in this, too. But it's all about *him.* And what he has to say."

I glanced at the prophet. He sat close to the television, leaning towards his frightened global audience, perhaps sitting with some invisible angel hovering beside him on the very couch where late one summer night as a young teen I'd touched my first girlfriend.

I turned my gaze to Jack and Mary, the godly couple who had patiently sown so much love and peace so deeply into my psyche that it was to them I had intuitively fled in an hour of crisis. And they had been there conveniently waiting for us, ready to drive out into a blizzard to pick up our crew and take us in. To shelter us from the storm and any dangers unknown.

"Whether I like it or not," I sighed again, "I've been chosen to serve him and the mission. We all have. I am not the man of the hour. Freak is. God is."

It took some silence, but Saundra eventually unfolded her arms and eased forward in my direction.

"The mission," she asked, "is the message, huh?"

"Yes. And the work Freak has been saved to do. I'm not saying what I believe—and what I don't believe—but with everything that has happened, and with what's on the television tonight, I guess it's time I put a little of my skepticism on hold for a while."

I met Saundra's eyes. "I guess," I finished, "that I need to stop filtering everything through my doubts. And it's about time I started listening a little better with my heart."

It had been a while since Saundra had been able to brush her hair. There was a boldness, an energy in her eyes, a sensuous abandon in the way the oversized, untucked flannel shirt she'd selected from the lost and found closet was rumpling and piling into her lap.

"And," she smiled, "what exactly is your heart saying?"

I hesitated. I suddenly struggled, barely able to restrain the instinctive rush. Maybe it was the lust Rider. Maybe it was a couple of decades of wolfish bad habits gone wild.

For a moment, all I could imagine was that my mission was *her*. My only heart's desire was to somehow convince Saundra to nestle into my chest. To con her, if necessary, into trusting me. That I could never be happy until I had gently taken her face in my hands... until I had tenderly smothered her impossibly alluring lips with my own. If only for one night. That was my heart's mission, and it trumped all others.

I made myself look away from her mouth.

Freak had begun rocking his shoulders, barely inches. His eyes were closed, and his jaw was trembling.

"What," asked Saundra again, "is your heart telling you?"

My mind flashed to my beastie. My rig was rolling over the cliff, tumbling and crashing into the ravine far below.

I focused on the praying Freak in the other room.

Somehow, I managed to timidly squeeze out a single word:

Jesus.

I closed my eyes. When I finally reopened them, Saundra was still waiting.

"My heart..." I softly restarted, discovering new strength. "My heart is telling me that King Jesus is on the move. My heart is declaring that you...me... all of us... we need to do what we can to help Freak prepare the world."

"For the disasters on Monday?"

"And for the probable return of the Lord Jesus Christ."

PART III

EASTER SUNDAY AND BEYOND

I awoke to the sound of a trumpeting shofar.

The wind beyond the windows of our little cabin had died during the night, so the air was deathly still. Except for that distant sound.

The unnerving blast of a ram's horn.

Well, not exactly a ram's horn. More like the magnificent long spiraled prong of an African antelope. A kudu, I think.

One of Mr. K's most cherished possessions.

I rolled from the honeymooners' fluffy mattress and bumped across cold floor shadows to the heavy drapes of the front window.

The sky was thick in a chilled gray that hung low over nearby peaks. The path Steve and I had slogged the night before was beginning to collapse and sink. Our tracks between the main house and the cabin were settling and fading beneath a couple inches of pre-dawn accumulation.

The horn sounded again.

It was awkwardly blown. The pitch cracked. The noise swelled, crescendoing until it at last broke in the midst of the release of the final note.

Another signature blast from Mr. K's chapped mountain-man lips.

Jack normally kept the impressive relic locked in his gun cabinet. The big rancher racked it among high-powered elk rifles, target shooters, and bird-gauge shot guns in the main-house trophy room. Jack only uncaged his prized shofar a few times each year. Only on special occasions.

Like dawn on Easter day.

I parted the drapes further and tucked my face between the lace curtains. I craned my neck, pressing one cheek snuggly into the window's frost.

Jack stood in his favorite dark cowboy hat, swaying a couple hundred yards up the hilled lane at the top of his porch. One elbow sagged, then rose to a gloved hand that firmly cupped the tapered horn of the long-forgotten beast. Jack's other arm stretched forward, cradling one of the shofar's curves, aiming his lips and breath through the ancient Jewish instrument towards targets unseen.

As with most of his other prized possessions, Jack referred to his horn by its nickname. The trumpet had been given to him decades ago as a special thank-you gift from a thickly bearded rabbi who had booked a cabin for a spiritual retreat from New York. The Jewish cleric had spent one month in silent solitude at the Diamond K, then abruptly departed in the night, leaving behind only a short handwritten note and this remarkable shofar.

"I've noticed you like to name your treasures," read the note. "This horn is to be called… Saint Michael."

Jack's closing bugle blast started strong, then predictably faltered. But not for lack of sincerity or effort. His amateur WASP lips were simply shot… Jack sputtered short on lungs long before completing his final tekiah and trill.

Blame it on the cold air.

And too few holidays in the year to master his art.

27

BACON AND HARD-BOILED EGGS

Breakfast was light and simple.

A few dozen eggs from the barn. A few pounds of bacon. A few stacks of sourdough pancakes. And a mixing bowl stirred full of yogurt and granola, with assorted fresh fruits on the side.

Mrs. K kept busy, bustling back and forth, refilling our plates and apologizing for not having had the time to whip up anything more substantial.

And worrying whether—given the collapsing of the world—she should plan on cooking up her annual Easter ham.

"It's a low, thick ceiling out there," observed Jack. "According to Cal's new phone, the weather app is calling for clouds and light snow off and on throughout the day. The storm stalled last night, and they're not expecting much activity until the next system bumps down from Wyoming sometime after supper tonight."

Cal reached for a hard-boiled egg. "Dad," he asked, "do you want me to do some snow plowing this morning? I could open the driveway as far as the road. Or I could leave us snowed in a little longer." He casually began to shake salt for his first bite. "But we don't need to get out, so maybe we should leave the drifts to slow down anyone else who might try to get in. What do you think?"

"Well," sighed Jack, "now there's a good question."

Jack extended his fingers for another strip of bacon. He sized it up, tested the grease, then waved it at Freak, playing the bacon like a favorite fishing rod. "With this break in the storm," said Jack, "the county trucks will have US 40 open again within an hour. They'll probably have our side road plowed as far as our ranch entrance by late-afternoon."

Mary smiled. "So," she asked, "does that mean we can have everyone over tonight for oikos? People have been calling and texting to see if we're going to cancel or not. With everything that's happened since last Sunday—and because it's Easter—it seems more important than ever to me that we meet this week."

"Oikos?" asked Saundra.

"Oh," Mary apologized. "That's just the word we use to describe our little house-church community."

Freak nodded. "Oikos is a Greek word from the Bible. It means household... extended family. During the early years of the Christian movement, believers often met in houses to share meals and to worship together."

"Most of us," said Mary, "go to regular churches on Sunday mornings. But on Sunday nights, a group of us have a potluck here on the ranch. We sing a few songs, pray together, and then we encourage each other in whatever challenges we face."

Jack glanced from his wife to Saundra. "We've become a wonderful little group to help support each other in the ways we try to serve the world. Every Sunday night, our oikos gatherings are like an intimate family reunion. You'd like it. Stick around long enough, and you'll see for yourself." Jack halved his bacon with a single chomp and then turned back to Freak. "What do you suggest?" he asked. "Should we plow our driveway open to the road, or should we leave ourselves plugged off for the day?"

Freak sat with the question, eyeing what was left of Jack's pork slice.

Saundra lowered her fork onto her sticky, berry-stained plate. "I don't mean to sound paranoid," she ventured, "but maybe we should stay cut off, with nobody coming and going. It's pretty clear there's an army of terrorists or something that wants us all dead." She drew Freak's gaze. "Or, at least, that wants the Reverend W.B. Jacobs to be silenced."

Freak nodded. "Yes. And it could be very helpful to have some warning and time to prepare if any kind of enemy was trying to slowly work their way up the drive to get to us. But I keep hearing the Lord say we're supposed to be bold. That we're supposed to raise our heads and to stand in faith in the midst of these dangerous times and violent shakings."

"That's in the Bible," agreed Jack, grinding the last of his meat. "Luke 21:28 is a favorite verse of mine. Something I have always carried around in my pocket for a time like this. *'When these things begin to happen, stand up and lift your heads, for your salvation draweth nigh.'* For thirty years, I've been watching—waiting—for the trials that have begun this week."

"What," asked Steve, "do you mean?"

"The Great Tribulation, son." Jack looked surprised. "The great global shaking... the time of sorrows and persecutions before the return of our King." Jack reached for another strip of bacon. "Maybe the next time Freak gives a speech, you should put down your camera for a few minutes and listen."

Steve winced. "I've been listening," he said. "I know how Freak interprets these events. But I didn't know every Christian looks at it all the same way that Freak does. I figured Freak's theories were from the fringe. Pretty radical, I mean...."

I tried not to smile. Jack was one of the most radical Christians I'd ever met. But he didn't see it that way, and he tended to get defensive whenever it came up like this. From Jack's perspective, his passionate no-holds-barred version of following Jesus was normal. The way every Christian was supposed to think and behave. The way Jesus taught, and pretty much how all of the true Christians of the early church lived.

At least from Jack's point of view.

"I'm not sure," said Jack, "how much Freak and I agree... and where we disagree. But there ain't a Christian in the world worth a lick of salt who isn't watching the skies and waiting for the return of the King."

Steve sheepishly returned to his eggs.

It dawned on me that Freak hadn't touched any bacon. I slid my gaze back up from the bacon platter to the prophet's scars.

The resemblance was a little unsettling.

"What's the matter, Freak," I asked, tying to lighten the mood, "how come you haven't tried any of Mrs. K's bacon? Did that shofar this morning turn your stomach sour... or *kosher*?"

Freak gave me another one of his protracted odd stares.

"Glad to see," he finally replied, "that you haven't lost your sense of humor. You've been unusually quiet this morning."

"Enjoy it," I grinned, "while you can."

"Seriously," he asked, "what's going on?"

It was my turn to hesitate.

I glanced at Saundra, then to the others. Then back to Freak.

"Okay," I said at last, "I hate to admit it, but that last sermon podcast of yours got to me. Maybe it was because I'd just been so out of control, and then you'd just prayed over me, but I felt some pretty heavy conviction while you were giving your End of Days speech to the camera."

Freak nodded, his face unmoved.

"I already talked with Saundra last night, and I guess I might as well go public with the rest of you today. I am painfully aware of how I've behaved like an idiot at times.

Not exactly a class act. I want to say again how sorry I am for how obnoxious I was yesterday."

Mrs. K offered an encouraging smile. "We've already accepted your apology, Mark. You know you're forgiven. You've come clean."

"Yes," I said, weighing her words. "And no." I thought some more. "I can believe you're willing to give me a pass for yesterday, but I still don't feel very clean. I feel like those bad habits Jack mentioned are still riding me. Sometimes I sort of snap. Or forget myself or something. It's me being a jerk... but it's not me. It's like I'm not myself... at least, not who I want to be." I shrugged. "Sorry," I mumbled, "I know I'm not making any sense."

Saundra quietly stared in my direction, but I avoided her eyes.

"So the thing is," I finished, "I want to work on doing better. Nobody likes a jerk."

Freak cleared his throat. "It's a tough battle, Mark," he said, his voice flat. "Even the Apostle Paul confessed in the Bible that he sometimes found himself doing the very things he hated to do. That's true for all of us. We just can't be in denial about what's going on. We have to pay attention to what we're doing... and why. And then we have to be intentional about how we deal with it."

"I have read the verse," I replied, starting to wonder why I'd even brought the subject up. "I know who the Apostle Paul is, and I've read his letters."

"Many theologians," Freak continued, "believe that when Paul spoke of a thorn in his flesh, he was referring to an afflicting demon. An unclean spirit that was assigned to him to constantly torment, tempt and discourage him. A Dark Rider."

Steve looked puzzled. "Freak," he asked, "are you saying we can blame the Devil for the bad stuff we do? That it boils down to sprinkling Holy Water and casting off Dark Riders so we can be better people?"

"Of course not," Freak replied. "We have free will. We make our choices. We form our habits, and we're accountable for what we do. That's part of what God is doing right now in history... he's showing every creature in heaven and on Earth what happens when...."

"Anyway," I interrupted. "Like I said, I'm sorry for yesterday, and some of my other stuff this past week. If the world is going to end, I don't want all of the people I die with to all think I'm a jerk. Starting today, I'm going to try to do better."

Jack smiled. "Let me know if you need any help, son. When it comes to helping folks kick bad habits, I've got a size 14 boot."

Steve shook his head. "Mark, did you just admit that Freak might be right about the world ending? Are you starting to doubt your doubts?"

"I'm not sure. But if Freak *is* right—and so far he's been right about a lot—then I've got some more work to do before I'm ready." I met Freak's eyes. "Before I'm ready for what might be coming next."

Freak grinned.

Jack wiped his freshly licked fingers on his chest. "Good boy," he winked, reaching for the last egg in the bowl. "It's about time you got back with the program."

"Easter," said Mrs. K, "is a perfect time to remember that we all can start over, thanks to Jesus and the power of the resurrection." Her face flashed a moment of distress. "Goodness," she exclaimed, "here it is Easter, and I guess we're not even going to church."

Jack pointed his egg at Freak. "We've got a preacher," he smiled. "And we've got plenty of Bibles." He turned back to his wife. "We're stuck on the ranch this morning, and we may have to skip oikos tonight. But one way or another, I'm sure that today we'll have some kind of Easter to remember."

"By the way, Jack," I smirked, "thanks for your classic Diamond K wakeup call this morning. But I have to confess... it did take me a while to recognize it was your Saint Michael shofar calling. For a minute, I thought it was Cal blasting his truck horn to clear out the geese."

I ducked to be safe, because it sure looked like Jack might let fly with that last hard-boiled egg.

28
EASTER SPAM

We emptied the table and finished in the kitchen, then gathered for a survey of the morning's cable news highlights.

Emergency rescue efforts and disaster relief responses filled the reports from California, Europe, and around the world. Clips from recent Freak recordings were seasoned into the mix here and there to vary the pace and to wrap the entire past week into one possibly connected narrative.

People were desperate to make sense of the unprecedented chaos and horrors of the past few days. The planet had not experienced a week like this since WWII.

The memory span of a lifetime.

But there were no new earthquakes, nor any significant new outbreaks of violence.

Freak had been right about a Sunday break.

"He called it exactly right for Easter," said one network anchor. "The prophet predicted that Saturday would be filled with natural calamities and continued terrors. And he also said today would be a day of calm."

Podcast footage of Freak's forecast for a reprieve appeared on an inset screen. A second cut showed Freak warning the world to prepare for the unleashing of unimaginably horrific events on Monday... to brace ourselves for the First Trumpet of the Apocalypse.

The anchor turned to his suited guest. "What," he asked, "do you make of this 'trumpet blast'? As an expert in the field of apocalyptic literature, do you put any stock in the prophet's references to the blowing of a trumpet?"

"The pastor," frowned the celebrity, "is a buffoon. Nobody with a reasonable grasp of the intertestamental period and the pseudepigraphic and apocalyptic literature of the early church takes any of these passages literally. Images of bowls of wrath, wax seals, and blasting trumpets are purely metaphoric... at best, allegoric and symbolic. Those of us with even one foot in the real world will not see—nor will we hear—a trumpet. What people see and hear in their private fantasies and within their sleeping dreams are between them and their therapists. As for me, and I hope for you, there will be no trumpets."

"You are certain of this?"

"The trumpets in the book of Revelation are no more literal than the two-edged sword that is said in Revelation 19:15 to be shooting from the Christ figure's mouth as he drops from the clouds in the midst of a million flapping angels. No serious modern interpreter would ever take such a passage as literal."

"But," smiled the journalist, "a week ago, I wouldn't have believed it possible for a televangelist to drop from the sky claiming to have a message from God... and then to have the entire world's prime-time shocked attention as he preaches from the Bible and makes accurate predictions about...."

The guest scowled. "As has already been said of Bill Jacobs and countless other fanatic fundamentalists before him, *even a broken clock gets the time right twice per day.* Trust me, the book of Revelation is a lovely piece of allegory. And there will be no trumpet on Monday."

The host straightened his stack of notes. "Prior to this past week," he pressed, "it is my understanding that many experts took the earthquakes and the 'wars and rumors of wars' of the past week to also be something less than... *literal.*"

Nonplused, the professor pressed back.

"There have always been earthquakes," he said, "and our planet has never known anything other than wars and rumors of wars since the emergence of man. If the prediction of such inevitabilities suddenly transforms a country bumpkin pastor into a mouthpiece of God—a semi-literate fool who is taken seriously by anyone who counts—then we live in a sad, sad world indeed."

Freak sat transfixed, hardly blinking.

Saundra found a scratchpad and began to furiously jot notes.

Cal disappeared to do his morning chores.

Mrs. K rose from beside Jack to attend to the computer at the front desk.

"These literalists," continued the scholar, "are irreconcilably inconsistent, even to the point of absurdity."

"For example?" asked the host.

"Take the fundamentalist dogma of a Pre-Tribulation rapture." The guest shook his head. "For years, Pastor Bill Jacobs has clamored every weekend on his television show that the only real Christians were those who believed in an escapist *Left Behind* type of doctrine, a fantasy theory within which Christians will magically disappear from Planet Earth when most of us least expect it. With everybody else in the world will being left behind."

"You don't accept this theory?"

The guest laughed. "Of course not. But let's stick to the pastor from California and his inconsistent predictions and his every-changing timelines. Jacobs has always been on record as *promising* that Christians will escape the Tribulation by being raptured *before* the blowing of the Trumpets of the Apocalypse. But now, he's *promising* that the Trumpet will blast tomorrow, *before* the rapture."

"Sir," asked the host, "has the prophet actually said *anything* about the rapture since he was miraculously saved on the Day of the Falling Skies?"

"Well, not exactly. But it is implied." The guest tugged his tie and laughed. "Jacobs predicted in yesterday's podcast that the First Trumpet will blow within the next 24 hours... and I'm still here today, right? Every Christian I know is still here. And I haven't seen any deserted piles of abandoned clothing anywhere."

He laughed again, then reached for the half-empty plastic bottle near his hand.

"So," sneered the scholar, lifting his water in a mock toast, "whatever happened to the so-called rapture that Jacobs and his fundamentalist cronies have been waiting for all of these years? If the rapture doesn't happen within the next few hours, then I guess all credibility and any remaining integrity of this so-called prophet goes down in the spectacular flames of his own arrogance and lies."

Jack raised his television remote control towards the screen. He countered the skeptical scholar's salute with a click of the Diamond K mute.

Then looked at Freak.

"It's a fair question," said Jack. "I'm not at all impressed with this arrogant faithless talking head, but he makes one very good point. Freak... *what about the rapture?*"

Freak studied the silent screen, then slowly turned to meet Jack's gaze.

"I'm working on it," said Freak. "But I've got to confess... so far, I'm hearing nothing from the Lord on this. If I had to guess, then I'd probably say...."

Suddenly, we all became aware of Mrs. K.

She stood, trembling at the edge of our conversation, holding a piece of paper within her quivering hands.

"Sorry to interrupt," she said, "I just printed this out. I didn't recognize the sender, and at first I thought it was a mistake or some sort of spam. But after reading it a couple times, I'm not too sure...."

She stepped forward to pass it to Freak, stopped, then turned to Saundra.

"Here," said Mrs. K, "maybe this is for you?"

Saundra rose to accept the printout. She quickly skimmed the email, gasped, then sank to the couch to read it again:

SUBJECT LINE — TJ: Happy Easter Sandi !

Yo, Sandi Patti ... I hope this Easter finds u happy and whole?
What's *NOT* shaking, baby?
A whole lot of us hit the hole and checked out early this week.
Not me. I was working the streets when the clock went off.
I tried tapping into yer droid, but got zip.
I got worried you might have checked out early yourself.

I called the Lollipop Shop, but got no K-girl & knew something wuz up.
G-bird man was chilling by the Licker Store, & he glued me in on you.
G-bird says K-girl heard the word, got smart, and flew the coop.
She's outa site 4 now.

Then I saw your latest masterpiece.

Borrowed a Budweiser's keys 2 reach 2 you.

Rumors of a stiff dude from your past who wants another run at u.

Git back with me, girl! Use this line 4 now.
I'm here 4 u. Use me!

Hugs and kisses... and whatever else you'll give me. — TJ

SETTING FOCUS

"It's from Tom Jackson," said Saundra. "Sometimes when I'm in a hurry at the station, I call him TJ for short. Whenever he wants to get on my nerves, he calls me Sandi Patti."

I looked up from the letter in my hands. "Hit the hole…" I said. "That means hit the grave, *killed*. The Lollipop Shop… the Licker Store… he means the *liquor* store in Silverthorne. Where Krissy works. K-girl."

"Obviously."

"And this G-bird man has got to be Pastor Gilford, from the church next to the liquor store."

"Right. He's avoiding all of the key words that might set off alarms for anyone with spider programs… anyone with crawler software and high-level monitoring access to the Internet."

Steve took the page from my hand and skimmed it for himself. "Anyone with *access*," he asked, "you mean, like agents from Homeland Security... or some other government surveillance organization?"

"He's being cautious," I said. "He knows something. But what the heck is this *stiff dude* business... about him wanting another shot at you? An old boyfriend?"

"Not likely," said Saundra. "Especially not in this context."

Freak motioned for Steve to pass him the email. Freak studied it carefully, then gave it to Jack.

"The note is asking," said Freak, "for Saundra to reply. What do you think... should we trust this contact, or not?"

Saundra took a sip of coffee. "I'm not sure. I'm pretty confident the note is authentic... that it was at least written and sent by TJ. I've gotten flirting emails from Tom Jackson before where he signed off with that exact same silly nonsense at the end."

"*Hugs and kisses,*" I recited, "*... and whatever else you'll give me.*"

Jack rose to his full imposing height. "I'm no computer nerd, but if you folks think hackers are clever enough to do word searches on emails in private accounts, then it seems to me they could have just as easily found Jackson's old office emails. Anybody could have copied that flirting line and pasted it here to fool Saundra." He shook his head. "You folks keep working on this. As for me... the best thing I can do is probably just head up to the loft and pray."

He started to move, then looked to me.

"Mark," said Jack, "you seem to be doing a lot better today."

"Yes," I said. "Maybe better by the minute." I pointed to the familiar heirloom clock that filled the far corner of the fireplace wall. "Ask me again in an hour."

"Good. I will. We've been praying for you. It'd be nice to have you back." He smiled. "All the way back to where you began with us as a child."

"Thanks," I grinned. "At peace at the Diamond K... that'd be nice again."

Freak turned to Mrs. K. "I'd be honored if you'd add your prayers to our work upstairs. I'll be heading up in a few minutes myself. Hopefully between the three of us— and the Lord—we'll get a few things sorted out and put in their proper place." He looked back to Saundra. "Any other thoughts?"

"Yes," she said, her voice tentative. "Whoever sent this note must have gotten the ranch's email address from Pastor Gilford. I think we need to trust Gilford, and we need to assume we're dealing with Tom Jackson at Channel 5 News. He suggests he's using a buddy's laptop or something, so it'll be hard for anyone to discover or trace our communications for a while. I say we should take advantage of this opportunity while we still can."

"What are you saying?"

"While you're up there praying in the loft," said Saundra, "you should ask the Lord if there's anything that he wants you to preach today. Seems like the world could use a really good Easter sermon right about now."

Steve transferred everything off from the camera memory cards, backing up the files on both the ranch's main computer and Cal's laptop. With plenty of freed memory, he began preparing for another fireside podcast.

Saundra replied to TJ's email with a test question only the real Jackson could answer. She quickly received a satisfactory reply. She informed him that some files would be coming his way in about an hour, and then she began helping Steve finalize the setup for Freak's holiday address to an ending world.

I mostly watched.

Unlike the previous day, I felt relaxed. Even excited.

I found it surprising that the previous day I'd judged my chair to be too lumpy. I replayed impressions of recent events. I tried to imagine what Freak might say when the camera was rolling once again. And I couldn't help but admire the courage and cool-headed efficiencies of the team busily working around me to save what they could of the world.

"Looks good," said Steve, pulling his eye from the viewfinder and giving her a thumbs up. "It's a great set. Serious, but intimate. The fireplace and lamps are perfect."

Saundra lifted herself out of Freak's dark recliner and stepped from the frame.

As she passed close, I suddenly blurted the question that had captured my imagination as I'd watched her and Steve tweaking the focus and angle of Freak's big chair.

"Saundra," I said, "help me out with something."

"Yes?"

"I'm dying to know… tell me about the test question. What exactly did you ask Tom a few minutes ago to determine for sure it was him at the other end of the emails?"

She placed a set of knuckles on her hip, then summoned a lovely, mischievous half smile. No lipstick. Hair loose. Nothing plastic or painted for her viewing fans.

Just herself, for her scrambling family at the mountain ranch.

"I asked him..." she replied, "something that nobody else had any business knowing."

"And...?"

"Like I said, something nobody else has any business knowing."

"C'mon," I grinned. "We're in this together, right?"

"Fine. I told him that if he was the real TJ," she winked, "then he could tell me about all of those hugs and kisses he mentioned. He should be able to write back and tell me exactly the *what*, the *when*... and the why of the... *whatever else.*"

I scratched my head and shrugged in feigned disinterest. "Oh, is that all? And his answer was...?"

Saundra smiled, then teasingly turned to leave.

"Aw, come on," I begged. "Wilt thou leave me so unsatisfied?"

"Fine," she said, tossing her hair. Meeting my eyes. "He correctly replied, and I quote: 'New Years Eve. One hug. One kiss. Nothing since... because Ms. Patti claims she has never ventured all the way down the road... and she'll never take that path with me.'"

I caught myself bursting in satisfaction.

"Hang on," she laughed. "TJ added a PS."

"No doubt."

"*But,* he added... *after this... Ms. Patty-Cakes is really going to owe me big.*"

I smiled as she rejoined Steve in some double-checking of the computer system at the front desk.

Up in the loft, prayers were rising and falling in melodic waves. Confident. Passionate. Searching. Their three voices wove in and out, taking turns, passing the torch, then sometimes overlapping in agreements and utterances that I could not quite understand.

Even as the world shuddered and convulsed, this faithful trio offered their services, lifting their hearts and pouring forth petitions for others from the humble choir loft above.

An image popped into my head, complete with lively tunes: The dance band on the Titanic.

A pathetic huddled team, soulfully playing *Nearer, my God, to Thee...* even as the iceberg ripped open their unsinkable ship like a can of sardines. Even as hundreds of screaming passengers were dumped out to helplessly plunge endlessly downward to a forever-icy black grave.

I tried to muster a sneer for the band... for the naive foolishness upstairs.

Could not.

Found myself somehow admiring them all the more. Somehow at peace, able only to smile at the fleeting image... and to dismiss it from my mind.

I strained again to hear what I could of their prayers. I might have caught them whispering my name, but couldn't be sure. I do know I heard the name of Jesus. Over and over. Jack called it. Freak prayed it. Mary sang it.

Without thinking, I echoed it.

Jesus.

In the spirit of the day, I finally attempted a simple prayer of my own.

"Lord have mercy," I murmured. "Jesus... please help Freak. Help the world. Help me. Be with us all. Thank you, Jesus. Amen."

Granted, it wasn't much.

But it was the best that I'd drummed up in a long time, and I felt better once I'd prayed it. In fact, it felt so good that I almost offered up another version of it all over again.

Almost.

The prophet descended from the loft. His steps were light, and there were holy embers in his eyes.

"God's on this," he declared. "And we need to start recording while the door is yet open. Let's roll!"

30
EASTER SERMON

"Today," said Freak, his face grim, "hundreds of millions of people around the planet are frightened." He took a deep breath. "And most of us... *should be terrified.*

"If you are watching this podcast, then you are still alive... and that means you still have time. I suggest you use your time wisely. I beg of you... listen very closely to what the Lord has put on my heart to share with you on this Easter day."

I caught a bit of motion from Steve. I shifted my attention from Freak sitting in the fireside chair to the cameraman standing behind the rifle tripod. His eyes were locked on the prophet through the viewfinder, but Steve was nodding, lifting a thumb for Saundra—or maybe for Freak—to telegraph that all was well on the technical side of the preacher's End-of-the-World address.

"In a few hours," Freak continued, "the time of the Great Tribulation will begin. So that you may trust my words in the days to come... know and confirm this: it will soon begin, and radiate outward... from the heart of Islam. The presence of Jesus is thin there... our Lord's protection and his restraining grace often grows weak where his authority is openly contested or denied. Demonic strongholds increase where brutality and the wicked ways of the Evil One are embraced.

"Suffering—and hell on earth—will soon be unleashed in the Middle East.

"As the scourge quickly spreads, horrors will be released upon the great planet Earth unlike anything in all of recorded history. In the past, we've measured our disasters and battles by fatalities and casualties numbered in the hundreds... thousands... occasionally, by the tens of thousands. Seldom more than that." He leaned forward. "Starting tomorrow, we shall often number them by the tens of thousands... hundreds of thousands... and millions."

He lifted his Bible towards the camera.

"If you are surprised by what I am saying, then you should listen all the more closely, because if you are surprised by these predictions... then you are not ready."

He lowered the Bible, but patted it gently.

"Science explains to us much about the *what*," he said, "but nothing about the *why*... nor anything about the what is *next*." He gingerly rubbed the big Bible's cover. "To answer the really important questions, we must raise our eyes from text books and test tubes to the author and giver of life... to the Lord God Almighty, and to his living Word... to his Son, the Lord of all that was... and all that is yet to come.”

I glanced to the heavy couch that had again been pulled to the far wall. Again, Mr. and Mrs. K were silently praying, hands entangled, heads down. Cal stood at the other end of the room, leaning against the kitchen doorway with a cup of coffee, eyes wide, his free hand absently scratching Rex behind the ear.

“Science would tell us that in the events of this past week, many thousands of people have died. My nearly 300 co-passengers on the flight over Colorado... dead. The thousands of others around the world who dropped from the clouds on *The Day of the Falling Skies*... dead. The dozens of journalists and vacationers who were incinerated and crushed in the rocket attacks against the lodge where I was staying... dead. Thousands of people in San Francisco and along the fault lines of California this weekend... dead. Thousands of people in European cities and villages around the world that were assaulted by terrorists or swept into outbreaks of revolution and violence this weekend on Good Friday and Black Saturday... dead.

“Most of you who are watching right now... in the days to come... dead.

“These are so-called *facts*... which can be confirmed, or that will be confirmed in the coming season of judgment.”

Freak squeezed his eyes, shaking his head.

Again he sighed deeply, then raised the Bible to line-of-sight between his ravaged left cheek and the unblinking lens of the world.

"Now hear from the Lord." Freak opened the Bible, never glancing down to the page. "We read in John's account of what he experienced that first Easter, some 2,000 years ago:

'Mary stood weeping outside of the tomb. And as she cried, she looked into the tomb and saw two angels clothed in white, seated where Jesus' body had been. One angel rested at the head of the ledge, and another at the foot.

They asked her, "Woman, why do you weep?"

"They have taken away my Lord," she replied, "and I don't know where they have put him."

But then, the woman turned around and saw Jesus standing there....'

'Where, O death, is your victory?
Where, O death, is your sting?'

Freak slowly closed the Bible.

"Science would tell us Jesus had died. That would be a so-called *fact*. If so, then in the days to come, you, too, will soon be declared dead. In the flesh... billions of us have now entered into the final season of our lives.

"A few of us will be granted the gift of quiet passings... strokes, heart attacks, health failures in the night. But most of us will suffer terrifying calamities... fires, horrible flesh-eating disease, starvation... bullets and bombs. We will not go quietly in the night. We will feel pain. We will bleed. We will be wracked with spasms and stabs beyond anything we've ever known. We will feel helpless, starved, abandoned... not in a clean hospital bed with an attending nurse—for the hospitals themselves will be overwhelmed or destroyed—but we will feel utterly alone... with no cup of cool, refreshing clean water. With no hope of recovery. With no professionals—or even loved ones—comforting us at our sides."

Freak raised his hand and pressed two fingers into the depths of his scars.

"Look at me," he demanded. "I was snatched from an exploding airplane on *The Day of the Falling Skies*. I was plucked from an exploding lodge, pulled from the screams as glass shattered and walls collapse around me in flames at the lodge. I have stared death full in the face. I have smelt the breath of death. And I have heard the living almighty voice of the one who is Lord over death itself.

'Where, O death, is your victory?
Where, O death, is your sting?'

"Science says you will die.
"But the Lord says that you shall live.
"Your heart will cease to beat. Your lungs will collapse, and your brain shall become as rotted meat.
"But you shall live.
"Ashes to burning ashes... flesh... to silent dust.
"But *you* shall live.
"Jesus was spat upon. He was whipped, stabbed, crucified. Bled out like a slab of beef in a slaughter house.
"And yet... he returned. He stood and spoke with those he loved beside his own empty tomb.
"And he is about to return again.
"Whatever happens to your body... you will soon face the Lord of heaven. The creator of our planet Earth. The

King of all space and time. The one who gave you life and holds your living spirit within his hand.

"And when your Lord calls your name, when your spirit is suddenly freed from your passing flesh... you will have to answer. How will you reply?"

Rex snapped his head to attention. Cal looked down.

I vaguely sensed a distant thumping.

The dog cocked his head, barked once, then bounded towards the north-facing window.

The thumping was rapidly growing louder.

"Do not put this off," urged Freak. "*Think* now. *Pray* now. *Bend* a knee before Jesus Christ... while you still can choose. If you wait, then this decision will be thrust upon you... by your own fainting heart at the sounding of the final trumpet. By the sight of Jesus returning with the vast multitude of his angel armies...."

The sound was suddenly nearly overhead.

The incessantly unnerving thumpf-sha-thumpf-sha of a descending helicopter.

I leapt from my chair and hurried to the window beside the dog. I peered through the lace curtains, taking care to remain hidden, as Cal slipped in alongside me.

It was a military helicopter.

From the barn rose the terrified whining of a mare.

Other horses immediately joined in a raucous chaos from the stables.

The descending camo-green Huey was one of the copters I'd grown accustomed to seeing and hearing during the past week. Numerous such crafts had shuttled back and forth between Fort Carson and the Breckenridge airport, and several had been dispatched to major wreckage sites scattered across Summit County.

This one was now hovering low, idling over Jack's half-buried rig in the drifted parking lot not far beyond my window's glass.

At once, Jack was touching my shoulder.

"Better step back," he whispered, careening his neck.

I didn't argue.

"Cal!" he softly commanded. "Fetch me Old Abe."

Cal leaned back and hurried off towards the gun case at the other end of the house.

From behind Jack, I shot a glance down the ranch's long drive to confirm that the county road was still unplowed. The heavy trucks had not yet ventured this far off from the main highway. I turned my attention to the others in the room.

Freak had paused. He'd closed his eyes. His lips were furiously busy, swept into the urgent task of flowing petitions.

Saundra, Steve and Mrs. K were all facing my direction. Each wavered in a posture of uncertainty, caught between rushing to a window or crawling beneath the massive dining room table in the other room.

Outside, the helicopter tilted one way, then another, then slowly drifted over Cal's truck. Back towards the house.

We could feel the blades.

The slashing rotary wings were not so much whirling as chopping the air. Lifting swirls of fresh white powder from the pre-dawn dusting. Rattling our windows, pulsing in the floorboards beneath our feet.

"Here," snapped Cal.

He'd returned fully loaded. He passed to his father the largest of the three semiautomatic rifles, then handed me my old favorite, a clean M1A wood-stock competition dandy. My trigger finger instantly tingled in remembrance of the curve and click of that deadly thin lever. I knew the feel of this gun almost as well as the familiar leather-wrapped grip of the steering wheel of my beloved beastie.

Ex-beastie.

Cal dropped to a knee to beside his father. Patted Rex upon the flank.

I checked and prepped my modified magazine.

It was hard to guess how many men there were.

Maybe eight.

The helicopter passed over the roof.

I could feel the pulse of the metallic creature deep within my ears. Could feel it in my lungs. Even at the back of my eyes. It was as if those thumpf-sha's were my own racing heart pumping adrenaline and blood through my skull and limbs.

Then, suddenly, the thrashing pulse accelerated into a buzz.

Dragon-like, the chopper swooped back over Jack's truck, then rose with a shimmering tail of falling crystals.

Finally, it shot back north the way it had come.

Back towards Hot Sulphur Springs.

Back towards the certainly-by-now reopened main highway from Summit County to the rest of the world.

31
WAR ROOM PLANNING

Freak finished his sermon.

Steve immediately threw himself into the task of editing and uploading files over to our TJ connection. Saundra assisted, shuffling back and forth between Steve's elbow at his improvised front desk work station and our little huddle of elbows pressed around the empty kitchen table in back.

"Who knows," said Cal, "how long before they'll be back here to land and force their way in...."

Trembling, Mary shifted a plate of cookies from the counter to our table, then sank among our ranks. "How do we know if they'll even return?" she questioned. "And who were they?"

"The chopper," I said, "was a military Huey. I've been watching them all week up in Summit County. But who's to say who might have been flying around behind the controls."

"To be honest," said Cal, "I didn't see any guns."

"I didn't, either," agreed Jack. "But I suppose with the cold and everything, they were locked shut pretty tight. I saw the pilot and a few moving shadows, maybe a pair of binoculars, but not much else." He patted the rifle against his side. He glanced at Freak. "What do you think, prophet? Does this situation call for a fight... or flight?"

Freak picked up one of Mary's cookies. He smiled faintly at Mrs. K, then returned it to the plate unbitten.

"*Not* fight," he said. "At least not yet. It's a fight we'd lose. Even if we held out through the first round, our resistance would only draw more and bigger guns into the fray. We've already faced rocket launchers at the lodge. If they've got a Huey, then they've got all of that... and more."

I cleared my throat. "Freak," I asked. "What is the Lord telling you we should do?"

All eyes turned my way. Some surprised, others curious.

"Look," I continued. "This dude accurately predicted catastrophic earthquakes... and a little while ago he told the entire planet that the Apocalypse was going to be unleashed on humanity in less than 24 hours. Sure... I'm interested in what Freak has to say right now. Who wouldn't be?"

Freak grinned. "Thanks," he said, "for that amazing vote of confidence."

Jack hoisted Old Abe up onto the table, then pushed the gun across to Freak.

"Fight," asked Jack again, "or flight?"

Freak studied the gun. He put a hand on it. He traced the contours of the barrel and scope with two fingers the way that had come to be his habit with his scars.

"No guns," he sighed at last, reopening his eyes. "The Lord has promised that this round will not be won by Diamond K weapons. At least not the bullets you three like to feed your guns."

"What about the Gideon?" I asked, turning to Jack. "Maybe we could hide out up at the old hunting cabin?"

The Diamond K had a series of cabins and outbuildings, mostly clustered within a short walk of the big house's main dining hall. The accommodations ranged from the tiny honeymoon cabin where Steve and I were staying, to the matched pair of Luke and John plywood bunkhouses which could sleep twenty guests each.

And then there was the Gideon.

The Gideon Refuge was set deep into the back of the ranch. The little camp butted against a rugged cliff and the protected wilderness of the Arapaho National Forest. It was equipped with a small generator, an outhouse and a hand pump, and it was nearly inaccessible even in the best of weather. It was more of a warrior's cave than a city-slicker's weekend retreat.

Jack reached for Old Abe and drew the rifle down into his lap.

He touched the contours that had just been stroked by Freak.

"Perhaps the Gideon could work," he said, shifting his grip from the rifle to his chin. "We might be able to crank up a snowmobile or two and give the Gideon a try. But I'm not sure how far we'd get. There's gotta be three to five feet of snow. We'd probably bog down somewhere along the way, and then we'd have to snowshoe in for the last bit of the trail. Nobody has been up to the Gideon since mid-November."

"Besides," added Cal, "if someone was after us, it'd be a slam-dunk to follow our tracks. And then they'd have us boxed in with our backs against the wall."

"At least," I said, "we'd see them coming. They could only come in by foot, and only from one direction. The trees are thick, and there's not a clearing anywhere close where they could land a helicopter."

"Who would go to the cabin?" asked Jack. "Freak, of course, but who else? I'm not sure I see how this all fits together...."

"Hey," said Steve, suddenly conspicuously filling the kitchen doorway. "You've got to check this out."

We followed Steve to what had become his command center at the registration roll top desk. He pointed at the monitor.

Freak's sermon clips were already going viral.

We watched for a moment, congratulating each other as Steve flicked us from site to site, showing us how quickly the host sources were multiplying and how exponentially the number of hits were soaring.

"Fantastic," said Freak again. "Good job, Steve. All of you!"

"Let's see," Saundra urged, "whether or not Tom Jackson was able to get any of this onto the Channel 5 news."

He had.

Cal was cranking the television's volume and showing highlights from Freak's sermon before we'd even all found our seats. The networks were picking up the feeds as well. Reporter Tom Jackson was talking around the edges of videos, running extended clips, and acting as if he hadn't a clue as to where the footage had come from, let alone how it had ended up on the Internet.

Yet acting as if the clips belonged to him alone.

"It figures," said Saundra. "Our necks... his scoop."

"This is good," nodded Freak. "The world will be without excuse."

We'd seen enough.

We were about to kill the TV to examine our options a second time when the room instantly fell into stunned a hush.

The reporter's parka was casually open, flapping over a plush knitted sweater vest. Her hood was pulled halfway back, enough for gorgeous blond hair to spill forward around and over a thick fur collar ruff.

She directed her question through rosy cheeks to the man who stood beside her at the edge of the mountain road. The treacherous snow-covered rising curve was familiar. The guardrail forever etched in my mind.

She swung her microphone to a person who should have been dead.

Our old pal from the lodge.

"Agent Wilcox," she asked, "I know this is an ongoing investigation, but what exactly is it you and your team are expecting to find?"

Wilcox bobbed his head. He glanced at the mic, then back to her eyes.

"Rachel," he said, "unfortunately, we don't know what to expect. One of our teams discovered the accident site earlier this morning. When the storm lifted, we immediately began doing helicopter sweeps... and I guess we got lucky. So far, we have been able to ascertain that this is in fact the vehicle Mark Hanson used to flee from Breckenridge. But as of yet, we have no reason to believe anyone is alive down there in the wreckage below."

"Certainly," she said, "you wouldn't expect to find the prophet in that wreckage? After all, his latest messages are hitting the air waves even as we speak."

"We don't know," said Wilcox, sounding matter of fact, "when those messages may have been recorded. For all we know, he may have recorded them last week. What we *do* know is his body has not yet been recovered from the lodge site, nor have the bodies of Mark Hanson and their reporter friend, Saundra Paige."

I glanced at Steve. He shook his head and muttered an echo of Saundra's *it figures*.

"Hey, Steve," I called, "maybe they found your goofy hat in the snow and decided to call that good enough."

"Tell that," Steve sighed, "to my momma."

We turned back to the screen.

"If the prophet has survived," asked the reporter, "then what are your plans?"

Wilcox hesitated. He tossed a look over his shoulder, past the guardrail to the plunging granite slide where even now a harnessed military rescue team was busily rigging their gear to rappel over the side for a hands-on inspection.

"All I can say," said Wilcox, turning back to the camera, "is that I was assigned to protect Pastor Jacobs. If I have failed, then I take full responsibility. But if he is still out there someplace—somehow still alive—then I can promise you we will find him... and we will bring him back in. We will *not* lose the pastor again."

"Why," asked the reporter, looking genuinely confused, "why is it so important for the prophet be under your protection? Perhaps Reverend Jacobs is safer off the radar and hiding out on his own than he would be if so many people knew exactly where he was."

Wilcox shot her an icy glare.

"Terrorists," he said, "are everywhere. They have struck once at the pastor, and if he is alive, they *will* strike again. Without our protection, it is only a matter of time before they find him. And the next time the terrorists lock him in their sights, this Freak fellow may not be so lucky as he has been thus far."

"Terrorists?" she asked. "Tell us more about these terrorists. Who are these terrorists, and what is their motivation for trying to silence the prophet?"

"Excuse me," Wilcox shrugged, indignantly distancing himself from her side. "I must attend to my team. I will let you know what we find."

REALITY CHECK

The silence lingered long after Cal had engaged the mute.

Finally, I stated the obvious.

"Two things," I declared. "First, we *were* being tracked. With all of the wind and all of the snow we've had for the past couple days, they never would have found my rig in that hidden ravine if there hadn't been some kind of electronic device planted on my beastie."

Jack agreed.

"Second," I said, "Wilcox is a worm. He had to be an insider with the attack. There's no way he could have fled the lodge fast enough to survive unless he already knew the missiles were on the way."

Saundra tugged her collar, lips white. "Wilcox met us at the elevator in the lobby," she said. "And then he disappeared. He just left us there to die...."

"No," I said. "He didn't simply leave us there. He walked us into their trap... he tried to kill us himself."

Steve rose. "I've got an idea," he said.

He glanced briefly at Saundra, then headed for the computer and the modem at the front desk. "Maybe," he muttered, not looking back, "I can come up with something to help remedy this situation."

The rest of us turned to Freak.

"You," said Jack, "heard the agent. It's only a matter of time. What do you want us to do?"

Freak lowered his head into his hands. "I'm not sure," he softly replied. "The Lord has still not yet spoken in regards to our next move."

"Fine," I said. "You wait for the Lord. Meanwhile, the rest of us need to be working on some kind of plan. The last thing any of us wants is for the Diamond K Ranch to be flattened to rubble in a lodge attack do-over. That snake Wilcox was right about at least one thing."

"What's that?" asked Cal.

"Next time," I sighed, "we might not get away."

Jack, Cal and I revisited the few options we'd covered before, and then we added a few more response schemes that weren't any better. Freak remained planted, head bowed, apparently oblivious to our rising frustrations.

Finally, Freak stood.

"The Devil," he said, eying us one by one, "has had his way with Agent Wilcox. Attachments. High priority assignments. I have seen Dark Riders. Maybe three. One of them appeared to be of a powerful order. I caught glimpses at the lodge, and now I'm certain."

"Three," I sighed. "Same as me?"

He studied my eyes. "Mark," he said. "We all get harassed by Dark Riders. Me. Mother Teresa. Jack. Even Jesus. It's not about whether or not they come around, or even if one or more has been assigned to you. It's about how you handle them when they go for your throat. When they go for your heart and mind. For your soul."

I hadn't looked at it that way before. Jesus had moved among the Dark Riders. And for a time, Satan himself had camped out with Jesus in the wilderness.

"This may appear," continued Freak, "to be a battle of flesh. A war we must fight with weapons of steel. But the Spirit has reminded me that we are contending against demonic enemies and powers. Against spiritual rulers and the veiled cosmic forces of the unseen world."

"Are you suggesting," I asked, "for us to merely roll over and pray?"

"No. Not *only* to pray. But it starts with that." He directed his voice towards Steve at the desk. "Steve," he called, "how soon before we might be able to record another podcast?"

Steve rose and approached us where we sat.

"Funny you should ask," he grinned. "I think we might be able to do one better. After the remark from Wilcox about your podcast being an old recording, I got it into my head to start working on something a bit different for our next broadcast."

Steve lifted his hand and shook a long coil of thin camera cable.

"Do you see this?" he asked, nodding at the cable. He then pointed towards the video recorder still in the other room. "And do you see that?" he smiled. "Well, how about if we link this and that..." he swung his arm, "to this other thing?"

He pointed to the work station computer where he'd spent the last five minutes establishing a live video conference hangout with Tom Jackson.

But not only with Tom Jackson, but also live with a network of media geeks scattered in a dozen cities far beyond the reach of Agent Wilcox and his men.

At least for now.

"Here we go again," I sighed, meeting Freak's eyes. "Better not hold anything back. Unleash whatever you've got. Make it one for the books."

Freak gave me one of his odd stares. "Why'?" he asked.

"Because... this might be the last sermon you ever get to preach."

Freak really was the right man for the job.

Within minutes, he was up to full throttle. Animated. Articulate. Full of stunning metaphors, stirring imagery.

He spoke again of humanity's sin, more of our need for a savior, more about the judgments soon to come. About rising evils and our need to help each other with acts of mercy in the midst of impending travails. And he waxed adamantly about the imminent return of Jesus the King.

And then he switched gears.

"Many of you," he said, "must now brace yourselves for what I can only call: *The Great Disappointment.*

"As church historians recall, this term has been used before. Over a hundred years ago, a group of convincing teachers created schemes and set dates for the return of Christ. And they broke the hearts of countless thousands.

"Unfortunately, we need to resurrect this term once again, because no other phrase will adequately capture the emotions many people will experience in the coming months. Millions of Christians throughout the world are about to be... *greatly...* disappointed."

Freak took a deep breath, then released a slow, sorrowful sigh.

"I confess with grief how I've been among those who've misled thousands. It was not intentional, but prior to this past week, I have misrepresented the dark days to come.

"Many popular writers and sincere pastors... many of *us...* we have taught an absurd doctrine in recent years. We've promised Christians to be completely spared the trials and horrors to come. We've generated charts and timelines, and we've offered false hopes for a supernatural pre-Tribulation event... an occurrence to provide followers of Christ a peaceful escape... an escape not actually described in scripture the way we have taught it.

"I speak, of course, of a dogmatic fantasy most commonly called... *The Rapture.*

"For my part in this misreading of scripture... I beg your forgiveness. It was not intentional. But like so many others, I was caught up in a misguided, popular fringe movement within the history of biblical interpretation...."

Freak shuddered.

"Sadly, I must warn you... do not be waiting for any sudden pre-Tribulation raptures. We must let go of the sensational *Left Behind* scenarios many of us in the Christian bubble have come to expect. There will be no abruptly empty cockpits. No mysteriously vacated cars. No magically swept church sidewalks with inexplicable piles of abandoned clothing and footless leather shoes.

"Until recently, virtually all Christians accepted the Bible's clear teaching: Christ will return one last time, with angels and power for all the world to see at the end of this age. Christians have also accepted God's promises of special honors for those who serve in times of trials and tribulations... those who suffer and die for the Lord.

"In the 19th century, a man named John Nelson Darby invented a new doctrine. He speculated how Christ might return twice more, not once as the Bible describes. Darby did not learn this teaching from respected teachers. As far as he knew, these were his own 'discoveries.' First, he claimed Christ would come back invisibly, to remove Christians from the planet in a way not described in the Bible. Then, Christ would return a second time, years later, exactly the way the Bible actually describes."

Freak touched his forehead, then leaned towards the live feed of the camera.

"The Lord has assured me.... Monday, we'll indeed see the beginning of the end. But there will be no evaporation of folks being teleported to heaven prior to tribulations. The rapture promised in the Bible will not happen until the very last day of this age, on *The Day of the Lord*, when Jesus will return with his angelic host with unmistakable glory... with his full power unleashed for all to see.

"Yes, the Lord loves his children. But not just some of his children... *all* of his children. Not only the saved, but the wretched and the lost as well."

He leaned back.

"Those of you who already know and obey the Lord have been chosen... chosen to *serve* him. *Not* to opt out of the work to be done in these our planet's final days. If you believe, then you have been chosen to hear and to obey in this hour of humanity's greatest need. I will speak more of this in the days to come. But for now, it is imperative for you to hear these words from the Lord....

"Do not grow faint... lift your heads... for the Holy Spirit is with you... even as our Lord Jesus draws nigh."

Mary stood fidgeting by the television. Hers was the task of monitoring the feed as it entered Steve's camera, as it launched into space and bounced from satellites back down to the millions of computers and televisions tuned in live from the four corners of the Earth.

She stood swaying, tossed between her focus on the movement of his lips on her muted television, and on his live and unsettling voice and presence across the room.

"Finally," said Freak, his voice and demeanor shifting yet again, "I must now speak of myself."

He lifted his hands in surrender.

"My motives—and even the authenticity of my messages—have been questioned. Fair enough. It is right to test my words. You *should* test my words. You should pray. Please... examine the scriptures. Discern together with those you trust in the days to come. But hear this: Satan wants me silenced. Or dead. The opposition is real."

He took another deep breath.

"But not just Satan. There are leaders in positions of power around the world, even here in America... people within our own democratic government... who want me silenced... or dead."

I glanced, stunned, at the others in the room.

They appeared as shocked as me; Freak had crossed the point of no return.

"Today, a short time ago, a certain government agent made a live report from a crash site near the Colorado mountain ranch where I now sit. This Agent Wilcox declared, in no uncertain terms, that he would find me. And I have no doubt he soon will. The abandoned vehicle he was searching was the very one I used while fleeing two days ago from the attack at the lodge. An attack this agent anticipated—or choreographed—in such a manner so he himself could survive... even as scores of others were consumed in the flames.

"The fact this agent so quickly found our SUV within a deep hidden ravine confirms our vehicle had been bugged... fitted with an electronic tracking device so we would remain on his radar at all times.

"I share this with you—not out of fear or self pity—but for the sake of the Lord's call upon my—*our*—final days.

"In the days of suffering and persecution to come, many of you will experience an increase in demonic oppression, as well as versions of what I've suffered in this past week. But take heart. The Lord will be with you... even as he has been with me every step of the way.

"I have been defamed. I have been attacked and pursued. I've been separated from my family. And I may yet be killed.

"But until my final breath, I will not forsake the mission of our returning King. I will not yield to Satan, nor will I forsake my service on the Lord's behalf.

"God's proclamation and his demonstrations of Grace and Truth... for a desperate, dying, broken world... *this* is my duty. My *privilege*. And this will carry me to the end."

He paused.

"I shall pray the same for you... as well."

33

EASTER ENCOUNTERS

Steve tested a look my way, then towards Saundra. He appeared uncertain whether to keep recording, or if he should sign off the broadcast on that climatic note.

If Freak caught the confusion, there was no indication as to his preference.

Freak dropped his head and began to loudly pray. Live. In front of the fireplace. Perpendicular to Mary and the image of himself streaming on the television's muted split-second delay.

We exchanged more glances and shrugs, then came to the unspoken consensus his prayers were probably an important part of the message, and maybe the prophet would eventually clue us in when he was finished by giving us some sort of *amen.*

Finally, Saundra stepped to Steve and began to whisper.

Then Rex jumped up, barked once, and I heard it again.

The distant whirlybird thumpf-sha of the returning Huey.

Jack and Cal reacted to the sound at the same time.

"*Freak,*" I hissed. "Heads up."

He opened his eyes.

I raised my hand and made a circling motion with my finger. "They're coming back," I said, softly mouthing the words from off screen. "What do you want us to do?"

Freak lowered his gaze from my finger to the cameraman's eyes.

"Steve," he instructed, his voice decisive. "Keep rolling." He turned back to his waiting audience beyond the lens. "They are coming for me now, even as you watch. In real time, you shall witness the confrontation of the Spirit... with the world, the flesh, and the Devil. Please pray. Pray the Lord's word to not be silenced in this hour of fierce testing."

Freak remained seated, but he shifted his attention towards Cal.

"The gun cabinet," asked Freak, "is it still open?"

Jack stood, his rifle already in hand. "If you're looking for Old Abe," he interjected, I'm already on it." He pulled the gun against his chest.

Instinctively, I located my own semiautomatic weapon leaning against the wall across the room.

"More guns and ammunition?" Cal asked.

"No," said Freak. "We do not need bullets. Nor guns."

"Then what?"

In what became loosely known as the most sensational moment in live television history, Freak stretched forth his hands.

"Bring me Saint Michael," he said. "Bring me the shofar."

Later, Saundra swore that for a brief instant, she saw the shimmering silhouettes of three enormous angels.

Freak's two celestial guardians stood flanking, fully armored, swords drawn, a bridled wildness radiating in their translucent bluish-white fire that took her breath.

But what nearly stopped her heart was the third angel, a much larger figure whom she'd never seen before. He was in the middle, behind and over the prophet, garbed in jewels and polished steel.

Standing. Waiting.

Holding his own magnificently glowing shofar.

Cal returned in seconds. He handed Freak the Diamond K horn, then quickly retreated from the camera's frame even as the thumping of the approaching chopper began to overtake the room.

Freak studied the instrument.

He hesitated, consuming precious moments he could hardly afford to waste.

He turned it end-for-end, testing the feel of it, breathing it in.

Slowly, he lifted the finely tapered hollow tip to meet his pursed, tremoring lips.

Whereas Jack had made a mess of it at dawn, Freak opened with a soulfully long, wonderfully resonating single note.

He built the sound, starting soft and low, then crescendoing into a surge of energy sufficient to raise goose bumps on my arm... and on perfect pitch.

I glanced to the TV area. Mary wavered at her post, quavering with the remote, her gaze moving back and forth between Freak with the primitive trumpet and the television screen with its satellite-bounced delay. Rex had moved to her side, but the dog's eyes were locked on the shofar. Or what was above the shofar.

Freak took another deep breath.

Then blew again.

This time, the sounding of staccatos and trills that Freak unleashed filled the room with such power and force that those of us standing fell to our knees.

Perhaps in her faint, Mary had inadvertently disengaged the mute. She may have momentarily bumped the volume control to its maximum setting. Maybe the effect was compounded by the thumping of that descending military Huey.

However it was, the shofar's blast quickly gathered an almost unearthly reverb, a harmonizing echo that elevated each note to the richness and force of a vast celestial warring chorus.

With trepidation and awe, I tried to regain my feet, then lost track of time and was swept from my wits.

I clenched my eyes in shudders... and wept.

I wanted it to end. Wished it never would.

When Freak finally lowered the horn, I shook my head.

I glanced to the grandfather clock with no idea how long we may have endured that incomprehensible declaration of intent. For some inexplicable reason, I half expected the pendulum to have stopped.

It had.

Each hand of the time keeper stretched perfectly upward or outward: the long arm pointing towards the heavens and sky, the shorter hand extending straight east, towards Freak. Towards the shofar and the rest of the world.

The time read exactly 3:00 PM.

It was only later that we did the math. 3:00 PM Colorado Mountain Time was Midnight in Jerusalem.

Monday morning in the Middle East.

The very hour Saudi Arabia began its preemptive invasion of Iran.

The hour when Iran countered with a small nuclear detonation.

The day when Turkey stepped into the fray, when Russia and NATO quickly followed, and when global events rapidly spiraled into WWIII.

Saundra stared, trembling. "Freak," she whispered, "How did you learn to play like that? Did you see...."

"Later," he replied, closing his eyes. When he reopened them, he gently passed the horn to Cal. "It has begun."

Outside, the helicopter blades slowed and dropped in pitch as the craft settled into the deep snowy plain of the parking pad below the main log house.

Jack stepped forward across the carpet. "Steve," he called, pointing towards the registration desk near the front door, "reposition your camera and equipment there.

And hide it from view." He turned to Freak. "You'd best lock yourself in the bathroom. Until we can get a fix on where this is headed, you need to stay out of sight."

Freak hesitated, then complied.

34
BACK FROM THE RUBBLE

"Mark," said Jack, "let me do the talking. Saundra, it's best if you stay out of sight in the kitchen with Mary. If this goes badly, it may fall to you alone to one day report how this went down."

Cal tossed Saundra his phone. "You might need this," he said. "No sense wasting the minutes from this month's bill. Lord only knows if I'll live through the next hour to ever use them myself."

We all scrambled.

Mary straight to the kitchen, Steve and Cal attending to the camera setup, and Saundra busily moving something around on the bookshelf before darting past my shoulder to join Mary among the pots and pans.

Rex growled.

A heavy pounding abruptly fell against the door.

Jack approached, then waited at the knob until the hinges and frame began to shake.

"Take it easy!" Jack loudly complained into the wood. He turned the latch and swung the door. "Show some respect."

Wilcox leaned, one fist poised, ready to pound again.

Behind Wilcox, their knees bent and military rifles at ready, fanned at least four men in camo fatigues.

"How can I help you?" asked Jack. His voice carried the patronizing edge I'd once heard him serve across this same threshold to a dinnertime salesman in an obnoxious suit.

Rex coiled low on the floor, concern rumbling deep within his throat.

"You can start," Wilcox commanded, "by calling off that mutt of yours. And then you can cooperate by dropping your gun."

Jack glanced to his right hand. He seemed genuinely surprised to discover Old Abe within his grip. He looked down at Rex and thought for a moment. "You first," he finally grinned, raising the rifle stock to meet his other hand. "This old boy comes with the house. So does the dog. You don't."

Wilcox nodded over his shoulder.

A cadre of government weapons instantly snapped up to their masters' cheeks. One of the barrels pointed down at Rex.

The agent smirked. "Naw," said Wilcox. "*You* first. These enforcers come with the authority of the United States government. The sovereignty of this house has just been trumped by Uncle Sam."

Jack frowned, more perturbed than concerned. "Show me," he said, "Uncle Sam's authority. Any thug can pull a gun. I wanna see badges and papers. Show me your search warrant."

It was Wilcox's turn to pause.

"You know," said Wilcox, lifting his chest, "parts of the West Coast are already under martial law. I wouldn't need a warrant in California right now, and I wouldn't need to explain a thing. Who knows, maybe Colorado will be next. Maybe even the whole country."

"But we're not there *yet*," Jack retorted. "I'm going to say it again. Show me your papers... or get the hell off my property. Now!"

Wilcox tilted his head just enough to see Cal with his rifle leveled across the top of the registration roll top desk. Steve was also leaning onto the desk, slightly to the side.

Then Wilcox spotted me standing in the kitchen doorway. Saundra and Mary were around the wall and out of view. Surprisingly calm.

Then again, the ladies had not yet seen the crouching warriors in the frost beyond the doorway, weapons drawn, battle gear clouded in foggy breaths of puffing steam.

I glanced at Steve.

Steve caught my eyes, then sent a darting glance to the bookshelf to my right.

"Hey, Mark," called Wilcox, "why don't you tell your rancher friend here to cool his jets. This visit doesn't have to end like another Gunfight at the O.K. Corral."

For the first time, it dawned on Wilcox that I, too, held a rifle. My barrel was down against my leg, but it was slowly rising in his direction even as he watched.

"Sure," I said, patting my now-leveled and loaded M1A. "I'd love to chat. But Mr. K has specifically requested for me to let him do all the talking. It's his ranch. His rules. So I guess you'll just have to convince him yourself to put down his gun."

Wilcox studied me. He did a quick visual sweep of the rest of what he could see.

"Where's that girlfriend of yours?" he finally sneered. "She was a pretty little thing. I miss seeing her around the lodge." He leaned to the right, half-pretending to peek around me into the kitchen. "Or have you moved on to another new girlfriend already so soon?"

It was all I could do to restrain my finger as it twitched against the trigger's edge.

"You snake," I spat. "Were you jealous, or what? You could have easily saved her."

"Saved who?" His teeth flashed artificially white. "I thought you kept telling me that you didn't need my help...."

"*Enough!*" demanded Jack.

He stepped his massive hulk nearly onto the agent's toes.

"We're American citizens," declared Jack. He tipped his head to look down into Wilcox's eyes. "We've broken no laws. You have no search warrant. And you're letting in a whole lot of cold mountain air. Now shut my door... and *git.*"

"Not," retorted Wilcox, "until we have what we came for. You others can hide out on this ranch for as long as you want, but we're not leaving without him." He raised his voice. "Now, where is... *the Freak*?"

"The Freak?" I asked. "Do you mean the Lord's prophet? The man who dropped from the sky with angels and messages from God... predictions from heaven for our shaken and broken world?"

"I mean," scowled Wilcox, "W.B. Jacobs. The blow-hard fraud who sows chaos and fear whenever he opens his damn mouth. We're taking him out of here... dead or alive. That man's big fat ego trip—and this little dog and pony show of *yours*—are now both officially coming to an end."

"Fine," I said. "I'll bring him out. But first, I've got a couple questions...."

"Shush," said Jack, wheeling on me with a cutting frown. "Mark, I thought I told you to let *me* do the talking."

"Hang on," laughed Wilcox, stepping past Jack and into the room. "I'll answer Mark's questions. And thanks for confirming he's here in the house. It's good to know we won't have to search the bunkhouses and barns to find him. What an idiot." He shook his head. "Go ahead. What do you want to know? *Shoot.*"

Wilcox chortled a snort, suddenly amused by his inadvertent choice of words. He pointed at our guns. "*Shoot...*" he said again, "if you've got the balls." He pretended to duck, then glanced for approval at the heavily armed men behind him outside the door.

"Go ahead," resumed Wilcox, clearly disappointed by the lack of response from his men. "What is it, Mark? Was there something you wanted to know?"

"We can do this," I said. "We can talk. And I can bring you Freak... if you promise again to leave the rest of us alone."

Wilcox nodded consent. "Wise decision."

"But," I said, "we can not talk with the door open... and with a pack of loaded M16's staring us in the face. Unless you're afraid to meet me one-on-one... how about if you tell your choir boys to stand down and step back. You can close the door, and we'll sort this out... off the record. And then, in a few minutes, I'll give you Freak without a shot, and without another word."

Wilcox weighed the proposal. He studied the ease with which we three Coloradans held our guns. Studied Rex.

"Sure," he smugly smiled, "you won me over when you promised to finally shut up. You call off the dog, and I'll call off my men."

I nodded.

"Remember now, they'll be right outside this door." He made a circling gesture around the premises. "And just so you know, the rest of my men are already in positions on every side."

Wilcox gestured to his troops. They stepped back, and he closed the door.

"Rex!" I pointed. "Kennel!" He reluctantly agreed.

As the dog disappeared from the room, I turned back to the preening Wilcox. "How'd you find us?" I asked.

"Not just you," scoffed the agent. "Don't you get the news out here in the woods? We found that stupid red car of yours as well."

"Rig," I frowned. "How'd you ever find my beastie... I thought I'd tucked her under a ton of snow. And hundreds of feet below anyone's possible view."

"Idiots. We had you bugged... and we started tracking you last weekend before you even left the hospital."

"And the ranch?"

"What kind of fools do you think you're dealing with?" he asked. "Those cute little podcasts of yours were full of clues, starting with that licensed ranch mutt of yours shoving his nose into the Freak's lap. In addition to the county pet registration records, there were all of those interior shots on the Diamond K website. How long did you think it'd take for us to catch up with you?"

"Just long enough," I grinned. "How about you, Wilcox... do you get the news?"

"What are you talking about?"

I turned towards the registration desk. "Steve," I called. "I think it's about time for you to raise your hands for Agent Wilcox."

Wilcox grinned.

Steve raised an elbow, then stepped back from the desk.

"Smile," said Steve, "you're on Candid Camera."

Steve pointed to the digital recorder he had tucked beneath his shirt folds on the top ledge of roll top.

Wilcox laughed.

"Idiots," he taunted.

Jack looked confused.

"I got the word," said Wilcox, "before we even landed. My men had traced the path of your live feed. As I left the Huey, I got a thumbs up that they were disabling your server line. I'm sure your podcast was off the air before I even reached your door. Nothing I've said ever made it to the news."

Steve's face fell.

Cal straightened.

"Hold on," I said. "Did you confess all of that stuff about shutting up Freak just to jerk us around? Because you *knew*—that we *thought*—that we were broadcasting on television live this whole time?"

"What a bunch of chumps. You should have seen your faces when you believed you had tricked me into admitting on camera how we wanted Freak dead. Idiots."

"As they say," I grinned, " I do not think you know the meaning of that word."

"*Idiots*?"

"Perhaps." I lowered my rifle and leaned it against the wall. "Freak," I called, "it's time for you to show your face."

A rustling and turning of the bathroom doorknob was followed by Freak's reemergence. He made his way to the front room. I nodded into the kitchen, and then Saundra and Mrs. K joined our circle as well.

"Freak," I asked, "how much of that did you hear?"

"Most of it," he sighed.

"And what do you make of all these threats?"

Freak shook his head. "The Lord has assured me that my days of preaching...."

"Are over," sneered Wilcox.

"But," said Freak, "the Lord has entrusted me with much more I must share...."

"It's about time for your last *amen*, pastor. No more hocus-pocus god-talk nonsense from your soapbox. Count yourself lucky you got away with it for a week."

"Perhaps you're right," continued Freak, "but I was also given a vision where I was roasting marshmallows around a Diamond K campfire this Spring with Ellen and my three children."

"Not marshmallows," said Wilcox, "trust me. If anything, it'll be a grenade that you'll be eating. I will personally shove one down your throat, if that's what it takes to finally shut you up."

Freak frowned. "Such hatred. It is unnatural. Agent Wilcox, surely you must see that? Don't let the Dark Riders...."

"Dark Riders?" retorted Wilcox. "You know nothing."

"The Devil," insisted Freak. "He's got his hooks on you."

"Have you looked in a mirror lately, you hypocrite? I'll tell you what's unnatural. It's you and your face... and your presumptuous arrogance. The world will be better off without you. Then maybe the rest of us can get back to business."

"You must resist this evil," whispered Freak, "or it will destroy you."

"No," said Wilcox. "It will destroy *you*."

I stepped forward. "Wilcox," I said. "Those are strong words. You seem pretty sure of yourself."

"Let's put it this way. I am."

"Wow," I said, "it makes me kinda sad you're so eager to kill my friend."

"Your friend?" Wilcox laughed. "So I guess he's made a believer out of you, too, huh?"

I thought for a moment.

"Who knows?" I shrugged. "Some of what the prophet says makes sense. But as far as I can tell, besides me, there must be millions of other American citizens who believe in the freedom of the press... and who are at least a little curious about what Freak thinks might happen next."

"What happens next," said Wilcox, "is that Freak says goodbye. And then within a few days, the world will have forgotten all about this man."

"You underestimate," I said, pointing at Freak, "the staying power of that face."

"I guess we'll see."

"And," I continued, "if those voters who have shown an interest in Freak learn it was their own leaders who put a bullet in the prophet's head, then maybe those citizens would lose confidence in the folks who are in charge."

"Mark," sighed Wilcox, "I think it's about time we got to the part where you hand Freak over to me... *without another word.* Because, truth is, nobody gives a rat's arse about anything you're saying."

Saundra stepped forward. "Wilcox," she sputtered, fists clenching, "some people *care* about the truth... and freedom of speech!"

"Please," he grinned, "not another Channel 5 lecture about the press and the sacred public trust. The people will believe the American government, and they will do as they are told. We haven't had a revolution in a long time, and we're not about to have one now. Not so long as the masses know we're in a world crisis. Not so long as they need our help."

"A crisis..." accused Saundra, "that *you* are contributing to!"

"Unfair," shrugged Wilcox. "All we're doing is shutting up another cult-type religious fruitcake. I'm just a public safety manager.. a patriot who has been empowered to control the panic and to hold this nation together as best we can."

"God's truth," said Freak, "shall not be silenced. Not even in the name of peace. It is a grievous thing to muzzle the word of the Lord."

"Whatever you say," sighed Wilcox. He straightened. "I think it's time to go."

He turned and reached for the door to summon his men.

"Hold on," I said, raising my fist. "Not so fast." I flipped my head at Jack.

Jack brushed himself forward to between Wilcox and the door, then clamped his boot to the floor to block the threshold.

Wilcox grinned. "Come, now...."

Suddenly, a sidearm materialized in Wilcox's right hand.

"I thought," said Wilcox, glaring at me as he shoved the Beretta into Jack's side, "we had an agreement."

I held up two empty hands. "I no longer make deals with the Devil," I said.

"Then," said Wilcox, "I must *not* be the Devil, because you made a deal with me... and I plan to hold you to it."

He gruffly budged and rotated the frustrated Jack into a position between him and the barrel of Cal's aimed rifle.

"Preacher," he demanded again, looking at Freak. "It's time to go. If you value the lives of these people, then let's giddy up... before it's going to take a mop to rub your friends off this pretty wood floor."

Freak reluctantly lifted his hands and stepped forward.

"Stop!" I demanded, calling Freak short. I turned to Wilcox. "I'm going to do this real slow," I said. "No derringer. I promise."

I slowly reached towards the bulge in my chest pocket.

"*Careful,*" said Wilcox.

"You, too," I smiled.

With exceedingly deliberate intention, I lowered a thumb and two fingers into my chest pocket. When my hand resurfaced, it was loaded with a black plastic television remote.

"No tricks here," I said. I winked at Steve. "Well, maybe one trick. Call it Saundra's little cell phone video chat conference call... her little cell tower Plan B."

I carefully turned, then pointed the television remote at the big flatscreen at the far end of the other room.

And pressed the *on* button.

We all watched as Wilcox flared into view on the screen.

I raised the sound to full volume.

Wilcox gawked in disbelief at the image of himself holding a gun to the innocent rancher's ribs.

"What the...?" gasped Wilcox.

A split second later, Wilcox heard his shocked complaint from the other room:

"What the...?"

PUNKED

"Until death do us part," I promised, my voice strong as I briskly stepped towards the confused agent who still pressed his gun into Jack's ribs—both at the closed exit, and upon the television screen in the other room. "From now until eternity...."

"What are you saying?" twitched Wilcox. "What's going on here?"

I stopped and turned. Then I casually centered myself within the frame of Agent Wilcox, Jack, and the gawking prophet.

I smiled at the discretely concealed camera phone on a facing shelf. It was propped among several disheveled books, exactly where Saundra had positioned it. Where she had linked it to her network of Internet allies and had begun streaming our front room activities moments before Wilcox had stepped through the door.

I lifted my right hand, as if for an oath.

"Henceforth," I vowed, "if any harm should come to the Reverend W.B. Jacobs, let it be known by one and all that any such harm is on account of the action—or the willful inaction—of Agent Wilcox... our military, and the United States Government."

Wilcox started to stammer.

He wheeled to tug the door for his escape. He found it suddenly sealed again by Jack's immovable size 14 boot.

"For the record," I continued, projecting my voice and gaze directly towards the cell phone's lens and mic, "it is entirely possible that this Wilcox man," I pointed, "is a rogue agent—acting *not* on the authority of the United States government—but of his own volition... in violation of the intent of his superiors when he was given the assignment of protecting Reverend Jacobs, God's prophet to America in these, our most dangerous of days."

I lowered my finger.

"Time will tell," I said. "Obviously, this treacherous rogue agent must be removed from this assignment immediately, because, by his own confession, he wants to see the prophet dead."

Wilcox twisted the gun deeper into Jack's ribs, but found the rancher unfazed.

"On the other hand," I said, again facing the lens and a countless throng of viewers, "*if* Freak is allowed to safely remain on this ranch, and *if* Freak is allowed in the coming days to freely communicate with the public, *then* the American people will know Freak is indeed under the effective and safe protection of our trustworthy military and our freedom-loving democratic government."

Saundra smiled.

"Further," I concluded, "under such conditions, it would then be reasonable to assume that all unlawful, lethal, and threatening activities of the past week were the work of Wilcox alone, and all such unlawful activities were conducted *without* the consent of our government, and without the approval of any of the agent's superiors."

Wilcox looked dazed. "You can't...."

"I just did," I smiled.

"But...."

There was another pounding on the door.

"Wilcox!" a voice shouted from the other side. "It's over. Put down your weapon. Now!"

Wilcox hesitated.

Jack deftly yanked the gun from the agent's hand, then opened the door.

The special ops team leader quickly stepped through, his own pistol drawn, but trained on Wilcox, not Jack. He wore a headset and mic beneath a camo helmet and frozen frown.

"They got it all," he said, his voice steel. "Wilcox... command says you are to desist with all intimidations and unlawful activities. You've been relieved."

The officer turned to Freak. "On the behalf of the United States Government, we apologize for any stress or inconvenience this rogue agent may have caused. My name is Sergeant Andrews, and I've been temporarily placed in charge. Let me assure you, I've been given strict orders. You will be safe and unharassed while under my team's protection. Until my superiors can sort this out and assign an appropriate new agent who is better able to serve and protect you, any and all of your concerns may be brought directly to me."

Two more soldiers stepped to the door.

"Agent Wilcox," the officer continued, "it is now time for you to leave."

"You can't...." Wilcox protested.

"I just did," the officer corrected. "And you no longer are giving the orders."

"Excuse me," I asked, stepping forward, "may I have a brief word with this scum bag before you haul him away?"

The officer eyed me, then glanced around the room. His focus darted several places, then located Cal's phone on the shelf. He touched a finger to his ear jack, listened, then turned back to me.

"Yes," he said. "Given what you've all been through this past week, you may speak your mind before he is removed from the premises. But keep it brief."

"Thank you." I turned to the reddening agent. "You know, Wilcox... Freak says you've been plagued by demons. He says you've got at least three Dark Riders haunting you, sometimes playing you like a puppet... just like me. What do you make of that kind of talk? Do you want to be set free by Jesus, or not?"

The agent studied me, then cleared his throat.

I jumped aside... barely in time to dodge a flying glob of spit.

"I think," he snarled, wiping his mouth with the back of his hand, "Freak doesn't know the half of what's really going on right now."

"Not cool," I said, pointing at the splotch of spittle on the floor. "Bad choice. Once again, someone else is now going to have to clean up your mess."

"Screw you."

I shook my head. "Freak says we all need to get our acts together... while there is still time. It looks to me like you've got a lot of work to do before the return of Jesus Christ."

Something flashed through the agent's eyes I'd never seen before. I felt hair rising on my arm. "To hell with you, Mark," he huskily whispered. "To hell with all of you."

Hmm.

"Me, maybe," I said, rolling my head and cracking my neck. I waved my hand at those who stood behind me. "But not them." I stepped to his face. "These people are all good with Jesus. And if they keep praying for me, maybe one of these days I'll be good with Jesus again myself."

"Get out while you can," hissed Wilcox. "The enemy is taking you down."

"Down?" I stroked my chin. "Well, on the up side... hanging out with Freak has had an interesting influence on me, at least in one regard."

"How?"

"Have you noticed the way Freak keeps pointing at his face and touching his scars whenever he talks about God. About God's *Grace*... and God's *Truth*?"

Wilcox shrugged. "Sure. What's your point?"

"Do you see my rifle over there? The fact that it's leaning against the wall—and not pressed between your eyes—that's Grace."

"And what's Truth?" smirked Wilcox."

I extended my empty hand, palm up.

"See this?" I asked, stretching and curling my fingers.

"Sure," he muttered, "big deal. Are you having a seizure, or what...."

Suddenly, I dropped my arm.

In a blink, I balled my hand into a low fist, then drove it upwards with all the strength and force I could muster.

I felt some teeth break. Maybe a jaw.

"That," I said, as Wilcox slumped to his knees, "is *Truth*."

36
DIGGING IN

A dazed and sputtering Wilcox was briskly dragged and lifted out the door.

Through the window, we watched as a pair of soldiers loaded the agent like a sack of flour, then found ourselves exchanging grins as the helicopter rose in a frosty swirl of dancing white puffs.

The remaining soldiers were barked into strategic positions around the quarters, where they waited, eyes alert, weapons ready.

A different helicopter, this one fully armored and weaponized, soon replaced the departed Wilcox whirly. Even as the freshly stirred flakes settled, a small unit of Army Rangers deftly spilled from both sides of the chopper. They displayed a special ops disciplined precision that confirmed them as upgrades from the first unit under the direction of our recently relieved Homeland Security representative.

All of this was observed while the seven of us debriefed and strategized beside the big room's open drapes.

"Yes," said Freak, shifting his weight. His focus passed through the expansive front window to the soldier planted on the snowy porch only a few feet beyond the glass. "I believe we can trust these men."

Jack followed Freak's gaze. "I agree," he nodded. "At least for now. Besides, what choice do we have?"

Saundra drew their attention back into our circle within the front room. "Well," she offered, "we have at least one other option. We could turn on the live video feed again. And then, in front of the whole world, we could demand to be flown off from this ranch and down to Denver."

"What's the matter?" I asked. "Have you so quickly tired of our family retreat?"

She hesitated.

"No," she apologized, "it's not that." She gave Jack and Mrs. K a tender nod. "You have both been wonderful."

Mrs. K smiled back. "It has been our honor...."

Saundra turned towards Freak. "No, I'm not tired of anyone. Besides, this is *my* story, and it's the story of the century... maybe of the millennium. After all I've been through, I'll be darned if I'll let go of it now. I have no intention of letting any of you out of my sights." Saundra gently bumped Rex away from her knee. "But there's no reason why we have to stay here on the ranch. With only one road in and out, until we leave this place, other people will hold all of the cards." She frowned through the window. "And all of the guns."

Jack smiled. "Not *all* the guns." He nodded at the wall. Old Abe leaned, resting easily within his reach. Jack stroked his thick white beard. "Saundra, are you really sure Denver is where you want to be?"

"It suddenly feels like we're being jailed here," she shrugged. "Like back at the lodge. Seeing the helicopter parked out there, and all of those armed soldiers standing around like prison guards with their rifles everywhere.... It's creeping me out."

I stepped forward.

"No offense," I said, as gently as I could, "but I've got to agree with Freak and Jack." I reached down, taking my turn to scratch the dog. "But Saundra, I agree with you that from here on out, we absolutely must *insist* upon our freedom. We need to be able to come and go from the Diamond K whenever and however we please. And we need to set our own terms about open communications with the media and the outside world. Still, if the government is willing to secure these premises, then we're probably one heck of a lot safer here than we'd be almost anyplace else."

Steve cleared his throat. "Safer?" he asked. "With Wilcox finally out of the picture, we should be okay now, right?"

Freak shook his head. "Wilcox was certainly in on some of this, but there's more going on here than he could have pulled off alone. What happened at the lodge was much bigger than Wilcox. As I've said all along, there are people in high places who fear and who hate the potential repercussions of my message... and behind those people are spiritual rulers and powers who are desperate to silence God's word." Freak closed his eyes for a moment, then opened them looking straight at me.

"And then," said Freak, "there is the whole business of the curses at the tree they skinned… those blood sacrifices and cult rituals. The threats made against me by the Sons of Thor…."

"Exactly!" insisted Saundra. "Which is why I think we need to somehow get out of the mountains and below everybody's radar. If we can get back to Denver, then we can find some new place to hide where nobody will…."

"No." Freak was emphatic. "The government is going to be even more vigilant about monitoring me after the embarrassment of this Wilcox debacle." He waved his hand at the window. "Look at this new team they just brought in. There will be no such thing as *below the radar*. Every move I make will be tracked. Every word I speak will be recorded. Every prediction…." He turned to me. "Mark, you understand what I'm saying, right?"

I wet my lips. "Saundra," I sighed, "you know Freak is going to have a lot more to say. I'm sick of trying to hide. And I'm tired of having to bounce signals around from laptop to laptop. We're 'out' in front of the public now. We need to embrace our new position and keep it that way. We need to trust the new team of soldiers to protect us. If they wanted to shut us down, with the kind of artillery they just flew in, they could have finished what Wilcox started without even bothering to land."

She squinted, furiously weighing my words.

"But," I said, "tomorrow—after tonight's snow moves out—maybe we can get the soldiers to take up less conspicuous positions further from the porch. Maybe in the trees, away from the house."

"So…" she asked, "for how long do you think we need to stay here?"

"Who knows?" I said. "It depends upon what happens next. And I suppose what happens next is between Freak… and God."

Freak stepped forward and put a hand on Saundra's shoulder.

"Saundra," he said, "we need you. I'm thinking we'll need to record a minimum of one podcast message and one interview per day. I'm going to need someone who I trust running all of the media aspects of this show. Other stations—and the networks—are going to want to come visit and to interview us here on the ranch. With the help of these soldiers and a crew you'll be able to put together, I'll need you to safely and effectively manage all of the endless moving parts." Freak turned to Steve. "You, too, Steve. You've both been stellar. But we've still got a long ways to go."

The reporter lifted an eyebrow in the direction of her cameraman. Steve replied with a wobbly thumbs up.

"Fine," she sighed. She glanced from Mrs. K to Cal, then dropped herself into a rustic cushioned sofa.

"So be it," she surrendered, adjusting the heavy throw pillow into the small of her back. "But if we're going to be staying here for a while, then I'm going to need a new phone."

"Of course," Freak concurred. "A new laptop as well. Plus a minimum of at least one full-time assistant."

Saundra massaged a wrinkle from the old shirt she'd rummaged from the ranch's lost and found.

"And," she said, "if you want me to return to the airwaves again—and to handle all of the media big shots as they come and go—then I'm going to need a professional-looking suit. Some shoes... some clothes from my apartment, plus a new outfit or two at least."

"Naturally," Freak winked. "Channel 5 would be crazy to disagree."

Saundra leaned forward, her voice regaining its commanding charm. "I'll call the station in the morning. I'll have the folks from wardrobe go shopping. With a light push, I'll bet they could deliver some real clothes up here for our next broadcast by late tomorrow afternoon."

"Of course," I smiled. "All it will take is a one push from Saundra Paige, and the Earth will move."

"What?" she demanded. "You don't think I need new clothes?"

"Personally," I said, "if I was you, I'd stick with the chic mountain look. You make it work. I think you look great in flannel."

She tipped her head, waiting.

"But," I continued, "if you're taking suggestions, then you might want to do something about your hair."

Saundra tossed me a scowl. She lifted her arms, gathered her hair, and then stuffed the knot behind her neck down into her back collar.

"Better?" she asked.

"Much," I said.

"Good. We certainly wouldn't want to upset the Louisville Slugger."

"Agreed," I nodded. "Now... if you could just do something about all of that smudged mascara."

I drew a fingertip beneath my eye, then swirled it around my cheek and across my chin as if to show her where.

"Funny," she grinned. "It can't possibly be that bad."

"I'm just saying," I laughed, "if I didn't know better, I mighta guessed you'd just stepped into the back end of a Diamond K pack mule...."

Fortunately, I was getting pretty good at dodging pillows.

37

WEE BOOTS

The short, wide-smiling African-American team leader from the combat Huey identified himself as Master Sergeant Brainerd.

"But you can call me Wee Daddy B," he bellowed, reaching to pump our arms. "My men are now all positioned. We'll be boots on the ground with you folks from here on out. Agent Wilcox and Sergeant Andrews are heading back to Fort Carson, so I'm your guy."

"Wee Daddy?" smiled the towering Jack. "You must be a real scrapper to be comfortable with a handle like Wee Daddy B."

"Yes, sir," he replied. "My other handle is Wee Daddy... *Wolverine.* My men settled on that second handle during our first tour. Once we were engaged, our enemy learned in a hurry that these boots were made for stomping. So I can assure you, there are no psychological insecurities on my side of the line."

Mrs. K stepped forward. "Well, Mr. Wolverine Boots, welcome to the Diamond K." Mary took her turn at the sergeant's hand. "Thank you for coming. We're so glad you've joined us."

"My pleasure, ma'am." He winked. "But let's try that name of mine one more time. Let's just go with Wee Daddy, if that's okay with you?" He finally let go of her hand and turned back to Jack. "My orders are to protect and to serve. And I can promise you that you are all now in the best of hands."

"Sounds great," said Jack. "Tell me more."

"Sir," he said, "this is the darnedest assignment I've ever been given. As you know, the military is pretty hamstrung by the law when it comes to operations on American soil."

Jack nodded.

Wee Daddy reached down and absently scratched the tail-wagging Rex. "But we suddenly find ourselves in extraordinary times."

The officer straightened. "We're the best that was immediately available, and for now, you're going to get the best our government can provide. I've been instructed to suspend many of our standard protocols. I'm to provide complete transparency and full disclosure in all matters. If possible, I'm to join your little family. I'm supposed to eat a few meals with you when I can, and if you'll let me, to be sitting in on most or all of your relevant discussions. My men and I will be at your disposal 24-7."

I met his eyes. "That didn't work so well," I said, "with the last guy they sent. I assume you'll understand why, after Wilcox, we might be reluctant to take your word about your team serving and protecting us."

"Understood. Due diligence on your part is commendable. But I can assure you that while my superiors have given me exceptional latitude on this assignment, I will not misuse your trust and that freedom in any way. The necessary paperwork is being put in place even as we speak. But given the extraordinary circumstances of the past week, I hope you'll be willing to be rid of Agent Wilcox and to now settle for my team's humble services. We'd like you to give your servants in uniform—and your government—another chance. Let us prove ourselves trustworthy. And, as I said, the operative word here is *transparency.*"

Saundra lifted an eyebrow. "Transparency? What do you mean by *transparency*?"

"It is my understanding," he replied, "unlike me and my team, Agent Wilcox was not accountable to any clearly defined line of command. He withheld information from you and those around him, and he intentionally misled you on a number of occasions. While you were on his watch, your lives were perhaps at risk."

"That," I said, "is putting it mildly. Wilcox had spy cams planted throughout our suite at the lodge. In *every* room."

"Yes sir, Mr. Hanson. May I call you Mark? According to the report I was given, Wilcox employed hidden cameras, audio bugs and GPS tracking devices without your consent. He also tried to win your favor through misdirection and outright lies. He apparently spent his entire assignment secretly manipulating situations trying to keep you silenced... or to make you dead."

"Today," I shrugged, "we planted our own spy cam. And, as a countermove, we did a bit of transmitting ourselves. Thanks to our last broadcast, the whole world already knows everything you've just admitted. Tell us something new."

"Transparency," he said. "That means I must confess right up front that by the time we've finished securing this compound, we'll have motion detectors, infrared night cameras and sufficient surveillance capabilities to monitor every conversation on this ranch... if we need to. Right through the walls. No bugs required. Anything short of sign language in the shower... theoretically, we will be able to have it on tape at the flick of a switch."

I winced at the mention of showers.

"But," he said, "as I've pledged, we're not going to misuse these resources. To be honest, it's in our own interest to show some integrity and to earn back your trust. And for you to share that restored trust with our nation. Given what's going on in the world right now, we need to pull together as a nation and to be strong. But, thanks to the whole Wilcox incident, the military and our government took a bruising black eye today."

"As I recall," I said, "we never asked for Wilcox. And it wasn't exactly a black eye. It was more like a tender jaw."

"Right," he winked. "I saw the clip. Nice shot."

"Thanks," I returned. "It was the highlight of my week. But I wasn't sure how it came off on the video. Maybe I'll watch for the replay on tonight's news."

"Speaking of surveillance and hidden cameras...." Wee Daddy turned to address Saundra. "This," he pointed to his right cheek, "is generally considered to be my better side."

For the first time, I caught sight of a long scar that disappeared into the hair on his left temple. Wee Daddy's single scar was nothing like Freak's patch of mangled face, but the original wound must have been substantial.

"So where are the rest of your devices?" he asked. "Am I live on Candid Camera, or are you going to spring it on me later when I least expect it?"

"No," said Freak stepping forward with an outstretched hand, "everything is off for the moment."

They shook long and hard, with mutual intentionality.

"You're a believer," said Freak at last, his voice warm and matter-of-fact.

"Yes, of course." Wee Daddy released the prophet's hand. "In the past ten years, I've hunkered down in more foxholes than craters on the moon. And as they say, there's no such thing as an atheist in the foxhole."

"Is your faith," asked Freak, "why they gave this assignment to you?"

"Only partly." He glanced around our circle. "Do you mind if we all sit down?"

"Goodness!" exclaimed Mrs. K. She blushed at the realization of how long it had been since she'd offered anyone cookies and milk. "Please," she implored, "let's all find seats in the big room. I'll put together a tray and I'll be right back. It'll only take a minute."

She vanished through the kitchen's swinging double doors.

"Nice scar," I said, tipping my head towards Wee Daddy's left cheek. "But after a week with the Reverend, it took me a while to even notice. What's the story?"

Wee Daddy reached for a second cookie. "Sure," he said, "I could tell you where and how I won that slice." He tested the balance of the snack, sizing it up as if it was a ninja star. *"But then I'd have to kill you."*

"Fine," I grinned, crossing my legs. "But with answers like that... then I guess we can know what to expect when you promise to bring us transparency."

"No, sir. With answers like that, you can know what to expect when I try to bring you a joke." He bit the cookie in half. With his left hand, he deftly snatched from mid-air several tiny falling crumbs. "Afghanistan. A knife. One of those foxhole ranger-grave experiences I mentioned in the other room. This scar came from the night I came to my senses about the miracles of God. It's a faith I'll hold for the rest of my life... however long or short that may be." He turned towards Freak. "Maybe that's the sort of question I should be taking up with the prophet. What do you say, Reverend Jacobs? Has the good Lord given you a date yet... for when it all ends?"

Freak leaned back in his chair. "You were starting to tell us," he said, "about how you got the assignment to serve and protect me and this ranch."

"Yes, sir." He finished the cookie and glanced at Mrs. K. "Delicious, ma'am. Not many homemade chocolate chips out there in the field. Could I impose upon you for another dozen of these for my men? Uncle Sam will gladly reimburse. I can request a check to be written to you personally, or to the Diamond K Ranch. Just submit an invoice for the full retail value." His face suddenly grew serious. "Which brings up another subject. How are you all set on vacancies right now?"

"For how many?" she asked. "And for how long?"

"Well," he replied, "for starters, for tonight. We'll sleep in shifts, of course, but we've been pushing almost non-stop for the past two days. If it wasn't so cold up here, and if the National Weather Service wasn't predicting more snow tonight, I wouldn't even ask...."

"Hush," she laughed. "Not another word. We'll give your team your own bunkhouse. Let's make it the Luke cabin. The Luke is close to the main drive, and it can sleep up to twenty men. It has a small kitchen, a shower, and everything you'll need. You'll be able to set up a private command office there, and you can stay as long as you need to." She glanced at her son. "Cal, when you're finished, maybe you would be willing to plow a path from here to the Luke? And then you can help me turn up the heat and get the place ready for our new friends."

Cal nodded.

The Army Ranger appeared delighted. "As I said, ma'am, Uncle Sam will reimburse the Diamond K for everything... at your peak season rates."

"Wee Daddy," asked Jack, apparently still amused by the novelty of the name, "while Cal has the truck fired up, should we have him plow the whole ranch drive all the way down to the road?"

"It's your call," he replied. "I was told a county truck will soon be opening things up as far as the entrance to your ranch. And I'm sure the driver would plow all the way up to your cabins if so requested. But this is private property, and we're going to respect your rights and to follow your wishes."

"Good answer," said Jack. "So, what do you suggest, Wee Daddy?"

"If I was you," he said, "I'd have Cal open her up. You'll be safe now that my team is hunkered down. And maybe you'd like to be able to freely come and go from the ranch without having to worry about getting stuck in your own drive. The snow is deep, and you know your own curves. No sense asking the county to do it, and then having twenty tons of a stranger's truck drop off the grade and start tearing through your favorite huckleberry patch."

"Makes sense."

"Gotta warn you, though," he said, "if you do decide to open her up, then we'll have to establish a checkpoint and roadblock at the ranch entrance. Which is no problem. The snow will melt sooner or later. We'll have to eventually set one up anyway."

Jack nodded, and Cal rose to fetch his boots.

I reflected on Wee Daddy's suggestion about his team being prepared to stick around until after the snow.

"As for this assignment," he continued, "they sent our team screaming through the clouds from Fort Carson to Summit County yesterday within minutes of the first explosion at the lodge. Special ops teams are scuttling everywhere around the world right now. Home and abroad. Those of us being deployed on American soil are a little uncomfortable with the situation, but we understand. Local resources and the National Guard are overwhelmed. Too much is happening too fast. The stakes are too high to be dragging our feet and second guessing our superiors."

"So," asked Jack, "you happened to be at Fort Carson, and someone high up made the call to send you our way?"

"They had our team secure the lodge site first, and then try to do some recon around the area. Despite the off-and-on storm, we were aiding the investigators as best we could right up until your latest broadcast this afternoon. We got the word immediately when the Wilcox scandal started hitting the news. They had us back on the Huey within minutes. I was briefed during the quick flight over. We passed the other chopper along the way."

"Recon?" I asked. "Can you tell us what you found around the lodge?"

"Full disclosure, right?" Wee Daddy laughed. "You're going to love this. Up on the drive above the lodge, we found some broken scraps off the rear end of a 2016 Suburban. You wouldn't happen to know anything about a hit-and-run on the hill, would you, Mark?"

"Maybe," I grinned.

"I'm pretty sure," he said, "those broken parts will match any scuffs the forensics team is able to salvage from the front end of your Ford. We'll know more for certain once they can more carefully examine your rig. Mark, do you care to confirm this theory and save us some time, or shall we have the team keep dabbing around for tiny clues?"

"Affirmative on the fender bender," I smirked. "Guilty as charged."

"So far," he said, "what's left of the Suburban remains off the grid. We did recover enough of their plate numbers from a stoplight cam to make a match and confirm the plates were lifted from a Denver minivan and transferred to the Suburban. Whoever these folks are, they somehow managed to get back onto the service road in the storm and slide their way down into a Breckenridge and a private locked garage or something before we could zero in on them. As you know, the entire Dillon basin is on high alert. It's going to be hard for them to slip the noose."

"We did," I said.

"Yes," he said, studying me. "But none of these characters are Mark Hanson." And then, lest it go to my head, he finished the thought. "None of them have been around here long enough to know the lay of the mountains the way you do. And remember... you were at the front edge of the confusion and storm. After another five minutes, you and your rig wouldn't have slipped out, either."

Satisfied, I let it go at that.

"What else," asked Freak, "can you tell us?"

"Not much is certain." Wee Daddy took a deep breath. "Wild theories are flying in every direction. Hopefully they'll drag something useful from Wilcox in the next day or so. Besides the earthquakes and tsunamis, there's a lot more going on right now than people realize. The intelligence community has been able to keep most of it out of the news." He turned to Saundra. "Ms. Paige, I'm trying to trust it's all for the best somehow... but you and these media leaks of yours have been driving the military and the government crazy."

The Ranger glanced at Freak, then sighed. "May I ask a favor?"

Saundra started to protest. "If you're asking that we censor the news...."

"Not that," said Wee Daddy, "something else."

Freak leaned forward. "How can we help?"

"I know," said Wee Daddy, "you're the real deal. I know you pray. Back on the base, I analyzed clips from a couple of your interviews." He glanced at Jack and Mary, then back to Freak. "Pray for us, pastor. Pray for me. For my team. Pray for all of the good guys who are busting their butts on this. We want the bad guys shut down, and we want peace, and we want to be back with our families, just like you. We're willing to put everything on the line and to do whatever we can. Whatever is best for our nation."

"For the world," corrected Freak. "God's Kingdom is coming... for the world. Not only for America."

Wee Daddy studied Freak. "Yes," he said at last, "for the world, too. But I don't have much influence right now beyond this ranch. So as far as I'm concerned, it's gotta start in America. Right here."

"We'll pray," Freak committed. "And I'm inviting you to join us in prayer whenever you are able." He glanced at Jack, waiting for an indication of agreement.

Jack cleared his throat. "For the King," he said. "We can pray right now."

"Yes," said Freak, turning back to Wee Daddy. "But first, we need to know one more thing. Something else to include in our prayers." Freak squinted, gently. "You're hurting, too, aren't you? Something from the lodge...."

"Yes," he said, slowly meeting Freak's eyes.

Wee Daddy's voice grew so quiet I needed to strain to follow the story.

"It was really bad... it was still fresh when we landed at the lodge," he said. "I could see immediately our team would need to take the lead. A lot of the local folks were shell shocked... rookies and volunteers fumbling around in a daze. We were the seasoned pros with all the training and all of the war experience, so it fell to us to wade into that smoking rubble and to forage through the carnage to check for faint pulses or any signs of life. And we had to manage the trauma of the civilian responders as well.

"With all of our training and everything we've been through on other assignments, it should have been familiar. But it wasn't. We knew those other guys, the team that had been assigned to you with the Humvees. As hard as it was to pick through the twisted armor of their vehicles and to confirm their deaths, we could almost do that part on autopilot. We've lost buddies before.

"But... to handle all of those charred and mangled civilian bodies...."

Wee Daddy took a moment to collect himself.

"That lodge wasn't some black dot on a map, some anonymous dirt village filled with land mines and enemy snipers on the other side of the world. This was American soil, a family ski resort in the Rockies. At the heart of our nation....

"These were carefree college kids who'd just happened to pick that lodge for Easter Break. Moms and dads on vacation... children the same ages of our own kids back home. Innocent folks with no idea... trying to...."

He slowly looked at Saundra.

"The worst of it," he said, "was in the press conference area. As you know, the lobby had been almost standing room only...."

Saundra turned away.

"Transparency," Wee Daddy said at last, his voice growing more assured. "I know it's not professional, but I'm telling you all of this because I'm serious about joining this family of yours here on the Diamond K. And I'm serious about wanting and needing your prayers. About doing this for God. Getting it right. The stakes are too high for any more screw ups."

"Were there *any* survivors?" asked Freak.

He shook his head. "None of the military. A few of the media people from the parking lot outside. A handful of guests—just barely—from the far ends of the lodge. That's it."

He turned to me. "I'm sorry, Mark. It took a while, but they did finally identify the deputy. Andy didn't make it. Neither did the young woman who was staying with you. Your girlfriend."

He met my eyes.

"Heather," I said.

"Yes." He nodded. "Heather was killed in the attack with all the rest."

The finality of the declaration caught me off guard. Of course she was dead. Any fool would have known as much. I'd been saying so from the hour of the first explosion.

Our wall of windows had faced the rockets. Had been marked for the first strike.

And that's where she'd been. Barely behind the glass.

Packing.

Fearful. Frustrated. Fuming over my refusal to leave.

Probably stuffing a nightie into that silly little daisy daypack of hers....

The others kept talking, kept looking my way. Extending hands.

They wanted to pray.

But I couldn't hear. Couldn't reply.

It was official. She was gone.

Like my beastie over the cliff. Buried under a ton of snow.

No, not like that.

My beastie could be hauled up. Towed out, flattened the rest of the way and recycled.

She was flesh. A soul.

Really gone.

I'd done it again.

Eventually, I excused myself and pushed my way from the room.

I discovered myself in the kitchen. I found my arm rising toward a top cupboard. Found myself blindly extending fingers into the cache of cheap wines Jack kept stashed for emergencies. For guest oversights. For the anniversaries and the special occasions of those who were too careless to even attend to the details of the most important days of their own lives.

I withdrew a heavy green bottle. Ignored the label.

Gathered my jacket; found my boots. Banged out the front door into the first flakes of the returning snow.

Managed to escape.

I unscrewed the cap and soaked my lips—my tongue— in the numbing drink.

And stumbled down the frozen path toward the Esther.

Alone.

PART IV

MOVING ON

In the following days, efforts were made to discuss what happened that night. The others wanted me to talk about my feelings. About Heather.

But there wasn't much I could spill.

I let the empty bottle lie.

Still, there was no way for me to avoid attending the extravagant Denver memorial service for all of the victims of the Breckenridge lodge attack only our team of four had escaped. I didn't want or need to talk about her, but I guess I had the decency to realize I needed to at least make a quiet appearance at the big church event.

The governor was slated to speak, as well as mayors and church representatives from the numerous communities who had taken hits or suffered losses. Each of the government agencies and media venues who'd sacrificed members from their ranks were in on it as well, planning a program, drawing up speaker lists, ordering cakes.

For me to skip the service would have been the greatest possible insult to Heather's family. Not that I planned to sit with them. I hardly knew their names. But the media had published what they knew of the facts of the attack, including stories of the four survivors from the targeted suite.

They had reported in detail how I'd whisked Freak, Steve, and Saundra away.

And now, they would report how I grieved for the pretty young preschool teacher who'd died in my room. While I was running from the lodge downstairs without her.

There was no way I could decline an invitation like that.

Freak offered to fly down with us for the day, but we all agreed his presence would only complicate an already over-hyped event. His attendance would only add stress to what promised to be an exhausting ordeal for everyone involved.

Besides, he hadn't been asked to speak.

38
THE DENVER SERVICE

The morning sky glared clear as we crunched through the ice-gravel remnants of recently plowed snow. We spoke little and monitored closely our leather-soled footing down the crystal slope to the helicopter rumbling in pre-flight prep on the parking area terrace below the main house.

"We'll be praying," said Wee Daddy, slapping the chopper's door. "And you won't have to worry about a thing. A pair of agents will meet you when you land. They've got a heavy set of wheels, plus a small escort. They know your itinerary, and they're on duty until they send you back to us tonight. You won't have to navigate a single detail without their help."

Saundra and Steve had flown in the Channel 5 News Chopper a few times, but never in anything like an armored Huey. Maybe it was our nerves as we anticipated the involuntary sobs and struggled to stifle our anxiety over the post-service reception awaiting us at the other end of our morning.

Perhaps it was the fumes. The sharp movements. The deep thumping.

Whatever it was, only minutes into the air, we all felt ill.

The flight up over the glaciered Continental Divide and down to the Mile High City seemed to last forever. By the time we finally bumped to rest on the concrete pad at the edge of Denver, we were already weary of the day and longing to be back at the quiet Diamond K.

With hardly a word, we clambered into the government SUV for our 15-minute drive to the church. One by one, we closed our eyes and drew within ourselves, trying to collect our nerves. To seek a place of peace within the recesses of our black attire and dark moods.

Our sable rig suddenly lurched over a chunk of some truck's freshly shucked ice.

"God," I mumbled, clutching the door. "I never should have...."

"God," Saundra whispered, drawing my eyes. "God is gracious. Lord... we beg that you have mercy. Christ have mercy... upon us all."

Security was tight in the event parking lot, and the typically rabid media behaved atypically reserved, as if on an unusually heavy leash. With so many of the fallen victims having been their colleagues, the pack had a hard time working up the spittle for their usual yelps and snaps.

They were grieving, too.

At exactly five minutes to the hour, we stepped through a north side entrance. We were ushered through the hundreds of milling mourners who'd lacked a golden ticket pass and had been unable to attain seats.

Heads turned. Conversations ceased.

Our little parade marched though their ranks in an awkward wave of growing recognition. And then we were seated.

Thankfully, organizers had reserved a half-hidden spot for us off from a side hallway near a middle entrance into the massive sanctuary. We flowed in, eyes lowered, only a few shuffling strides. Steve and I settled, Saundra between us, trying to see as much and as little as we could manage.

It had been a long time since I'd sat in such a cavernous venue. It'd been a long time since I'd cushioned myself into theater church seating, filed among so many thousands of attenders all perfectly rowed and decked in their somber-best hues.

In vain, I scanned the crowd for Heather's family—for anyone I knew—then quickly abandoned the folly. In my hands, I discovered a rolled service program.

According to the bulletin, the softly strumming stage-right band included guest musicians from the churches of several of the victims. Below, on the main floor, one huge section was filled with hundreds of military uniforms; the complementing quarter was lined with the dark crisp shoulders of the finest of Colorado's first responders.

I wondered how many of Andy's friends were there... how many officers and deputies had been allowed to leave their posts for the day to pay their respects for a fallen brother and a rock-solid friend.

The program menu mentioned there would be other funeral services in the coming week. Private gatherings. Graveside committals and church memorial events in towns scattered throughout Colorado. Even in other states.

But today's extravaganza was billed as the biggie.

Precisely at the top of the hour, a kilted cadre of emerald bagpipers entered the stage. They jerk-stepped with their Amazing Grace to a perfectly centered halt, did a bit more twirling and unearthly honking, then yielded to the first of many speakers.

The mega-church host pastor who opened the ceremonies offered an appropriately warm and formal greeting. He led a brief prayer, and then he read the long list of names. The alphabetical victims rapidly faded in, then dissolved out, one photo slide on the jumbotron each.

The host was followed by numerous others, a litany that was interspersed with rounds of projected slides and sentimental melodies from the guest band. It was all very dignified.

Perfectly planned.

They'd even choreographed the event for an occasional stress-relieving chuckle.

I followed what I could handle.

That amounted to almost everything from the first speaker up to Heather. Not much after her moment and passing slide.

I remember hearing her name. Seeing her graduation day smile fill the screen, then watching her fluffed hair and bright eyes fading to black almost as fast as they had arrived.

Like Heather, I faded in and out for the remaining two hours.

But I do vividly remember the final lines of the last cleric, a square-suited, white-collared gentleman who sauntered as if in no hurry to yield the stage to dismissal. He remained a blur until half way through his shtick, when I suddenly realized he had been invoking the name *Freak*.

"Unlike this man, this *Freak*," he nearly coughed the name, "I do *not* believe it is a preacher's right to interpret current events, let alone to frighten the flock. It is not a shepherd's task to declare who is to blame for earthquakes, tsunamis, and the world's most violent and senseless of tragedies. Historical analysis is the responsibility of academians and politicians, not of the clergy. Thoughtful citizens will leave it to the experts to sort out what they can from the random and horrific events of the past few weeks."

The speaker finger-pressed his thin spectacles tightly to his thick brows.

"It is the clergy's task to calm the sheep."

He swept an open palm over the auditorium, then drew his hand around until it was stretched towards the enormous cairn of potted flowers opposite of the band. The arrangements were woven together into a fittingly glorious cascade of floral remembrances.

"Yes," he said, "our nation—and our world—have suffered some disturbing and confusing shocks. Closer to home, here in Colorado, we were stunned on the Day of the Falling Skies, when nearly 300 innocents lost their lives in our Summit County apportionment of the sorrows allotted for humanity to endure that day."

He shuffled his notes, then pressed forward with an affected nod.

"And today, we now remember those who lost their lives in the recent explosions at the Breckenridge lodge."

Thousands of lungs simultaneously filled and slowly exhaled during an appropriately reflective pause.

"In the midst of such loss and pain," the churchman continued, "it is natural for us to lament. It is easy for us to feel as if we are experiencing what the Freak has metaphorically preached as... *The End of the World.*"

He patted the unopened Bible on the podium below his notes.

"The Bible tells us that the creative force of the cosmos is one of generative love... not destructive rage. From the thrones of heaven flow rivers of eternal energy and life... not flames."

He leaned forward.

"Do not be deceived by the wild-eyed sensationalisms of the televangelist W.B. Jacobs. Do not yield to his talk of devils and his antics of despair. Do not surrender to fear. Do not abandon your hopes... for you shall yet receive your due blessings as a spiritual sojourner who patiently strives for the betterment of this verdant planet we call home."

He leaned back. Tapped his glasses. Inhaled for a big finish.

"I exhort you—all of us—to leave this place encouraged. To depart from our time here together knowing that your investments in this world will pay their dividends. That you can be lifted and inspired by those who we release today. And you can eagerly anticipate a day, when your time here on earth has finished, when you, too... will rest in peace."

He raised both hands, then added a grin wide enough to nearly meet his wrists.

"Brothers and sisters, family and friends... the universe has *NOT* begun to end. It has barely begun to begin. Creation and life are gifts freely given with no strings attached. We have come a long way in these past billions of years, and our destiny assures us... we still have a long way to go."

He expanded his embrace of the air.

"Humanity's time is not over. It has only begun... and there is much we must yet do."

He dropped one arm.

"Do not despair. Press on, my friends, press on."

He closed his eyes. Squeezed them for all through the jumbotron to see.

Then he raised a sweeping open palm to the stars.

"May the Lord of Love and Life have mercy upon those we remember, and upon us all. May the cosmos we call home receive and comfort... those who *were*... *we* who are... and those who are yet to come. Amen."

39
WAR AND PEACE

Even before the memorial service in Denver, Jack and Mary had already canceled all reservations, and they stopped booking any new guests for the coming season.

Between the media crews and the comings and goings of an endless stream of special visitors, the ranch would remain plenty busy without having to entertain strangers who could squat in cabins and expect to be waited upon for days at a time.

Or so Jack said.

In truth, Wee Daddy and Jack had probably agreed not to expose any more innocent bystanders to the sort of collateral devastation we'd suffered at the lodge.

We settled into Diamond K rhythms, and, as the Denver memorial service celebrity cleric so blithely put it, we pressed on.

I'd help Cal and Jack with chores. I'd assist Saundra and Steve with their interviews. We'd share meals. We'd pray. We'd watch the news. We'd host Jack and Mary's intimate house-church community in the big room on Sunday nights.

And—when I could—I'd squeeze in a few hours here and there to pluck away on a project Freak somehow wrangled me into accepting.

"I know," Freak urged, "how you hate to write. So don't write. Just jot a few notes. Some impressions. Some bits and pieces from conversations as they come to mind."

"What's the point?" I protested. "If the world is going to end soon anyway, nobody's ever going to read...."

"Trust me," he smiled. "This is important. Besides, it's not like you have anything better to do."

I had a hard time arguing. The thought of moving back to Denver... of going back to my job, of going back to anything....

"Don't," he said, "make this so difficult. Don't bind yourself up trying to pretend you're some sort of Hemingway or Fitzgerald. And don't worry about organizing your thoughts. Just write down whatever bobs to the surface. If the Lord tarries, then you may have the time to clean up your notes and put everything into some kind of chronological order later."

"Sounds like a lot of bother...."

"If you're lucky," he laughed, "maybe the Lord will help you with this. Maybe it'll sell. And maybe God will reward you with the cash to buy a new rig...."

"Nice try with the carrot, but nobody cares about a school teacher's amateur opinions...."

"Are you kidding? Not opinions. *Facts*. The whole world wants the rest of our story... the honest inside scoop, directly from the man who saw me fall and who has been here at my side every step...."

Freak moved towards the window.

"Believe me," he pleaded, motioning at another television van beginning to unload. "People want to know what's been going on behind the scenes. Make yourself useful. Give this an honest shot."

"Useful? Like I haven't been useful already? Don't forget who it was who dug you up from the snow...."

"All right," Freak smiled, rotating back my way. "Not *that* again. We've all got *new* assignments now. And unless you've got your eye on another preacher to dig from the dead, this assignment is yours."

"So," I sighed, "I guess I'm now officially taking my orders from the Freak who fell to Earth."

"Not from me," he beamed. "From God. He's the one who dropped this assignment into your lap. Of all the people in all the world, he chose you...."

"All right," I grinned, raising my hand. "Not *that* again, either. Fine. I'll give it a try. No promises. Nothing fancy."

"Nothing fancy," nodded Freak.

"A few paragraphs each day," I said. "And I'm only doing this for the official record. Only because documentation might come in handy if I have to stand up in court and testify...."

"Perfect," Freak nodded. "Do what you can. That's all he asks."

The unprecedented earthquakes and disasters along America's west coast eventually subsided. Their fury spent, those first tectonic shifts gave way to the heart-wrenching tasks of mass burials. Of cleanups and the relocation of millions of bewildered and injured survivors. Death tolls and missing person estimates for the San Francisco Bay area alone approached nearly one hundred thousand. California property losses racked up into the many hundreds of billions.

Meanwhile, the war reports of destruction and mayhem from the other side of the globe kept piling on, complete with frightening live images and staggering reports of radiation and horrific deaths.

The American President began a series of weekly addresses, casting hope. Dedicating resources. Promising a better day.

According to Wee Daddy, the investigation into the individuals or the organization behind the attack at the lodge was going slow. Wilcox was locked in an isolated federal cell behind a row of expensive lawyers. He was pacing and cursing, but not saying a word of any use.

Freak and Jack agreed we should stay current on major world events. But they insisted we should limit our news intake to the primetime hour of each evening. It became a sacred hour. A somber time of gathered gasps and shared sighs, followed each night by a time of communal prayer.

I more or less participated in those prayers—as best I could—from a wobbly stool I'd tucked into the darkest corner of the candle-lit loft. I'd gaze at the shelves of matching Bibles and commentaries, the stacks of inspirational magazines and self-help devotionals. The carved figurines and the handmade tapestries. Anything to keep my eyes from lingering too long on my friends as they prayed.

My mind would wander, and then be pulled back.

Stuff happened while they prayed that I couldn't explain.

I didn't buy it all, but they were sincere, and I had to admire their commitment. They worshipped the King. They prayed for the world, for the lost.

For each other.

For me.

Wee Daddy kept his word to serve and protect during those tumultuous months that came to be known as *The Season of the First Trumpet*.

Freak used the phrase often in his podcasts, and he managed to slip it in several times with nearly every conversation with the media. By the end of his first week of ranch interviews, almost everyone in the news business was speaking the same language.

The fact that a broad-based consensus emerged about our planet experiencing what could be called *The Season of the First Trumpet* was frightening.

It implied a concession... that at least one more Trumpet was yet to come.

Despite pundits and clerics who claimed otherwise, a pervasive resignation emerged among common people—and much of the media—for the likelihood of worse days still to come.

Then again, maybe the press only leveraged Freak's brand of doom to sell their news.

"Picture a speeding train," suggested one program host. She tapped her folder until her skeptical guest frowned.

"This speeding train represents modern history. The train is over a mile long, and it is racing down a mountain... 150 boxcars filled with everything you can imagine. Thousands of tons of freight. Fresh produce, washing machines, electronics, automobiles, coal. You name it. At the bottom of the steep grade is a wide turn... no problem. Except someone loosened a track on the bend."

She lowered her notes. "Suddenly, the front locomotive hits the bad section of rails. The loose track breaks free."

She leaned towards her guest, then nearly whispered.

"You tell me... what happens next?"

Journalists would wait turns, working up the queue until their slot to spend an afternoon with Freak. They'd ask about falling from the plane. About fleeing from the lodge. About blowing the shofar.

They would try to generate fresh questions, new ways to uncover unusual aspects of Freak's story no none had heard.

They would endure the obligatory lecture from Freak about Truth and Grace, complete with his trademark finger illustrations as he drew floating lines down his left and right cheeks.

And, without fail, they would conclude with some version of the one question none of them could resist:

"Has the Lord given you any new predictions or observations for the coming week?"

"Yes," Freak would inevitably reply, "the Lord has declared... he is on the move."

Then Freak would offer something new.

"Our government," said Freak, "needs to stop debating carbon emissions and to start preparing our response systems for the Second Trumpet. Volcanoes are churning, building energy to blacken the skies and clog our rivers. Our priorities need to shift from distant minutia to the clouds of fire and ash looming only months away."

Freak was an equal-opportunity offender. He managed to tick off everyone... from the President to the Pope.

Hate mail arrived daily from every quarter. From Green Peace... to the pastors of obscure churches in the south.

He was forever stirring up the bees.

"Yes," said Freak, "I know many fine Christians who've taught the sacred Darby Doctrine of a pre-Tribulation rapture. In seminary, I was taught the dogma myself... and I confused those speculations with the gospel for most of my adult life. But look around. The tribulation has begun, and we're all still here. God has forgiven me, and he'll forgive my colleagues as well. It's time for every God-fearing pastor to face the facts and dig in with the truth."

"This Freak," buzzed one especially agitated critic, "he reminds me of a junkyard dog who has slipped his chain. He's growling and terrorizing the entire neighborhood. He's out there snapping and barking with a reckless abandon totally unacceptable for any leader, let alone a man of the cloth. Somebody needs to muzzle this guy." The commentator cleared his throat. "He fancies himself some kind of a savior. If you ask me, this mad-dog prophet of the Apocalypse is nothing more than a menace."

The mad-dog prophet's "predictions" and "observations" were sometimes almost poetic—and only vaguely specific—but his top lines were forever quotable.

Not particularly barking-like at all.

Speaking to a foreign journalist, he might say, "Officials in Nairobi should begin preparing for troubles in their streets. God loves Kenya, but the Devil is running amok. God will not ignore the lawless marauding. Christians in Kenya most resist the Dark Riders, or beware a greater wrath to come."

Or he might smile and nod to a religious network reporter. "Yes, God is pleased with those preparing to assist in California. But the Lord reminds us to travel light. We must pray and worship as a team. We must build rhythms of work and rest into our efforts. In our own strength and pride, we will fail. Seek people of peace, call upon the Lord, and only then will we produce lasting fruit to please the King."

He might touch his scars and sigh to an international correspondent. "The towers of Tokyo... soon shall shake. Teach us, Lord, to number our days, so we may gain wisdom and turn to you while the sun yet lights the day."

Pundits went ballistic and stocks tumbled the week Freak unflinchingly declared: "Wall Street should brace itself for another ditch. Russia is about to make a move. Blessed is the investor who piles wealth where neither moth can nibble, nor rust can reach. *Bank only on the Lord.*"

Bloggers snatched up phrases like "Bank only on the Lord." Such lines became known as *Freakisms*, and the prophet's best line of the day would sometimes go viral.

At the end of each interview, the mad-dog of the Apocalypse would finish with a prayer.

Freak's interview prayers were occasionally omitted. But, more often than not, at least a few sentences of each prayer would somehow survive through the final edit.

Some people complained that Freak's prayers were aired on the basis of crass corporate profit motivations. They claimed networks were pandering to the frightened masses; focus groups were rumored to have responded favorably whenever Freak was presented as *hyper-spiritual.*

"It's lousy," groused an MSNBC guest analyst. "It's manipulative. It's ratings-driven journalism at its worst. The private whisperings of a fanatic have nothing to do with the nightly news. To include these closed-eyed fantasies of this back-woods, snake-oil showman only prove precisely how crazy the world has become. His prayers never should have made it to the air."

"Agreed," smiled Freak turning to me from the couch. "But God is good."

Freak dropped the critic to mute, then closed his eyes.

"Lord, confirm the fumbling words of your back-woods servant," he whispered, "so *your* Word may be known by all... and it may be rightly obeyed by all those who will."

And then Freak slipped into that kind of mumbling I could never quite understand.

Presumably to work up another semi-specific Freakism or prayer for the next day's news.

Wee Daddy sometimes joined us for meals and prayers. He participated in many of our discussions, and he kept us up to date on what he could. He was gracious, focused, quick witted, and pragmatically insightful in surprising ways.

"No, Jack," he said, his second day on the ranch. "I don't think you should be leaving Old Abe sitting around with a shell in the chamber." He sprinkled more pepper over his stew. "You need to put your gun away."

Wee Daddy replaced the shaker at the center of the table. "But leave the gun cabinet unlocked. If you're going to need your rifle, you're going to need it in a hurry."

He turned to Cal. "All of them. Keep your weapons ready." He laughed and looked at Freak. "And I'm talking about the shofar, as well."

"Speaking of which," said Jack, turning toward Freak, "how'd you learn to play the horn like that? I've never heard anything like it. I'm surprised you didn't shatter a few windows."

Freak lowered his spoon. "I played trumpet in the band."

"Right," I laughed. "John Philip Sousa on a cornet... First Trumpet of the Apocalypse on a shofar... same thing."

Freak studied me. "My grandfather owned a small ram's horn of his own. He kept it hid, mostly under a thick coat of dust. It was pushed way back on a top shelf.

Every once in a while one nobody was around, I'd pull it out and give it a few toots."

"That," said Jack, "was more than a little toot."

"This time," smiled Freak at last, "I had some help."

Saundra refolded her napkin. "Jack," she asked, "did you see them... the angels?"

He hadn't. So she explained, and that's when we did the math and realized the clock had stopped at midnight in Jerusalem. Monday morning, the day after Easter in the Middle East.

A few non-uniformed men were added to Wee Daddy's team in the bunkhouse, but Wee Daddy himself continued to be our primary point of contact. As necessary, we developed shopping lists. Wee Daddy did his best to broker our requests and to supply our needs, so we seldom had real cause to leave the ranch.

His men were always polite and vigilant. When required, they could be firm, which was especially important at the check station they built at the Diamond K's entrance. By the end of the first week, they were turning away dozens of vehicles a day.

Belligerent television crews without prior clearances would always raise a fuss when turned away. But it was the paparazzi and the religious pilgrims who became the biggest nuisance. They often travelled light, and they were forever trying to sneak into the ranch from vehicles parked far from the blocked front gate.

Saundra got her new phone. We all got new phones. But Saundra's arrived with a new Neiman Marcus wardrobe from the Cherry Creek Shopping Center. She also received an expanded production crew that included an intern assistant and one of the top field people from the Channel 5 network.

She established her media center at the Apostle John, a spacious two-bedroom cabin with beds for her team a short distance from the main house. The cabin was soon tethered with cables and power cords to a satellite truck on one side, matched by a studio support van on the other.

"Off to the John?" I would ask.

Saundra would sometimes smile, if only to shut me down.

Weather and lighting permitting, Freak's daily guest interviews were conducted on the outdoor log furniture and along the post-and-timber rails of the John's front porch. Otherwise, recording was handled inside the cabin using Saundra's efficient fireside hearth set, complete with fixed lights, tripods and equipment ready for uplinking at a moment's notice.

Saundra continued to sleep alone in the guest suite in the big house. Steve and I settled into the Esther Cabin by adding a twin bed we pushed to beneath the north window. We kept the fridge stocked with snacks and beer, and we grew relatively comfortable in our humble home at the far end of cabin row.

Given the circumstances, my boss—the principal at the high school where I'd taught for several years—readily agreed to grant me an open-ended leave of absence.

"Call it an extended spring break," he said from the phone. "You're welcomed back whenever you're ready. But you've got to promise," he chortled, "that you won't bring any of those terrorists when you return. Your new substitute says you've got more than enough terrorists in your World Lit class already."

Freak moved out of the big house into the cabin next to Steve and me near the end of the gravel drive.

His was the Ruth House, a family unit with an outdated VHS entertainment system flanked by a couple hundred family-fare tapes.

It also happened to be the only cabin without a fireplace.

Perfect for Freak and his wife... and their three little wildlings.

If the Ruth had been equipped with a fireplace, then one of Freak's boys would have gotten stuck in the chimney for sure. The other would have found the matches and burned the place flat for an encore.

Freak's wife and kids arrived two days after the departure of Agent Wilcox. They were found at a cheap motel outside of Salt Lake City. Ellen was tearfully holed up with her three children in a single small room.

Not knowing if she'd find her husband, nor trusting whether she'd find another room anywhere up the road, she dared not move. According to the nightly news, because of the devastation of so many major cities along the Pacific coast, motel vacancies inland to as far as Denver were almost impossible to find.

Upon learning Ellen's whereabouts, Freak immediately petitioned Wee Daddy for assistance. The government obliged by dispatching Wee Daddy's chopper and a couple of his men for the family's retrieval from Utah yet the same day.

We all stood with Freak on the porch for the Huey's return. Jack chewed a cigar stub in his favorite wide-brimmed hat with a rattlesnake band. Mary leaned on his arm in a light Navajo blanket shawl. Saundra wore a denim vest and matching slit skirt. Freak tugged on a windbreaker, in black slacks and tennis shoes.

"Hang on there, tiger," laughed Wee Daddy, gently anchoring Freak's arm. "Let's give them a minute to slow their blades."

The moment Wee Daddy released, Freak bounded from the porch. He skipped steps and reached the settling aircraft like a man half his age.

"Micah," he shouted, extending his arms into the open door. "Eli... Miriam!"

I glanced at Saundra, who stood transfixed.

For a guy who'd been so tight-lipped about his offspring, Freak's exuberance hit me as a bit of a wonder.

For a woman who'd never mentioned kids, Saundra's fascination provided an equal surprise.

Freak scooped out the tallest boy first. He hugged him hard, then plucked the smaller two as a pair, one giggling from each arm.

Wee Daddy's team attempted an assist, but found themselves quickly dismissed.

Ellen emerged last, her smile broad but uncertain, her footing hesitant as Freak guided her down onto the frozen, freshly plowed pad.

She was a large woman. Not so large as she'd appeared in her driveway on that first news clip over a week before, but big all the same.

The rest of us moved down from the porch to add our greetings.

A short distance from the chopper, I noticed glistening streaks on Ellen's round cheeks as her husband held tight and their children orbited in a circle-dance among the rays of the sinking sun.

Ellen murmured the name 'Benny,' and then something I could not hear.

"Honey," he replied, "you have no idea...."

The whispered rest was lost into the collar of an oversized military parka she'd been loaned for the ride.

This time, Saundra met my gaze.

Beyond her, Jack and Mary paused, arm and arm, lost in the parent zone. Steve shook his head, then turned back to the house, apparently ready to return inside to the fire.

Wee Daddy signaled to his men, and they quickly began unloading the family's gear.

DOCUMENTATION

Mary loved to feed her guests, but she had the grace to share the honors. During our third Sunday oikos meeting together on the ranch, with the New York film crew constantly underfoot, she forced herself to focus only on a few desserts.

"Mrs. K," I laughed, trying to ignore the camera, "nobody makes a fruit pie as good as yours." I placed my first of two tall green bottles to beside a heaping basket of steaming rolls.

I turned to Saundra. Her hair was pulled back above a stylish western outfit. I realized for the first time how long her hair had grown. With the new growth and mountain weather, her dark lowlights were fading into the rich natural hues of a cornsilk blonde, with faint, soft flowing hints of mid-season rust.

The heels of Saundra's boots lifted slightly from the floor as she leaned into the table and reached across the wide varnished tabletop planks.

"Saundra," I said, pointing at her with my remaining bottle, "I'm telling you... Mary's pies take the cake."

Saundra grinned, then continued dealing her white plates to the dozen Navajo placemats lining the sides of the long table.

She rocked back to the floor, smiled at me, then restocked her arm from the tall stack of ceramic plates on the knotted pine sidebar.

"Seriously," I said, "Of all the pies in all the world...."

"Hush," glowed Mrs. K, shuffling past my flatteries. She nestled her fresh sweet dish atop the sidebar among several aromatic contenders. "Gloria's recipe is every bit as good as mine...."

"Nonsense," chirped Gloria, "everyone knows nothing comes close to a Diamond K berry."

"Whoa," cried Lou. The balding widower was relatively new to the group. He wore oversized pants and an untucked shirt, perhaps to help mask his limp. Lou had retired into a small grove of flat-tired trailers a few miles outside of Granby. He was a likable, gregarious round fellow, who seemed to have difficulty keeping his eyes off the widow Shirl. "Are we talking about just pies," asked Lou, "or are we including cobblers and cakes? Because, if you're going to throw other desserts in with the pies...."

"If you're going to start throwing pies," I joked, "then I'd better get a bucket and mop."

"I'm just saying," said Lou, "that I'm going to have to cast my vote for Shirl's angel food. Nothing quite like it...."

Shirl fled in a fluttering blush towards the swinging double doors.

"You two," I said with a laugh. "Why don't you just get married and be done with it?" I walked the second bottle of wine to its place beside the bread basket at the table's head. "The suspense of all this unfinished love is killing me."

The award-winning filmmaker tipped his shoulder and executed a pull back, bending his knees and physically withdrawing slightly from the camera as he widened his shot. His tight leather duckbill cap fused so comfortably with his buzzed scalp that Mary never thought to ask Cary to remove it, even during prayers.

Cary pivoted around his low tripod. He finally released us from the shot, then silently panned left.

The six of us in the dining table area collectively exhaled in relief, thankful to be at last set free from Cary's probing lens. Lou followed Shirl into the kitchen to help retrieve the rest of the desserts.

Completing his 180, the director zoomed across the great room to the pensive Freak, who sat in soft lamplight on a cushioned rocker. Beyond Freak's bowed head was a window filled with distant peaks and darkening clouds. Freak's scars faced the camera, though his gaze probed deeply through the pages of his Bible. He flipped and paused somewhere past the middle, perhaps within the pages of the prophets.

The somber scene was broken only by an occasional bob, a reaching for the water goblet on the floor near his feet.

Saundra, at Freak's urging, had orchestrated this show.

A Colorado State University talk radio host had contacted Freak for permission to do a 30-minute documentary. The student's request prompted Freak to explore other options, more far-reaching venues. Through Saundra's television network connections, she hooked our ranch team up with one of the most respected independent film crews in North America.

Within a week, we'd completed and notarized a contract, a copy of which now rested in the roll top registration desk. Freak reviewed the documents with Cary, and then they stapled it inside the folder now bulging with our Sunday group's collection of signed releases.

The film company's working mandate was to answer the questions now haunting hundreds of millions of people around the world. The questions asked continuously for the past few weeks, ever since the blowing of the First Trumpet at midnight, the hour of the breakout of World War III:

"Who is this guy really...
... and how much does he really know?"

Cary's small team arrived from the East Coast and moved into the Matthew cabin on Thursday. Mary stocked their shelves with a wide range of foods, which they seemed to appreciate. But they couldn't seem to get over the fact they weren't given a set of keys for their doors.

"Look," I said, standing with Steve on their front porch, "there's not a safer place right now on the entire planet." I presented Cary with the cold six-pack from under my arm. "Isn't that right, Steve."

Steve nodded.

I pointed to the parking lot. "Do you see the weapons on that armored Huey down there? There's more firepower on that one attack helicopter than you'll find in all of Denmark's military put together."

Cary followed my gaze.

"And," I continued, sweeping my arm to cover the nearby forest, "do you see all of the Army Rangers... hiding up there in the trees? I'm telling you, these guys are vigilant and ready for anything. They're up there 24-7, locked and loaded with their assault rifles and night goggles... clinging to the branches in their flak jackets and camo fatigues."

Cary tugged on his cap. "Soldiers are hiding in the trees? I don't see any soldiers...."

"Of course not!" I said. "That's exactly my point. That's how good they are!"

Cary studied me a moment. He looked at Steve, then busted a grin.

"Fine," he laughed. "And thanks for the beer."

"Of course," I smiled. "But just don't get careless and start chucking your empties into the pines."

Once settled, Cary's team began filming immediately. They tried to capture it all.

One-on-one interviews with each of us.

Shots of meals, chores, prayer times.

Footage of Saundra working with Freak on Friday's podcast.

Coverage of a network reporter interviewing the prophet for the nightly news.

Wee Daddy's men cleaning their weapons.

Everything.

They continued roving and filming all the way into our weekly Sunday night missional community potluck. The house church gathering. The oikos.

Cary attached himself to Freak and those of us on the meal prep assignments in the main house. He busied himself covering our activities from the tripod he'd positioned at the center of the great room.

The rest of Cary's film team was dispatched to the barn. They were up in the haymow with Jack, Cal, Steve, and Ellen, along with a pair of the younger parents. The adults were playing games and rollicking with Rex and a hive of happily buzzing grandchildren and offspring. Tossing beanbags and balls and spinning laughter among the green, sweet-smelling stacks of baled hay.

Saundra closed one eye, then lowered her knees slightly away from the table.

She leaned to the right, a dinner plate still in her grip. She tilted her head to see around the back of the stooped cinematographer's shoulders. She adjusted until her line of sight was aligned with the rising trajectory, from Cary's low tripod slightly upward towards Freak's profile against the distant window and the brooding sky.

She leaned until she discovered what the cameraman had selected to see.

Then straightened. Then smiled my way.

"Nice frame," I observed, "right?"

"These guys are good," she answered. "Cary started with us over here, but he knew where he was going to go with the shot before he even began to roll. Come see."

I stepped to her side.

Saundra lowered herself again, then extended her arm and stretched a finger. I moved closer, slightly behind her. I bent and tipped a cheek until my gaze was flowing directly up Saundra's arm, from her shoulder to her wrist... and beyond.

There, past her soft cornsilk, far off from the end of her fingertip, I saw what caused her smile.

"Who would have thought..." she absently sighed.

Saundra let down her arm and started to rise.

And bumped my cheek.

"Sorry," she sputtered.

For a split second, Saundra struggled to balance.

Instinctively, I reached for an elbow. Steadied her.

"Sorry," she said again, finding her feet. She cleared her throat and gently shucked my hand. "I guess I lost track...."

I stiffened and withdrew.

"Brilliant," I sniffed, rolling my neck. "Pure genius."

My retreat gave her some distance, but her gaze dropped to the floor as she turned my way, as if to double-check the space between our boots. She returned to my eyes, faintly flushed.

"It's funny," she said, tugging a sleeve, "how I never really paid attention to the cross on Jack's sign before. I never noticed how you can see it from here, on the hill above the helicopter in the parking lot."

"It was a good call," I said, giving her another step of grace.

I casually directed Saundra's attention back to Cary, who had stopped filming and was gathering his equipment. "He's wrapping up his B-roll shots, but I'm sure something from this past couple of minutes will make it into his final edit. This is better than your run-of-the mill supplemental fill footage. He might even get a title shot from this."

I glanced again.

The maestro had lined it up perfectly.

Freak. The Bible in his lap.

And the cross on the Diamond K welcome sign beyond the window... merging into the profile of Freak's shadowed raw scars.

Henry, one of the Sunday night regulars, raised an eyebrow as I returned to the kitchen for another handful of spoons.

"Hey," asked the blue-jeaned rancher, pausing in front of his vat, "how many mouths are we feeding tonight? Are we setting up an extra table for the film crew, or what?"

I patted him on the back as I passed. "Of course," I said. I stopped in front of the silverware bins beside the sink. "Can you imagine Mary *not* demanding that they stuff their cheeks? These skinny boys are from New York City. In Mary's mind, New York is practically Europe. Mrs. K is worried they've never had an American, protein-balanced meal in their lives."

Henry looked my way. "Do you think," he worried, "they'll edit their documentary to make us all look like a bunch dim-witted hicks?"

He tested a dab of the ruby-brown sauce from his pork and beans. He smiled, tonked his wooden spoon, then lowered the heat.

I finished counting my spoons, then looked back towards the stove.

"Of course not," I assured him, "their documentary is going to include footage of Saundra and me. Not *everybody* in the film is going to look like a dim-witted hick."

Henry snapped up his spoon and shouldered it like a tiny rifle. With me in the sights.

"And how," I laughed, "could they resist including a few shots of you, Deadeye Dick, with daggers in his bloodshot eyes?"

"Right," he smiled, lowering his spoon. He wrung another splash from his fingers into the expanding collection of stains on the kitchen towel dangling from his belt. "But I'm still not sure we should have agreed to letting them film tonight's oikos meeting without getting some more guarantees... without praying it out for another week or two...."

I'd known Henry and his wife for almost as long as I'd known Mary and Jack. Some of the other members of the Diamond K Fellowship were less known to me, but the Walaces were third generation ranchers. They worked the land and raised livestock along the Colorado River a couple of ridges north of the Diamond K. Their claim to fame was the small herd of buffalo they grazed near the road.

Jack would sometimes help a few of his Diamond K guests saddle up and ride the rugged horse trails over to the neighboring Double Bar W Buffalo Ranch. Tourists and ranch guests never seemed to tire of seeing how close they could get to those shaggy black beasts on Henry's ranch. Zoom lenses not withstanding.

"Naw," I drawled, "we needed to pull the trigger on this right away. Timing is everything when it comes to getting free publicity. Freak said we needed to rush to git 'er done while we still had time." I rattled my spoons. "Like Freak likes to say, *ya gotta fry the bacon... while the grill's still hot.*"

"Right," chuckled Henry. "Now I know you're lying." He reached for a serving ladle. "Reverend Jacobs would never talk that way about hog meat."

"How so?" I asked.

"Because, when he came in here an hour ago for some water, he caught me chopping pork for the beans. I offered him a dice, and he wouldn't so much as take a second peek. He appeared almost ill... just from the smell."

Jack prayed up a dandy, then launched us into our Sunday night feast.

To make space for the film crew—and against Cary's protests—Ellen and two of the others had settled the toddlers onto benches and into highchairs around the kitchen table beyond the double doors. The giggles and cries and the gibberish from Freak's kids and the other four children provided a homey humming soundtrack from the adjacent room.

We all noticed the New York boys were hitting more on the breads and salads than on the barbecued meats. None of them complained, and we made no jokes of it. Until finally, I couldn't stand it any longer.

"Look, guys," I said, "I hope you don't take this the wrong way. But you really ought to try the ribs. How are you going to understand our table and this community if you refuse to dig in?" I added a wry wink. "I mean, if you were filming in Africa right now, you'd be giving it the old college try... trying to gulp down at least *one* of their flame-roasted grubs, right?"

Cary smiled.

"Sure," he said, glancing over his crew. "One bug-sized nibble each. I insist." He stretched his fork for a rib. "When in Rome..." he shivered, "swallow their grub." He tossed me a good-natured smirk.

"Maybe you'll thank me later," I grinned. "But whatever you do, please don't slaughter me in the edit. I made a joke about Saundra's hair once, and she retaliated by airing a shot of me puking onto my shoes."

Saundra faked a frown. "That was outside of the hospital, before we'd even met. For all I knew, you were just another ski bum who'd drunk himself witless." Her eyes twinkled. "Now that I think of it...."

"Please..." I said, faking a wound, "take into consideration the escalated level of my trauma at the time. If you'll recall, I'd recently witnessed a terrorist attack. And don't forget who I'd just pulled from the snow." I glanced Freak's way. The man of the hour was suddenly impossible to read. "Freak?" I asked, "if you'd been me, you would have tossed your cookies, too... right?"

He hesitated. Long enough to make me squirm.

"Sure," he smiled at last. "If I'd dug the bloody likes of me from six feet of snow, I'd have gotten sick, same as you." He put down his napkin. "Especially if I'd been sloshing around mountain curves at 80 mph with a half dozen beers in my belly… and not a drop of common sense between my ears." He reached for his water. "Mark, the way you drive, the biggest miracle of the year was that you didn't get us both killed on the road. The airplane explosion was nothing compared to the horrors of that ride."

Jack cleared his throat with a gentle, "Enough." He reached for the ladle rising from Henry's enormous tin pot. "No more about them grubs and vomit. Some of us are trying to enjoy these beans."

Randal, the senior of Cary's assistant cameramen, got up from the table several times throughout our meal to record a few handheld clips. Randal was a tight-pants health club specimen. His chestnut cheeks and chiseled profile bore witness to a lucky combination of unlikely genetics and expensive spa trainers.

I wanted to ask Randal to stay in his seat. To warn him about how he was destroying good conversations by befuddling the women every time he stood. But I thought better, choosing instead to focus on how little the cameraman probably grasped of the sublimated social debaucheries buried within Chaucer's great tale of the Miller's ruse.

I stole a quick peek down the table towards Saundra's end.

Yes, Saundra would understand the subtleties of British Literature; she would appreciate the ironic nuances of the Canterbury pilgrimage.

That is, if she wasn't so darned preoccupied with the sculptured hams of the visiting cameraman.

I glanced back at the crouching New Yorker. Randal was clearly comfortable in his own vigorously glowing hide. For all I knew, he held an English degree from NYU. With a minor in the British classics.

I decided to scoop more beans. To dwell on less trivial matters.

In addition to Randal's handheld work, a second camera was mounted on a tripod to my left. It recorded continuously throughout the meal, unattended, filming with Freak anchored at the high end of the frame. Four microphones were positioned around and over our gathering, inches above the line of sight.

Shannon, the sound and lighting technician, stood once or twice, as if to check on his equipment, then immediately sat down. He nodded and politely smiled a few times, but he lowered his head into his hands off and on throughout the meal, until we all were certain something was wrong.

As we approached desserts, I caught Freak's attention and tipped my head towards the troubled guest. Freak floated back a quick acknowledgment, then flicked me an inconspicuous thumbs up.

After the meal, during cleanup, Cal reached for his guitar from beside the hearth.

Cal was immediately joined by Rhonda, a twenty-something waitress from Kremmling. Rhonda was lovely and sweet—in a country sort of way—and she really seemed to enjoy strumming, harmonizing, and bumping knees with Cal. She also happened to be surprisingly good on the mandolin.

Henry soon sidled in among the birds, positioning himself behind their shoulders on a low stool. Within a few measures, he was confirming their buoyant rhythms with a cheerful banter of whacks and taps upon his thigh-held drums.

The rest of us finished in the dining area and the kitchen. One-by-one, we joined the music in the great room's transformed landscape of orbiting couches and chairs.

"Ellen," said Mary, "you need a break. Let me herd the kids into the sunroom. I'll put in a Veggie Tales video and close the door. Let me babysit, and you can forget about them for a couple of hours. I insist."

The prophet's wife smiled a thanks.

Meanwhile, the film crew continued to wrangle their equipment from the dining area over into our gathered community space. They were creating a fresh gangly outer ring of lights, cameras and mics.

"Our huddle," I laughed, "is starting to feel like a fishbowl."

Steve took the bait.

"A goldfish," he grinned, motioning towards Saundra.

"Guppy," I said, waving at Lou.

"Starfish," said Steve, nodding at Freak.

"Trout," I countered, tipping towards Cal.

"Tuna," he said, squatting forward, with Jack in his sights.

I pointed towards my roommate's belly and bowed knees. "Frog," I chuckled.

Jack lifted his head and stared over his reading glasses. "Enough," he frowned. The rancher adjusted his glasses, then returned to flipping through his Bible, stopping here and there where he'd placed stickies and notes.

I leaned towards Steve, then gestured towards Jack. "Shamu," I whispered. "Shamu, *not* tuna. Game over. I win."

"Blowfish," he coughed.

I coughed back and settled for a draw.

In recent years, I'd never stuck around on Sunday nights, so this was only my third oikos gathering. But I'd already learned all of their names. It surprised me to realize how comfortable I felt with this group. As the last of the couch cushions and chairs filled with stragglers from the bathroom and kitchen, I swapped a few lines and tapped my foot to the background tunes of Cal, Rhonda and Hank.

Saundra appeared mesmerized by Cary, studying the director's bustling preparations, and how he handled his team. I followed her gaze.

Cary and Randal already had two fixed cameras positioned, while Shannon struggled to finish plugging together his soundboard with the last of his booms. The youngest member of the crew, a stringy gaffer whose name I'd not yet found the trick to remember, stepped over to help Shannon untangle some cords from a shotgun mic. The young man put a hand on Shannon's shoulder, then looked to Cary with concern.

Cary took Shannon aside for a brief whisper.

And perhaps to slip him a few pills.

Eventually, everything was in place, and we were ready to begin.

41
FOOD FOR THE SOUL

"Pretend like we're not even here," Cary smiled, tapping the bill of his cap.

He stepped behind his tripod, then signaled to his crew. A couple lights came up, a boom swung a few inches, and his team immediately began to record.

"Sorry," said Jack. "But it doesn't work that way."

"Huh?" Cary poked his head around his camera. "What do you mean?"

"I may host these gatherings, but I don't run the show."

"I still don't follow." Cary stepped to his camera's side. "Is Freak in charge then, or what? I thought we'd agreed for this to work, we'd all need to...."

"Right," replied Jack. "For this to work, we agreed upon no acting. No faking. No staged lines." He swept a gaze around Cary's crew. "Go ahead and keep recording. We've begun. But don't assume for a moment we can ignore the reality of each of you being here."

Henry hit a quick thump-da-thump-*thump* on his bongos. "Gentlemen," he laughed, "you are all now officially into something—shall we say—way over your heads."

Because of the floods and gels, it was hard to clearly see some of their expressions. But at least two of Cary's men were obviously nervously shifting from left to right.

"Listen," I said, addressing their fears. "Lighten up. These church folks are not some sort of hillbilly cult militia. Really. Just because they like to shoot wild animals and butcher cows, I promise... they're not planning to mount or stuff any of you... let alone to pack you into the huge coffin freezer they keep in the cellar." I winked at Steve. "That would be ridiculous, right?"

Randal frowned.

The gaffer glanced at the picture window, which had become a huge night mirror beyond Freak's scars. His eyes flashed around the room. His gaze stopped short on a few of the antler racks and game trophies mounted upon the walls. He turned back to Cary with a shrug, perhaps realizing for the first time how far they were from New York's Finest.

"Come on," I laughed, "I'm just messing with you."

Saundra glared. "Don't listen to Mark," she said. "Sometimes he just gets that way."

"Of course," smiled Cary. "There's always a Mark." He turned to Jack. "But what did you mean... about *you* not being in charge? This is your group, isn't it?"

"It's the Lord's group," answered Jack. "It's *his* meeting. We merely try to listen... and to obey. God is in charge. Not Freak. Not me. The Holy Spirit."

"But you told me you have a lesson or something to teach tonight, right?"

"Sure. Plus some prayer items and a few worship songs we'll probably sing. But we might never get there." Jack looked back at Cary's team. "You all need to feel free to ask questions. Whenever we have guests, folks interrupt with questions all the time. That's how we roll. Often, our best meetings are when those questions become the agenda. And you need to feel free to challenge anything you hear. Anything less, and your footage here tonight will be a fraud. Understood?"

Jack refused to budge until he had collected from each of them some sort of reluctant consent.

We did sing a few songs.

Jack's planned teaching, though, was bumped to another week.

Once Cary and his team settled into their roles as participant-observers, the meeting took off in a whole different direction.

Things got frisky.

The boys from New York flexed their knuckles.

"So," said Cary, "you're saying I live by hope and faith every single day, even though I'll swear on my mother's cookbook I don't believe in God?"

"Yes and no. It's complicated." Jack sipped from his water. "We blur words like trust and belief with the word *faith*, but for a Christian, there's a kind of faith that is much bigger...."

"Faith," said Shirl, "is everything."

Randal swung his camera towards Shirl, but when it became clear she had nothing to add, he followed Cary's eyes and tracked over to Freak.

Cary pressed, adding an edge to his voice. "Reverend Jacobs, you folks here on the ranch have got it made. Great food, beautiful scenery, friendships. Meanwhile, you're preaching to the rest of the world that we're all going to end up in hell. According to you, the rest of us have got nothing to look forward to but more and more suffering... ending in our own total annihilation."

"Always," said Freak, "there is hope." He looked at Shannon. "Even in the midst of suffering, there can be Grace. For each of us, from the first miracle of our conception, until the last miracle of our passing from this life to the next... there is always hope... always the possibility of more miracles... more mercy...."

"Riddles," shrugged Cary. "Your opinions are pretty hard to take."

"First," said Freak, his tone not at all defensive, "I speak here of more than mere opinions. These are facts. As I once told Mark, to the person who says everything is a matter of personal preferences, I say: *tell that to gravity*."

Freak tapped his scars.

"Second," he continued, "it is an inaccurate and unfair characterization of my position to say I believe all of the world will suffer and go to hell while I hide out above it all at a mountain retreat. I have already experienced a good measure of suffering, and I am certain there is more suffering for me yet to come."

"Pardon me," said Shannon, "but I find your message a real downer. You speak of hope, but I'm just not seeing it."

"For you, Shannon—for everyone—the possibilities for miracles and Grace will exist until the very last moment of the final hour. But it takes obedience to live into these realities. It takes faith to appropriate the miracles of Grace."

"Again," said Cary, "you're losing me."

Jack cleared his throat. "Guys, if you're going to come away with anything from your week here on the ranch, then it'd better be an understanding of what faith means to our community. Faith defines and drives everything we do at the Diamond K."

"Go on," said Cary. "What does faith mean to you?"

Jack looked at Freak. "Help me out here, Bill. I like the way you describe it when you talk about the diving board."

"Some people," said Freak, "think faith is like jumping off a high dive at the pool."

"I suppose," said Cary. "That makes sense. But...."

"But," interrupted Freak, "such a definition is wrong. Jumping off a high dive takes *courage*. Not faith. If you've ever been around a pool, then you've seen others dive. You've learned how the water can smack and sting, but you know even a belly flop won't kill you. *Courage* is trusting the water, which is seen... trusting in resources and skills that are tangible and known."

Randal lifted his head from behind his camera's display. "Then what's faith?"

"Faith," said Freak, "is diving into the same pool... except this time, when you look down from the board... all you see is dry concrete. No water. Not a single drop."

"Who in their right mind...?" sputtered Shannon. "A person would have to be crazy to jump into anything under those conditions."

"Maybe," said Freak.

Freak waited until Shannon leaned forward, perturbed, demanding the prophet to continue.

"But," posed Freak, "what if you believed in a powerful God? A God who could do the seemingly impossible? And what if you believed God had specifically asked you to trust him... and to jump, despite what you fear might happen? What if you hear the Lord saying, 'Let me worry about the water'?"

"There," Randal blurted. "This is exactly why you religious people are so dangerous." He leveled a finger. "You know you sound crazy when you talk like that, right?"

"Yes," nodded Freak. "And your concern is well based. Some people do crazy things in the name of faith. And that is precisely why faith generally needs to be discerned and worked out within the context of a mature community. Like what you see here tonight. If our friend, Steve," Freak pointed, "if Steve showed up at oikos one night and said God told him to jump off a cliff, then we'd all have to have a good talk with him. And we'd all have to pray together, and to listen to what God might *really* be saying."

I laughed. "For example, God might be telling our community it is time for us to strong-arm Steve into getting back onto his daily medications."

Steve chuckled.

From beside Shirl on the couch, Lou squinted at Steve. Lou's voice suddenly cracked with concern. "Steve, are you...?"

"Not to worry," laughed Steve, holding up a hand. "I'm still on my meds."

Lou slumped back with a sigh. Then scratched his head.

"As I said," resumed Freak, "with a little prayer and care, our community would probably be able to talk Steve out of his dive."

Randal glanced back through his camera. "It's your *probably*," he muttered, "that worries me."

Steve gestured in agreement. "But what if I refused to be dissuaded? What if I refused to let you talk me out of making my leap of faith?"

"Well," I grinned, "as they say, faith sometimes gets messy. Literally."

Shannon nearly exploded. "How can you joke about what he said! We're talking about a guy dying. This stuff is life and death...."

"Everything," said Freak, "is life and death. The stakes are higher than you think... for every choice we make."

"Fruitcakes," Randal frowned. "The world is going to be *sooo* much better when we finally outgrow religion...."

I looked at Cary. The director's eyes were alert, darting, monitoring the unusual interaction between his crew and the subjects of their assignment. With some careful editing, he'd harvest some engaging clips for sure.

Saundra stirred. "It's not fair," she said, "to assume the world will be better off without Christianity." She met Randal's stare. "I'm sure you know that Hitler's Germany had abandoned traditional Christianity to pursue their vision of a better humanity without the constraints of almost everything Jesus ever taught or stood for, right?"

She cautiously glanced at Cary, then back to Randal. "Forget about the millions of deaths in China and North Korea, because accurate records from those nations are pretty hard to confirm. But we do know Stalin was an atheist. In terms of sheer numbers, the horrors he 'accomplished' in thirty years were beyond anything in the history of our planet. Together with his Christ-rejecting Soviet cohorts, somewhere around 50,000,000 people were killed...."

"Fine," Randal snapped. "What's your point?"

"*Sooo*," said Saundra, "my point is *not* that atheists are worse than Christians, but rather, that humans can be awful. People can be terrible, no matter what they profess they do or don't believe. It's just plain naive to think if we move away from Christianity, then somehow the world will be less wicked and more humane. History proves otherwise."

Cary cleared his throat. "Jack, is this what you do every week? Argue about religion for two hours?"

"Of course not," replied the big rancher. "But this week is special." He smiled. "Then again, every week is special. We take it as the Lord brings it."

Shannon shook his head. "Back to the swimming pool. Finish your simile, pastor. How is faith like diving into an empty pool?"

Freak lowered his glass. "As I said, it takes only courage to leap into water. After a few jumps, then even the need for courage diminishes. Diving becomes fun and easy."

Freak took a deep breath. "On the other hand, despite what some people teach... true faith is seldom—if ever—something that feels *fun and easy* at the time you must step out and test that faith."

We waited.

"Faith," he said at last, "is when you think you know what God wants you to do. And then you do it... even when you are unable to see for sure what might happen next. If you complain to God about not seeing any water in the pool, then God answers, 'You just jump. I've got this covered. Water is one of my specialties.' To hear and obey God, with something to lose and so much unseen... it can be brutal."

"Sane people," muttered Randal again, "do *not* jump into empty pools."

Freak sighed. "It's a metaphor, Randal. But that's exactly how it sometimes feels when you have to step out in faith."

"Please," probed Cary, signaling for Randal to zoom, "give us an example that makes more sense... if faith can even make sense in the first place."

Freak leaned back. "The classic list of examples of faith is found in the Bible, in the book of Hebrews, chapter 11. The list includes people like Noah, who built an ark under clear skies in anticipation of a flood still many years beyond the horizon. And Rahab, who risked her life in Jericho to save some Jewish spies. Rahab makes for a great story, by the way. Adventure, intrigue, sex, war.... And a happy ending. The world eventually got it's greatest king out that one. Check out Matthew 1:5 to see what I mean."

Gloria winked. Saundra tugged on her shirt sleeve.

"My favorite," continued Freak, "is Abraham. Here we have a guy who left a comfortable life for a dangerous country he'd never seen. God told him to act, and Abraham did. He jumped into an empty pool. But if you read the story, you discover Abraham never saw the pool fill up before he hit. I guess you could say God only gave him about ten inches of water. He basically smacked. Abraham was promised millions of descendants, but he only lived to see it starting to come together at the end of his life. He only ever saw a few... the rest remained unseen. Faith is like that sometimes. God tells us to do something, and we never really see the *how*... nor the final outcome... let alone the why."

"Fine," said Cary, gently gesturing for Freak to continue. "But what about *you*, Reverend Jacobs? For most of us, the Bible is pretty abstract. Make it more real."

"Real?"

"Give us," pressed Cary, "an example from your own life. What has faith meant to you? What does faith look like... in the midst of the risks and chaos of the real world?"

Freak considered the question.

"A number of times in my life," he said, "I've been like the Bible prophet Elisha. I've felt God calling me to leave a productive farm and to follow unknown paths by faith. I felt called by God to burn my plow and slaughter my oxen for a meal... so there was no way I could return to what I'd been doing if things didn't work out. For example, I cashed out my family inheritance in order to purchase television time for my first season of preaching broadcasts."

Freak squeezed Ellen's knee. She met his gaze, then sheepishly looked away.

Randal shifted behind his camera. "I'm sure that was difficult, but most of us can hardly imagine a family inheritance in the first place. I don't mean to sound harsh, but to my ears, investing a little free money on a long shot business gamble is hardly like diving into an empty pool. Is that the best you've got?"

Freak studied him. Sipped from his water.

"There are those," he said at last, putting down his empty glass, "who hate me because, in faith, I'm speaking out about the End of Days, risking everything to say what God is calling me to say. There are people—and powers— who despise my presumption to speak for the Lord. Even now, there is a conspiracy rising... to bring me down if I refuse to stop preaching.... They *all* want me silenced. They all want me dead...."

His voice trailed off.

The room grew uncomfortably still.

Saundra started to clear her throat, then stopped.

From the sunroom floated the faint riff of a Veggie Tales tune.

Finally, Randal broke the fragile quiet.

"They all want you dead?" challenged Randal. "Jitters and butterflies like that could be viewed—at least by some people—as a little bit paranoid... don't you think? Conspiracy theories and delusions seem to be the stock and trade of almost every street preacher when it comes to the End of Days...."

I caught myself in a scoff. Several heads turned in my direction. I licked my lips and tried to let it go, but found that I couldn't.

They waited as I took a moment to find my voice.

"Randal," I said, my jaw tight, "you are probably a very bright fellow back in New York, in your studio." He met my eyes. "But the next time you leave the city and tromp onto someone else's turf... do your damn homework... or shut your damn mouth."

Several of the women gasped.

Randal's expression froze.

Saundra, Steve and Freak held steady.

They'd been there.

At the lodge.

And at the tree.

Cary coughed. "Randal," he apologized, "is a good man. He's just doing his job... he's just fishing for good footage. Jack told us we should freely challenge and engage...."

"You asked," said Freak, "what faith means to me today. As always, it comes down to making choices. Deciding whether to listen. And whether or not to leap...."

Freak's attention moved around the room. "For the time being," he said, "I am protected. As Cary put it, I've got it made. The courageous soldiers outside have set up a perimeter of technology and deadly weapons." He spread his hands. "Also, we enjoy the protection of the unseen guards. The Lord has provided a squad of mighty angels, spiritual warriors who've been assigned to each of us... and to this ranch."

He looked at Jack. "This community. Your prayers. I find myself secure in a fortress of warriors and friends. Staying here requires no courage. And no faith."

He looked back to Cary.

"But... soon... I must leave this fortress."

"And that," said Freak, turning to me, "will be my dive into an empty pool."

42

OF MIRACLES AND MEN

"Sorry," I said, my voice low. "I guess I sort of snapped."

Randal shifted awkwardly. "My mistake," he murmured, pretending to tighten a knob on his tripod. Avoiding my eyes. "I wasn't thinking about your girlfriend... about the attack at the lodge."

"It's okay," I replied. "I've got to get used to people not knowing. It's been a while, and not everybody will have heard about all of the stuff Freak and I have been through together in the past month."

We were beyond earshot of the others, who were using the ten minute break to grab snacks. To refresh their glasses and use the bathrooms. To light a few candles and to dim the overheads. Only Freak had not stirred from his chair.

Only Freak remained in his seat, faintly rocking already, waiting for us to return for a time of closing prayers.

"Anyway," I said, "I'm good... if you're good?"

"We're good," said Randal. He met my eyes. "It took me a minute, but I think I now understand. For you, it's probably like it was for a lot of us New Yorkers after 9/11. I was pretty young, but I still remember how people who'd never been anywhere near the rubble and the ashes of Ground Zero would pop off, trying to tell us how we should feel, and what we should think. That everything was okay. But we knew better...."

I heard a bathroom door open. "Hang on," said Randal. "I'd better use the restroom before we get restarted."

"I've got a list," said Jack, "of some stuff we're going to pray through tonight before we end." He made an effort to connect with the film team. "But, as always, anything the Lord raises up is fair game. We can pray for anything the Spirit brings to mind. You guys are free to join us. Or to make any special requests."

Several of the Diamond K regulars smiled and nodded enthusiastically.

Gloria rolled forward on the couch. "We'd love to pray for you," she said. "Is there anything we can lift up to the Lord... any special concerns... or thanksgivings?"

The guys were shifting again, looking around the room.

"Gentlemen," said Jack, addressing the director, "we've got to go back to what I said before. We might end up praying for you. We cannot pretend you're not here."

Cary nodded. "We get it." His voice wavered for the first time since they'd arrived.

"It's okay," continued Jack, "if you want to record our time of prayer. In fact, Freak told me he is certain God *wants* you to record this. Are you going to be able to get what you need with the lighting this low?"

"We'll be fine," said Cary. "Just do your thing."

Jack smiled. "Okay, then. Each week before we pray, we always remind each other of a few things... whatever the Lord puts on our hearts. That sets a good tone for our prayers, and then we try to pray as the Lord leads. Anyone?"

Henry half-lifted a hand. "Prayer is talking to God... and God encourages us to call him Father when we pray."

"Prayer," said Gloria, "is a conversation with the Lord. It should be both talking... and listening."

Rhonda reached over and squeezed Cal's hand. "Jesus liked to pray with his friends. Lots of his prayers were community experiences... where he said things like, '*our* Father,' and 'give to *us* our daily bread.' There is a special blessing when we pray together... in unity."

"Good," said Jack. "And you all know my favorite. Every week, I like to remind us that when Jesus taught us to pray, he said we should mention that we want God's Kingdom to come to earth... for his presence to be among us, as it is in heaven." He touched his heart. "For the love of the King. Anyone else?" Jack waited a moment. "Okay, then... let's pray." And they began.

It was pretty standard stuff. Not too formal. Heartfelt. People taking turns.

And then, ten minutes into the flow, the wind changed.

"Lord," prayed Freak, "I think I'm hearing something. Please confirm if you want us to go in that direction."

After a moment, Gloria's voice broke the silence.

"*New York*," said Gloria. "The Spirit is asking us to pray for our guest... for Shannon... for him to be healed."

I cracked an eyelid long enough to observe Freak and Shannon locked in on each other. I wasn't sure how it might look on film—if they caught me staring—so I half-squinted back closed. For the next couple minutes, I tried to not turn my head too much between them, until I finally gave up and let myself watch it all play out, eyes wide open. No longer caring what anybody might think.

"Within the Kingdom of God," prayed Freak, "there is no sickness. No death. Thank you, Jesus, because you brought your Kingdom to Earth. Thank you for teaching us to boldly pray for your Kingdom to be among us."

"Thank you," whispered Ellen, from near Freak's side. "Thank you, Jesus, for your power to heal."

"In the Kingdom of God," Freak prayed again, "your name is honored... your power is seen, and your love is known by every living creature."

"Thank you," said Gloria. Her subdued praise was so charged that my hair tingled at the base of my neck.

"Tumors," said Freak, his voice definitive, "are of this *broken* world." He stretched a hand. "Shannon," he urged, "would you like to experience the *restoration* found in the Kingdom of God?"

Freak gestured. "Shannon, are you ready to be healed?"

The next 10 minutes were intense.

Shannon got angry, but he stayed engaged.

There were prayers, and lots of passion. I was surprised by Freak's wife, Ellen, who really got into it. She was the first to slip into tongues. To weep. To hum.

Once Shannon said yes, his migraine-like symptoms abated almost immediately.

His inoperable brain tumor took a little longer.

"You know," objected Shannon, "I don't believe in any of this...."

"God loves you," whispered Freak, touching Shannon's forehead. "It's a gift. No strings attached. The Lord wants you to be healed."

"I don't want religion," said Shannon. "I don't want your rules. I've been learning how to stop fighting my fate, to make my peace. I'm ready to die."

Freak pulled his hand from Shannon's brow.

"You're ready to die?" he asked. "Really?"

"I've accepted my destiny," he softened. "Sooner or later, we all die. I promised Cary to help him with this one last project. Colorado was always on my bucket list. After this... that's it."

People were quietly swaying around the circle. Some with closed eyes, others not.

Ellen began rocking, gently waving her hand and humming the refrain from one of her ancient hymns.

Freak gently reached again. He cupped Shannon's head.

"Soon enough," said Freak, "every man, woman and child on Earth will face the Lord. Don't spit at God's Grace... with your meeting so close at hand. Trust him. Accept his gift. It is a sign for you." He paused. "And for the world."

"For the world?"

"For you," cooed Freak, "and for those who do not yet believe. There are those who will see and hear... and they will find hope. They will come to believe the Lord is mighty to save." Freak asked again, his tone commanding. "Shannon, will you receive?"

"What am I supposed to do?"

"There's a relationship between receiving and faith."

Freak began gently stroking behind Shannon's head, from his spine upwards. Towards the sky.

"To receive from the King," said Freak, "is an act of trust. It is to have faith that there is no poison in the Master's wine. Will you receive the cup of blessing? Will you drink deeply from the King's cup?"

"Yes," shuddered Shannon.

And then he was healed.

Cary's team was confused, torn between filming and huddling around their friend.

Shannon spoke in a cascade of tumbling images. Recounting about a heat surging through his skull... and of a sudden, crisp release.

There was no doubt in his mind something happened.

Something which he insisted would be confirmed by lab tests when they returned to New York.

I approached Cary and Saundra, standing at the side.

"Saundra," said the director, "you're a trained professional. How can you be so certain?"

She rotated from Cary to meet my gaze. "You felt it, Mark... didn't you?"

"Sure," I grinned, stopping as close as an uninvited guest might dare. "Nobody knows how to heat up a prayer meeting like our friend, Freak."

"So," Cary asked, shifting to me, "you're supposed to be his *wingman* or something. You've been around him from the start. Do you agree with Saundra? Was Shannon healed? Did we witness... did we just record a supernatural event on film?"

"It's not," I shrugged, "like Freak has never cured cancer before. You heard about the preacher over in Summit County, right?"

"Yes, we've done some background work on the Reverend Gilford. We'll be heading over to Silverthorne on Tuesday. We've got an interview scheduled that same day with Kristen—the woman with the web site—as well."

"Gotta love Krissy's new poster," I said, recreating it in the air with my hands. *"End of the World? Ask Freak!"*

Cary tugged his cap. "So, Saundra... if the lab results are clear, would you call this a documented miracle... or not? I'm still trying to wrap my head around what happened a few minutes ago. Trying to decide if I can even include this footage in my film...."

She smiled. "You're the director. You know Shannon. It's your call."

"The industry," he sighed, "insists it is bad journalism when a filming crew crosses the line... when reporters start becoming their own story. This could destroy my reputation."

"Welcome," said Saundra, "to the club. Steve and I had to cross that line a long time ago. But it's not like we had any choice about it." She patted Cary's sleeve. "Apparently, neither do you."

Cary withdrew his arm. "We've always got a choice. Of course we can edit ourselves out of this story... if that's what we need to do."

"A choice?" I shook my head. "Good luck with that." I felt my stomach suddenly in a churn. I glanced across the room. Freak and Jack were whispering, studying the bachelor Lou.

Cary waited.

"You have only been around him," I said, taking a breath, "for a few days. But even *you* can see something is going on here...."

"And?"

"And... I'm not sure anyone gets to stand on the sidelines anymore."

My neck grew hot. I watched as Jack stepped away from Freak and disappeared up the stairs to the loft.

"According to Freak," I said, turning back to Cary, "from now on, nobody gets to sit and watch."

Cary started to object. He was interrupted by a small commotion over by Freak.

"Get your camera rolling," I sighed. "If you're going to be hanging around the Freak, then you're going to have to learn... it ain't over... till it's over."

Randal had already found a good angle. The gaffer was repositioning a boom. Shannon was observing, listening carefully, swaying in with the others who were gathering into a tight huddle.

"Lou," said Freak. "In heaven, old wounds are healed. How about that limp of yours? Show me where it hurts."

Lou hesitated. He straightened his shoulders away from Shirl, then tipped a few inches sideways. "Here," he said, touching his upper hip. "And down to right there...." He slid the heel of his palm down to his outer knee.

Lou leaned back upright, self-consciously, then began to fidget. His eyes darted from Freak to Shirl, and then to the film crew bobbing and circling his couch.

Freak nodded. "The King is coming," he said. "The Lord of heaven and Earth wants the world to know he is on the move. Grace and Truth abound."

Ellen rustled with an *Amen.*

Cary was already tracking in tight from his tripod. Randal was back with a wider shot, hand held, over Freak's shoulder, Lou opposite, uncertain.

"Lou," asked Freak, "would you like to be healed? Will you receive this gift from the King?"

The balding bachelor grasped his paunch with his left hand, breathing hard. "Yes," he said at last, his other hand reaching to clutch his knee, "I would like to be healed."

Freak moved forward, receiving from Jack's outstretched hand a small bottle of anointing oil. Freak uncorked, then lifted the little vial.

"In the Bible," said Freak, "instructions are given in James 5:11 for God's leaders to pray for healing. We are told to anoint the sick with oil in the name of the Lord. May I anoint you, Lou, in the name of the Lord? And may I lay hands upon your limp?"

Lou indicated permission.

"Nothing magical," said Freak, his voice low. "There is no witchcraft or alchemy in this bottle. The oil came from the kitchen cupboard. It's the same olive oil Mary uses for cooking. It was poured into this little ordinary bottle and prayed over in the prayer loft... in order to be set aside—consecrated—for healing. But we do not believe in superstition and magic. We believe in the power of the

Lord. We simply use oil as a physical symbol to represent the Holy Spirit. This oil symbolizes the power King Jesus provides, to soothe, to comfort… and to heal."

Freak placed his fingertip on the open vial's top, then tipped it for a healthy dab.

"Lou," he asked again, "do you receive the healing of the Lord?"

"Yes," said Lou, his voice quivering.

"Then," Freak continued, "I anoint you…" he slowly marked Lou's forehead with a glistening wet cross, "in the name of the Father… and the Son… and the Holy Spirit."

Upon the word *Spirit*, Lou shuddered.

Lou squeezed his eyes and trembled. "It's hot," he whispered, eyes still pinched. "But it's icy, too."

Freak withdrew his finger, then floated the same hand down to Lou's hip.

"Sickness and death," Freak declared, "I curse you in the name of the Lord Jesus Christ. In the name of the Father's Kingdom… through the power of the Holy Spirit… be gone!" He gave Lou's joint a firm smack.

Freak's hand slid down to Lou's knee.

"Flesh and blood," he said, staring at Lou's leg, "bone and sinew… you are of the King. I speak the resurrection power of Jesus Christ into your disobedience. I command restoration and life into you… in the name of the Father, the Son, and the Holy Spirit. Be healed!"

The leg jerked.

True to form, Saundra later insisted she observed a white flash.

She recalled catching a quick glimmer, a lightning bolt of sorts, supposedly entering Lou's forehead through the mark of the cross, then enveloping his body... then flaring around his hip and knee.

For my part, I might have felt a little whip of heat. Maybe not. It could have been my nerves. Perhaps the power of suggestion. Who knows.

Anyway, a minute later, Shirl was weeping, and Lou was dancing around the big room, hopping on both legs like a teenager at his first kegger.

With no limp.

It all made for great cinematographic storytelling. Lots of "Praise Jesus" and "Hallelujah" yelping. All of the usual sorts of hugs and shows of thanks and tears.

Cary and his team stayed at it, trying to capture what they could of the theatrics. Trying off-and-on at the same time to calm Shannon and to process with their friend what had happened to him as well.

Almost as an afterthought, Freak stepped to where I leaned by the kitchen door.

"It's time," he said, his eyes piercing.

"For what?"

"John," he whispered, "in God's Kingdom, there are no Dark Riders."

"*Mark*," I corrected him.

"John," he said again, "in the Kingdom, there is no shame and guilt. Mark, would you like to be delivered tonight... to finally be set free?"

I studied him. Hard.

"With all these cameras," I said at last, "you're getting a little full of yourself, eh?"

"Full of the *Spirit*," he grinned. "I can feel the power. And I can feel your pain... your internal struggle. You've got something in your past... a death. You've never let go. And the Riders... the bondage of the enemy...."

"What," I asked, "are you trying to do?"

"You know," he smiled, his lips smug. "You know."

"Forget it," I said. "I'm not your dog."

"Steady," he whispered, stretching for my arm.

"Just like that?" I asked, pulling away. "You think you're going to fix me and solve all of my problems with two dabs of olive oil and a couple of stupid prayers?"

He reached for me again, this time catching my wrist. I didn't want to make a scene, but his grip was surprisingly firm. He was leading me away from my wall. I tugged against his insistence, resisting as best I could short of becoming violent.

Sharp waves and tiny silver spasms began shooting up my spine, into my eyes.

Saundra stopped clapping to the music in the other room. Began drifting our way.

"Freak," I shrugged, "Thanks for the offer, but...."

Others were sensing something. Were shushing. Even the fat bachelor had finally stopped dancing. Now it was Lou, making his way over towards me.

My turn to make monkey faces and to sob into my hands for all of the world to see.

"*John*," Freak urged, "the Lord wants to do this... to set you free from...."

"My name," I nearly spat, "is *not* John."

Randal smelled the blood and sensed Freak calling for an extreme tight zoom.

Cary was back behind his tripod, a seasoned navy gunner, with me in his sights. The gaffer swung a boom nearly into my face.

"No more Dark Riders," repeated Freak. "No more guilt. No more haunting memories. No more shame...."

I felt a choking within my throat. Could hardly breathe. I glanced left, then right, confirming that the others were coagulating. They were closing around me in a tightening tourniquet.

Freak's voice grew husky. "Deliverance, Mark... you can be set free. Right now. The Lord wants this for you. To expose the secrets and the enemy in all his lies. To expel the Dark Riders in all their filth...." His lips were almost to my ear. "Say the word...."

Maybe the prophet should have leaned in from the other side.

From where I stood, all I could see was cameras... and Freak's rotting pink scars barely inches from my nose.

I pushed him off with a single hard shove.

"Stop it!" The words left my throat in an almost growl. "I didn't invite you into my grill. Now leave me alone."

"Mark!" Freak recoiled. He glanced at Cary, then over at the probing shotgun mic. "Don't be selfish, Mark," he said, dropping his voice. "This is bigger than you. We *need* to do this... so others may see and believe. This is for the world." His voice swelled. "You *must* know it's time for this to end...."

"Exactly... now *stop!*" I shook. "Enough of this Freak-show circus nonsense."

"Get ahold of yourself," he implored, eyes darting towards the nearest lens.

I lifted a fist. "Screw the cameras! Screw the world. I'm sick of all your presumption and arrogance. Now back off, Freak."

"*Mark....*"

"*No*, damn it!"

He froze. They all froze.

"Listen, Jacobs," I accused, "if you've got such a sizzling hand tonight, then why don't you go play some poker? Better yet, why don't you lay your red-hot hand right *here*."

I raised my hand and slapped the left side of my face... the place where Freak wore his marbled pink pride. "If you're going to play Hollywood, how about if you play with yourself for a change?"

"Please," pleaded Freak, "the Lord is ready right now to...."

"To nothing." I cruelly slapped my face again. "End it, Freak. Prove to everyone once and for all. On film. Wipe your own filth from your own mangled self...."

I heard mutterings and sobbings from the sides, but I couldn't stop.

"Physician..." I demanded, "heal thyself!"

"Mark!" It was Jack. He pressed forward, ready to take me down.

"Sorry, Jack," I said, holding him off with a raised arm. "I'm out of here." I turned back to Freak. "But seriously, Jacobs, clean yourself up, and then we'll talk."

Ellen convulsed. Freak straightened, rising to his full height.

"Some wounds," he intoned, "are meant to be carried...."

"*You* carry *your* wounds, Freak..." I countered, rising, stepping to meet his face, "and I'll carry *mine*."

I jabbed a fingertip into his chest. "Go to hell."

With that, I whirled and stormed for the door.

CINDERS

"Not pretty," sighed Steve.

I took another shallow hit from the amber bottle.

"Not pretty," I agreed. "Did I actually tell him to go to hell... on camera? What an idiot. What a train wreck...."

Steve swirled his tall glass. "You should have seen Saundra's face. It was pitiful. After you left, she started crying. I think she had mascara streaks all the way down her neck." He emptied what was left, then reached for another beer. "She was still crying when I left. In the kitchen, with Mrs. K...."

I tossed him the bottle opener. "If you're trying to make me feel better, it's not working."

Steve looked at the brewery's churchkey, but made no move to use it.

We'd been sitting for a while. The cabin was warm, the fireplace hot, but I couldn't shake the chill. Probably too many frosty long necks.

"Sometimes," I said, "junk just gushes out of my mouth. I don't even know where it comes from... it's not who I want to be." I started to tip my beer, then lowered it without a taste. "What a jerk."

"You... or Freak?"

"Exactly," I grinned. I tabled my IPA, then slowly stood to select another split log. More fuel for the flickering hearth. "That's what I'm talking about. A real moron... hopeless."

Through the window, I could see a single yellow light dimly glowing in the front room of the Ruth cabin next door. Beyond Freak's window, darkness all the way down the cabin row to the big porch light of the distant main house. Blackness into the forest and everywhere else. Nothing in the sky but a clouded shroud of ominous abyss.

I dug for a heavy log, groping for one with dry bark. Better for a quick start and slow burn. I tonged out an old charred remnant, stirred it from the ashes, then used the poker to roll and nest my addition among the embers. I leaned in, deep into the glowing hot hearthstones, blowing lightly where I saw life. A few snapping pops and cinder sparks later, the bark caught, my cheeks singed, and I ran out of tasks for the fussing.

"Steve," I said, slinking back into my chair, my eyes raw and blinking, "I'm hopeless."

My watery gaze panned around the cabin. The LED digits of the clock on the shelf beside my bed pulsed with each damping blink of my lids. Dirty socks were piled low, neglected, biding time for a Monday wash they'd probably miss. Across the room, an improvised pine table workstation awaited, its surface cluttered with stained mugs, pencils, and a notepad littered with the latest of my random scribbles.

Closed, charging beside the pad, rested the laptop Saundra had loaned me from Channel 5, their mobile unit's electronic stash.

My memoir days were over. I could see that.

So much for the good life.

I would need to return Saundra's computer in the morning... on my way out.

Freak should have given Saundra the project in the first place. It'd been interesting for me at times, remembering, trying to put things into words. But it had also been slow, and sometimes embarrassingly painful. I'd leave Saundra what was there. I'd let her decide what to erase after I was gone. But with my beastie dead and buried, what would I drive....

"Hey," asked Steve, forcing me to refocus, "do you think Cary will use the footage of you and Freak... of your little... misunderstanding?"

"Misunderstanding? Is *that* what that was?" I tried to laugh. "To be honest, I think we *do* understand each other... and all too well."

"So, do you think they'll keep the footage, or not?"

"Who knows. We all signed over our legal recourse the moment we submitted our notarized forms. It's Cary's call." I noticed the cap still on Steve's bottle. "I guess what Cary decides might boil down to how things work out for Shannon. On what the test results show when they return to New York in a few days. Those results will probably tip him one way or another on how he wants his film to play. Positive press for Freak... or an investigative exposé on an End-Times charlatan."

"Right."

Hmm.

"Mark... what do *you* think? Was Shannon healed... was it a miracle? I mean, Lou stopped limping, but Lou's deal could be adrenaline and manipulated thinking, something temporary. But for Shannon, there's got to be all kinds of recent X-rays and scans and stuff they'll be able to compare at the clinic."

Steve waited. Eventually, he got around to using his bottle opener.

"Sure," I said, at last. "It was a miracle. Freak drives me crazy, but he's the real deal. God uses him. *Why* God wants to work that way, is beyond me. But at the end of the day, we both know this guy... he's God's guy."

Steve nodded. "It's good to hear you say so, Mark. Maybe there's hope for you yet."

I half-heartedly flicked a bottle cap towards Steve. It was a token protestation. I could barely work up the smile to accompany my finger's snap.

Steve let the cap bounce off his chest and land in his lap. He looked down, and didn't bother to lift it.

I got to wondering again about what I'd have to do for wheels to get back to Denver. And if I could face going back to my classes, to grading stacks of plagiarized and dim-witted essays....

About the time we needed to consider another log, we heard something outside.

The noises were coming from the porch of the Ruth. A soft pounding on Freak's door, followed by two or three muffled voices. Nothing frantic, but one of the voices was clearly Saundra's.

I rose to my feet and glanced at the clock. It was late. Minutes to midnight.

From our window, I could see Freak in his open doorway. Talking with a bundled Saundra, who shifted, gesturing beside a stout man in military garb. Wee Daddy.

They looked my way. Two of them hesitantly waved towards my bleak silhouette at the drapes. Then disappeared through the Ruth's closing front door.

44
NIGHT CALL

Ten minutes later, they were on our porch.

Wee Daddy grinned. "Good evening." He stood with his flashlight down, enough to illuminate steps, not blinding our eyes. "You've got some friends here who would like to talk."

Steve bumped past me to Saundra before I could move. He wrapped her in a bearish hug.

Maybe not down to her neck, but her makeup had flowed. Had probably been smudged around by a sleeve without the benefit of a mirror. Her hair was a mess. Saundra met my eyes over Steve's shoulder, then quickly buried any remaining dignity among wet sobs somewhere below Steve's ear.

I turned to Freak. Extended my hand. Dropped it.

We met, arms awkwardly wide, and embraced.

From deep, unexpectedly, rose unwieldy sobs of my own, matched in force only by the shuddering within Freak's chest.

It took awhile, but we untangled. Exchanged partners. Then cried some more.

Wee Daddy sniffled. Cleared his throat. Coughed. "May I remind you," he said at last, "that one of us is on the clock right now?"

I loosened my embrace. I let my hands uncross in back and slide down to the top of Saundra's hips.

"I couldn't sleep," she said, finally letting go of my shoulders and stepping inside. She looked down, nervously swiping a matted frock of hair from her eyes as she brushed past my side.

"Right." My voice cracked. "No pajamas on this end, either."

Wee Daddy laughed. "None of us could sleep. But at least I was getting paid to be awake. It was my watch. So when this little lady started stumbling around in the dark, I knew something was up."

I glanced at Freak, then back to Saundra. "I really blew it this time," I choked. "I wish I hadn't...."

Steve and Freak had arranged chairs and had summoned a couple extras over for Saundra and me. But neither Saundra nor I moved from the entrance rug.

"Listen," said Wee Daddy, "the way I hear it, there's been some grabbing and shoving tonight. Even a little bit of finger jabbing. As you know, we have a zero tolerance for that sort of behavior here at the Diamond K." He smirked in my direction. "Saundra—your little snitch here—has already filed a full report."

She glanced my way, embarrassed, then over to Steve.

"Wee Daddy," she explained, "is here to help us sort this out. An objective third party. A peacemaker."

The Army Ranger rocked on his heels. "Of course, you may not know this, but in my line of work, training in conflict resolution is one of the hurdles we have to jump in order to earn these bars." He thumped his uniform insignia. "I'm practically a certifiable psychotic-therapist." He jostled his sidearm. "Blessed are the peace-keepers. And blessed be the inventor of the peace-keeper's quick-snap holster. Never met a quarrel I couldn't quell as fast as a speeding bullet."

"A peace-*keeper*?" smiled Steve.

"And don't make me use it." Wee Daddy patted his gun a second time.

"Is anyone thirsty," I asked, starting towards the kitchen. "Can I get anyone something to drink?"

Freak took a sweeping inventory of our scattered empties. "Yes," he smiled, refraining from his usual frown, "water would be nice."

Saundra met my eyes. "Mark, you and Freak really unraveled. It felt like everything we'd worked so long and hard to put together... was suddenly coming undone."

I gestured assent. "Water?"

"Sure," she sighed, loosening her coat. "I'm sorry. I just feel so exhausted and worried. Like everything is draining out of me...."

"They make tissues for that," I smiled, staying with her eyes, hoping for a flicker of response. I motioned to the box of tissues on the end table near Steve.

She glanced, then smiled, faintly.

I returned with two waters, then found my seat.

"Hey," blurted Wee Daddy, "what am I, chopped salad?"

"Sorry," I apologized, starting to rise. "I'll get you some water, too."

"Naw. Not while I'm on duty." He turned for the doorknob. "It looks like you four lovebirds have got it from here."

As Wee Daddy stepped through the door, he stopped.

"Let me know in the morning," he called back, "what you decide. In the spirit of complete transparency, I've gotta tell ya, I think it's a bad idea. A logistical and security nightmare. But it's your call. However, if you do decide to go... then I'll need to start pulling things together right away."

Saundra waved, and Wee Daddy was gone.

We tested the silence for a few moments, then Freak took the lead.

"Thanks, Saundra," said Freak, putting down his glass. "We needed to...." He sighed. "You've been great, Saundra. In so many ways...."

Her eyes were filling again. She reached for a tissue. Steve handed her the box.

Freak restarted, this time looking at me. "Ellen went to bed an hour ago. Angry." He wet his lips. "At me... not you."

I waited.

"Ellen said you were justified, Mark." Freak swallowed. "She said I started slipping back into my old ways. She said you were right about the cameras... about me getting manipulative and full of myself. Feeling high from all of the interviews and important prophecies... playing Hollywood...putting you into an impossible situation...."

"Listen, Freak... Bill." I waited until I was certain he wouldn't interrupt. "You pushed some buttons. But I swung back at you with a baseball bat. An atomic bomb." It was my turn to swallow. "I was out of control. I said some things... I told you to go to hell...."

I picked up one of my empty beer bottles. I rolled the cold brown cylinder between my damp palms, stared through the glass to my shoes. "Bill," I said, looking up. "I'm sorry. *Really* sorry...."

Saundra quivered, cleaning up her sniffles, dabbing her cheeks.

Freak's scars glowed soft, familiar, almost beautifully surreal in the angle of the fire and the low lamplight from the end table.

"This was a test," said Freak. "God wanted us to know."

"So," I said, "then I guess we failed the exam, huh?"

"No," said Freak, "we're passing. Right now." He reached for one of Saundra's tissues, then blew his nose.

Freak met my uncertain gaze. "There never was any doubt about whether or not we'd screw up as a team. But we needed to know... would we bail as a community, or would we work it out and press through?"

I weighed his words. We all did.

"If you're right," I said at last, "then what's next? What happens if we survive this test?"

"You're the school teacher," Freak smiled. "You tell me."

I shivered in an unexpected draft. I rose and found a cabin couch blanket for Saundra. She received it with a red-eyed thanks. I made my way to the wood stack beside the hearth.

"If we passed some kind of test," I said, selecting a particularly thin, tapered piece of kindling, "then it's not going to get any easier." I pointed my thick splinter towards Freak. "Is it?"

"No," said Freak. "It's not going to get any easier. The hardest is yet to come."

I tossed in my stick. I rummaged for a couple of agreeably dry, white split logs, then stoked the re-surging flames. Satisfied, I returned to my circle of friends.

"Dark Riders," I said, slipping back into my seat. "Freak... was this their work? In me... in you?"

"Not *in*," he said, "More like *on*. And only partly."

"What do you mean?"

"Sometimes," said Freak, his smile sad, "when the copy machine jams, it's not the work of demons. It's because someone got lazy and didn't read the manual. Or they got careless, and didn't load the paper straight."

"Lazy," I asked. "Careless? Sounds like the first two lines on my resume."

Freak grinned. "Better than mine. Try *arrogant. Stubborn.* And *insecure.*"

"Let's do better," I said. "We can both do better. If it's going to get harder, then we're going to have to. But you need to know.... You're going to have to take it easy with the pushing. I'm making progress, but I'm not there yet. I need more time."

"Agreed." He reached for his water. "I can see it now. I pushed first, not you. And if it's any consolation, there's nothing either of us could ever do, that God couldn't undo with a snap of his finger. Ultimately, this is his show, not ours. We just need to hang in there with him. With each other."

Saundra crumpled her tissue. She couldn't decide where to put it. "Guys," she said, stuffing the wad into her glass, "you two scared me tonight. We don't have time for this. There's too much to do. According to the news, things are getting worse. The world needs to hear from Freak... from God."

Steve bobbed his head. "Another bomb went off in London. The accusations and the threats are getting out of hand."

"Something is up," Freak concurred. "I'm waiting to hear more from the Lord. But I wasn't kidding about diving into an empty pool. Our next step is going to be a big one. It's going to feel like we're free-falling into a concrete pit."

I glanced again at the clock. It was a new day. Black, but new.

"You called me John," I said, facing Freak. "How'd you know? A word from the Lord?"

"Yes... and no." Freak smiled, faintly. "Cary and I reviewed all of the releases before the oikos meeting tonight. You signed yours: *J. Mark Hanson.* I asked, and the Lord confirmed. Your legal, baptized Christian name is... John Mark. Same as in the Bible."

Saundra laughed.

"What," asked Steve, "is so funny? Why are you all smirking?"

"Because," she said, patting Steve's knee, "John Mark is considered by many experts to be the author of the Gospel of Mark... probably the oldest written account we have of the life of Jesus. John Mark was also a sidekick of the Apostle Paul. And, according to some experts, he was the rich young man who shook his head and walked away the first time Jesus invited him to follow."

"Just for the record," I said, shaking my head, "he was probably also the young man who lost his shorts in the Garden of Gethsemane. When the soldiers grabbed Jesus and the disciples, John Mark slipped their grip by shucking his linen and running off naked through the trees." I grinned. "Now you know why I dropped the *John* part."

"Here," said Saundra, her eyes catching the light, "would this help?"

She tossed me her blanket.

I caught it, then made a show of arranging and rearranging it delicately upon my lap. I looked up.

"Saundra," I asked, "what was Wee Daddy talking about? He said something about a security nightmare... about making arrangements in the morning?"

"Right," she said, suddenly somber. "When I couldn't sleep because I was so upset, I caught up on some news feeds and checked my emails. And then when I still couldn't sleep, I left the house, praying to work out the stuff that had fallen apart tonight."

"Saundra," I gently asked again, "what did Wee Daddy mean when he talked about making arrangements in the morning?"

Saundra glanced from face to face. "Are any of you country music fans? Has anyone ever heard of the Western pop star, Nellie Foxton?"

We all indicated some level of familiarity.

"Well," said Saundra, "Nellie's agent dropped me a note today. More of an invitation. Come to find out, it's *Christian...* country pop star Nellie Foxton."

"And?" Steve leaned forward. "Nellie is a babe. Her tour is swinging through Denver this spring. Does she want to meet Freak while she's in Colorado, or what?"

"The concert," said Saundra, "is at the Red Rocks Amphitheatre. They've got over 9,000 tickets, but less than two thousand have sold. They're running into the same problem most promoters are having with major league sports events. Fans are staying home because of the terrorist threats. And her concert is only two weeks away."

"So?" asked Steve, his eyes eager.

"So... Foxton wants Freak to join her on the stage."

45

THE REST OF THE STORY

After breakfast, Saundra and Steve met with Wee Daddy to begin devising security and media strategies for the upcoming Nellie Foxton event at Red Rocks.

Freak and I met with Cary.

"What you saw last night," I said, "is part of who we are. But that's not the whole picture."

"Of course not," said Cary.

He sipped from his labeled water, then returned the plastic bottle to the weathered planks beneath his red alligator skin boots. For this particular shot, Cary had positioned himself within the frame, letting his off-camera team record our conversation from calculated angles. He was just a regular guy, kicking back in a Polo Ralph

Lauren Western plaid shirt, relaxing in a rustic rocking chair on a Colorado cabin porch. Tugging on his European duckbill cap. Shooting the breeze with a couple of other regular guys. Talking about life. About the tensions and the back-and-forths of friendships. About God's timeline for the impending global meltdown. About World War III.

Just the usual end-of-the world grist.

The New York filmmaker let his gaze drift past our cushioned log chairs. His attention meandered down from our perch on cabin row at the edge of the forest into the greening valley and the blooming wild flowers below the Diamond K stables. Randal's camera followed the director's gaze to the panorama of grazing livestock, to the white-streaked cobalt sky and to the soaring snowcapped peaks. Eventually, almost reluctantly, Cary brought the shot back to his circled team, back to Freak and me, where we waited in our blue denim shirts and loose-fitting jeans.

"I've been making films for a long time," he said. "I know how these things work. Even professionals can occasionally slip from character. Especially when the cameras catch them off guard... and the floodlights glare too brightly in their eyes."

Freak nodded. "All the same, Mark and I wanted to debrief a little. Thanks for meeting with us, and for recording this part of our story, too. I'm not sure if you'll get any usable footage, but you never know."

"You never know," Cary smiled. He looked at Shannon, who all but glowed. The sound and lighting tech had risen from sleep headache free for the first time in months. Shannon claimed his vision was more clear than he could remember. His exuberant appreciation seemed to bounce between Freak and the brilliant mid-morning landscape of the mountain ranch.

"If nothing else," added Cary, "we'll get some fantastic B roll. A day like this makes me want to hang around for another week."

I smiled. "Jack and Mary would like that. She would probably do your wash."

Even Randal seemed to feel it, seemed at peace sipping coffee behind his camera in the spring rays. Drips from the season's last fingers of melting ice on the cabin's tin roof splashed softly, rhythmically, rippling into the tiny, clear stone-littered puddles below the eaves.

"There!" I whispered.

I tapped Cary's arm and pointed off the porch. Randal pivoted around his tripod, then began probing the conifers up the steep incline north of the cabin. Birds darted and sang among the shrinking snow patches in the shadowed coves of the tallest pines. Randal glanced away from his camera to double-check where I was pointing, and then found the prize.

A tawny young mule deer was nibbling fresh growth, a large ear twitching each time she raised her head and looked our way. She took two steps, then disappeared for a moment behind a thicket of budding bushes and tangled brush.

"Keep watching," I whispered. "She's not alone."

A moment later, two more appeared.

We watched in silence as the three of them floated amongst the shadows and sunbeams a mere thirty paces above our unlikely nest of split rails, varied opinions, and state-of-the-art electronics.

Freak cleared his throat. "What happened to Shannon last night," he said, "was real. Tests will confirm that Shannon's tumor is gone. But what happened last night between me and Mark... was also real."

"Of course." Cary rocked forward, away from Freak, towards me. "Mark, last night... you shouted... you cursed him... you shoved him. How often does it get like that?"

I gave the question some time. "Like *that*? Never. That was the hottest it's ever gotten. I've brushed him off and yelled at him a few times. Freak drives me crazy when he presses me too hard about my issues. In some ways, we're a lot alike." I turned to Freak. "We've known that from the beginning. But I guess we're in this together... so even when it gets rough, we keep working it out as we go."

"Working it out?"

"Last night, around midnight, we sat with Saundra and Steve. We hugged and wept. We talked and prayed for over an hour. The four of us have gone through a lot together."

For the second time, my phone vibrated. I ignored the plea, again leaving the annoyance unattended in my chest pocket beneath my open coat.

Freak turned his head down from the three deer to meet Cary's gaze. "Mark was right to call me out last night. The Lord uses me... God wants to use us all. But none of us are perfect. Or above correction." He patted his knee. "As for me... I'm as flawed as it gets. And just because the Lord uses me from time to time, I don't get a pass for being rude."

"Rude?" I gently smirked.

"For being..." Freak winced, "a pompous ass."

Cary redirected my way. "What's it like... hanging out day and night with a pompous ass?"

"A pompous ass," I laughed, "who happens to heal strangers and to predict the future with unnerving accuracy. When it comes to asses, he's of the sort that'll drive anyone crazy. Freak is so spiritual, sometimes he literally scares me. I've seen a lot. I don't know how to make sense of it all, but I'm past questioning whether God is using him or not."

"If your friend is so full of God, then how can he be so... rude... at the very same time?"

"Blame free will," I said. "We all make countless choices each day. Some of those choices are bound to be bad. Blame our bad choices on ignorance... maybe blame the selfish, self-serving nature of our species. And when it comes to being fallen, as far as I know, Freak currently holds the world record."

Cary smiled. "He called you *John* last night. You seemed to take offense at that. What was that all about?"

"My legal name," I said, glancing at Freak, "is John Mark Hanson. That's how I was baptized. It's a family tradition to name Hanson boys with J's. My dad's name is Jeffrey. My grandfather's name was James. As a little kid in Sunday school, Mrs. Barskal did a whole lesson about the John-Mark in the Bible, and she made a big deal in front of the other students about how John Mark was my name. She thought I'd be flattered or inspired or something. But it backfired. Kids started teasing me, and then it was *John-Mark* for the rest of the year. *John-Mark* did this, and *John-Mark* said that. So, the next year in elementary school, I told my teacher that my parents called me Mark. And I've managed to keep it Mark ever since."

"But," pressed Cary, "why all of your hostility around the name? You were pretty upset...."

"It's a long story. Part of it is about who John-Mark was in the Bible, and who I was as a kid. Who I still am. The bottom line is that ever since then, only my mom calls me John, and she only says *John* when she's trying to push me around. Freak blindsided me when he came up with that name and hit my manipulation reflex button. Kinda like you said a while ago... I got caught off guard in the glare of the bright lights."

Cary leaned back, apparently searching—or waiting—for where the conversation would venture next.

"Speaking of secret names," I said, "Freak, I keep meaning to ask... what's up with your wife calling you *Benny*?"

Cary lifted an eyebrow. Freak hesitated. Frowned.

"I know," I continued, "prior to your fall, you went by the name W.B. Jacobs, or Bill for short. Does the name *Bill* come from the B, or from William?"

"From William," said Freak, his voice flat. "My full name is William B. Jacobs. Bill Jacobs for short. As you know, I now prefer... *Freak*."

Cary tossed Randal a signal, apparently calling for a tight zoom on the prophet's face.

"Interesting," said Cary. "*Benny*... Benjamin, perhaps?"

Freak closed his eyes. When he finally opened them, his composure was resigned. "Like Mark, we have a tradition in the Jacobs family. We honor our ancestry with our middle names, even though our heritage has been thinly masked ever since my great grandfather's arrival in

America over a century ago. Benny is Ellen's affectionate house name for her man... for Benzion. For me."

"Ben-zion?" Cary grinned. "*Son of Jerusalem.* That's about as Jewish as it gets."

Freak remained quiet.

"Jacobs..." ventured Cary. "So I'm guessing *Jacobs* is short for... Jacobowitz... or Jacoby, perhaps?"

"Jacobi," said Freak. "With an *i*, not a *y*. It's Ashkenazic."

"So, you are Jewish?"

"My great grandfather was a rabbi... Benzion Jacobi immigrated by way of Prussia. Like everyone else, he Americanized his name at Ellis Island."

"A rabbi?" I whistled.

Freak squared his shoulders. "Not just a rabbi. A Jewish mystic. He fled Europe with his family because he feared the unification of the Central Powers... and he saw the coming of the Great War."

"He *saw*..." I asked, "he predicted the coming of WWI?"

"Lots of people saw the coming of a massive European conflict," said Freak. "Half of the world felt it was inevitable. But my great grandfather saw some of the specifics. Battles. Trench lines. Weapons. Airplanes." Freak unconsciously floated two fingers down the contours of his left cheek. "And then, before he died, Benzion accurately prophesied WWII. With the holocaust. And the atomic bomb. In vivid detail."

"You have proof?" asked Cary. "Anyone can make claims after the fact...."

"Hand-written journals," said Freak. "Family legends. I come from a long line of rabbis, and not all of them were known for coloring inside of the lines. I doubt we've got anything concrete enough to stand up in a court of law."

"So, *Benny...*" I flashed him an exaggerated wink, "when were you going to let me in on all of this?"

"I wasn't." Freak dropped his hand. "I've built my career as an Evangelical Christian. I *am* an Evangelical Christian. But with my audience and revenue streams so heavily dependent upon my appeal to fundamentalists, I've had to be very careful. As you know, many conservative Christians are fearful and suspicious when it comes to...."

"Jews?" offered Cary with a smirk.

"No," said Freak, less than amused. "Conservative Christians tend to be very supportive of Israel. I've known them to spend their life savings on Holy Land tours. They send money to Israel, and they study Jewish history... they preach a form of Zionism almost every time they teach from the Old Testament."

"Then what's the problem?" Cary asked, glancing to me.

"Mysticism," I replied. "It's Benzion's non-Christian mystic angle that could derail the whole conservative train. That particular type of supernatural thing would be a hard thing for some folks to swallow. If the rabbi got his insights directly from interpretations of the Bible, they'd listen... but to get those predictions from private visions or something...."

"There's more," sighed Freak. "In his dated journals, Benzion claimed to 'see' a lot of things that even many open-minded people might find pretty difficult to accept."

"Such as?" I asked.

"Such as *my* birth... his great-grandson, little Benzion. And my role in history. That God would speak to the entire planet through his heir... in the midst of earthquakes, disasters, and the wars of the End of Days. He even gave a date. He said the First Trumpet of the Apocalypse would be blown during the time of Nisan, the season of the *former rains*... of this year."

"Nisan?" asked Cary.

"Basically, March-April," said Freak. "Precisely predicted, accurately fulfilled."

Hmm.

"For me," said Freak, "to make such claims for myself...that my birth and my role in End of Days history had been predicted.... Well, it couldn't be done. It would be seen as self-validation. Self-promotion. The ultimate presumption. The grandiose delusions... of a pompous ass."

"But," I objected, "it could have gotten some folks switching over to your side much sooner."

"Not to mention," Freak said, "getting the opposition against me into place much sooner as well. Thankfully, God had a better idea when it came to validating my message." He touched his scars yet again. "Besides, I wasn't ready to speak with any kind of authority yet.... not until a month ago. Especially because I was wrong about so many of my other predictions prior to my fall...."

Again, there was a faint humming rattle at my chest.

Freak tipped a questioning look towards my vibrating phone.

I fished out the device and glanced at the number. "My dad," I said. "I'll call him back when we're done."

Cary had been rocking, ever so slightly. He stopped. "Benzion. Ben-*zion*...."

"Please." Freak held up his hand. "Now look at who is being rude."

"Reverend Jacobs," smiled Cary, "if all you say is true, then you really *do* believe you're a chosen spokesman for God? That it's your job to tell the rest of us about all of the judgments and the suffering we must face?"

"God," said Freak, "wants to heal this broken world and to set things right. Sometimes, it takes pain to drive people to their knees... sometimes it takes suffering to humble the proud and to bring people to a place where they will soulfully cry out for the Lord's help."

Cary shrugged. "So you're saying the end justifies the means? God makes us suffer for our own good... as if that's some sort of gift to us? This doesn't sound like Grace to me. It sounds like violence. Abuse."

Freak paused. He met Shannon's eyes, then glanced down the gravel lane of cabin row.

I followed his gaze towards the big house. Jack was stepping down from the porch in his big dark hat. Rex was bounding at the rancher's heels.

"In the Bible," said Freak, "there's this incredible line. Perhaps one of the most astonishing verses in all of scripture. In the book of Hebrews, it says Jesus himself was perfected through suffering. The implication was that without suffering, even Jesus could not be all God wanted him to be."

"Whatever." Cary shrugged. "When you start quoting about Jesus, I start feeling like you're trying to convert me. Let's get back to the here and now. The global meltdown that seems to have begun. I'm hearing you say the end justifies the means, and you believe it's only for our own good God is smashing the world and ignoring the pain of the innocent?"

"God," said Freak, his tone emphatic, "never looks away. He's here—with us—in the very midst of the very worst we'll ever face. He ignores nothing."

"So, I ask again," demanded Cary, his face exasperated, "if God loves us, and if God has the power to change things, why does he allow the innocent to suffer?"

Freak studied Cary for a long time.

"Wrong question," said Freak at last.

Freak looked to the sky, then back at Cary. "In a broken, sin-riddled world," he said, "with Satan and evil all around us on every side... people *will* suffer. There's no way around it."

"Then what *is* the right question?"

"The correct question is not *why* does the world suffer... but for how long."

"And?"

Freak sighed. "Not much longer, my friend. Very soon, the Lord will complete his plan to bring this groaning mess to a climax... and then, to an astonishing end."

Cary turned back to me. "Do you agree with his assessment? Is Armageddon somehow a good thing, and is the end of the world really close at hand?"

"Anyone can see," I said, "God is doing something special right now. And it is clear Freak has been chosen by God. Freak has been given a special message to share during this critical moment in human history."

"Would you say," asked Cary, "that Freak is your leader? Are you—and your friends here at the ranch—are you all following the Reverend Jacobs... because you believe God has chosen him to start a new religion...."

I laughed. "No," I said, waving a hand, "we're not looking for a new religion. Let alone a new leader."

Cary waited.

Jack was almost to our cabin. The big rancher's strides were long, and he was chewing his cigar stub with unusual vigor.

Rex suddenly caught wind of the deer. He yelped once, then bolted for forest.

Jack shouted a sharp rebuke, immediately followed by a slap to his thigh and a snapped command. The black Lab reluctantly looped wide and fell back to Jack's side, head down, tongue long, eyes darting.

But the deer were gone.

"To be honest," I confessed, turning back to Cary, "I've never been much of a follower. Maybe that's part of my problem."

"And yet," coaxed Cary, "here you are, sitting with me, making apologies for your all-too-human leader."

"Am I?" I stiffened. "I guess I'd have to think about that. I kinda thought I was apologizing more for myself." I reached for my water bottle. "No... I'm not apologizing for anything." I unscrewed the loose cap and took a shallow wash. "I'm just trying to be honest. Trying to say *what is*... as best I can."

I replaced the cap. I found the bottle rolling between my palms.

"I guess," I reflected out loud, "I'm more of a witness than a follower." I glanced at Freak. "But I'm not just a witness. I suppose I'm a participant-observer. Like I said last night, I'm not sure anyone gets to sit and watch from the sidelines anymore."

Cary waited.

"The sidelines and balcony loft disappear," I said at last, "when the whole world has become the stage."

"Stage?" asked Cary. "A stage is a pretty controlled environment. I'm thinking this planet is more like a three-ring circus… filled with nothing but animal acts."

"But is there a ringmaster?" I asked. "That's the question we need to address."

Freak studied me. "Oh, there's a ringmaster all right. And he's just maneuvered some of us into ring number three."

Jack commanded Rex to sit, then waited until I'd finished with Cary. We'd all eaten breakfast together, yet Jack couldn't resist tapping the brim of his hat and mumbling several fresh greetings and inane exchanges before asking me to step off with him for a word. We found a lone ponderosa pine a short walk below the cabin, then locked eyes.

"Your dad," he said with a squint, "has been trying to reach you all morning."

I patted my chest. "I was about to call him. What's up?"

"He asked me to tell you he couldn't sleep last night. He kept having some kind of premonition or something."

"That's not like him," I said, suddenly on guard.

"He said he wants me to send you home to Denver. Right away. Or else he'll come up here and get you himself."

"Why the threat?"

"Apparently, your dad had a reoccurring vision. He kept seeing you getting caught up in some sort of explosion again. He said you and Freak were like fish in a cement barrel, swimming around with thousands of people in some kind of huge red bowl or something."

"Red Rocks Amphitheatre," I said. "But how did he know?"

"He didn't. And I didn't say a word. You'll have to tell him yourself."

Hmm.

"He also said, and I quote: 'Tell that boy of mine... this time... he's not going to be able to just hop into his Ford and drive away.'"

"Of course not." I tried to grin. "My crushed beastie is still at the bottom of the ravine."

Jack took a deep breath. "You know that's not what he meant."

"Yes. I know."

I looked eastward, towards the brilliant sun high above the distant Indian Peaks. The sky was clear, save for three silvery jet plumes. The manufactured clouds stretched for countless miles, parallel, before feathering off into the oblivion of thin air. The planes themselves were no longer anywhere to be seen.

I turned back to meet Jack's waiting gaze. "Is that all he said?"

"No. One more thing." Jack put a hand on my shoulder.

"Your father said the inside of the red bowl..." Jack puffed, then squeezed my neck, "was splattered and running with streams of thick blood."

PART V
RED ROCKS

Freak agreed to appear on stage with Nellie Foxton only on the condition the event would be accessible throughout the world as a free broadcast. He didn't care whether the evening was recorded by a Colorado public-access station and then simultaneously streamed via the Internet, or whether a major network took the bait.

Anything live, free, and reliable would do.

Saundra and Foxton's agent immediately began consulting with lawyers and negotiating with Red Rocks officials to re-write contracts to make it happen. A Denver community service channel manager was alerted to the opportunity, and she promptly pledged to dedicate all of their resources to six hours of continuous coverage—before, during and after the event. Word of her station's offer made it into a Freak podcast later the same day, and a bidding war for exclusive rights quickly ensued.

A global cable network with proven simultaneous Internet broadcasting capacity ultimately inked the winning proposal.

PRIORITIES

Jack eventually ceased pacing. He gruffly snatched a throw pillow and lowered himself huffing into the couch beside his wife.

"I'm worried," he said, gesturing towards the nightly news. "All of this publicity...."

"...*is good*," finished Saundra. "Freak wants this. The *movement* needs this."

"The movement?" I asked. "Since when has Freak become a movement?"

Saundra hesitated. She glanced over her shoulder towards coffee smells beyond the kitchen's double doors.

"*Freak...*" she said, her voice barely audible above the banter of an insurance commercial, "*he* is *not* the movement. But the people who've been stirred by

Freak's messages... they are the ones who are creating a movement. And that's a good thing."

"Wonderful," I said. "Good for ticket sales. And good for ratings. Maybe good for your career. Am I missing something?"

"This is the sort of development," she said, ignoring my remark, "that could change the course of history. With a little luck, perhaps God will...."

"Will what?" Freak stopped behind Saundra, a plate with a sandwich in one hand, an unopened bottle of water in the other. "With a little *luck*..." he frowned, "what exactly is it you hope our God will do?"

Saundra tugged her sleeve. "I only meant *luck* as a figure of speech. All I'm trying to say is we don't know for certain what God plans to do, but if we're lucky, then...." She caught herself, then looked down in embarrassment.

Freak extended his plate. "Here, Saundra. You were on the phone straight through lunch again. You must be starved." She received the plate with hardly a glance. "Your lips are dry," he added. "You'll need this to wash it down."

"I'm sorry," she apologized, licking her lips and taking the water with her free hand. "Everything has been a blur since last Sunday."

"We're all spinning in a dozen directions, and you even more. Don't be so hard on yourself. God has got this."

Saundra glanced at the sandwich in her hand, then looked up. "Yes, I do feel like God is bringing everything together." She placed the plate on the end table, then nervously unscrewed the bottle's cap. "Only a few tickets are left to sell, and according to the latest news polls, millions of people are planning to watch the event live on cable." Her words tumbled. "Nellie's agent says they've adjusted the program to free up time in the middle for your talk, and she's really excited to meet you, and to finally be able to sing some of her old favorites... praise songs from her church band days, before she became so famous. Almost 7,000 more tickets have already sold...."

Freak stepped around the couch and pulled in a rocker.

"Take a deep breath," he urged, patting Saundra's knee. "And no more caffeine. Try the water."

She took a quick sip.

"There you go," Freak smiled. "You've done an amazing job."

Steve agreed. "Saundra," he chuckled, "those guys from New York should have made a second documentary before they left. About you. I've never seen anyone get so much done so fast. The fact you got a Denver stage crew to build Freak's prop so quickly... that alone should win you an award. I don't know how you even found time to ever recharge your phone."

Saundra glanced my way. "It *is* a movement. You know that, right?" She gulped twice more from her bottle. "At first—the first week after Freak's fall—all we had was the news coverage. And then it was Krissy's website. And then all of the blogs. And then after we came here to the Diamond K—after Wilcox—it was the daily podcasts, and the guest interviews, and all of those people who were trying to sneak in so they could catch a glimpse of Freak here at the ranch...."

"Yes," I smiled. "And then came more blogs, more websites, more posters. More new silkscreened shirt designs. Then came the *Freak for President* bumper stickers, followed by the keychains, water bottles, and coffee mugs. And now ticket sales. Scalpers are hustling out-of-staters for $250 and up per seat. Freak is becoming an underground industry all his own."

Jack turned off the television.

"Mark," he said, "you're forgetting about the ripples. Freak might still be the biggest splash in the pond, but the waves are building. They're moving outward." Jack reached down to Rex beside Mary's leg. He scratched the black Lab's neck, then turned back to me. "I think Saundra is right. In the past month, scholars and pastors who never paid attention to the End of Days are suddenly doing research. And they have to, because people are showing up in their classes and at their churches. Everybody is asking for answers."

"And," rushed Saundra, "people are praying together. They're forming small study groups and local disaster response networks. People who've ignored religion all of their lives are suddenly worried about judgment... they're helping with needy victims and the poor, and they're trying to clean up their lives. And millions of people are buying books about the resurrection and the return of Jesus as King."

"The problem," sighed Freak, "is that a lot of what's bouncing around out there right now is still wrong. Sloppy research. Bad theology. Deceptive doctrines. People remain confused about the reality of demons, and misinformed about a rapture."

"But," said Saundra, "all of these new study groups and emergency support teams... that's a good thing, right?"

"Our challenge," said Freak, "is to get them to see how their prayer and study groups should also be rolling up their sleeves and grabbing towels." He looked around the room. "And conversely, how those service and response groups should also be fighting on a spiritual level, praying and doing studies."

I grinned. "Preach it, Rev."

"That model," said Freak, not turning from Saundra, "is the only option Jesus ever gave for confronting Satan's schemes and for engaging the desperate needs of our world. Anything less than a balanced community of Grace and Truth is a lazy, self-serving perversion of the Christlike way established by Jesus himself."

"Yes," said Saundra, twisting and untwisting the bottle's cap, "which is exactly why this Red Rocks event is so important. People need to hear the message. They need to see Freak—to see you in real time—and to hear the word of the Lord directly from the prophet's mouth. They need your help to know how God wants them to obey and to serve others in this season of global shaking."

Freak rocked in silence until Saundra grew still.

"There's something else," said Freak. "There's one more thing we still need to talk about." He turned to me. "It's about your father's dream...."

"Listen," I complained, "I thought we were finished with all of his nonsense. People have nightmares all the time. Whenever people anticipate something big, they get anxious. And then they have bad dreams."

Freak cleared his throat. "Mark, I've given this a lot of prayer. We all have."

Hmm. Well, almost everyone.

Freak continued. "Jack and I were discussing it this morning. He agrees with me. Because we've received no additional confirmation of your dad's premonitions, we're not willing to cancel my appearance."

"You *see*," I said, "that's what I'm talking about. My dad got a little nervous. He was...."

"No," said Freak, rocking forward, "I'm worried we're dealing with something more than a random nightmare."

I let him gently rock a few times in silence, hoping he'd eventually feel awkward enough to change the subject.

"Mark," he said at last, halting towards me, knees bent, "I want you to stay here on the ranch with Jack and Mary. I don't want you with us next weekend at Red Rocks."

"What?"

"You're not going."

To his credit, Freak addressed my eyes. "I've already informed Wee Daddy you'll be staying behind with Jack and Mary, along with the rest of my family. A couple Grand County Sheriff deputies will swing by to cover around here for the day. Wee Daddy and his team will be with the rest of us at the event."

Mrs. K folded and unfolded her hands. She caught sight of the untouched sandwich on the end table beside Saundra. "Pastor Jacobs," she said, rising and starting towards the kitchen, "let me make you another sandwich." She disappeared without looking back.

"Why?" I asked at last.

"As I said," repeated Dave Freak, "I am seriously concerned about your father's dreams. I think it is highly probable we may experience an attack."

"You're leaving me behind... with your kids?"

"Not just my kids. Also my wife. And with Jack and Mary, and Cal. And with your work."

"Soooo…" I said, my tone low, cheeks tight, "you're dumping me. And you want it to look like you're protecting me from danger… as if you're leaving me behind for my own good?"

"No." Freak's voice dropped to matter-of-fact. "I would not presume to protect the one who has saved my life twice in the past month. I am only trying to protect the mission."

"The mission?"

"The mission," said Freak, "is not *me*. And it's not you. The mission is God's message."

"But," I protested, "at Red Rocks, you'll be sharing God's message. What does the message have to do with me staying behind?"

"Again," he said, "God has not confirmed an attack. But I am *deeply* concerned about what might happen at the concert." He pointed at Saundra, then Steve. "Let me be clear. People may die." He forced them to consider. "I am not going to insist, but I strongly encourage you both to stay here on the ranch with Mark."

Steve swiped his mouth. Rubbed a hand on his thigh.

Saundra just stared.

"Freak," I said, "you're not making sense. You're willing to go there and die. You're willing to let Saundra die. Steve die. But not me. After all we've been through, suddenly I'm not good enough to tag along,…."

"Listen, Mark…." Freak touched his face. "If I was certain of an attack, then I wouldn't let Saundra and Steve attend, either. I would call off the entire event…."

I drew a deep breath. "I thought I was your wingman. That's all I've been hearing from you since you started jerking me around our very first day in the hospital, when you whispered up to me through the gauze of your bandaged face... when you insisted God had chosen wisely...."

"You *are* my wingman. My witness." He checked on Saundra, then returned to me. "Mark... I need to know... how is the writing going?"

"What?"

"How close are you to being done with your account?"

"Are you *kidding*?" I started to rise, then caught myself. Collected myself. "What in the world difference does in make how my writing is going?"

Freak held up his hand.

"Mark," he said, "your account... counts. More than you know. Every life that is lived... is the writing of a story. But only you, John-Mark...."

Freak granted me a wince, then continued.

"Mark, you have been called to not only live the story of your own life, but to record this chapter of mine. If I die next week, it will be your witness of these events that keeps the message alive...."

"Forget it," I said. "I'm not willing to hide out here on the ranch. Like it or not, I'm *going*."

Rex raised an ear from beside Jack's feet. He cocked his head my way, blinked, then lowered his jowls back to the floor. He settled between his paws, then closed his eyes.

"It's a free country," sighed Freak. "If you can land a ticket, and if you can find a way to get there, nobody is going to stop you from taking a seat at Red Rocks. But,

Mark... if you're planning on hitching a cheap helicopter ride to Denver, let it go. Wee Daddy has already agreed to not let you aboard."

"Jerk," I spat.

I started to add something. Drew another deep breath instead. Glanced around.

Saundra met my gaze, her eyes full.

"Are you going?" I asked.

She nodded yes.

I glanced to Steve. He looked at his shoes, then shrugged a yes.

Damn.

Jack stood. He stepped towards me, over the dog. Squeezed my shoulder, then strode to the kitchen to join his wife.

Freak waited.

A soft sniffle rose from the couch. Saundra's fingers were poised at her temple. She met my vacant daze, then brushed back a blonde lock, tucking it behind her ear. The passing of her hand revealed a single wet streak, a glistening line along the graceful contour of her reddening nose. The line swelled bright over the pink of her lip, then emptied into the thin blackness of her quivering mouth.

I wanted to release her, but couldn't.

Couldn't think of where else to look.

I finally stood and made for the door.

47
THE PLANET'S STAGE

"Hang on," said Cal. "I'll be right back."

He dashed up the porch steps and disappeared through the front door with a bang.

I reached for Freak's hand. "Good luck," I said. "Knock 'em dead."

Freak squeezed long after I'd finished my goodbye. He held our parting shake into a hint of pain.

"Not luck," he said, finally letting go.

"Right."

He lifted his hand, palm high. "May the Lord bless you... and may he keep you safe... may he keep us all safe... until we meet again."

"Sure." I slapped his shoulder. "Now get out of here. Enjoy yourself. But just go. I've got some work to do."

Freak stepped back with a resigned nod.

Jack stepped in front of me and reached for Freak's hand. "We'll be watching... praying."

They shook. Jack moved back and adjusted the cigar stub between his teeth.

The front door banged a second time.

"Here," panted Cal, stepping close. "Hopefully, you won't need this. But I think I'm supposed to give it to you to bring... just in case."

Cal extended his arms, cradling in his hands Saint Michael. The shofar.

Freak gingerly received the offering. He studied it for a moment, again testing its curves and balance. He met Cal's eyes and smiled a thanks. Then, abruptly, the prophet tucked the horn beneath his arm.

He retreated from our Diamond K troupe to kneel and hug whispers amongst his children and wife. I caught Ellen murmuring a *Benny* or two, along with a few personal directions, and then I dialed back to see what else was going on around the ranch.

Wee Daddy's team had almost finished loading. For the first time in a while, he was wearing his black flak jacket. The Army Ranger was all eyes. He glanced at me, then lightly grazed a palm along the side of his holstered sidearm. And winked. Then got back to business.

I called to Steve, "Keep an eye on them for me, okay?" Steve tossed me an ironic salute, then did a quick-draw motion from the camera bag on his hip, as if he was pulling a pistol instead of a camera.

I saluted back, then laughed as Steve joined the others who were being herded by Wee Daddy from the shadow of the big house down the short gentle grade towards the morning sunlight. The special ops armored Huey throbbed and whined, impatiently vibrating on the parking pad below.

Saundra took a few steps, then spun. She squinted into the sun above the roof. She started to shield her eyes, to wave, then awkwardly hurried forward for a fleeting embrace.

"I'm sorry," she choked. "But Freak is right. If anything happens...."

"Be safe," I whispered.

And they were gone.

In August of 1964, the Beatles played Red Rocks during their first American tour.

Almost every big name in entertainment, from Sonny & Cher to Jimi Hendrix, has faced the lights and rubbed their hands over the irresistible, cavernous sandstone contours of the enveloping Stage Rock. James Taylor, Pearl Jam, Rush... countless others have said the Denver foothills park is the most amazing performance venue in the world.

Because of the jaw-dropping formations creating the world's only natural acoustically perfect amphitheater, Stevie Nicks, The Moody Blues with the Colorado Symphony, U2, John Tesh, and numerous others have booked the Rocks for some of the most spectacular live concert videos ever made. The Grateful Dead, John Denver, Willie Nelson... they played the majestic setting with its panoramic view of Denver so often they appear on poster plaques along the walls of the on-site museum gift store.

In July of 1984, twenty years after the Beatles, my folks drove us up to the hogback for Amy Grant's first appearance at the Rocks. I'd never heard of John Lennon, but Amy Grant I knew. I'd never been to Red Rocks, but I'd seen a postcard, and I'd heard the rumors and the legends.

I remember leaning back and forth in the back seat between the right and left windows, annoying my sisters on both sides as our family's car slowly climbed up from the park entrance.

"It's like *Mars*," I cried, too excited to contain myself.

I pressed past my sister and craned my neck.

"Look," I marveled, pointing at the monstrous outcroppings and the soaring stacked-slab spires. "It's like the pictures in my space book."

My father frowned. "Not Mars." He tapped his brakes. "What you see here is the history of our planet. This is raw, exposed Earth... dating back thousands of years... to the days of Noah's flood."

He cranked hard around a small chunk of rock debris crumbling on the narrow, shoulderless asphalt drive.

We were deep into the park, negotiating bumper-to-bumper fumes through a tight set of 5 mph winding turns. We stopped again, still a half mile below our graveled parking destination.

"God," he added, "left these monuments here so we could remember his power. And his wrath. Same as with the rainbows."

I leaned forward into the gap between my parents' seats. I wedged my hand and chin into the side of my father's headrest. "My Sunday School teacher says rainbows remind us of God's love."

"That... too." He pulled his elbow back into the car. "Mostly that."

I leaned away from the Old Spice of his neck and slumped into my seat. I carefully unrolled my program and flattened it upon my thigh. "She's pretty, isn't she, Dad? Amy Grant?"

He glanced at my mother, then snapped his attention back to another curve.

"Amy Grant," said my mother, "sings like an angel. That's because she sings to God."

Tail lights flickered, and an annoyingly familiar green minivan forced us to yet another halt. "Over one hundred years ago," said my father, "this place was called the Garden of the Angels." He stretched his arm out the window and pointed upwards. "Do you see those two huge rocks up there? Those are called monoliths. Each of them is taller than Niagara Falls. The one that sticks straight up on the right goes by the name of... *Creation Rock*."

I followed his finger.

"We'll be sitting," he finished, "between those two monoliths. We'll be sitting in what will seem like a huge triangular bowl, tilted as if pouring out towards Denver. There will be one monolith at each of the top two corners, and the enormous stage rock at the bottom. We'll be able to see the skyline of Denver in the distance, over the top of Stage Rock. When it gets dark, the lights of Denver will be amazing."

"So," I asked, "are we going to be sitting down by the stage, or where?"

"Our seats," he answered, "are on long wooden benches built into huge curving concrete steps. They made 70 rows with painted lines and numbers for each person. Our tickets are for five spots on the north side of the bowl."

He removed his foot from the brake, and we began again to move.

"The seats for our family are at the base of Creation Rock... 300 feet below the throne of God."

Those of us who'd been left at the ranch gathered in the big house around the flat screen for the half-hour pre-concert show. We got it in HD, live via satellite, 6 PM Mountain Time.

The network had flown in their A-team for the event. They were kept busy, clambering about in the thin air for audience interviews and live shots from around the venue. The broadcaster's New York studio team provided production support, complete with panel commentary, file clips, and expert remote opinions. Most of it focused on Freak and his mixed record as a prophet. I appeared in the background of one or two clips, and Saundra might have flashed through maybe three times.

Nellie Foxton hardly appeared at all.

Five minutes from showtime, a spike-heeled celebrity collared an unshaved blue jacket whose bottom filled a seat-and-a half at the end of row 58.

"Sir?" she asked. "Do you mind if I ask you about your shirt?"

The surprised man glanced up. From someplace between his nachos and a wide plastic cup of draft beer, he did a double-take. He smirked, then indicated he had a minute to talk.

The feathered brunette leaned forward. "Sir," she asked again, "could you tell me about your shirt?"

The man grinned as she leaned even tighter, her bright nails within scratching distance as she thrust her enormous mic beneath his chin. He met her blouse, then passed his treasures to the thin man on his left. He removed his sweat-stained ball cap and scratched his thinning crown. He studied the reporter's painted brows and powdered face, then flattered her with a gap-toothed flash of country-western approval.

"Your shirt?" she asked a third time, now forcing her smile, giving him a few inches to collect the required thoughts.

He replaced his cap, then flapped open his unzipped jacket. "This shirt?" he asked. He patted the black and white T-shirt that barely canvassed his rolling girth.

She hurried a yes.

"Wednesday," he said, "I bought this here shirt from a guy on the 16th Street Mall." He rubbed the lettering and read the sentiment upside down by heart. *"End of the World? Ask Freak!"* He dropped his hand. "It cost me fifteen bucks... but I liked it more than any of the others. I bought it so I'd have something to wear tonight for this show. My brother got us all some tickets from where he works...."

"And *why*," she prodded, "did you choose this *particular* shirt?"

"It wasn't exactly my size, but it was my thoughts. I've been following this preacher feller on television ever since he fell from that plane. And I'm hoping tonight he'll give us the date."

"The date?"

"Of course. For the end of the world. I want to know whether to keep paying my child support."

Ever since the 1971 Jethro Tull riot at Red Rocks—with its swooping police helicopters and its tear gas bungled response—security has been tight on the days of concerts. For the Foxton and Freak event, it was by far the tightest anyone had ever seen. Wee Daddy kept a few of his men out of sight, but half his team was stationed with loaded weapons in the most strategic and visibly prominent positions in the bowl. Park security agents and Denver law enforcement officers were everywhere, rifling fanny packs, sniffing containers, and patting down the guests.

But at 6:30 PM, when two raised drumsticks swayed on the stage, then snapped four quick pace-setting clicks, all was forgiven. Forgotten.

The band exploded, and the show was on.

Nellie Foxton apparated from the smoke beneath an oversized white cowboy hat in a swell of rousing thunderclaps and cheers.

Flashing lights, colored smoke, and a swirling galaxy of lasers served in concert to complement Foxton's bling-glittering ensemble. The impact of her kaleidoscope entrance was mitigated only slightly by the dying grays of a thinly clouded sky. Darkness was still technically almost an hour out, but the rapidly deepening shadows of Mount

Morrison and the Front Range peaks to the west provided a golden opportunity for pre-sunset effects.

Her plan was to open with a few of her pop tour favorites. Then she would transition into a short religious set. She would yield the stage at 7:00 PM to Freak. After Freak, she'd retake the audience. She would perform a few more Christian tunes, then close the night with kettledrums, fireworks and the best of her traveling light show routines. The grand finale was anticipated to be especially spectacular beneath the drama of the stars and the firefly clouds of the distant Denver skyline.

For thirty minutes, Foxton proved herself to be every bit the high-powered professional her reputation claimed. Beautiful, passionate, and a very captivating performer.

She had drawn some fans, and her edgy cherubic delivery was truly inspired.

But the audience had come for Freak.

Foxton had the good sense to wrap it on time at 7:00. Then to slip off to dry down and regroup with her band for their later return.

Maybe even to listen to Freak from the side.

For all I knew, she might have been a real Christian, not just an entrepreneur leveraging Freak's global notoriety to revive her sagging tour.

I never did find out for sure.

The glaring lights dimmed.

Waves of dark hush washed through the crowd. Camera crews panned the audience, pausing here and there to catch the murmurs of soft prayers that immediately began wafting upward from the primordial basin of the Red Rocks bowl. Silent hands began to appear, rising from 70 rows of plank-and-concrete benches, from thousands of ticket-matching numbered slots.

From the uncertain, hopeful congregation that had assembled for heaven's word.

Stage hands smoothly rolled from the shadows, gracefully positioning a towering Reformation-style pulpit at center stage. The elevated podium box was stained in deep cherry, but remained inaccessible until a second team floated forward with a triple-deck set of wooden handrails and stairs. A final team followed, as if upon skates, swinging into place behind the pulpit with an imposing, soaring sounding board of antiquated design. The towering backstop was hooded with an ornately finished canopy that tilted upward, perfectly matching the former two props in visual splendor and resonant deep tones.

Then all went black.

Suddenly, a single, piercing small spot flickered white into the silence. The beam steadied, then slowly began to move. It swelled and swirled into pirouettes about the stage. Finally, it slowed again, wide and intensely bright. It locked, centered upon an empty target, the lectern's vacant book-stand high upon the pulpit's top rail some fifteen feet above the stage.

Freak quietly strode into the light, reverently cradling a large black book.

He climbed to the box. Opened Jack's big leather Bible from the Diamond K, and placed it upon the lectern.

Then, before the camera could complete its dramatic zoom, Freak dropped his chin to his chest. And buried his face in open hands.

And prayed.

A lesser man would have kept it short.

Praying is generally not considered a spectator event, and only an elite few of the thousands who had gathered that night were able to hang in there with Freak for the full seven minutes.

In stage time, 420 seconds of motionless silence is equal in human years to about the time between Noah's Ark and *Star Trek, the Next Generation.*

Long before Freak finally raised his face, the huge off-stage stadium screen began switching to crowd shots and audience zooms. Several of the less mature or more irreligious youths began whistling and flashing pen lights, then making animal noises to draw the camera's lights. Their hoots and yelps of satisfaction played better than Freak's prayer at both ends—the amphitheater's restless bench seats, and the millions of emptying couch cushions scattered in hundreds of cities across the world.

I found it fascinating. For awhile.

A few minutes in, I cracked the silence of our local crowd. "You know," I said, directing Cal's attention towards the absurdity on the screen, "in the 1970's, Steve Martin won a Grammy for his *Wild and Crazy Guy* album... which he recorded on that *very* stage."

Cal stifled a snicker.

"Cal," I continued, pointing at the young man who'd just struck a pose while baptizing himself with a beer, "take note of the sacrilegious consequences of underage drinking... not to mention the inherent dangers of live broadcasting. *This* is why they hire professional actors for reality TV."

Eventually, the network applied a bit of sideline voiceover. A minute later, they added into the screen an inset box filled by a somber-faced New York talking head with a tie.

Jack fumed. Prayed. Fumed some more.

"Hey," I chided, "maybe you shouldn't have glued all the pages shut before you loaned him that Bible of yours."

Jack slammed a palm to his thigh. "Enough!"

The big rancher slipped from his seat to his knees.

He resumed praying, this time in moans and muffled vows. I admired him there on the floor like that, in front of both wives and all of the kids. But I had a hard time deciding whether his growl had been to silence my sarcasm, or to stir the frozen prophet's stew.

Probably about the time Nellie Foxton was thumb-flipping a coin whether to retire from show business or to shove the wheeled pulpit off from the stage to reclaim her night, the prophet did stir.

Raised his head.

For the second time, waves of hush spread through the crowd. It started in the low rows, where folks could see with their bare eyes. Then it moved upwards, onto a Jumbo-Vision tight zoom. Until at last, every ticket holder got their fill... and all were still.

Freak's face was hideous. And glisteningly drenched.

He waited.

Soaked in sweat and tears, contorted in anguish, the prophet slowly blinked as the audience struggled to adjust.

I'd forgotten.

Only a handful of people had ever seen Freak up close in person before, and never like this. The audience had been denied anything but a long wide shot when he'd first stepped into the light and had ascended the stairs. And then, at the top of the pulpit, he'd dropped so quickly into the shadows of prayer, they'd still not yet seen.

Now, many were forced to turn away.

Whoever made the call in the booth to hold the frame of that extreme close up so long was probably fired after the show.

From his chin to his left eye, there rose a wide swath of twenty-foot, deeply furrowed scars. Beneath the harsh lights of the planet's rock stage, the rawness of Truth shimmered like I'd never seen. It glimmered and stunned in the ravaging hues of sob-wetted flames. It turned stomachs and stopped hearts.

The shock of that image was enough to shut the mouth of even a fool.

I'd forgotten.

48
A HARVEST OF WEEDS

"Grace to you, and peace," Freak whispered at last. "From God our Father, who loves you all." His voice gathered force. "And warnings to the world... from our returning King... the Lord Jesus Christ."

The tech wizards had been warned of Freak's habits. Their fingers were poised; they were sliding soundboard levels immediately upon the word, *Grace.* By the time Freak hit *"our returning Lord,"* a majestic reverb filled the entire shuddering earthen arena. It raised hair and shook the rocks.

Freak let it settle.

He repositioned the large Bible. Flipped a few pages, and then raised his eyes.

"It is not my goal tonight to frighten you... but to fortify you for the sake of the Lord. Many of us are weak. Too weak for the days to come."

He started with the front rows. Slowly, he began viewing—showing—turning his mis-matched cheeks from north to south. He didn't stop until he had attained the upper west deck and the highest rows. From there, he floated to the right. He climbed Creation Rock, then raised his chin to the heavens.

"Jesus Christ," he said again, finally lowering his gaze, "spoke often of God's Kingdom... and of his own return to set things right. He warned us to be ready. To serve and endure during times of great testing.

"Tonight, we shall read from Matthew 13, starting at verse 24." He found the spot with his finger.

But the pastor's wrist slipped from the page as the story took over... as the message welled from the deep and began to flow through his hands and lips.

Jesus told them another parable.
The Kingdom of heaven, said Jesus, is like this:
There once was a farmer. The man sowed good seed upon the
soil. But one night, an enemy crept into the field and salted the
land with the seeds of poisonous weeds. With the damage done,
the evil one slinked off into the darkest of shadows....

Freak finished his paraphrase.

He paused. He glanced back into the Bible, then up.

"Tonight," he said, "I offer you no slick, Hollywood-choreographed video music clips. No color-coded info-graphic charts. No timelines. Merely the word of the Lord."

With both hands, he lifted Jack's heavy pulpit Bible, then slowly returned it to the lectern.

"It is customary," said Freak, "for preachers to interpret the words of holy scripture. But in this rare case, Jesus himself explains *exactly* what his story was meant to say. In verse 36, his disciples beg him for an interpretation, so Jesus obliges with an unnerving prophetic vision of judgment... of the season of harvest... of the End of Days... when the Lion of Judah shall roar. When Jesus himself shall return with his vast angel armies to complete his work as the triumphant King."

The broadcasting network team was running again, caught up in the full-throttle adrenaline rush that keeps them in the field. All five cameras were finding good shots; producers were making the right cuts; a slow-starting program had suddenly lifted off into an unforgettable one-man show.

"Jesus," said Freak, "explicitly identifies the adversary in the night. He calls his enemy... *the Devil*. God declares throughout scripture that Satan—and Satan's demonic minions—are real. Jesus insists these unseen alien spirits move among us in the shadows. They have entered into the history of our planet from another realm. These Dark Riders of the night sow into our lives—and into our world—their seeds of poison... and death."

Freak paused, then punched his words. "Do you *understand*... demons... are *real?*"

He allowed a scattering of murmured yeses and amen's to rise from the crowd.

"Jesus," continued Freak, his delivery falling into a cadence, "speaks of a day of harvest to arrive at the end of this age. He declares that the Lord's harvest workers are mighty spirits, and his holy warriors shall successfully gather up the wicked... then cast them into a roaring fire."

Again, Freak waited, then punched his words.

"Brothers and sisters... do you *understand*... *holy angels*... are sharpening their sickles and scythes. And even now... they are assembling, preparing for a rapidly approaching... *return of the King?*"

This time, Freak's pause was rewarded by louder agreements. Even a spattering of shouted praise.

The screen cut to a gray-haired woman on her feet, both hands high, her chain-and-cross necklace bouncing atop her NFL team jacket. She rose and fell wildly, clapping and shouting from her sneaker-tips that she *did* understand.

"*Jesus*," said Freak, "reveals here in his own interpretation of his own words, that prior to his return, the wicked and the righteous shall commingle. Their stalks shall rise from roots that are intertwined. The world will be filled with good... *and bad.* Love and hate. With suffering and joy. With horrors and *hope*... up until the very day of the King's return."

Freak patted the text.

"Jesus speaks here of... *no* rapture. Of *no*... pre-harvest escape. Only of *his* promise... that his people will be grain, and they shall remain and be ready until the day of harvest, producing fruit even amongst the weeds... up until the day the weeds are burned."

"Do you *understand*... *the wicked*... shall be gathered... and *burned?*"

An audience-directed microphone collected a confused jumble of mixed responses.

A quick cut to the gray-haired woman revealed she'd stopped bouncing; she appeared uncertain as to where to go with her hands.

"As in the days of Noah, Jesus says in Matthew 24:39, those who ignore and disobey the Lord may watch and scoff, but it is *they* who are swept away and removed in judgment. As Jesus declared, it is the wicked who are *taken away...* and it is the *righteous* who are saved. It is they—those who serve the Lord—who shall be, like Noah... *left behind.*"

Freak swept an arm over the congregation. Then he centered his trembling hand over the Bible. He raised it high, fingers wide.

"Many of you here tonight—and throughout the world—you are still hoping for a pre-suffering magical teleportation. A pre-tribulation rapture, as it has been called. You believe in the return of the King. But contrary to the clear teachings of scripture, you don't plan to be here on that day. You imagine yourselves as an elite few, the *evaporating elect.* You imagine yourselves as the few privileged Christians of history who will be scooped into heaven and spared their assigned work and the cross of grief Jesus himself commanded the church to bear. You expect to be spared the very tasks that have been assigned to the followers of the King for the past 2,000 years. You plan to miss it all... with only your shoes and shorts being... *left behind.*"

The broadcast team cut to a nervously swaying pair of 40-somethings. They sat close, clutching each other in disconcerted frowns.

The screen flared with another tight Freak zoom.

"Brothers and sisters... have you seriously considered the spiritual bankruptcy of your most cherished of fantasies and fears?"

The elderly woman who had stopped bouncing was now fidgeting with her cross, clutching it to her chest.

She darted a self-conscious glance at the camera. Licked her lips.

Sat.

Freak leaned forward.

"*Left behind!*"

On the word *behind*, Freak slapped his hands with a resounding whack. The pulpit mic caught the smack. Boosted it. Thousands of ticket-holders responded with an involuntary, collective wince.

"Not just your shoes and your shorts... but you want to believe people will be left behind. Your neighbors. Your co-workers. Millions of people in Chicago, New York, Dallas... London, Paris, Rome.... Hundreds of millions of people in India, China, Africa. Billions of people around the world. *Left behind.*" His voice dropped. "To burn."

The screen cut to a shaking young redhead in slacks. She was snapping and unsnapping her windbreaker, twitching her attention between the jumbotron, the probing glare of the handheld camera light, and Freak on the stage.

"Love the Lord your God... with all of your heart, soul, mind and strength. And love your neighbor as yourself." Freak closed his eyes. Drew a long breath.

"*How dare you!* How dare you presume you're a follower of Jesus the King... when you fantasize... about leaving your neighbors behind... to burn!"

Murmurs of restless disapproval began moving through the crowd. Camera's were picking it up, relaying the discontent via satellite to around the world.

"*Jesus*," Freak roared, "suffered and loved the world with his dying breath. The early disciples... they suffered and they loved the Lord and the lost... to their dying breath. In the past century, millions of Christians around the world have suffered grievously, all the while... loving the Lord and the lost... with their dying breath."

Again, his voice dropped low. Almost lifeless.

"Tonight, even as we bask here in the beauty and the safety of this natural Colorado mountain fortress, elsewhere in the world, throughout the Middle East... Indonesia... Africa... thousands of Christians are suffering and loving the lost... with their dying breath."

He slammed his fist to the pulpit rail.

"How *dare* you... fantasize of your own easy out... with the suffering neighbor whom you were *commanded* by the King to love... being *left behind.*"

The camera caught a wide shot of a small group near the front, all milling about their seats in matching hats. They were shaking their heads side to side, loudly grumbling, gesturing their flowering disdain, moving as if about to walk out in disgust.

Freak spotted them. Stared them back into their seats.

"Now," he challenged, meeting their rejection with a pointing finger, "the Lord your God requires those who have ears for his word... to hear and obey."

He drew his arm inward.

He raised two fingers to his healthy right cheek.

"Grace," he said, tapping lightly.

He moved the fingers over the bridge of his nose.

"Truth," he finished, slicing sharply downward, as if with a knife.

The big screen did its work.

"Now, perhaps more than at any other time in history, the King is calling forth those who will faithfully— courageously—serve in love. Those who will obey... even into sacrifice... even into suffering... and even into death. Do not be deceived. The worst for our world is yet to come. Those who refuse to hear the Lord and to release their delusions of blissful escape... they are destined for a *great* disappointment.

"The Darby Doctrine of a rapture escape is lie. The Great Tribulation has begun. And it is about to get worse."

An elderly gentleman had slid from his bench. He was nearly fetal, covering his ears, rocking, his head between his knees. The woman beside him was stroking his back, trying to coax him into a sip of water.

The sound techs were adjusting their levels, raising isolated pockets of crowd noises. Amplifying complaints with a scattering of boos.

"As Jesus urged in Revelation 2:25, *'Until my return... hold on firmly to what you have.'* Brothers and sisters, it will not be easy. But like Jesus himself, and as with all of the greatest saints of the past 2,000 years, we must hold on. We must be willing to face the suffering and trials. We must endure in faith until the last day, when Jesus promises angels will sweep in among us and gather up and remove the weeds."

Freak himself began to rock.

"Will you choose... to radically serve? To obey and persevere... to the very end? Or will you fall away, in these, the darkest of days that are falling even now as I speak. How will you choose?"

I forced my attention away from the screen to Jack. To Mary, Ellen, and Cal. They sat oblivious to me, frozen in various postures of recoil and concern.

A few rapid shallow sighs. Soft prayers.

When my focus returned to the screen, Freak was gesturing off stage, into the shadows. With silence from the pulpit, a gathering storm of crowd noises began filling the air. Hecklers were growing bold.

Suddenly, Saundra stepped into the brilliant bright light. She strode hesitantly towards the pulpit. Bearing the shofar.

She awkwardly reached her free hand to the bottom handrail, then steadied herself and began an ascent.

Freak met her at the second flight, on the center deck.

It was then the audience began to realize the drama that had begun to build.

For the third time in the night, waves of hush swept through the audience. Heads turned and mouths clamped as the two embraced.

Freak received the horn. Each of them turned and returned—up and down—to where they'd last stood. As Saundra slipped from the circle of light, I thought I caught a dark figure in the shadows by the huge speaker stack at the edge of the stage. But maybe not.

Freak waited in the spotlight, high in the pulpit box, ignoring the crowd, re-testing the balance and the curve of the ancient Jewish Saint Michael horn.

When at last the prophet lifted his gaze, the congregation was waiting, leaning forward in tense anticipation and awe.

"The Lord," said Freak, his voice calm, "is not willing for any to perish. Nor should be... *you*."

He raised the primitive instrument almost to his lips.

"Trumpets announce celebrations, battles... and the arrival of lords."

Freak extended an arm and leveled the horn, aiming to the center of the crowd.

"How do you choose to respond? Will you serve in faithful readiness... waiting here, doing your part among your dying neighbors until the very day of the return of your King?"

He closed his eyes.

"Or... not?"

And then... he began to blow.

49
LIGHTS OUT

When not hosting the likes of Bono and Freak, the Red Rocks Amphitheatre campus is just another Denver City Park. Sort of. People can drive the ten miles west of Denver to explore the 868-acre attraction almost any time, so long as there's not a paid event.

They can picnic, hike, watch deer, mountain bike, even walk the dog. Out-of-state visitors are often particularly intrigued by the authentic Jurassic period fossils and exposed dinosaur footprints found in the rock slabs along the park's connecting trails.

But the most popular thing to do at the base of Mount Morrison is simply to stride out onto the Red Rocks open stage.

To goof around.

For one brief moment, anyone can be an opera star. A jazz saxophonist. A preacher.

I've heard some pretty good performances from Sunday afternoon drumming classes that have slipped out onto the stage with their rag-tag bands of congas, bongos, cajons... and their five-gallon plastic pails.

Aspiring comedians and *Romeo and Juliet* flops take their turns, queuing up to bounce their favorite lines.

Little kids are always a hoot. Shouting, snorting, making fart noises under their lifted shirts. It's cheap family entertainment to test the Rocks phenomenon by whispering jokes from the stage to parents who stand small and far away on the high back deck.

The amphitheater acoustics are so incredible it's not uncommon for someone on the stage to sneeze, and then for dozens of *God Bless You*'s to waft back from loitering visitors scattered throughout the vast soaring incline of almost 10,000 seats.

So when Freak lifted the shofar to his lips—when he sucked in his first deep breath to blow—most of the locals had a rough expectation about what might come next. They'd heard replays on YouTube and television from the Easter weekend when Freak blew the First Trumpet. And when it came to sound, they figured they knew what the Red Rocks could do.

But they were wrong.

In the history of the planet, an elevated pulpit with a massive sounding board backdrop had never played host to a shofar in a sanctuary anywhere near the equal to the Red Rocks open-sky cathedral.

This was a new sound... without earthly precedent.

The sound technicians might have played with the notes a bit as well.

Maybe not.

Survivors complained the next day of headaches, nausea, chills, even hallucinations... some of which they attributed to the shofar; not everything was blamed upon what happened a few moments later, when Freak finally lowered the horn.

Even on the couch, a satellite bounce away, I felt the tingling of goose bumps. A dizzying wave of humbling amazement.

Euphoric... afraid.

I became aware of the fact I'd stopped breathing.

How Freak was able to continue to blow the succession of repeating notes so long, rising and falling, trilling at the end... I can only guess.

When at last the prophet lowered the trumpet, my ears continued to ring. My vision remained blurred.

"Jack..." I started to say, turning when I'd finally regained my composure.

But I never finished.

The flat screen flashed white. Accompanied by a corresponding *ka-Boom!*

Investigators later confirmed the number three.

Thankfully, only one of the men made it all the way into the bleachers.

Jump bombers.

A local Denver reporter coined the phrase, and the name stuck.

The terrorists commandeered a FedEx Cessna 208 Caravan and flew to within three miles of Morrison. They'd descended towards Denver International Airport strictly according to an approved TSA and FAA flight plan.

South of Red Rocks, the pilot suddenly notified the DIA tower of equipment failure. Executing an emergency maneuver, he gained altitude and veered hard to the north. With a little coaching from the tower, the pilot corrected, adjusted altitude, then returned to his scheduled approach.

The aircraft was shot down over a flat ranch ten minutes east of Denver. The chuted pilot was never found, but the black box confirmed the final minutes of flight were completed on autopilot.

It was during the plane's brief veer to the north when the suicide divers had bailed.

Head first. In visored, aerodynamic crash helmets.

Free fall.

The jump bombers streaked in modified wingsuits strapped with five explosive belts each. Arms, legs, and torsos. Free from the drag of parachutes, and weighted with C4 and hundreds of ball bearings, they attained terminal velocities of over 200 miles per hour.

One-way tickets to heaven.

Or straight to hell.

The huge Red Rocks parking lamps, along with the stadium aisle lights, had provided a bull's-eye seen for miles. They'd apparently been trained for inverted freeflying, and they must have continuously adjusted their fins and bomb-strapped bodies throughout their plunge. If not for a flukish gust of evening breeze, the attackers would have racked up even higher tolls of carnage, nightmares, tears, and death.

As it was, one of the living missiles smacked in the Upper North Lot, less than fifty yards from the target. A half dozen vehicles. Lots of glass. No casualties.

The second glanced against the south outside face of Ship Rock. The massive sandstone formation shielded the unprepared audience from injury, but the explosion drove through the attached structures and did considerable damage to the Ship Rock Grille and the Red Rocks Visitor Center. Fourteen injuries; two deaths.

The third jumper torpedoed with a deafening boom into Row 35, seat 63. Pretty much dead center.

Many of the injuries and fatalities were caused by the scattering and piercing of secondary elements. Splinters of wood from the benches. Chunks of cement. The jewelry and bones of those sitting within thirty seats of Ground Zero.

279 injuries. 106 deaths.

With shock waves instantly felt around the world.

Only one camera team was neutralized upon impact.

The four others continued recording from their posts, swinging their cameras, coached by the technology and the level-headed expertise of their studio counterparts half a continent away.

Later, sense was made of the chaos.

But in the midst, even we who participated through distant screens received a sickening barrage of images and sounds that left us traumatized and numb. Snapshots wide, then tight. Audio silent... then layered with wails and mournful screams.

I caught sight of Wee Daddy, wrestling with Freak.

The soldier was shown struggling with the prophet, dragging Freak from a crumpled body near the front of the stage, pulling him away to beneath the iron catwalks along the face of the Stage Rock's hollowed lee.

According to Saundra, the victims' blood flowed all the way down to the mosh pit at the base of the stage.

There, it mingled with a pool of deep red from the lower seats.

Along with a splash of life from her cameraman.

A single random steel ball had shattered Steve's skull.

In shock and tears, we gathered the next day at the ranch.

"Steve was filming," sobbed Saundra, "in front of the speaker stack. I *told* him to come and stand by me, to the side, *behind* the equipment. But Steve insisted on getting closer. He insisted nobody would notice him as long as he stood there in the dark. He'd inched himself as close to the pulpit as the shadows allowed. He wanted to get footage for our project that nobody else could get."

Saundra shook her head. "Steve said this event was too historic… too important to film from only off stage."

Freak sat beside his wife, opposite of Saundra.

Motionless.

The silent prophet's face was fixed. His flesh was as gray and red as stone.

"When Freak began to blow the Second Trumpet," Saundra continued, looking at me, "Steve stepped even closer. And then he went down on one knee and stuck out a hand to hold steady while he kept recording. I tried to call him back. But then the sound took over, and then the explosion... I lost track... and then everything went crazy. And Steve fell, and his body started to...."

Saundra began crying, almost hysterically, brushing away Mary's calming hand. She spun her tear-streaked face towards Freak.

"*You*," she accused, "they are saying *you* did this. That you *knew* all along... right down to the minute. You made me bring the shofar out to you, and then you blew it right at the very spot where the jumper hit...."

Jack sidled in tight, pinching Saundra between his hip and his wife. He draped himself around her shoulders, blanketing her heaves with his massive arm.

"Saundra," he hushed, "those critics know nothing. And they don't believe...."

"*Believe*?" she wept. "Believe *what*?"

Jack hesitated. Searched for an answer.

Found only a room full of pain-laden stares.

"Say something," Saundra wept, her eyes pleading with Freak. "*Anything.*"

The prophet remained still for what seemed an eternity. Finally, he rose. Started for the front door.

"Next time," muttered Freak, "Saint Michael will have to blow his own damn horn. I'm tired of being used."

He turned the knob.

"I'm done."

Most of us made it down to Denver for Steve's funeral.

Not Freak.

Freak mumbled he didn't want to make any of the focus about him. That the victims should be honored. Laid to rest... in peace. Not in the circus his presence would evoke. He claimed he didn't want to have to lie if anyone asked him about what had happened.

Nor about what he thought was going to happen next.

He said people really wouldn't want to know. Humans were never made to absorb death on such a scale.

I wasn't sure whether to believe Jacobs or not.

He'd become himself like a man who was dead.

But Freak was right about one thing: what happened next was not good.

Shortly after the Second Trumpet, the planet was rocked by an unprecedented series of catastrophic earthquakes, followed by devastating tsunamis.

Meanwhile, the ocean floor let loose with a string of deep-sea volcanic eruptions that quickly reduced much of the world's fishing industry to empty nets and bankruptcies.

Ocean temperatures rose. Currents shifted. Fish and sea creatures began sloshing back and forth with the tides. The stench of death rose along the beaches of every continent.

The epicenter of one of the biggest quakes was beneath the Olympic Peninsula, near Seattle. That disaster of shaking and destructive waves was followed by mudslides and flows, then a series of deep grumblings from the molten bowels of Mount Rainier.

What was left of America's Pacific Northwest flew into a state of justifiable panic.

The President of the United States faced his people yet again. Another emergency address, vainly attempting to steady the collapsing markets and to calm his nation with promises no one believed he could keep.

Many universities suspended classes for the summer. Some churches filled to capacity. Others all but closed.

Congress rushed to patch together a massive piece of provisional legislation addressing the most pressing needs.

World leaders posed and postured. Armies raged, and cities from Lisbon to the Pacific Rim crackled with the violence of anarchy and flames.

"Benny," Ellen softly urged, "come back to us. We need you."

Freak lifted his eyes. He forced a feeble smile for his wife, then dropped his black brows deep back into his hands.

"Benny," she implored again, "we're at the table. Your children are hungry. Your friends are waiting. Give us a prayer."

Nothing.

"Bless this food," Jack prayed at last, "for though we are sinners, we are still your sheep. We yearn for your green pastures... for your renewing waters... and for your grace and peace...."

Freak pushed himself away from the table and rose.

"There will be no peace," he said, staring at his empty plate, "until the end."

He lifted his eyes to me. "Welcome to the Apocalypse."

And then he left.

INTO SUMMER

Without a roommate, things got a little lonely for me on the ranch.

Freak had never been that great of company, and now, even those occasional smiles the prophet used to contribute were all but gone.

There was a big hole where Steve had been.

I pulled the linens off Steve's empty bed, and I stacked his few clothes and possessions in a couple boxes in the cabin's only closet.

I was surprised to discover a Bible in his drawer, a worn paperback edition from the ranch's set in the loft.

Yellow sticky notes flagged a few pages, with arrows pointing to verses in Isaiah, Matthew, and The Apocalypse of John.

Revelation 3:20.

"Behold! I stand at the door and knock...."

I carefully closed the book and placed it on top of the sheets inside the last carton. I folded down the cardboard flaps, then walked the box to join the others in the tiny back room.

At the funeral, his family promised to come visit in a few weeks, to see where Steve had spent his last days. To retrieve his things.

But they never showed.

I started helping Cal with chores.

I spent unhurried time with those who would have me.

And I worked as best I could on completing my journals.

Wee Daddy's team stayed with us, rotating in and out as they took their leaves. Freak needed them more than ever. Public opinion was splitting, and not exactly down the middle. For every positive commentary or letter of support, Freak was trashed by a group of protestors, and then blasted in a blog. Or threatened by something in the mail.

Insults arrived from all directions.

The attacks were particularly painful for Freak when they were launched by respected church leaders and the religious media. His predictions of a "Great Disappointment" were beginning to prove accurate. Millions of Christians were questioning whether a time of tribulation had begun, and they were wondering if they'd been robbed of their highly anticipated rapture escape.

The "evaporating elect" were indeed left behind with the rest of us. The wheat and weeds would apparently commingle until his return, exactly as Jesus had said.

For some Christians, the easiest way to manage their confusion and pain was to blame the messenger. Not the preachers and the fictions they'd been so eager to believe, but the prophet who'd exposed the lies on the world's stage.

They took out their frustrations on Freak.

At least at first.

Before they directed their anger towards God, who they felt had somehow let them down.

Saundra continued to hang around the ranch.

Channel 5 left her with a tripod and a good camera, along with a few pieces of broadcasting equipment. Her people were betting that the logjam with Freak would eventually break, and they wanted her to remain embedded and ready to beam it up when the big day came.

But because Freak had stopped granting interviews and doing daily podcasts, the rest of her station's crew was shuffled back to Denver.

We still held our Sunday night oikos gatherings, but a darkness hung over much of our time together. Freak wouldn't pray.

He wouldn't even read a few lines from the Bible. Would not be consoled.

"Hey," I joked, "lucky for Lou, those healing oils really hit the spot. No more pain. No limp. And it's been a month. Maybe it's time we called another press conference."

Freak stared.

"Better yet," I added, groping for any kind of response, "let's call Krissy and see if she'd like to start selling bottles of Lucky Lou's Armageddon Oil on her website. We could bottle it right here on the ranch. It'd be something we could do… for the *profit*."

Freak stood and left without a word.

The days grew longer, warmer.

At times, I became lost in my writing. The challenge of putting into words the remarkable events since the Day of the Falling Skies was a powerful distraction. We'd been through a lot, and Freak had become more alive in my memories than he was across the table.

Saundra discovered the video files Steve transferred to the ranch's hard drive. Upon request, Channel 5 also provided the files from his camera, which had been recovered on the Red Rocks stage. She spent countless hours combing them for cogent bites, editing and splicing together the documentary Steve would never finish.

She also spent long stretches of time on the Internet, researching and jotting notes on various theories about the End of Days. A few of her friends came to visit, and she drove down to Denver a couple times. For the most part, though, she seemed content to spend her days at the ranch.

"I was long overdue for a vacation anyway," she smiled. "This slow pace is nice for a change."

When the slow pace became too much, Saundra would sometimes help Mary with ranch duties. Or even join Cal and me in the barns for our daily chores.

One especially quiet weekend, while passing out oats, I convinced Saundra to go for a horseback ride. Cal confirmed that without the ranch's usual stream of guests, the horses were growing restless and fat.

"Come on," I laughed. "You'd be doing the ponies a big favor."

"Okay," she smiled. "I suppose it's about time I leaned to ride. But I'm going to need to borrow some clothes from the lost and found again." She batted her eyes. "My regular clothes are probably all too tight. I guess me and the ponies could both use the exercise."

Cal and I put her on Old Buck, a gentle veteran of the trails, and she took right to it. Rex tagged along, the weather held, and the afternoon went well.

Pretty soon, we were saddling and riding into the hills and down along the river a few times each week, a bit further each time.

We all felt sorry for Ellen.

Freak's wife had her hands full, having to deal with her husband's despondency, and having to manage the young ones with so little help. Saundra and I got to talking about it, and we ended up volunteering to take the children down to the resort's thermal pool in Hot Sulphur Springs.

The kids happily splashed around for hours.

On our lounge chairs in the sun beside the pool, I was reminded of how beautiful the news lady really was.

I forced myself to come up with a lame one-liner about her tan.

Saundra hesitated. Studied me. Adjusted her sunglasses. Then finally replied with a faint smile.

She lowered her water bottle to the concrete deck beside her chair. "I miss him."

I nodded. "Me, too."

She lifted her hand from the bottle. She floated it outward, awkwardly extending it in my direction.

I stretched my hand as far as I could reach.

Our fingertips barely touched.

But it was enough.

In late June, I was sipping ice water with Freak in the shade of his cabin's front porch. Our attempt at civility was awkward for us both. But I'd said yes to Jack and Saundra, and I didn't want to report I'd failed to follow through. They'd insisted it was my unique place in life—in the midst of the End of Days—to coach Freak into at least pretending he still retained an ounce of his former humanity.

Even a mustard seed of hope from Freak would do.

Especially with how badly the war was going on the other side of the planet. The scale of losses was staggering, and it appeared inevitable for America to soon be sucked deeper into the fray.

The world needed another word from the mad-dog prophet.

Perhaps not Truth, but surely some Grace.

"The journals," I said at last, grasping for a point of contact, "I've almost finished writing the first drafts."

Freak nodded.

"I've pretty much covered from the morning of your fall, all the way up to when Cary and his film crew flew out here to work on their documentary."

"Good." Freak sipped from his glass. "They did a fine job."

"Darn right," I said, my laugh hollow. "It's a lucky thing Shannon got his clean bill of health when they got back to New York. Without that, Cary might have thrown us both under the bus. He certainly had the footage. Not to mention a few of the details he could have played up about your prophetic Jewish heritage. But the whole time he was editing their film, he was sitting right there with Shannon in the room. With living proof...."

"Proof?" asked Freak. "Proof of what?"

I decided to let it go.

Down below, beneath the lone pine, Freak's two sons and daughter were playing tall-grass tag with Rex. The black Lab suddenly caught the buzz of a hummingbird. The game quickly expanded to include wild flowers, dandelion puffs, and the flutterings of white butterflies.

Young voices and playful barks floated up to the porch shadows, rising and falling with innocence. Effervescent with the joy of life. Bubbling with latent potential.

"Your kids," I said, "they're okay." I swirled the ice in my glass. "They've started to grow on me."

Hmm.

"Freak," I continued, "would you mind if Saundra and I took them over to Hot Sulphur Springs for another dip in the pool?"

I tasted the rim of my glass. "It's supposed to get pretty hot again tomorrow. And I think a drive over to the pool to play with some other children would do your kids some good."

Freak turned.

"My kids?" He surprised me with a smirk. "Sure, Mark. They told me they had fun the last time they went. Micah says you tell funny jokes. So I guess, if Ellen says yes... then it's okay with me. Take my kids."

I put down my water. "Based upon your expression, and the tone of your voice... I'm not sure what it is you're really trying to say."

"I'm saying," he smiled, "I think it's a good idea for you to take Saundra to the pool tomorrow. I'm sure your time with her will be very rewarding."

"Wait a minute...."

"And I'm also saying it's okay if you want to invite my children to come along. By taking my kids, I'm sure Saundra will feel much less embarrassed saying yes when you work up the nerve to ask her."

"So... am I to understand you think this whole thing is really about me spending more time with Saundra?"

"If the swimsuit fits...."

"Whoa," I grinned, "are you suddenly developing a little sense of irony on me? Was that supposed to be some kind of a joke?"

He replied with a good-natured snort.

"What's the matter?" I asked. "Has the Dark Rider begun to loosen his grip on your tongue?"

Freak laughed, softly. A flicker of life all the same. His first in a long time.

I gave us each a moment to savor the breakthrough.

"There," I said, meeting his gaze. "That wasn't so bad, was it?"

He shrugged, eyes pleased.

He lifted a hand to return a wave to his little girl.

Miriam.

Freak saved the rest of his thoughts for another day.

By the Fourth of July weekend, Freak was making good progress.

He still wouldn't pray, but at least he'd participate and finish a full entree at the long table.

And he'd fallen back into the habit of hugging his kids and laughing with them off and on throughout the day. Miriam. Eli. And Micah.

Even smiling and talking with his wife.

Ellen.

Who I once caught squeezing his hand with a nod.

The front door opened in a bang.

"Freak," called Wee Daddy, "we've got somebody here who wants to see you."

We all looked up from our plates.

Wee Daddy stood on the entrance rug. His boots were caked in gray mud, and he didn't seem interested in loosening the laces only to re-string them a few minutes later.

Behind him leaned a familiar face. And beside that man, another, although I couldn't put a name to him. The face I did recognize began nervously poking from side to side, glancing around Wee Daddy towards Freak, towards our quiet table deep within the big house.

Shannon.

And the young gaffer.

Mary leapt from the table and gathered them from the door, dirty boots and all.

"I've got to sweep and vacuum tonight anyway," she apologized. "You boys need to sit down and have some berry pie." She started toward the double doors. "Three plates, three forks... right?"

Afterwards, Ellen took the children out for a sunset walk. Some of us busied ourselves in the kitchen. Wee Daddy returned to his men.

Freak retired with his visitors to the guest lounge area by the cold hearth.

Jack tapped me on the shoulder. "*Go*," he said. He dropped his hand and rolled it in the air towards the other room. "Get out there. The prophet needs you right now more than we do in here at the sink." He touched his heart. "For the love of the King."

Saundra agreed.

I dried my hands, kissed Mary on the cheek, then took a deep breath.

"For the love of the King," I whispered.

I tapped my heart. Then pushed through the double doors.

The three of them were hunched forward in gentle conversation.

The gaffer's name was Charlie.

I stood there above them, not certain what I should say or do.

"It *was* a miracle," said Charlie. "And, Reverend Jacobs... you *did* change our lives. Ever since we got back, we keep reviewing over and over all of the footage from our time in Colorado. Especially when you prayed over Shannon. And we've been studying some of your old YouTube clips. And the footage from the Second Trumpet... from Red Rocks. We're still trying to figure out what it all means."

"Good," sighed Freak. "That's a good start."

"We'd given up all hope. The doctors said Shannon's tumor was too far along. But then, when you healed him...."

"*God*," I said, my voice soft.

I took a seat amongst them. "It is only *God* who heals."

"Yes, but...."

"Listen," I said. "I know this guy." I leaned over and patted Freak's knee.

"Trust me," I smiled, "Freak is just another junkyard dog breaking loose from his chains. Trying to run around free in the neighborhood for a while. Maybe even to sneak into the big top tent to get in on an act. But take it from me... it is *God* who runs the show."

"The show?"

"The miracles. The prophecies. History. It's all one big dog and pony circus. The ringmaster runs it. Freak has just become part of the drama in ring number three."

Freak studied me.

"And," I said, "right now, Freak is taking a little break. He's catching his breath after his last performance. Getting ready for the big finish."

I leaned back.

"Am I correct?" I asked.

"Sure," he reluctantly smiled. "It's the ringmaster's show."

"And," I added, "you're free to perform in the final act, right?"

"Yes," Freak nodded at last. "Unleashed... to serve and obey."

EPILOGUE

"Freak... I think I'm done. At least with the first draft."

I slid the thick three-ring binder to him across the worn table.

He picked it up. "Heavy."

"Right back at you, Bro."

He grinned.

Freak opened the cover and fanned through some random pages. He paused now and again to read a few lines. A passage caught his attention. He squinted for a minute, then looked up.

"You're being a little hard on yourself, don't you think?"

"Maybe. I couldn't seem to keep it from getting personal."

Freak nodded. "Well, I did encourage the painful truth, right?"

"Agreed. But if you think I come off looking like a loser, wait until you get to the parts I wrote about you."

He patted the binder. "When I'm done, would it be okay if I let Saundra give this a read?"

I frowned. "I'm not sure. Saundra probably knows me too well already."

"Grace and Truth," laughed Freak. "It'll set you free. Besides, she could clean up your punctuation. For an English teacher, you should be ashamed of yourself."

"I am. But it's not about me, remember?"

He turned to the last page. Read it. Looked up.

Smiled.

"Okay," I said. "I did my part. Now you do yours."

"What do you mean?"

"You told me to be brutally honest. About you, about me, about all of it. You said each of us writes a story with our lives, but my assignment was to record this chapter of *your* life, so that...."

"That what?"

"I'm not sure. What *is* next... *Benzion*?"

"Mark, I don't know. I'm not sure."

"So you say. Not that I believe you for one single minute."

I got up. "Why don't you read everything I've recorded so far...." I leaned over the table and tapped the manuscript. "And then, when you've finished this, you can get back to me about the next chapter... if the Spirit so moves."

He studied me. Nodded.

I walked around to his side of the table and reached past his arm. I flipped the manuscript all the way back to beginning.

"Here," I said, pointing to the top of the first page. "Start here."

I withdrew my hand and started to leave, then stopped and turned to meet his eyes.

"Oh, by the way," I said, my voice as casual as I could force it, "I got an interesting phone call from my father today."

"And?"

"Well, my dad was up at our family's cabin on Bootlegger Lake this morning. He decided to check in on your tree." I shrugged. "You remember the tree, right?"

Freak frowned. "Now you're jerking me around."

"Do you remember how they'd stripped the bark all the way around to kill it? How they'd hacked and peeled a three-foot wide girdle into the heartwood core, and how they had gouged that pagan symbol... and smeared it all with blood?"

Freak leaned forward. "Come on, Mark... tell me. Quit playing games."

"Anyway, I just thought you might like to know. Maybe we can go check it out when you're done reading...."

"Mark!"

"Fine, I'll tell you." I let my eyes sparkle. "Dad says the bark has grown back. He says it appears as if your gnarly old ponderosa is going to pull through after all." I folded my arms. "My dad knows trees, and he's calling it a miracle."

Freak hesitated. Smiled.

"Finish your homework," I said, uncrossing my arms, "and then maybe you and Saundra can head over there with me in a day or two to check it out."

Freak nodded, then started to read.

Out loud.
The words were familiar. They were mine.
But the story was his.
And mine.

He was still reading aloud, oblivious to me, when I finally stepped from the cabin to begin my long walk back to the big house. Even as the door closed, his voice was building a curious edge, an excited anticipation of what the next page might bring.

As if he didn't know every detail of what would happen next, but he had a pretty good idea where it all was going. And how the story would end.

As if he believed the worst—and the best—was yet to come.

——— END BOOK II———

DAVE CHEADLE has published over 150 articles and five books, including the award-winning first volume of the Freak Trilogy, *Freak Fall*.

His fiction, social history research, and religious writing has appeared in St. Anthony Messenger, Cornerstone, The Church Herald, Sports Collectors Digest, and dozens of other venues. His first novel, *Family Ashes*, debuted 15 years ago as a Rocky Mountain Fiction Writers Colorado Gold finalist.

Cheadle's non-fiction works have appeared in publications ranging from Persimmon Hill to Victorian Decorating and Lifestyle Magazine. He has served as the managing editor for two nationally circulated collectibles magazines, and he is the author of the definitive work on 19th Century lithographed business advertising cards, *Victorian Trade Cards: Historical Reference and Value Guide*.

Cheadle has taught high school writing, photography, literature and history. In the 1980's his high school journalism program was recognized with the highest honors in the state of Colorado. In 1989 he led a team of high school newspaper editors to Germany—loaded with cameras and equipment from three Denver television stations—to provide live reporting on the collapse of the Berlin Wall.

He lives in Colorado where he founded and now leads the CenterPoint Missional Community movement in Denver. He is the father of two college graduates, and he has been married for 33 years.

For more information about *Freak Fall*, *Freak Unleashed*, or *Freak Ending*, or to order books, visit: www.FreakTrilogy.com.